UNKNOWN ENEMY

UNKNOWN ENEMY

A NOVEL

KARL GOODMAN

Covenant Communications, Inc.

Cover image by Steve Taylor © Digital Vision/Getty Images, Inc.

Cover design copyrighted 2006 by Covenant Communications, Inc.

Published by Covenant Communications, Inc.
American Fork, Utah

Printed in Canada
First Printing: January 2006

11 10 09 08 07 06   10 9 8 7 6 5 4 3 2

ISBN 1-59156-855-2

This novel is dedicated to the woman who has accompanied me on so many of life's adventures: raising children, serving in the Church, and visiting places we love—Spain, Mexico, and Central America. We have witnessed the hand of Heavenly Father many times in our life, and have seen many beautiful places and people as we've served three missions for the Church. Wilma is my lovely wife and my one and only love.

CHAPTER ONE

Adnan Ahman was picked up by a Soviet-made Hind attack helicopter near the small town of San Juan del Sur. The helicopter had Sandinista markings. Whether it belonged to Nicaragua's army or was disguised to look like it, Adnan did not know. His prospective arms sale was to a group of insurgents who fought the Sandinistas. Besides the pilot, there was a small man with a big weapon. Adnan was blindfolded by the small man, and the chopper headed out over Lake Nicaragua.

Upon landing, the buzz of insects, the cry of birds, and the sweltering humidity told Adnan that he was surrounded by jungle. The blindfold was removed, and the pilot told Adnan to get out. The only landmark was the towering mantle of deep green jungle trees.

The pilot led the way along a narrow descending trail, the man with the gun never more than a few paces behind. In five minutes, the trail opened onto a cleared compound. In the middle of the compound was a large, oblong building constructed from tree trunks set in the ground. The branching forks of the corner posts held intersecting log beams and rafters, over which thatched guano palm fronds were placed. The pilot motioned for Adnan to step inside. Three men seated on stools looked up as he entered.

A big, older man motioned to a three-legged stool. Adnan looked around briefly and sat down. Crude stools and tables made of woven vines and reeds comprised the furnishings.

The older man did not offer a hand, but asked, "You Adnan Ahman?"

Adnan merely nodded his head in assent.

"I'm Valderas." Nodding at the others, he said, "Miguel and Jaime."

Adnan studied the three men. The older man, tall and large for a Central American and sporting a bushy mustache, returned his stare. Adnan placed the slender, handsome one, called Jaime, third in the power structure. The one called Miguel toyed nervously with his pistol. He was a powerfully muscled man, not quite as tall as Adnan's own six feet. He was, Adnan decided, clearly the most dangerous of the three—perhaps second in power only because men would rather follow him than face him. Adnan would make his pitch to Valderas.

The bargaining started, and then one they called Dama Mariposa entered the jungle encampment. He had a vague feeling that he knew her. She was pretty, despite the fact that she wore a bulky camouflage uniform. A pistol was holstered around her slim waist, and a Belgian FAL hung loosely by lanyard behind her back. She turned smoldering, nearly black eyes toward him, and he remembered where he had seen her before. It had been during the Sandinista revolution. He decided that she probably would not recognize him.

The occasion had been in Commander Cero's field headquarters. She had worn a uniform that did nothing to hide her femininity. Adnan had supposed her to be an attractive camp ornament and had made advances toward her. She had slapped his face, and he'd viciously returned it. Commander Cero's displeasure had been evident, but it was clear that Cero desperately needed weapons.

Here in El Cinco's jungle headquarters, Adnan studied the girl again. He searched his memory for her name. It had not been Dama Mariposa then. Finally he dismissed her as a rather dangerous showpiece.

The bargaining continued. Valderas said, "I'll give you four hundred a weapon."

Adnan responded, "I have to cover freighting—"

Dama Mariposa interrupted. "Valderas, if you agree to buy weapons from this man and check them before accepting delivery, you'll find half of them no good—and the ammunition won't perform to specification in the field."

Furious, Adnan snapped, "That's ridiculous! I sell only the best . . ."

Dama's interruption was calm. "Carlos Salguero would not agree."

Finally, eyes blazing in anger, he stopped talking, looked directly at her for the first time, and demanded, "Just who is Carlos Salguero?"

"Carlos Salguero was my friend, until a rifle Commander Cero bought from you blew up in his face."

"You have mistaken me for someone else. I never sold rifles to Cero."

"I admit you look different." There was conviction in her words. "But, my *compas* will tell you, I can hear accents and remember voices and faces—even disguised faces. You, for instance, despite the name Adnan Ahman, are *Norte Americano*. You sold faulty weapons to Commander Cero all right." She turned to Valderas. "I wouldn't buy a gun from him if General Ortega were armed and standing in front of me and I had nothing but my bare hands to fight him!"

Adnan knew it would be futile to argue against her testimony. He blustered, "Under combat conditions, weapons are not always properly treated. I'm not res—"

A pistol jumped into her hand, accelerating Adnan's heartbeat, interrupting his words. How Adnan hated a showoff woman!

Her eyes sparked. "Are you saying I don't know how to care for my weapons?"

"I wasn't speaking of you. I referred to Cero."

"You just did not *know* you spoke of me. I was Cero's ordnance officer." She waggled the pistol at him. "Are you saying I don't know my guns?"

He said lamely, "Well, what did you expect for the price?"

She returned the pistol to its holster. "A weapon you can depend on! I don't care that a gun's old if it does its job. What good is a weapon, no matter the price, if it blows up in your face?"

She caused another acceleration of his heartbeat when she hitched her shoulder and pointed the Belgian FAL automatic rifle at his heart. "Besides, M16s don't compare with a weapon like this!"

There was just the slightest trembling of her finger hovering near the trigger. There was no trembling in her voice. "If I didn't fear the eternal consequence of deliberate murder, Señor Ahman, you would die right now to pay for my friend Carlos."

Adnan did not let his slip of composure show. "I can supply you with FALs if that's your weapon choice—if you can pay for them."

Her eyes didn't budge from his. "How much? Delivered along the Rio Colorado in Costa Rica?"

Adnan did mental calculations before answering. "Twenty-five hundred dollars a rifle, if you order a hundred. You'd have to arrange—"

Again she interrupted. "We just received a shipment of FALs that cost less than one thousand American dollars each—and they were delivered on the Rio Colorado along with fifty thousand rounds of ammunition!"

Adnan had difficulty keeping his temper in check. His hand itched to slap her insolent face. Still his voice was flat. "You lie. There is no way you could buy a Belgian FAL for a thousand dollars." He turned and made appeal to Valderas. "I didn't come to Nicaragua to play games. Who is this woman, anyway? This Dama Mariposa?" Adnan had never been able to properly roll a

Spanish *r*. "I've got other business—you agreed that you would—"

The man called Jaime interrupted, stabbing a finger at Adnan. "If Dama votes against buying from him, then I vote with her." Voice intent, he spoke to Adnan. "She tells the truth in saying the last shipment of FALs cost one thousand dollars each. And don't call her, or, for that matter, any person here, a liar!"

Adnan hardly knew what to say. He turned back to Valderas. Before he could speak, Valderas looked at Dama Mariposa and said, "We could use some M16s, because they're cheaper. You sure you're against buying from him, Dama?"

"The first time he sold inferior guns was his fault. But if we buy from him again, knowing he sells bad weapons, we have only ourselves to blame."

Valderas stood up. His voice rumbled. "She speaks truly in two ways. You ask who she is? No person in Nicaragua is more expert on weapons than Dama Mariposa. You were foolish to violate her trust the first time. And our last weapons did cost one thousand dollars each. Good-bye, Señor Ahman."

Adnan stood up. The venomous hatred in his eyes spilled over on Dama Mariposa. It was dangerous for anyone to interfere in his business, especially a woman. He thought, *You could . . . No, you* will *end up dead, pretty butterfly lady. Very dead.*

Miguel stood up. "Valderas, do you remember that Carlos was my friend?" The muscles on his arm rippled as he poked a finger at Adnan. "How about I take Señor Ahman to the Miskitos near San Pedro del Norte? They'd either teach him not to sell bad weapons or feed him to the fish."

Jaime said, "Or me? I didn't even know Carlos, but I'd drop this Ahman off right in the middle of Managua—from five thousand feet."

"No, gentlemen. Vanson will return him as he brought him. Don't forget that we must deal with other gun sellers in the future." Valderas laughed heartily and clapped Adnan on the shoulder.

"Señor Ahman, you've made yourself unpopular with mis compas. Don't return to this part of Nicaragua."

Adnan started to speak in anger. "I'll travel where I—"

There was the deadliest chill in the voice of Valderas. "You should leave quietly and soon—or I will change my mind and let Miguel take you to the Miskitos of San Pedro del Norte as he has asked."

Adnan did not understand the full significance of being taken to the Miskitos, but he did understand he was no longer welcome at this jungle outpost. He walked quietly from the headquarters of the group called El Cinco. He wondered how to go about finding the location, because he *would* take care of the woman, Dama Mariposa.

On the flight back to San Juan del Sur, he thought, *That woman remembers me too well. If by some accident she sees a picture of me in the newspaper . . .* He did not take the thought to its conclusion. He knew that she had to be a dead woman. He, Adnan Ahman, had too much to lose in being recognized.

* * *

The failed arms deal left the four people in silence, each thinking. Several minutes passed, and Valderas broke the silence as the muffled *whuff-whuff* of helicopter blades lifting against the tropical air reached their ears. "How did you come up with the ridiculous price of one thousand dollars per FAL, Dama?"

She laughed. "It wasn't ridiculous. I figured the price of renting your boat for a couple of days and divided it by the hundred FALs we got in our last raid. It came out about a thousand dollars each. I was generous in paying you rent. I wanted to be sure you made a good profit."

They all joined in laughter at her joke.

Valderas said, "I think you made an enemy, Dama. If the acid from his eyes had splashed on you, you would be losing all your lovely skin."

She laughed easily. "Who worries about *bichos?* He's an insect, and I'd squash him if he gave me the slightest excuse—and besides, Valderas, you know I never lose."

* * *

From the beautiful mountaintop chalet, a short helicopter ride could take a person to Vail or to Denver. The native stone walls of the house seemed a natural extension of the rugged rocks of the mountain. Large windows afforded a commanding view of the valley below through the tops of spruce and pine trees. Inside, massive stone fireplaces joined the rugged beauty of the mountain stone with functional use. Hewn wooden beams gave solid support for the roof, which often carried deep snow loads in the winter.

As the morning fire's dying embers whitened into ash in the rough stone fireplace, W. Andrew Morgan's eyes strayed toward the German Luger pistol mounted above the mantel. As always, the Luger triggered a flood of bitter memories.

He had joined the army near the end of World War II, and his father had engineered an officer commission for him. He was sent into the Battle of the Bulge as a replacement in the Second Infantry Division, the famous Indian Head Patch. He survived a vicious attack on a bunker that he claimed to have defended. In the heat of the battle he had actually hidden himself in the snowy forest and made his way back to the battle as reinforcing troops arrived. He had no substantiation for his claims, but he became a war hero.

He was in a London pub the day before he was to be shipped back to the United States. A small-statured, black-haired boy sidled up to him and showed him a German Luger that was for sale for twenty dollars. Morgan wanted a German gun to corroborate his war story and bought it.

The sights and sounds of that day were still clear in his mind—the smell of the lifting fog and salty sea; the crisp coffee served by the Salvation Army; the acrid tang of tobacco smoke as the GIs lit up; the line of soldiers seated on duffel bags containing all their personal possessions.

A sudden stir at the front of the line had brought the GIs to a nervous attention. Hoarse whispers came down the line. "Duffel-bag check."

Morgan started in concern. "What are they checkin' for?"

A grizzled officer near Morgan said, "Who knows? I heard they're checking for smuggled weapons—and if they catch you with one, even a German one, it's a two- to five-year sentence."

Just then the boy who had sold the gun walked up and whispered, "Hey, GI Joe. I take your Luger on ship for you, five dollar."

The older officer asked with a profanity, "How you goin' to do that, kid?"

The boy pointed to the constant movement of crates taken up by cranes attached to nets made of aging gray hemp rope. "Easy. When it's dark."

The grizzled one asked, "How you goin' to find us on the ship?"

The boy shrugged. "I can't find you." He pointed. "*You* find *me* by where the chain goes in the hole in the ship. Nine o'clock, exact."

Morgan and the gray-haired soldier waited in vain for the boy to meet them by the anchor chain at nine o'clock that night. Finally it dawned on Morgan that by this time the boy had already sold the Luger again.

Morgan's eyes drifted back to the pistol. He had always suspected that the giver of the pistol knew the truth of his story, but because the giver was a close friend of his father, he felt obliged to display it. Today, he angrily vowed anew that he would get rid of that gun.

The drumbeat of helicopter blades on thin Colorado mountain air intruded on his reverie. Morgan did not go out to the helicopter pad to meet Paul Gentry, liaison officer between the president and the National Security Council. Gentry entered, and the men greeted each other civilly but not warmly. Morgan pointed to a leather chair. Gentry sat on the edge of the seat.

Without preamble, Morgan demanded, "Give me your report."

"The president will ask for a hundred million for the Contras."

"Who'll be responsible for spending the money?"

"Bermudez, Calero, and Cruz."

Morgan's eyes glazed as he sat in deep thought. *Bermudez was Somosa's top military aide, and Calero is the darling of the U.S. banking industry. I'll have to find out about Cruz.*

Morgan allowed Gentry to sit in silence for a moment, then asked, "How long can the Contras hold out without U.S. aid?"

Gentry shook his head decisively. "They can't. The Contras don't have the support of Nicaraguans, and they have no money of their own."

Morgan stared into the gray ashes of the fire. Finally he said, "Your reports have not included a group who operates in southern Nicaragua—called El Cinco."

"I'm aware of El Cinco."

"How much do you know of its leadership?"

"We know a couple of names. Valderas. Another called Miguel. Communist sources list one called Jaime. No last names for the last two."

"Make your next report complete. El Cinco means the five. I want their full names and background information. One of those is female. She's an agent of the Sandinistas, and she endangers the whole project. I want her gone—eliminated."

Paul Gentry seemed hesitant in following these instructions. "I've heard a little about her, but I'm not at all sure we—"

Morgan cut him short. "I think El Cinco is a significant organization. Its strength lies in the unspoken support of

Nicaraguans—a hope that El Cinco can become a power to represent the people." He turned back to the fireplace. "We must find, protect, and support any group that can bring about the downfall of the Sandinistas—even if that means the death of one individual. I want a positive report in four weeks."

When Paul Gentry still hesitated, Morgan spoke in icy words. "I hope I don't have to remind you of your military fiasco in Da Nang and the effect it would have on your career if made public."

Paul Gentry held his anger in check. In truth, he wasn't really concerned about his military actions in Da Nang any longer. But there wasn't much sense in antagonizing Morgan, and it could mean a black mark against a nearly perfect military record. He just hoped Morgan didn't know about his other indiscretion in Da Nang. The meeting was at an end.

* * *

Leon Hardesty sat in a comfortable leather chair in the disguised CIA headquarters in Limón, Costa Rica. He stared at the paper in his hand and then crumpled it and threw it into the waste basket. He spun in the chair and stared at the bold colors of the Matisse prints on one wall. After a moment, and in great agitation, he spun the chair again and went to the waste basket, retrieved the paper, and smoothed it out. He sat in a secretary's swivel chair at the keyboard of the computer and began to tap in the information to open a new file. The first words on the screen read:

> TOP SECRET
> THE GENTRY DIRECTIVE
> RE: FEMALE LEADER OF EL CINCO

Then followed a list of charges against this unnamed person.

CHAPTER TWO

JOHN TANNER CARRIED ONLY the small case he had stored overhead in the luggage rack. He noticed the man coming off the plane behind him because he was so ugly. The man's dark, flat face looked like it had met head-on with a bus, and though his features had been flattened, he'd have left his mark on the bus too.

Following the directions of the arrows, John walked down the San Jose airport halls. A tall man, dressed in a fashionable off-white seersucker business suit, passed the barrier going the wrong way. He spoke in Spanish. "Come with me."

John put out his hand and asked, "Leon Hardesty?"

"Wait until we're in the car."

John Tanner was whisked through the formalities of entering Costa Rica. John wondered if the officials noticed the VIP treatment given to one wearing denim pants, a suede leather vest worn over a faded red shirt, and a once cream-colored sombrero. It would be difficult for a casual observer to decide if this *vaquero* was Anglo or native.

Outside of the terminal, John noticed the ugly man who had gotten off the plane behind him standing at the curb. He had made it through *inmigración* as quickly as John had. He wore no hat, and the folds of skin at the base of his closely cropped, grizzled gray head of hair accentuated his obesity. A business suit completed the grim caricature.

John asked if Hardesty recognized the man, and after a brief hesitation was answered shortly, "Fiero Rinskin. Sometimes works for the Company."

A car whisked up to the curb, and Hardesty motioned for him to get in the back. The car sped along a divided highway toward the congestion of the city. Large stands of coffee bean trees grew up the sides of the hills. The roadside was filled with sign boards and all the trappings of commerce. They entered a parking lot next to a sign labeled *COLEGIO DE ABOGADO*. Hardesty led the way to a stately dining room. Its brick-red tiled floors shone brilliantly. Graceful columns supported the roof structure. A curving staircase led to a balcony. They were ushered to a table set with fine linen and silver.

Keenly aware of his cowboy garb, John said, "I don't understand the significance of calling this place the Colegio de Abogado."

Hardesty murmured, *"Momento."* He signaled the waiter and ordered drinks.

John asked for an orange soda.

Hardesty continued. "It's a private club—for practicing attorneys."

Steak smothered in a mushroom white sauce arrived, and Hardesty spoke in Spanish. "You come highly recommended."

John spoke in English. "Thank you. I—"

Hardesty interrupted in Spanish, "I need a case officer to pass as native Nicaraguan, so I must hear your Spanish. Tell me about your last assignment."

"I've been working in Panama City for several months—"

Hardesty interrupted. "What are your goals with the Company?"

He started to explain and was interrupted again. "Where were you born?"

"Colonia Dublan, Mexico."

"What was your father doing in Dublan, Mexico?"

"He worked on a large cattle ranch."

Hardesty threw a curve. "You look like a gringo to me."

John answered, his lie a practiced casualness. Since he needed to pass as a native, he said simply, "I'm Nica, *hecho y derecho*—tried and true."

"You a Sandinista?"

This test question required a politic answer. "I want what's best for my people. What about you? Are you Nica, Sandinista, or Somocista?"

Hardesty chuckled. "Good answer. You went to BYU in Utah?"

"Yes. A bachelor's in animal husbandry and a master's in international business."

"You a Mormon?"

"Yes."

"Orthodox?"

"If by orthodox you mean am I committed to the goals and ideals of the Church, then yes, I am."

"Doesn't that commitment interfere with your work for the Company?"

"Panama wasn't my first assignment. My feelings and commitment for the Church haven't interfered with anything I've had to do so far."

"I noticed that you lied very casually to me when I said you looked like a gringo—doesn't that go against your teachings?"

John flushed. "I supposed you were testing me. I wasn't lying any more than if in playing a role on stage I spoke the lines my part called for."

Hardesty grinned, nodded slightly, then asked, "You have a girlfriend?"

"Not at present."

"Ever have one?"

"Of course. A girl I met in Mexico—Colonia Juarez, one of the Mormon Colonies." John half expected that Hardesty would

ask what the Mormon Colonies were, but he didn't. John
continued, "We kind of grew up together. Her name was Juliana
Brown." He wondered if Hardesty would recognize the name,
for Juliana, too, worked for the Company. They had trained
together after the Y. If Hardesty recognized the name, he said
nothing.

"What do you know about the political situation in
Nicaragua?"

Prior to being sent to meet with Leon Hardesty, John had
heard that there was a coveted assignment that would include a
lot of travel in Nicaragua, some good adventure, as well as some
danger. He had hoped he would get the assignment and sensed
that the answer to this question would determine whether the
assignment would be his or not.

He expressed himself thoughtfully. "You may already know
that I spent two years in Honduras for my church. It was a totally
different kind of work, but we couldn't help but get a picture of
what was going on in Nicaragua."

For the first time John had the feeling that Hardesty was
really listening to his answers. He continued. "I even met a few
people who had left Nicaragua trying to find some kind of
asylum. My understanding is that the Somosa family and their
supporters, the Somocistas, ruled Nicaragua for many years, and
by nature of past connections continued that rule until a group
called Sandinistas rebelled and gained power. The problem was
that the Sandinistas were not completely in favor of a democracy
and even had some communists aboard. Then a group of rebels
called Contras, and I've heard they are U.S. supported, fought
and are still fighting to take back control—and that's about
what Nicaragua's political situation is today."

Hardesty had listened carefully to John. "I'd give you a
passing grade on your summary." Then, dinner completed, he
said to John, "Your Spanish is better than most gringos, so you'll
do. Your assignment is in San Carlos, Nicaragua. Cover: Boquis

Cattle Ranch. Your job with Boquis is to build a better herd. As for the Company, there're rumors of another group of insurgents called El Cinco. They operate along Rio San Juan—that borders the rangeland of Boquis. If El Cinco doesn't turn out to be communist, we hope to merge them with the Contras to open a southern front. The Company might invest training and weaponry in El Cinco. Penetrate the group. Find out if they have communist leanings, and evaluate their leadership. There is one of particular interest, a female—Paul Gentry says that her name is rumored to be Dama Mariposa. We want a complete report on her. By the way, if you slip up, we never heard of you."

Hardesty motioned to the waiter for the bill.

John tipped his glass, and ice clicked against his teeth. He thought, *A lady leader named Dama Mariposa? Wonder why the CIA wants a complete report on her?* He looked directly into Hardesty's eyes. "Is this a hazardous duty assignment for which I'll get extra pay?"

The waiter appeared and handed Hardesty a bill. "Not exactly. But whatever you can pry out of Boquis is yours to keep."

Hardesty stood up and shook his hand. "You have reservations on an Aeronica flight in one hour. You'll be met by an operative in Managua. He'll turn a Ford pickup to your use. It's a rough ride from Managua to San Carlos, but you can make it." He handed him a packet of papers. "Proof of Nicaraguan citizenship and a map to get you to the Boquis ranch. Spend a couple of days in San Carlos, and rent a *pensión* to stay at before you present yourself to Ernesto Boquis. You've got six months, but I want monthly reports, in person, in Limón. Good luck."

* * *

John was met in Managua by an operative of the CIA who gave him information about Ernesto Boquis and his ranching operation. "Here's your contract with Boquis Cattle Ranch.

There's a small branch of Banco Managua in San Carlos. Go to the bank and ask for Umberto and open an account. Umberto's not with the Company, but he can help you find a pensión and can introduce you to Eduardo Solano, a feed-store owner and also the owner of a hacienda bordering Boquis land. He's your starting place in San Carlos. Boquis will likely have an account with Solano, so use him as much as you can. You should only contact me in case of great emergency. Any questions?"

John had many questions, but he simply shook his head.

The highway leading down El Lago de Nicaragua was poorly maintained, but compared to the road from San Miguelito to San Carlos, which was barely more than a trail following the power lines, it was very good. Many times John was glad that the Ford pickup was equipped with four-wheel drive. He was glad for the excellent cover identification, for he was stopped often by soldiers on the drive down to San Carlos.

Umberto was very cooperative and did help him find a pensión. He also introduced John to Eduardo Solano.

Solano was tall, and his black hair was streaked with iron gray. His black eyes regarded John steadily when Umberto introduced the men.

John explained to Señor Solano, "I've been hired to build up the herds of Boquis Cattle Ranch. Before I make any suggestions, with your help, I'd like to look over the rangeland where their cattle graze without their vaqueros knowing I'm doing it— a college man's ideas are not always well accepted by the cowhands."

Solano's wife was in the store that day. As Solano presented her to John, he looked at John to help him with his name.

John used the Spanish pronunciation, accenting the last syllable. "Juan Tah*nair*. I'm pleased to know you, Señora Solano."

Solano said to his wife, "I want to help Señor Tanner if I can. Perhaps we can invite him to dinner this evening?"

She looked doubtful. "Katia is coming today."

"Si. I know. It would be good for Katia to meet someone new."

Her face brightened. "*Claro que si*. Please, Señor Tanner, dine with us?"

John said, "I would love to, but only if you will call me Juan."

Mr. Solano said, "And you must call me Eduardo. My truck is . . ."

"I have a pickup. I'll follow you. Then I can drive back to my pensión."

Hacienda Solano was on a dirt road a half hour's drive out of San Carlos and toward the hills. The house was a large, well-kept, stuccoed-adobe structure. The orange tiles of the roof were aging and in some places covered with moss. Thick vines, blossoming with purple bougainvillea, splashed color across the colonnades in front.

"This is a magnificent home and ranch. How much stock do you run, Don Eduardo?" John said, using the respectful Spanish title.

"Fewer than a hundred head. The Sandinistas conscripted most of my cattle and divided my land between four of their former commanders."

A massive stone fireplace filled one wall of the stately living room. Leather-upholstered chairs and sofas were placed on the polished quarry-tile floor.

A young woman was seated in a soft chair by a window; a book was open in her hand. She had been staring at the mountain rising in the background. She stirred from her reverie and embraced Eduardo. "*Hola,* Papa. Are you well?"

She wore a red and white plaid cotton blouse, jeans, and distinctly feminine cowboy boots.

Eduardo returned her embrace and then pushed her away and looked at her. "Si. Despite your men's clothing, you are more beautiful than ever, *mi hija*—my daughter."

She blushed and said, "Papa!"

Eduardo hugged her again, then turning to John, he said, "Katia, this is Juan Tanner. He's in San Carlos to inspect the Boquis cattle herds."

When she looked at him, it seemed to John as if the warm brown of her eyes changed to a cold, piercing black. If Eduardo noticed her coolness, he ignored it.

John held out his hand. "*Mucho gusto,* Katia."

After a moment of hesitation, Katia took his hand. Her voice was toneless. "Hola, Señor Tanner."

Eduardo said, "I invited Juan to stay for dinner. Why don't you show him the horses while I help Mama in the kitchen."

John wondered if Eduardo needed to help Mrs. Solano, or if he hoped that leaving them alone would help overcome Katia's chilly greeting.

Some of Katia's warmth returned. She hugged her father again. "It's good to see you, Papa."

After Eduardo left the room, they stood in silence for a moment. Finally Katia sighed and said, "Perhaps it would be easier for both of us if I did show you the grounds and horses."

John tried a smile. "Whatever would make it easier on both of us."

They stood for a moment on the wide veranda. She had expressive eyes like her mother but was tall and lean like her father. She pointed. "That hill was the southern border of the ranch. Then it turned west to the waters of Lago de Nicaragua, and east to the range of hills that you see. That was the hacienda I was raised on—ten thousand hectares—that my father lost to the revolution . . ." Her words trailed off.

She turned suddenly to John and demanded, "What part of the United States are you from, Señor Tanner?"

John was surprised. "Would you believe me if I said I was from Mexico?"

"Not for a minute. Everything about you cries *Americano! Americano!*"

John was sure he could bluff it out. Yet he said, "I've been told that my accent is perfect. But I'll tell you where I'm from if you'll tell me what things are hollering Americano so loudly."

She turned away and stared at the mountains. "Your accent *is* nearly perfect, but it's not the way you speak words. It's other things that you could never fake. The way you speak so casually—and something in your eyes. Maybe freedom. Freedom we in Nicaragua have—have rarely known."

"I didn't think I'd said that much."

"You spoke only three sentences. But one would have been sufficient. Where *are* you from?"

"I really was born in Mexico. Colonia Dublan, Mexico." John would never be able to explain why he went on to say, "But when I was fourteen years old I moved to *Los Estados Unidos.* To a town called Payson, in Utah."

"And the CIA helped you perfect your Spanish?"

"No. I was also a missionary for my church for two years in Honduras. Mostly around Tegucigalpa." John hoped that Katia would not ask him directly if he worked for the CIA. He did not want to lie to her.

"Most gringos can't speak Spanish without an accent. You have done well."

Katia looked toward the house. It was clear she wished they would be called to dinner. She said, "Come, Señor Tanner. I'll show you our horses."

As she started toward the stable, John reached out and caught her hand. She spun around, anger sparking from her eyes. John released her hand quickly. "Please, Katia. Can't you just call me Juan?"

She regarded him silently.

John said, "How about a truce, then? Just for dinner. So your folks won't be—be uncomfortable."

There was just the hint of a thaw as her eyes seemed to change from smoldering black to a dark hue of brown. She

spoke in English for the first time. "Okay, but I will not call you
Juan to help you hide your American self. I call you in
English—Chohn." It was clear she could not make the English *j*
sound.

John smiled. "Fair enough. But my friends call me Johnnie."

Katia reverted to Spanish. "If you ask me to be your friend,
then you ask for a dangerous friend, Chohnee. So . . . a truce.
Then maybe later you will tell me what you *really* do in San
Carlos."

They walked slowly toward the stables, and Eduardo stepped
onto the veranda. "Katia! Juan! Come to dinner."

When they entered the dining room, a tall young man was
seated at the table. John noticed that Katia greeted him very
coolly. He was introduced as David Solano, Katia's younger
brother.

If, during the course of the meal, anyone wondered why
Katia called their guest Chohnee, no one asked. The only one
who did not join freely in the conversation was the young man.
David's deliberate manner made John think he would be inflex-
ible in his thinking.

After dinner, Eduardo invited John to join them in the living
room.

John said, "I've imposed on your hospitality enough for
today, Don Eduardo. Perhaps I can stop by tomorrow for the
discussion I mentioned?"

Eduardo hesitated for a moment and then speaking to his
daughter, said, "Katia, Juan wants to inspect the Boquis cattle.
Could you go with him and be a guide for him tomorrow?
Perhaps David—"

David interrupted sharply. "No! I have business in San
Carlos."

Katia looked speculatively at John. "I too have business, but
I suppose Chohnee could come with me. We will be able to look
at some Boquis cattle."

Eduardo said, "You wouldn't have to worry, Juan. Katia's been riding those hills since she was a small child."

Katia asked, "Chohnee, do you think I can give you the answers you want?"

John had a disquieting thought that he would likely be answering more questions than Katia. He managed a smile. "Great. What time?"

She gestured broadly. "Anytime works for me."

"How about—say, ten?"

Her smile was slightly wicked. "You don't look like you have bad gringo habits of getting up so late. Can you be here at eight?"

"Sure. Eight sharp. Will we take my four-wheel-drive pickup?"

Katia's laugh filled the room. "There is no pickup, not even with four driving wheels, that can go where we will go. Do you ride horses?"

John said matter-of-factly, "I ride well enough." Then he turned to Señora Solano. "*Muchas gracias* for a delicious dinner."

Katia followed him onto the front veranda. "Just come to the stable in the morning. The horses will be ready."

* * *

John debated a moment and then rolled a scrap of scarlet cloth and tied it around his neck to form a colorful tie. He spoke to the image in the mirror. "Vanity of vanities saith the preacher."

As he studied himself further, he realized that he had thickened through the torso since his rodeoing days at Payson High. He first tucked his denim pant legs into the top of his boots and then, not liking the effect, pulled them out, partially hiding his worn cowboy boots. Then he slipped on the suede vest. Finally he fitted the faded cream-colored hat on his head, covering his shiny black hair. A final glance in the mirror gave him satisfaction. He was tall and still fairly lean. He *could* pass for a Nicaraguan *vaquero*.

He arrived at the Solano residence promptly at eight o'clock. Eduardo was standing, looking up at Katia who was already mounted on a small, but sleekly muscular, dappled gray Appaloosa. Katia wore a red and white poncho-like *huipil,* a kind of blanket with a hole for her head to pass through, that hid her body as well as the saddle that she sat on so gracefully. The only other parts of clothing that John could see were her dainty cowboy boots and what looked like the legs of camouflage pants.

Eduardo handed John the reins for a large, shiny chestnut and greeted him with the comment, "Sometimes he's a bit skittish with a new rider."

John swung into the saddle. Eduardo nodded in approval as John gently checked the horse's dancing movements and clucked at the prancing horse.

Katia looked at John and asked, "Are you ready, Chohnee?" She urged her horse into a smooth lope.

Eduardo waved, and John's mount leaped to catch up with Katia. As soon as they were far enough away that Eduardo could not hear, Katia called to him, "At least if you *are* CIA, you ride well."

John did not respond.

In a half hour's time they had ridden over the first low hill. Forests of fragrantly pungent pine, eucalyptus, and guanacaste quickly hid the Hacienda Solano from view. They rode in silence, the only sound that of the horses' hooves striking the ground and the rattling of occasional rocks being dislodged as the riders made their way up the steep rocky incline of the trail. Both horses were blowing from their exertions. After an hour they topped the hill, and Katia turned her horse into a clearing. She swung lithely down and tied the Appaloosa to the gnarled branch of a eucalyptus tree.

As Katia's huipil cleared the saddle, a Belgian FAL automatic rifle was revealed, nestled in a holster attached to the saddle.

John sat on his horse in silence and watched Katia's movements.

She glanced up at him and, pointing to an outcropping of rock, said, "That's a good place to watch for action in the valley."

John tethered his horse close to Katia's. The horses were hidden from the view of any inquiring eyes by the trees. Katia took a pair of binoculars from the saddlebags and moved to the cluster of large boulders. At no time did she allow herself to be silhouetted against the sky, and she kept herself hidden from below. John mused, *She's a darned thorough professional.*

At the largest boulder, she slipped the huipil over her head, revealing a camouflage fatigue uniform. The .38-caliber pistol holstered around her waist seemed to leap out at John. She folded the huipil and placed it on one of the smaller boulders as a pillow for her elbows. She focused the binoculars and quickly scanned the valley.

John looked into the deep green vale. Tan and gray Brahman cattle grazed contentedly in several small clusters. After a moment, John sat on his heels near a boulder ten feet from where Katia was watching the scene below. He pulled a blade of sweet green grass and idly chewed on the end. After a time he asked, "You often run into bear in these hills?"

Katia didn't even look at him. "Bear? What do you mean?"

"Well, you seem particularly well armed to snoop on grazing cattle."

Katia turned and her brown eyes met his gaze steadily. "And you seem particularly uninterested in *checking out* the cattle yourself."

"I had in mind to check them up close. Can't tell a whole heck of a lot from this far away—even if I had brought binoculars."

Katia's laugh reminded John of the unexpected sound of wind chimes. "Would you know what to look for, Chohnee?"

John flushed slightly. "I was raised on a ranch. Beef cattle."

She stood up, placed the binoculars on the boulder, and turned to face John. Was it his imagination, or did her hand hover very near the pistol?

She said, "There's a horse. Nothing stops you from checking the cattle up close, though I can't think why you would bother. I don't for one minute think you care how El Rancho Boquis cares for its cattle. Is it time yet, Chohnee, for you tell me what you *really* do in Nicaragua?"

John suddenly felt very uncomfortable. He was unarmed. He slowly stood up, measuring the chance of reaching Katia before she could get her pistol out of the holster. Chills played up and down his back as she smoothly extracted the now deadly-looking .38 from its holster.

His words were hesitant. "What's with the gun? You aiming at me?"

"No, Chohnee. The target is the bear behind you."

At just that moment one of the horses whinnied and stamped a hoof. John, in reflex action, sprang to his left and rolled on the ground coming up on his feet facing the horses, his hands outstretched.

Again laughter rippled from Katia's lips. "The only bears in the forests of Nicaragua are communist and more dangerous than your Davy Crockett bears." The laughter in her voice was matched by laughter in her eyes.

During the short interval of his defensive movement, the gun had been returned to its holster. She picked up the binoculars and turned to watch the valley below, but, not able to contain her mirth, she shook with laughter.

John roughly spun her around. "That was not funny!"

John's breath was taken away as he stared into her face. Her shiny black hair was slightly windblown. Though she wore no makeup, her dusky cheeks were naturally rouged. Sunlight sparkled from her warm brown eyes, and her even white teeth shone brightly in her wide smile. His anger evaporated as quickly as dew on a summer morning.

"I'm sorry, Chohnee . . ." She burst into a peal of laughter. "I couldn't help—I went to school in Florida, and I heard a song." She began to sing, "Davy—Davy Crockett killed him a bear when he was only three." She convulsed into giggles again and said, "I wondered—and yet I was impressed. You looked as if you really would attack with no weapon but your hands."

Finally John himself laughed. "I guess I did look foolish."

With these words Katia's mirth vanished. "You did more than look foolish. You've acted foolishly. You follow someone you don't know out into country you are not familiar with, and you have no weapon. That's . . ."

"But I followed someone I trust . . ."

Katia's words were harsh. "That is most foolish of all! In Nicaragua today, you trust no one. Despite the victory of the Sandinistas, we are still in revolution. No one knows what side anyone else is on. Trust is destroyed! Someday it might return, but for now you trust no one!"

Her mood change was complete. The tears that had formed in her eyes were clearly no longer tears of mirth. She turned around and put the binoculars back up to her eyes. An immediate resolve that went against every element of his CIA training formed in his mind.

He moved close to her and took her hand in his. At first she tried to pull away, but John held her tightly to his side. He didn't say anything for a time. Finally she relaxed slightly, and they leaned against the rock, watching the peaceful scene below. Light clouds drifted overhead, occasionally casting patches of shadow on the lush green of the grazing land. The cattle either quietly munched on grass or lay contentedly chewing cud in the shade of the few trees dotting the valley floor.

John said, "If trust returns to your land, it must begin somewhere. If you never learn to trust anyone, no one will ever learn to trust you."

Katia turned to look into his eyes. "If I ever meet someone worthy of trust, I'll try your idea."

John spoke quietly. "From when you first met me, you suspected that I'm CIA. Everything I know tells me I should not admit I am. But I do because I trust you, Katia."

Katia shrugged. "So you admit what I already knew. So what? Two questions are more important to me."

"And they are?"

Katia's perplexity was clear. "First you—you seem such a decent person. How can you—can you work for the CIA?"

"I don't understand your question. I have deep feelings of empathy, of loyalty to the people of Central America. I was born in Mexico—raised and worked with the *campesinos*. I want to help them get civil and economic freedom. And while we're asking questions, why do your people have such distrust for the CIA—for the United States for that matter?"

Placing the binoculars to her eyes, she scanned the valley again. Clearly she had more on her mind than guiding him to grazing Boquis cattle.

"Well, what are your reasons for not trusting us?"

"Experience. Our experience with the United States tells us that your meddling only makes our lives more difficult. And even if it made our lives better, don't you think we have the right of self-determination?"

"But that's what we're trying to do. Help you gain democracy! And how has our so-called meddling made your lives more difficult?"

"Chohnee, don't try to make me think you're a child in understanding. Tell me—who is the biggest crime boss in the United States?"

"Crime boss? What's that got to do—"

"Just tell me, if you know."

"I *don't* know—I've heard the name Andrew Luciano."

"What if a foreign power helped make him president of the United States, then fixed it so your army enforced his will on your people and kept him and his sons after him in power. Would you be happy with that foreign power?"

"Of course not! But who has—"

"The United States put Anastasio Somoza in power clear back in 1937, and you trained his national guard and kept him and his family in power while they raped and looted our country until the Sandinistas kicked them out in 1979. The first Somoza had *nothing* before the U.S. put him in charge of the national guard. When his son was kicked out, he had several hundred million dollars and owned a fourth of the farmland of Nicaragua! All of that stolen from the people of my land!

"Perhaps my two years in the United States spoiled me for living in my own country. Your people have freedom, and though your system isn't perfect, at least you have some degree of self-determination. I don't understand! Your people permit the CIA to do things in a foreign country that you'd never allow in the United States, and you justify it by saying you're helping us gain civil liberties or economic stability. And the truth is, you aren't trying to give us democracy at all! You're protecting your bankers or your foreign capital investments!"

Katia paused and then looked straight into John's eyes. "And the CIA? Every time I—it's strange, Chohnee. There's some-thing about you. When I met you yesterday, I knew you were CIA, and you didn't lie to me. I guess I really want to trust you, to believe what you say about your motivation. But your CIA— my experience is they lie when the truth would serve a better purpose!"

John removed his hand from Katia's. He wanted to argue, felt the need to refute her words, but he recognized the seeds of truth in her indictment. He said quietly, "You throw powerful punches, Katia."

"Believe it or not, I feel badly because I've started to like you, Chohn Tanner. And so I hate to ask, but my next question is more important, because my first was to satisfy curiosity. The second is for my country." She paused.

"What is your assignment for the CIA in Nicaragua?"

John stood in silence for a time. "Since I am CIA, and you believe that we always lie, why would you believe what I tell you?"

"I've asked myself the same question."

He turned and walked toward the horses.

Katia took the .38 from the holster. Her words were strained. "Be careful, Chohnee. I have to know your assignment with the CIA. I like you, but my country comes first. Stay away from the rifle on my horse."

John turned and faced her but continued walking backward toward the horses. "If you shoot me, Katia, you'll have to do it face-to-face."

Katia raised the .38 to the level twice. John continued walking backward toward the horses. Finally, she turned to the boulder and stared down into the valley. John turned and pulled the Belgian-made rifle from the holster attached to Katia's saddle. Then he walked back to where Katia stood with the pistol still in her hand. He placed the rifle on the large rock in front of her.

He put one hand on each shoulder and turned her to face him. "That's what trust is all about."

Her eyes were troubled. "That was more stupid than trusting. I could have shot you."

"But you didn't because of my trust."

"Your brave experiment didn't prove anything, because I don't know if I didn't shoot you because of trust or because— because I like you."

"Whatever the reason, I'll tell you what I'm doing in Nicaragua. We believe there is a group of insurgents known as El Cinco who operate along Rio San Juan. I'm to find them and report my opinion as to whether they should receive assistance from the U.S. to help overthrow the Ortega brothers." He said nothing of his instructions to look for signs of communism in the group.

Katia's words did not match the expression of relief that seemed to cross her face. "You saw my rifle. Don't you think you told me too much?"

John shrugged his shoulders. "I know that most of the FALs come from Cuba. *Que sera, sera.*" After a moment he continued. "I guess that just to keep my story legitimate, I'd better ride down and take a look at the cattle."

Katia didn't say anything.

"Would you consider coming with me—or maybe your business up here on the hill isn't finished yet?"

"As a matter of fact, no, it isn't. I need to stay here till twelve o'clock." She glanced at her watch. "Nearly an hour from now."

"I don't suppose it would do any good to ask what you're looking for?"

"No, it wouldn't. Did you bring lunch with you?"

John pulled a small plastic bag of trail mix from his pocket.

She made a face. "Chohnee, if you wait till I can ride down with you, I have a nice lunch in my saddlebags." She pointed to a tree on the valley floor. "We'll have a picnic right there."

"Sounds like an offer I can't refuse." He shook some of the trail mix into his hand and then held the bag out to Katia.

Both munched on the mix, and John leaned over a boulder and studied the floor of the valley. He pointed to a trail coming into the valley and crossing the stream. "Where does that trail come from? Looks like it gets a lot of use."

Katia picked up the binoculars and studied the hills across from them. "What's your all-time favorite movie?"

"It's an oldie. *Cyrano de Bergerac.* Let me borrow the binoculars for a minute." He focused on the south end of the valley. "How long would it take by horse to reach El Rio San Juan?"

Leaning back against the boulder, Katia smiled. "Who knows? I never heard of *Cyrano de Bergerac.* What's your favorite TV show?"

"I don't usually watch TV. Is the valley on the other side of this hill as natural a route into Costa Rica as this one?"

"Did I tell you that my Appaloosa is named Sandinita? Or that the horse Papa let you ride is called Sandino?"

John turned abruptly and focused on the other end of the valley. He let some excitement rise in his voice. "Look! There are horses loaded with crates just crossing the stream!"

Katia leaped across the space between them, grabbed the binoculars from John, and quickly surveyed the scene. "Where? I don't see . . ."

John's laughter bubbled up from his belly. He felt good. "So. We're expecting a shipment of arms. Are we guards, or do we intercept it?"

For just the briefest moment, anger stormed across Katia's face. Rapidly her composure returned. "Think you're smart, don't you? Well, you didn't find out anything. Anyone would be curious to see horses loaded with crates out here in the middle of Boquis grazing land!"

John started to shake out another handful of trail mix. Katia grabbed the bag. "Don't eat any more! I've got a nice lunch, and you'll spoil your appetite. Furthermore, unless you want a frosty silence between now and twelve o'clock, you better find something innocuous to talk about."

John took the small package back from Katia and put it into his pocket. "All right. Why don't you tell me about your two years in Florida. It would be interesting to hear your reactions to us gringos."

She spread her huipil on the ground and sat on it, leaning the rifle against the boulder. "Okay. You keep lookout." A faint smile played over her lips. "You know what to look for." She continued.

"I went to Florida right after I finished what you would call high school. Papa wanted me to go to university in the United States. Somoza was in power. Papa still owned all of the hacienda. I stayed in a dormitory in Miami. It was exciting. An American boy fell in love with me."

* * *

After careful research, Adnan Ahman came to the conclusion that the group known as El Cinco centered its operations along the Rio San Juan. Dama Mariposa should easily be found there. Adnan began to put out through underworld sources that he would pay a healthy fee for her destruction. It wasn't long before word came to him of a professional killer named Fiero Rinskin, whose work, Adnan learned, centered in Central America. Adnan made arrangements to meet with the man. He was intrigued that a man so ugly could work unnoticed.

Adnan kept a large sum of money in a nameless account at the Bank of Managua, whose manager he had easily bought off. He obtained a safety deposit box and made arrangements with the manager that if a person came to him with a newspaper article telling of the death of one Dama Mariposa along with the box key, he was to allow that person access to the deposit box.

Adnan brought Fiero to the bank and withdrew ten thousand American dollars. Fiero watched as he put the money in the deposit box and gave him the key to the box. Then he explained his arrangement with the bank manager.

And so, an unwritten contract was agreed to between Fiero and Adnan. Fiero had the only key to the box itself—but that did not give him access to the box. The second "key" was that of a reliable newspaper article telling of Dama Mariposa's death.

Adnan felt that the balance was sufficient to insure that the man with such high recommendations and such revolting features would without doubt pursue the matter to its completion. He didn't really care whether Fiero or some other thug was successful, just that the woman who posed such a threat of exposing his real identity was dead.

CHAPTER THREE

KATIA KEPT JOHN SMILING and laughing with the story of her American adventure. At twelve o'clock, Katia made one more survey of the valley with the binoculars. "It's lunchtime, Chohnee." She swung into the saddle, and the Appaloosa began to dance. "The score is tied—one apiece. One for me, because of the bear, and one for you, because of the crates on the horses. I challenge . . ."

John interrupted. "Don't I get a score for taking your rifle?"

"No, because I call foul on that play. For the championship, we race to the tree close by the river." Then pointing, she said, "We'll have a picnic by that tree right there—loser serves lunch."

"No fair! You know the territory."

"But you ride the bigger and faster horse."

"No chance! There has to be some balance for knowledge of terrain."

She pointed to a large tree. From that point out on to the flat of the valley floor, grass covered the ground. "Okay. At that big tree, you turn right. I'll wait till you get to the first little tree at the bottom of the hill before I start."

"I'd hate to have Sandino step in a hole and break a leg. Besides, that's such a head start, you'd probably call foul if I beat you."

Katia's little mare was dancing all over the trail and seemed as excited at the prospect of a race as Katia. "You don't have to worry about Sandino. He has eyes in his feet. You only have to be brave enough to ride him. Get going! I can't hold Sandinita much longer. And as for a foul, you'll call foul this time!" Katia's laughter and excitement was infectious.

"All right! You're on! Turn to the right after that last tree?"

"Si, Chohnee, and I warn you, I'm tricky—and I never lose!"

John urged Sandino into a lope and called back, "Until this time!"

John reached the tree and looked up the hill. The gray Appaloosa was still dancing. He waved and called, "If you're ready, Katia, then go!"

John watched in open-mouthed wonder as Katia ignored the trail and urged her pony over the side of the steep hill. Sandinita was as surefooted as a deer, and in a headlong rush, she bounded around trees and boulders in a spectacular churning of dust and dirt. Katia had already covered more than half the distance to the tree that was John's starting point.

John held Sandino slightly in check. He would let him open up when he reached level ground. Just as he approached the tree where he was to turn to the right, the little gray Appaloosa burst out of a ravine and headed in a hard, fully stretched-out gallop straight for John and his horse. Katia, her hair flying in the wind, leaned nearly flat over the shoulder of the small horse.

John thought, *Surely she wouldn't be crazy enough to ram me at dead gallop?* But as the little horse pounded down the grassy incline and Katia showed no sign of turning her, John pulled on the reins to turn his horse.

Katia flashed by and let out a piercing scream. "Kiri! Kiri!" At the same time, her hand slashed down. She held a short length of pine branch and hit Sandino on his flank, causing him to shy in full stride. The unexpected sidewise movement of the horse nearly flung John from the saddle.

Katia's exultant laugh tumbled by, and John regained his seat, urging Sandino into a hard gallop. If he could cut between

Katia and the tree that marked the turn, he could still move in front of Sandinita and let his own larger, faster horse have its head. He gauged carefully and cut in as closely as he dared to miss the trunk and low-hanging branches.

Katia's hand flashed again, this time grabbing a branch and pulling it with her. She let it go just in time for it to whip back and slash at John. In reflex action, he pulled the reins hard to the left and threw his right hand up to protect his face. Sandino responded to the command to change directions in the midst of the hard turn, and once again John was nearly unseated.

By the time Sandino regained his stride, Katia, on her little Appaloosa, was halfway to the picnic tree. The little gray's legs were driving as pistons, in a flat-out, impossible-to-beat run. John let his horse finish the race in an easy gallop. As he rode up to the tree, Katia was leading Sandinita in an easy walk around the tree. Sandinita was somewhat lathered.

John chuckled. "You are one crazy lady!"

She said with a saucy smile, "You're not the first to notice, Chohnee."

John swung down from his saddle and pulled a handful of dry grass and began to rub sweat from the flanks of the Appaloosa.

"You know, Chohn Tanner, I like you more and more. You lose a hard race and don't complain, and the first thing you think of is the horses."

"Well, the horses did their part, and you warned me that you cheat."

"No, no, Chohnee! I don't cheat. I'm just tricky, that's all."

John picked up the reins to both horses and said, "Okay, you're one *tricky,* crazy lady. Let's walk the horses over to the stream."

"The grass is too tall. We'll ride. You won't forget you have to serve me lunch?"

They rode the horses through knee-high grass to the sparkling stream. A cluster of tan cattle watching them approach grudgingly moved a few meters and stared at them in suspicion.

John said, "This is a good place for a picnic."

Katia glanced toward the outcropping of rock where they had spent the morning. "No. We have to eat by the tree I showed you."

At the tree, Katia spread her huipil on the ground. "The food is in the right-hand saddlebag."

The food had been neatly rolled in a white cloth. Katia leaned against the gnarled brown tree trunk. A slight breeze toyed with her curly black hair. Her lovely, dusky skin was a smooth contrast to the bark of the tree.

John fumbled with the cloth for a moment.

Katia laughed lightly. "Spread the cloth out first and then place the food—oh—never mind." She took the cloth from him. "If you serve, you'll probably spill the food."

Soon the cloth was covered with rolled, meat-stuffed tortillas, small fruit *tortas,* a bunch of bananas, and two metal cups. Two place settings were marked by a cloth napkin, a fork, and spoon. She handed a canteen to John and said, "You can at least pour the chocolate."

He poured the chocolate and then took his watch from his pocket. The silver case had an elaborately carved design. Flipping open the lid, John checked to see that it was just twelve thirty.

The tinkling sound of music danced lightly in the air. Katia reached out for the watch. Her fingers traced the tiny figure etched on the back. "It's beautiful. The girl under the tree? Is she someone special, Chohnee?"

John smiled. "Unless I count you, there's no one special."

Katia said, "I've heard the song, but I can't remember the words."

"Yesterday." John spoke the words. "I believe in yesterday."

Katia snapped the lid closed at the end of the refrain. "The song is beautiful, but sad. I believe in yesterday too, but I believe in today more."

John put the watch in his pocket, picked up one of the tin cups, and held it up in a toast. "To today, then, Katia—and to us."

Katia said, "Just to today, Chohnee."

As they ate, John said, "Something puzzles me. How come the Sandinistas spared Boquis's land and chopped up your father's so much?"

Katia's face clouded. "Ernesto Boquis is an opportunist. His politics are like a reed that bends whatever direction the wind blows. My father's an idealist. Papa wanted Somoza gone, but he didn't give indiscriminate support to the Sandinistas. As a result, Boquis is favored, while Papa's land was divided as spoils for the victors." She paused and then said intensely, "I hate the Ortega brothers and what they are doing to Nicaragua." Then with an effort, she smiled and said, "But let's not spoil our picnic with politics. What did you mean when you said you were a missionary for your church?"

The request was unexpected, and John hesitated a moment, pondering whether to pass lightly over the question or to really tell Katia about the Church.

His answer was long enough in coming that Katia said, "Saying you were a missionary was just part of your CIA cover. You don't look like you were a missionary."

John grinned. "I can't help but wonder what you think a missionary is supposed to look like. I hesitated because I haven't asked the golden questions for a long time."

"I don't know what you mean, the golden questions."

"What do you know about the Mormon Church? Do you want to know more?"

"You're a Mormon, then?"

"Yes. What do you know about the Mormons?"

"Not much. I've heard there used to be Mormons in Nicaragua. I haven't heard anything about them since the revolution."

"Then would you like to know more?"

"You ask the question like you're serious. Maybe sometime I should learn about the Mormons. For now, just tell me if you really were a missionary."

John drew his finger over his chest. "Cross my heart. For two years, starting when I was nineteen, my work in Honduras was to tell people about Jesus Christ and Joseph Smith."

When Katia continued eating in silence, John said, "You're supposed to ask who Joseph Smith was."

"I know. But I don't want to talk about the political problems of Nicaragua right now, and I don't want to talk about religion either."

"How about I tell you what a Mormon missionary's supposed to look like?"

"You're just trying to trick me into letting you tell me about your religion. So—it's a beautiful day, isn't it?"

Katia had successfully deflected the conversation from either subject that John wanted to talk about. When there was not a scrap of food left on the cloth, John said, "I have never eaten such good food."

Katia laughed and stood up. "Mama said you looked like a man who could eat a lot. The only thing I worry about is if you can ride now."

John groaned. "Ride? Where to?"

Katia's tone and expression were suddenly serious. "I don't know if things will work. Your assignment with the CIA—it wouldn't work with any other person—but maybe with you—if you want it to."

"I guess you know that you're not making sense. If what will work?"

"Yesterday I told you if you ask me to be a friend, you ask for a dangerous friend. Today I tried to show you how dangerous. You passed my tests. But I'm not the only one to decide."

"I still don't have the faintest idea what you're talking about."

"You don't have to decide right now. Decide after tonight."

Suddenly the warm brown of her eyes seemed to turn to the same chilly black that John had seen the first moment he met her. "If you lied to me, it will be too bad for . . ."

John's voice was hard. "Don't say another word, Katia. I haven't lied to you about anything. So don't spoil our good feelings making threats you don't have to make."

Gradually the cold blackness left Katia's eyes and was replaced by dancing shades of various brown. The slightest wind-chime laughter rippled from Katia's lips. "I think I like trusting someone, Chohnee."

It seemed to John that her slightly parted lips were giving an invitation, and he pulled her closer. For just the briefest moment she allowed her lips to touch his, then she pushed him gently, but firmly, away.

"It can't be for us, Chohnee. I think—for me, the thing of most importance is freedom for my country."

She rolled the few utensils in the cloth and replaced them in the saddlebag. Then she took a small compact kit of makeup from the other bag and pretended to apply makeup. John looked up to the outcropping of rock and saw the round spots of reflected light bouncing off the boulders.

He watched but saw no responding signal from the rocks on the hill.

Katia swung into her saddle. As John mounted Sandino, he asked, "How do you know he got the message, since he didn't respond?"

Katia smiled at him. "You're quite good, Chohnee."

"I try to stay alert. It's kept me alive—till now."

"Are you showing off, or do you really want to know?"

John laughed. "You don't miss much yourself. I guess I just wanted you to know that you haven't hooked yourself up to a *cuerno verde.*"

Katia giggled. "Green horn? I've never heard of an animal with a green horn. It must lose something in the translation. But you handle yourself well enough to suit me."

Katia turned her horse up the trail.

John asked, "Do I blindly follow, or can I know where we're going?"

Katia pointed. "Up there, the path splits. Our trail crosses the ridge and drops down to the Rio San Juan. We keep a boat . . ."

"Am I permitted to know who 'we' is?"

"Do you know who the Sandinistas *really* are?"

"I think so, and I don't mind that they overthrew Somoza. Where we run into differences is in the support they received from the communists—and of course, eventually turning communist themselves."

Katia asked, "And it never occurred to you that if your government had helped the Sandinistas, communist support would have been refused?"

"I—ah, I wasn't much aware, and I certainly wasn't in a position to affect U.S. foreign policy. But I note you don't deny that the Sandinistas have turned communist."

Katia frowned slightly. "My father's not communist, and though he was wealthy, he supported the overthrow of Somoza. You see, the Sandinistas became *Los Muchachos,* our boys. In 1980, if your newly elected president hadn't been so afraid of communists under every bush, rock, and tree—if he'd been willing to help, the Sandinista junta would have had no reason to turn communist—and I admit some did."

They rode for a time. The only sound was the occasional cry of a bird and horse hooves striking dirt and rocks along the trail. There was a cluster of Brahman cattle grazing in deep grass.

Katia said, "I don't mean to tell you your business, but if you don't take a look at some Boquis cattle soon, you won't get to see any."

John smiled. "I saw some when we had our picnic, and I can tell quite a bit just riding this close to them."

Katia laughed. "Oh, a great expert? What can you tell just riding by?"

John pulled up on the reins and leaned over the saddle horn. "Go ahead. Laugh. But just for example, what difference do you see in the coat of hair on the cattle there and the coat of hair on both these horses?"

Katia studied the animals. "The horse's hair is smoother and shinier, but that's because we groom the horses. Nobody grooms a steer on the range."

"There's more to it than that. I'd bet a month's wages you feed both these horses grain. Right?"

"You mean I do that to keep Sandinita's hair shiny?"

"Yep. If she's healthy, her hair will be shiny whether she's groomed or not. Grass doesn't give the animals all the nutrients they need."

"But no one could afford to haul grain to the hills for the cattle."

"True. But it wouldn't take much to haul up some mineral blocks. Another thing. See how narrow they are in the fore-quarters? I guess I'd say that one of my first concerns would be to improve breeding stock."

"I have to admit, I'm impressed, Chohnee."

"So do I know enough about the Sandinistas yet, to find out who 'we' is?"

"Not yet. The Sandinistas, at first, were true patriots. They wanted freedom for Nicaragua. But they took over a bankrupt government, billions of dollars in debt, mostly to United States banks—an indebtedness that had served no purpose but to enrich Somoza. The Sandinistas had to claim that bankruptcy or try to make good on the debt."

"It wasn't much of a choice. You said they needed help desperately, and if they defaulted on their loans they would have received no help from the United States."

Katia raised her hands in a gesture of pleading. "For the sake of argument, agree that the Sandinistas, at first, were patriots and had honorable intentions. If you do that, I promise I won't remind you that we got very little help from the United States anyway."

John said, "You've already reminded me of that, but go ahead."

"Okay. Not only were we billions of dollars in debt, but also our country was in a state of ruin from the revolution; our factories were idle. Worse, no crops had been planted or harvested for two years, and even if the factories were producing or we had crops to sell, we had no ready market. We had thirty-five percent unemployment. People were desperate just to get food to eat. Despite these problems, everyone had great hope. Euphoria was in the air. The dictator Somoza was gone. Better days were here."

John watched as Katia sat on her horse, her fists clenched at her side. "And then reality set in. The job was too massive for us. We had no one to run the country but *paisanos!* We are only a few years into freedom, and already we are fragmented in our goals. People are losing their patience. They are tired of empty bellies and empty promises—and who can blame them?"

Katia turned away from John and wiped the tears that had started to fall from her eyes.

The impact of her words and the emotion with which she had spoken them were strong in John's mind. "I think that I understand your feelings."

Katia gave him a small smile. "We'd better get started. We still have a couple of hours' ride ahead of us, and it's nearly three o'clock."

"I still don't know who 'we' is. For that matter, who are you?"

Katia's face seemed bleak as she replied, "Nowadays, I am most often called Dama Mariposa."

Chills coursed up and down John's back. Suddenly it seemed the group he had sought was too easily found. Leon Hardesty's words came into his mind. *There is one of particular interest, a female . . . We want a complete report on her.* John impulsively resolved, *I will surely know more about this beautiful girl and what makes her tick before I report to anyone.*

He exclaimed, "You're one of El Cinco!"

Katia turned to face John, one hand clutching the saddle horn. "The original leaders of the Sandinista movement united to expel Somoza. Now they've fragmented into three groups— one, and the largest, communist. And I hate communism for destroying Nicaragua's chance at freedom! Another group strives for personal gain, and I hate them for selfishness. But the third, El Cinco, still wants freedom. And that is who *we* are. Sandinistas, *hecho y derecho*. Tried and true."

She urged her mount down along the trail. "Follow me, Chohnee! For today at five o'clock I want you to meet them."

John had to follow or be left behind.

CHAPTER FOUR

THE TRAIL WOUND DOWN the mountain and, in a series of switchbacks, dropped slowly in elevation. The cool fragrance of the timbered hills gave way to the heat and humidity of the lowlands. Tall forest trees were replaced by tangles of amate and huge mahagua trees. Ferns and vines grew in profusion and threatened to overrun the trail. It was quiet, except for the occasional cries of birds.

Katia turned in her saddle and spoke hesitantly. "It's—it's not too late. You could be in some danger . . ." Her words trailed off.

John continued riding in silence.

"You should know that the communists are bringing in a shipment of arms tonight that we'll try to take. The weaponry will come by boat along the Rio San Juan. Then it's transferred to horses along the Los Chiles trail."

"You'd take them along the trail?"

"No. They're most vulnerable when they shift the cargo from the boat."

"Are we—are we on the same side, Katia?"

After a pause, Katia answered, "I don't think so, Chohnee. But our short-term goals are the same. You want the overthrow of the Sandinistas. So do we—and whatever weapons we take strengthen us and weaken them."

Without warning, their way was blocked by three men sitting astride small but tough-looking ponies. None of the men spoke. They just sat holding automatic rifles carelessly pointed in John's general direction.

Katia said easily, "Hola, Miguel. *Que pasa?*"

"Hola, Dama. We were told to expect you. Efrain also."

Katia asked, "Has he arrived?"

Miguel shrugged his shoulders. "*No se.* I haven't heard."

Katia started forward, but not one of the rifles moved from alignment with John's body.

Miguel spoke. "Nobody said a stranger would join us."

Katia said, "It's okay. This is Juan—of Honduras. I brought him."

"I don't care who brought him. He doesn't stir from here without the vote of El Cinco. And I vote to drop him where he sits."

Katia said calmly, "Fortunately you only have one vote. We'll take him to *casa central*. I'll explain why I have . . ."

"You don't listen well, Dama. I said he doesn't move from here without the vote of El Cinco."

"Very well. Send Jaime for Efrain, if he's arrived, and Valderas." Miguel waved the automatic rifle and said, "Go get them, Jaime."

Jaime turned his horse and galloped down the trail toward the river.

After a tense and silent wait of fifteen minutes, the sound of horses' hooves pounding along the dirt trail announced the return of the men. The first rider wore camouflage fatigues, a weapon holstered around his waist, and a cloth hat hung over his belt. His face was weathered and brown. His hair was silvering, and his mustache was gray.

John's stomach muscles tightened as recognition came. The man was Colonel Efrain Montenegro. Company files listed him as a Sandinista, probably communist. Jaime was the second rider. The other rider, about sixty years old, had a deeply tanned face and a bushy gray mustache. He wore a faded blue cowboy shirt, dungarees, and a neat, wide-brimmed straw hat. Despite the paunch of his belly, he rode his dancing bay horse gracefully. He carried no weapon, though a Belgian automatic rifle was holstered to his black saddle. The saddle was ornately tooled and decorated with bangles of silver.

Miguel's attention was not diverted by the arrival of the riders.

Katia spoke to the older man first. "Hola, Valderas."

Valderas swept off his straw hat, revealing iron gray hair, and though he never left the saddle, he made a gallant bow to Katia. "Hola, Dama. It's always a pleasure for these tired old eyes to look upon your beauty."

Katia laughed good-naturedly. "Your flattery is good for my spirits." She turned to the other rider. "It's good to see you, Efrain. How goes it in Managua?"

"Tense, as usual." His eyes hardly left John as he responded to Katia.

Katia started without preamble. "Compas, this is Juan of Honduras. He brings information about a shipment of arms."

John hid his surprise at Katia's announcement.

Montenegro asked, "Where do you obtain your information?"

John said, "My sources are my own, Colonel Montenegro."

"And just how do you know me, Juan?" Montenegro asked sharply.

John mentioned battles in which Montenegro had received help from now-dead commanders. "I was with Montes at Matagalpa in '78 and with Recinos at Leon in March of '79." He felt justified in his lie.

Montenegro's features lightened, and a broad smile enlivened his face. "Of course! When Dama said you were from Honduras, my mind was thrown off track." Turning to Valderas, he asked, "You have any questions for Juan?"

Miguel interrupted. "I've got a question!" He demanded of John, "Why is a Honduran involved in Nicaragua's affairs?"

John said simply, "I'm not Honduran. I only lived in Tegucigalpa for a couple of years. The lady here might have misunderstood me."

Miguel growled. "How do we know your information isn't a trap?"

Katia's laughter caused Miguel to flush in more anger. "How could he set a trap in our own territory? We cover every trail between San Carlos and Concepción. We—"

"Enough!" Montenegro said. "Dama speaks for Juan. That's sufficient for me. It's time to vote." He turned first to Valderas.

Valderas said simply, "He looks good to me."

Katia said, "For Juan and Nicaragua."

Montenegro looked at Miguel, who spat on the ground. "*Nunca!* Never!"

Finally he turned to Jaime.

Jaime said, "Si."

Montenegro shrugged. "Four to one. Miguel, since you dissent, you watch Juan. If you find good reason, then shoot him."

Katia spoke up fiercely. "If you shoot him, Miguel, you'd better look quickly to me—for my face will be the last thing you ever see!"

Montenegro looked from Katia to Miguel. "I'd have preferred unity." He paused and asked John, "When does this shipment of arms pass through?"

"Tonight—but I'm not sure I want to proceed." John nodded his head at Miguel. "With your instruction to shoot me if he wants, I had just as well take my chances now."

Montenegro said, "Juan, you've nothing to fear if you don't intend to betray us. Where will—"

Katia interrupted smoothly. "We're wasting time!"

"That's right. Let's go!" Montenegro turned his horse down the trail.

John followed behind Katia and felt an uncomfortable chill play up and down his back as Miguel urged his horse into file right behind him.

They followed the trail through deep, oppressively close jungle for a couple of kilometers before coming to a stream. There they turned and followed the streambed for another half kilometer.

Hidden deep in a vale and only visible from a bend in the streambed was a large palm-thatched building. A young man leaning on a three-foot machete watched the horses splash out of the stream and the riders dismount. John groaned when he finally got out of his saddle. He walked stiffly around the clearing and bent and stretched his back to get rid of the kinks and pain. The young man holstered the machete and then took the reins of Katia's horse.

"Hola, Pablo." Katia nodded toward John's mount. "Please, take good care of these two." Then she blew the young man a kiss.

Pablo flushed, but replied, "Okay, Dama."

Valderas called to the only man whom John had not heard named, "Halcón, take care of our horses."

The floor of the thatched building was hard-packed dirt, and a single bare lightbulb, signaling a generator somewhere, hung in the middle of the room. A radio transmission unit was separated from the rest of the area by a thatched screen. A man, earphones over his head, sat at the radio console.

Montenegro nodded at a stool, and John sat at the table, as did the others. Montenegro said, "Let's make this quick. I have to return to Managua tonight. Juan, what does the shipment consist of?"

"Ten cases of FALs and some ammo. You could take it when they transfer the crates from the boat at the Los Chiles trail. But I wouldn't presume to tell you your business." John paused and asked, "What do you have to lose?"

Miguel shook a *cigarillo* from a packet, put it between his lips, and dragged a match along the edge of a small box. He blew a white stream of smoke at John. "Much, if you're not what Dama says you are."

John said evenly, "And you have your instructions in that event."

Miguel drew in another draft of smoke, blew that also at John, and said, "And don't think for one moment I would not follow them—to the letter."

John stood and said, "If you are man enough."

Miguel started to rise from the stool he was seated on, his anger evident. *"Gallo insolente."*

Montenegro roared, "Miguel, sit down and be quiet! Your insolent rooster would be crazy to ride into our territory and insult us if he wanted to double-cross us." He turned to John and spoke in a reasoning tone. "Juan, Miguel will fight any man, anytime, any place, for any reason—and would most likely win. So, *por favor,* don't try to pick a fight with him."

John stood, hands tensed at his sides. "I'll back off when he does."

Montenegro showed a moment's exasperation, then spoke to the group. "If the shipment is what he says, it will be worth taking. Agreed?"

He received a nod of approval from everyone except Miguel, who looked sourly at the table and muttered, "No."

"Your negative vote is duly noted, Miguel." Montenegro then began reviewing the plan of action. "Valderas, check out the boat and be sure it's ready for action. Your assignment will be the river, as usual." He looked at Katia. "Dama, normally you would work with Jaime. Do you want to do that, or would you prefer to show Juan . . ."

Miguel interrupted. "I'll work with the gallo. I can train him best. Besides if you don't let Jaime work with Dama, he might cry."

Jaime's handsome dark face flushed in deep anger. "Someday, Miguel, you'll go too far and I . . ."

Miguel looked at Jaime coldly. "Yes? You'll what?"

Montenegro jumped to his feet, tipping over the bench. In two strides he circled the table and stood looking down on

Miguel. He thundered, "Great heaven! What's got into you, Miguel? You trying to tear El Cinco apart? Maybe you've forgotten who brought Halcón to us unannounced."

Miguel looked startled. "That was different."

"It was no different! We trusted your judgment then as we must trust Dama's now."

It took a moment, but finally Miguel said, "Okay. I'll take Halcón. El gallo will go with Dama as you suggested."

Montenegro looked around the group. "You all know what to do. Do your work well. As usual, in my absence, Valderas is in charge."

They all stood up as Montenegro left the room. A variety of salutes accompanied him from the building. Valderas said, "I better check the boat."

Katia called to the radio operator, "Ramon! I need to send a message so Papa won't worry." She turned to John. "Wait for me here."

John waited for Katia and thought it interesting that no one asked about his qualifications. No one asked where he was from. No one asked about his next of kin in the event of the worst. Based on Katia's recommendation alone he had been accepted as an equal in their company—except for Miguel, who, John realized, was watching him closely.

Miguel spoke to him. "You fight as good as you talk, Gallo?"

John looked him steadily in the eye. "I get along."

With a big grin, Miguel stuck out his hand and said, "I think maybe you do, *hombre*."

John took his hand, and for a moment they tested each other's grip.

John followed Katia around behind headquarters to a pole corral. Sandino and Sandinita had been unsaddled and were quietly eating grass hay. Katia vaulted over the pole fence and into the corral. The little Appaloosa began to dance and nuzzle up to Katia. She pet her mount and said, "I'm sorry, but I need you for more work tonight."

John had to be firm with Sandino; the big horse was not too interested in being put back to work. By contrast, the little Sandinita seemed eager and anxious to please Katia.

Katia swung gracefully up into the saddle. "Ready, Chohnee?"

John glanced up. "Not exactly. We're going after the bad guys, right?"

"Bad guys? Well—yes, that's right."

"I don't have any defense except my hands, and though they can be certified as deadly weapons, I don't think I'll get close enough to use them."

Katia smiled. "I did warn you that I'm a dangerous friend."

John still had not mounted. "You said dangerous, not plain deadly."

"Well then, if you must have weapons, come with me. Miguel is in charge of issuing equipment to new recruits."

John swung into the saddle. As they rode back along the trail toward headquarters, Katia asked, "Were you serious about your hands, Chohnee?"

"Do you want to throw that .38 away and try me?"

Katia spurred Sandinita into a run, calling back, "No! I have better weapons than my fists. Haven't you noticed?"

John wondered if she meant dirty tricks like spooking horses with screams and pine branch switches, or her natural beauty and charm. He didn't feel like sitting on a running horse and so allowed her to precede him by several horse lengths.

John rode to where Katia and Miguel talked. A padlock hung in the hasp of the open door to the steel-paneled armory. Miguel's black eyes sparkled and he grinned constantly. He seemed excited in anticipation of the coming action. "Hey, Gallo! What weapon do you want?"

"What've you got?"

"Name it. See if I can't come up with it."

"Depends on what I have to do. But if you have a .22-caliber Remington rifle, a couple of extra clips of ammo, and let me back 'em up with a Remington long rifle pistol in a holster, I'd feel comfortable. Especially if you could give me a few grenades that I could clip to my belt."

Miguel grinned and disappeared into the armory. He returned in a moment with the specified weaponry. He said, "The pistol is not a Remington but it's just as good. In an emergency you can hand load the pistol from .22 clips. The grenades, you might not know . . ."

While Miguel talked, John opened the breech of the .22. Then he snapped it closed, and his response proved that he was no stranger to the grenades either. "They're Chinese." He took a grenade in his hand. "You twist and pull like this, and the pin comes out when you take it off the belt. They've got a three-second fuse."

Miguel grinned hugely. "Usually."

John nodded grimly. "Yeah. Usually."

Miguel said to Katia, "You picked a live one, all right."

"He told me he wasn't a cuerno verde."

Miguel was clearly puzzled. He muttered, "Cuerno verde—green horn?" Then as they rode away, Miguel hollered at them, "Hey, compas, have a good time!"

John asked sarcastically, "He think we're going to a party?"

Katia answered without a smile. "For him it *is* a party. It will be a sad day for Miguel when the revolution is over."

After a time, they splashed out of the riverbed, and John followed behind on the narrow and darkening trail to a marshy area where the waters of the river flowed quietly by. Heavy logs, flattened on top and still bearing machete scars, spanned the wet portion of the marsh. The logs angled up to join with others projecting out over the river to form a substantial dock.

Katia said, "We wait here. But first we have to hide the horses."

They entered what seemed solid jungle but which quickly gave way to a clearing that had a pole corral to contain the horses. Katia rummaged in the saddlebags, saying, "Pablo put rations and a radio in our saddlebags."

Katia hung infrared binoculars over her shoulder, slipped a box of rations in her pocket, and struggled with ammunition for the FAL.

John said, "You can't pack all that stuff through the jungle." He handed Katia two FAL clips and tied two over his shoulder along with a light backpack. "That's why I like a .22. It's light-weight, and you don't need a truck to haul the ammo."

Back at the dock, Katia pointed to a tall, heavily branched mahagua tree at the edge of the small grassy glen. Large vines twined round and round the trunk. Using the vines as a ladder, they began climbing. Shortly, they were on a platform large enough for several people. A full moon, just clearing the tops of the jungle trees, allowed mellow light to filter down through the thin cover of leaves. John glanced out across the river and back along the trail. It was clear they would not be approached by surprise.

Katia pulled a sharp knife from a holster strapped to the calf of her leg and hidden by her camouflage uniform. Taking a box of rations, she opened a tin of meat and handed it along with two hard biscuits to John. She said, "Valderas cruises the San Juan halfway between us and Jaime's post. Where they land won't matter because any of us can contact Valderas. Other options fall to Miguel . . . and I hope they don't come to him. He enjoys his work too much. If they come to our post while they unload the boat, Valderas brings his boat in and blocks their escape. We come up—"

John interrupted, *"We?* Who's *we?"*

"Us. You and me."

"Us? Just us? We don't have any backup?"

"We don't need backup. Except the leader, they'll be in it for a few dollars. They won't fight. We give them a chance, they'll run without firing a shot. And the gunrunner doesn't want his boat ruined. You and I just have to mop up what few people are left. There's nothing to it."

"Sounds like a crazy plan to me!"

"It's not crazy. It works. You want out?"

Embarrassed, John said, "Course not."

"The men who bring the horses and carry the weapons and ammunition are destitute paisanos. I would never kill one of them—as they would never kill me. But Miguel . . ." She seemed to search for the proper expression of her feelings. Then she laughed aloud. "When you stood up to Miguel today, for just that moment I could have kissed you."

John smiled at her. "It's not too late."

Ignoring his words, Katia said, "At first there was no El Cinco. Only Valderas and Montenegro. Then they brought in Miguel. For a time there was just the three of them. Efrain brought me in, and soon I stood ahead of Miguel in making decisions. It was bad because not only is Miguel very macho, but at first he wanted me for his woman."

By now, despite the bright moon, it was quite dark. She stood and surveyed the river in both directions with the infrared binoculars. Then she sat down and leaned against the tree trunk.

In the pale moonlight, John could see the smoldering of Katia's brown eyes. Her words were barely a whisper. "It was hard to make him understand that I am no man's woman." She lapsed into a brooding silence, and soon her eyes closed. Her even breathing made John think she slept.

He thought, *I could easily fall in love with you, Katia Solano, most beautiful and dangerous butterfly.*

The humid air had cooled slightly. John picked up the binoculars, which had slipped from Katia's fingers, and he alternated between watching the river and watching the trail.

Katia had slept for nearly two hours when the squawk of the radio brought her into instant wakefulness. She picked up the radio and promptly responded with a single word—"Mariposa."

Valderas's voice came through static. "Jaime reports a boat in his sector. I'm moving to cover his position."

"Acknowledged. Over and out." Katia stood up and stretched briefly. "You should have wakened me."

"Nothing moved. If it had, I'd have let you know. What do we do now?"

"We just stay right here. It's not comfortable, but it's safe."

John stretched out on the woven branches. "Suits me." He lay, head cradled on his small backpack, thinking that it seemed impossible that he had only known her for two days. He looked at the moon. It seemed as if he could reach out and touch it. His body was tired, but sleep was far from his mind. There were many unfamiliar night sounds, the calling of different kinds of birds, the cries of animals he could not identify. Slightly below the register of all these sounds was an almost unnoticed throbbing. Then he realized it was a man-made sound, and he sat up.

Katia had already placed the infrared binoculars to her eyes and was scanning along the river. Suddenly she thrust the binoculars at John and said urgently, "Watch the trail! A boat approaches the dock."

She began calling quietly into the radio. "Valderas. Come in. Valderas. Valderas, can you hear me? Valderas!"

The only response on the radio was the rasping and crackling of interference.

John grabbed her arm. "There are horses—six—ten."

Katia tried the radio again. "Valderas! Come in! Come in!" Finally she said, "Blast! He's out of range. What happened? There couldn't be two—or could there? Let me see the binoculars."

The horses were now close enough that the riders could be seen herding them into a group near the logs that formed the ramp to the dock. The boat became visible, and John watched as it, too, moved quietly into place.

Katia was fuming. "Something is all fouled up!" She nearly shouted into the radio, "Valderas! Valderas! Come in!"

John took the radio from her and hissed, "Be quiet! They're too close!"

Katia pointed. Two men were already struggling with a long case from the boat. "Look! Belgian FALs. That's *my* shipment!"

John asked, "Do you think those men would really scatter and leave if you started shooting at them?"

"Why? We don't have a chance without Valderas's boat to cut them off."

"Would they cut and run?"

"I don't know *what* they would do without Valderas to block the gunrunners' boat. Most likely they'd make a rush for the boat carrying whatever they had left and head out on the river."

John studied the boat. The deck floated four feet out of the water. If he could get close enough—and lucky enough . . . "I'm going to try to disable the boat. When you hear a grenade blow, you start shooting."

Katia humphed. "And you thought my plan was crazy."

"I just want to know if you think they'll stand and fight."

"One thing I know. They won't stand and fight."

With those words, John had already started over the side of the platform.

Katia whispered, "Be careful, Chohnee."

Slipping from tree to tree and moving quietly, John made his way to the river. At the water's edge, he placed the .22 and extra clips of ammunition on a log lodged against the bank. He pulled off his boots and entered the water, silently swimming a sidestroke as far as he dared. Then, taking a deep breath, he swam underwater, going rapidly as the current helped to move him through the water. When he reached the white hull of the boat, he surfaced. It seemed to him that each movement was sending loud signals of splashing water. He leaned his back against the hull and twisted a grenade loose from his webbed belt. He turned and lobbed the grenade as he would a baseball

on an easy throw from shortstop to first base. Then he dived
underwater and swam hard and fast, away from the boat.

He didn't hear the explosion, but rather felt a surge as if a
large wave pushed his body upstream. A pounding pressure and
red glow filled his mind. Gasping for breath, he surfaced to see
that his work had been done well. A hole had opened in the hull
of the boat, allowing the churning waters of the San Juan to
enter.

The night seemed silent for a moment. Then the staccato
roar of a machine gun split the quiet. Branches and leaves began
to disintegrate just inches over the heads of the unmoving men
on the shore, galvanizing them into chaotic action. At first some
started toward the boat, and then as they saw that the boat was
disabled, the first man turned abruptly back and knocked the
two behind him into the river. Others, in a dash, jumped on
startled, rearing horses and began whipping them into a gallop
back along the trail.

John pulled himself out of the water and looked briefly
around. He could hardly believe the little glade was empty. He
could not see one person. Katia had been exactly right. Given a
chance, the campesinos had all run away. He struggled to get his
wet feet into his cowboy boots. A slight movement caused him
to glance up, and he saw two men on the dock. One of the men
pulled a pistol and fired. The bullet thumped into the ground
near John's feet. In a roll, John came into a prone firing position.
The little .22 began spitting potentially deadly chunks of metal
at his assailants. His first shots were warnings; he didn't want to
kill any more than Katia did.

With the heavy, rapping bark of a Belgian FAL, bullets
chewed up the ground in front of John's attackers. Katia called,
"Throw down your weapons, hombres. You don't need to die,
but if you don't surrender, you will!"

There seemed to John something very familiar about one of
the men. He stood insolent and tall, unbowed despite having

dropped his weapon. As recognition came, John whispered his name. "David Solano."

Just at this moment, Katia came up from the side. She was clearly exercising great control over her emotions. She said quietly. "Hola, David. Why—what are you doing here? Do you fight for the communists?"

The young man did not seem shaken. He sneered and asked sarcastically, "Perhaps the more important question is what are *you* doing here, allied with thieves and bandits? I, at least, am loyal to Nicaragua."

John watched Katia struggle with the urge to argue with David. Finally she said, "I had hoped you would resist. But I suppose the brainwashing at the youth camps started when you were too young."

David said, "The real problem is that it started too late for you, Katia. You were too steeped in Eduardo Solano's brand of materialism."

"You are really far gone when you speak of Papa that way."

David's derision was clear. "Yes. Papa, the capitalist. He *would* be upset." He turned to the man standing by him and said, "Let's go."

The man did not stir. "I have no desire to die."

David said, "She won't shoot. Not her own little brother. Her papa would never forgive her."

The man said, "I'm not her brother. I'm not moving."

"Coward! She won't shoot you!" With these words David turned toward the path leading into the jungle and, ignoring Katia, started walking away.

John watched Katia for just a moment. He could see the anguish on her face. As her automatic rifle dropped from the ready position, barrel pointing toward the ground, John raised his little .22 rifle, took careful aim, and fired as short a burst as he could. Six bullets plowed in rapid succession into a tree a few scant inches from David's head. Bark splintered off and smashed into his face. He froze midstride.

John's voice was hard. "I'm not your brother, either, David. One more step, and the next shot will be in your leg."

David slowly raised his hands above his head.

John demanded, "Now turn around really slow and move back over here." Without taking his eyes from David, he said to Katia, "Cut the straps from the binoculars. We'll use them to tie David."

Katia whispered hesitantly, "David—would—not betray me."

John muttered, "You might be willing to bet on that. I'm not. Get the straps. If you let him go, the Sandinistas would know in a day where you are and what you do. And the day after that, your operation would be ended—and you'd be lucky to be alive."

As Katia cut the straps, John waved his .22 rifle at the other prisoner. "Tie him up. And if he gets loose—"

"Don't worry, señor, I'm not on anyone's side. I just handle my boat." The man looked sadly in the direction of his damaged boat. "At least, I used to handle a boat."

David was barely made secure when a rumble from up river drew their attention. Katia looked toward the river and shouted, "It's Valderas!"

La Dorotea came in a roar of foaming wake and stopped at the dock. Katia ran out onto the dock as Valderas jumped from the boat.

Katia asked, "What happened?"

Valderas was serious. "I got to Punta Verde and there was nothing around. Both men swear that there was a boat, but right after they called me, the boat pulled off."

Katia asked, "When the boat left, why didn't he call you back?"

"I don't know, but as soon as I knew there wasn't a boat there, I headed right back here. I tried to get you to answer on the radio, but I didn't get any response."

"We were a little busy."

"How did you manage to get that boat in such bad shape, Dama?"

Katia waved her arm toward where John stood, water still dripping from his clothing, his .22 rifle casually hanging in the crook of his arm. "You might want to hear it from Chohnee. It was his doing."

Valderas walked down the logs and said, "Hey, Gallo! So you fixed up the boat over there."

"Yeah. Dropped a grenade in it by accident."

"I bet it was an accident." He nodded his head at the two men John guarded. "Find out who they are yet?"

John pointed carelessly with the .22 rifle. "That one's the owner of the boat. Don't know this other fellow."

Valderas called to Katia, "What do you want to do with your prisoners?"

Katia's eyes dropped. "I have nothing against them. You decide."

Valderas said to the boat owner, "You work for the wrong people, *amigo*. If I help you fix your boat, will you promise not to work for the communists?"

The man stared at Valderas. "You would help me repair my boat?"

"The communists have nothing they can give to Nicaraguans except more poverty and more misery. El Cinco wants Nicaragua for Nicaraguans. For proof I will not only help you repair your boat, but I will also send business your way, but only if I have your word you won't deal with the communists again."

The man looked troubled. "I'd gladly make that promise, but I didn't know I worked for the communists this time." He pointed to David. "He told me he would pay me to use my boat. Now it's ruined. How can I know . . . ?"

"I'm Valderas. *I* will know. You work with me in the future. Agreed?"

"Si. From now, you are *mi jefe*—my chief."

"How are you called, amigo?"

"I'm Alonso."

"Welcome then, Alonso." Speaking to Katia, he asked about the other prisoner. "How about this one?"

John watched as Katia looked her brother in the eyes and said without expression, "He's nothing to me. Do with him what you will."

John noted that David accepted her words as impassively as if he had not heard her speak. He wondered at the course of human lives. How brother and sister could become enemies. Dispassionate enemies.

Jerking his head toward David, Valderas said, "I'll take this one with me and leave two men with you to guard the arms. I'll call headquarters and have horses here by morning to pick up the weapons."

Valderas put his arm over Alonso's shoulder. "Come with me. We'll return in the morning with a craftsman and material to mend your boat." To David, he motioned toward the boat. "Come on. In front of us."

Katia nodded at John. He followed her in silence to the base of the lookout tree. "It will be better to spend the night up there. We'll just have to trade off watching the guns till Valderas gets someone else here."

They climbed the tree again, and Katia leaned against the trunk. John stretched out on the airy platform. His body ached in every joint, and though he would have preferred a bed and surely needed a better pillow than his backpack, the woven branches and vines would have to do. John sensed that Katia was not in a mood for talk. Considering the events of the night, especially the betrayal by her brother, he didn't blame her.

Katia murmured, "Chohnee, I'm very . . ." Her words trailed off.

He wondered at the mellow brown of her eyes, opened so wide the soft full moon was reflected in them. She turned and looked toward the star-filled sky. The moon continued in its course across the heavens, imparting a mellow, romantic light. Tears trickled down her smooth cheeks. "Sometimes I'm so alone—and what I must do seems impossible . . ."

Her face was hauntingly sad. John moved closer and wiped the tears from her cheeks. She was so close and her lips so inviting. He let his lips touch hers softly and tenderly. Her lips trembled slightly, and she did not pull away or push his face from hers. She whispered, "Don't get wrong ideas, Chohnee—love can't be for . . ."

John's pressing lips prevented her from saying more.

CHAPTER FIVE

J OHN ALTERNATED HIS TIME between the El Cinco operation and El Rancho Boquis. Inspections and planning completed, he asked for a meeting with Ernesto Boquis. He wanted immediate inoculation and antibiotic treatment for all the stock, and mineral blocks in all locations where cattle grazed. He also wanted to bring in a new stock of bulls. His plans were accepted, and he was given a free hand to put them into operation.

With his first month behind him, John traveled to Limón in Costa Rica to make a personal report to Hardesty. The meeting between the two men took place in the restaurant of the Hotel Las Olas.

Hardesty opened the meeting with a strong request for knowledge of the female leader in El Cinco, whom he said had been proven to be Dama Mariposa. "I get the impression that Paul Gentry is being pressed very hard by some big wheel, somebody named Morgan, for information about her. Paul said that he doesn't think Morgan knows her by name; he just keeps telling Paul to get rid of the female leader of El Cinco. Paul, in turn is putting a lot of pressure on me. Paul says Morgan is positive the group called El Cinco is communist."

John said, "Well, I'm just as sure the group is not communist. I've worked on several raids with them. Of course, I've only met Montenegro one time."

"Okay. But what about this Dama Mariposa?"

John hesitated in giving an answer, then thinking to protect Katia, he said, "I'm not sure there is such a person. I've only heard rumors about her. Mostly from you." And then he quickly changed the subject. "I'd like to expand operations on the Rio San Juan. But I'll need funding."

"Have you determined El Cinco's method of operation and goals?"

"I've never been in any official planning meeting, but I am getting much closer to being trusted to that point. Once in a while they stage a raid on some small town or position held by the Sandinistas."

"How can we benefit from an operation on the Rio San Juan?"

"It'll give me more legitimacy with El Cinco, and I'm confident we can pick up a lot more information that way. They have very little money, so mostly they obtain weaponry by intercepting arms shipments intended for the Sandinistas. They train and arm men at El Cinco headquarters and send them back to their villages to await a call to join in the overthrow of the Ortegas when the time is judged to be right."

"Have you an idea exactly what they're doing?"

"As nearly as I can tell, what I just said is all they're doing: acquiring weaponry, training some paisanos, and sending them home armed, with instructions to be ready to respond to a call to fight when things are ready."

Hardesty stroked his chin momentarily. "So that means the Sandinistas are losing weaponry and the support of the people of Nicaragua." He thought about it for a few moments, then said, "All right. If you are sure they are not communist, then your actions will be of benefit. At the Banco Managua, you'll have one hundred fifty thousand córdobas a month, and that's not as much as it sounds."

John smiled. "I know. About a thousand American dollars a month. But I appreciate it, and it'll be used wisely."

Hardesty said, "It better be. You'll have to account for it monthly . . . matter of fact, we better make it twice a month if you expand things. We'll get you a room here at Hotel Las Olas. We need to keep your business separate so nobody will connect you to the Company."

"Great. Thanks, Lee."

"Then I'll see you in a couple of weeks . . . and you better make it worthwhile. Good luck, Tanner."

* * *

Pablo, shirtless, was scraping paint and doing odd jobs on Valderas's boat, *La Dorotea*. The assignment served a dual purpose. It kept the boat in top-notch condition and provided a guard to this one unprotected approach to the Hacienda Medina, which was also headquarters for El Cinco. Pablo was just eighteen years old, but he had spent seven of those years as a revolutionary. His parents had been among the many casualties of the Sandinista revolution. Disillusioned in the result of the revolution, Pablo joined yet another revolutionary group, El Cinco. He had been with Valderas ever since his parents had died.

The sun was warm. Pablo liked watching the water flow by. It was quiet and tranquil, and he enjoyed the smell of the big river. Huge trees and heavy undergrowth rolled down to the edge of the river in dense masses. Pablo looked across the river and briefly watched an alligator as it sunned itself on one of the few spits of sand that broke the monotony of the greenery.

The stuttering sound of an engine, a distinct miss marring the throb, came floating down the river. Pablo watched a freighting boat approach. A short railing, long in need of polish, encircled the blunted bow of the once-white boat. The name, *El Chilito*, was painted across the shabby, weather-beaten hull. The dilapidated appearance of the boat took Pablo's mind back to

instructions that he had received from Valderas when he had
been given responsibility for the care of the boat he now stood
on. The boat had been named for Valderas's wife, Dorotea.
Pablo had been deeply impressed when the very tough and
strong man he had come to love as a father, had tears well in his
eyes in speaking of his wife. Valderas was concerned that the
boat be kept in immaculate condition. He had told Pablo
exactly how he wanted the boat to be kept to make it a good
example of Dorotea's name.

A few hundred meters upriver, the boat, *El Chilito,* interrupted its slow headway down the Rio San Juan and nosed in
toward the dock that serviced the hacienda.

Pablo flicked on the radio in Valderas's boat and alerted
some troops not too far away. He slipped his shirt back on and
then slung an M16 rifle over his shoulder and stood on the
dock. When it became clear that the boat intended to dock,
Pablo snapped a bullet into the chamber of the rifle and stood,
watchfully alert. A man on the deck of the boat held a coil of
rope.

Pablo called, "This is a private dock! What do you want?"

The pilot leaned out of his cabin and called back, "I've got
engine trouble! I just want to pull in long enough to check it."

Pablo hesitated. It would be most suspicious to refuse to
allow a boat to dock briefly if it was in trouble. There were
plenty of men on duty close by. He nodded for the mooring
rope.

Pablo kept alert watch while the pilot of the boat opened the
cover to the engine to check wires and connections. The man
who had thrown the rope to Pablo lounged against the cabin of
the boat. He lit a cigarette and threw the match into the river.
His questions seemed rambling and desultory. What's life like
here on the river so far from towns? What kind of action to
make things interesting? Any jobs available out here? What
about girls?

Pablo's responses were casual, giving no information. He became instantly alert, however, when the man asked if he'd ever heard of a beautiful revolutionary called Dama Mariposa. The man would like to meet her.

Pablo answered, "I've heard stories of such a woman. But I think it's somebody's pipe dream. Anyway, I've never met her."

After a bit of tinkering, the pilot tried the engine a couple of times, but it would not start. Finally he called to Pablo, "I need some parts. Is there any way I can get a call to San Carlos to see if some parts can be sent down on a boat coming this way?"

Pablo hesitated, then jumped onto the deck of Valderas's boat and used the radio to call the hacienda. Valderas told him that he would send a mechanic to look at the boat. Pablo asked, "Is Dama at the compound?"

"Si. Why?"

"Maybe you better tell her that some guy on the boat's asking questions about Dama Mariposa."

"Okay, Pablo. I'll tell her."

Pablo then returned to the dock and hollered at the pilot. "You're in luck. We have an excellent mechanic. He'll fix your boat for you."

The pilot waved his thanks and tried the engine again. It fired immediately in a smooth rumble. He called, "Hey! Guess my luck is really good. Doesn't look like I need your mechanic."

The man who had asked all the questions jumped onto the dock, untied the rope, and quickly jumped back aboard. The boat drifted out into the stream momentarily and then roared on down the Rio San Juan. Just as the boat moved out of sight, Dama Mariposa came galloping up on her little Appaloosa pony.

She called to Pablo, "Where's my admirer?"

Pablo grinned and pointed down the river. "You're too late, Dama. He's headed downriver."

"How long ago?"

"Not five minutes."

She waved and turned her pony.

Pablo hollered, "Where you going?"

"I'm taking the trail to the loop on the San Juan." She waved binoculars at Pablo. "I want to get a look at the man asking about me."

Pablo immediately called for the hidden troops. Dama would cross the point of land that projected out like a thumb and caused Rio San Juan to make a huge bend, and arrive before the stranger's boat could get there. He yelled for the men to get in the boat, and then he fired up the engine. The gray rump of Dama's little Appaloosa was just flouncing around a bend in the trail when Pablo headed the boat out into the mainstream of the Rio San Juan.

He proceeded downstream and had just completed making the bend in the river when he saw the boat named *El Chilito* idling against the bank. Two men were hunched on the bank by the side of a fallen log. Dama was leaning against a gray-barked tree trunk casually taking pot shots at them.

As Valderas's boat approached, the pilot of *El Chilito* reversed the engine. The propeller violently churned the water as he backed into the stream. The men who were pinned down by Dama Mariposa angrily called for help. The captain of *El Chilito,* ignoring the demands of the men on shore, headed his boat in a foaming wake downstream.

Pablo stood in the bow of Valderas's boat, and holding his rifle steady on the men on shore, demanded that they drop their weapons. With Dama Mariposa's rifle also trained on them, they meekly raised their arms and let them rest on their heads.

Pablo had one of his men take the controls, and then he jumped onto the spit of muddy sand. He called to Dama, who was directing the prisoners toward the boat. "Dama, you loco! You should have waited. I'd have come with you!"

"Hola, Pablo. I didn't need help. I had the situation under control."

He said sarcastically, "I could see you did." Then he relented. "How did you know they were coming back along that trail?"

Dama smiled easily. "You never heard of woman's intuition?"

Pablo said, "Seriously. I was a little suspicious at first, but when they went on down the river, I thought everything was okay. How'd you know?"

"Anyone that really knows about Dama Mariposa knows where to find me. Because of my feelings here," she pounded on her stomach, "I knew they were after me."

"Please, Dama. Always have someone with you. You're too important to El Cinco."

Just three days later, Pablo accompanied Dama to San Carlos. On the return trip, Sandinita began to dance and prick her ears forward. Both Pablo and Dama became immediately alert when they caught the scent of tobacco smoke as it wafted up the hillside, warning them that someone waited along the trail. El Cinco's strict training was to not give their position away with tobacco smoke. And so a second attempt on Katia's life had been thwarted.

Katia was definite. "We'll take them to Valderas. He can do with them what he wants."

They rode silently down the trail to El Cinco headquarters where they delivered the prisoners to Valderas. Pablo angrily tried to tell him that he needed to restrict Dama's activities. But he seemed to brush it off. Pablo said fiercely, almost with tears in his eyes, "She hasn't got enough sense to see what's going to happen if we're not more careful for her!"

Perhaps because they were involved in a dangerous and revolutionary lifestyle, Valderas merely said, "Dama's a good soldier, and besides, she's always warned by her sixth sense. Still, I'll try to talk to her."

Dama showed no outward concern. "Don't worry about me. I never lose!"

* * *

John returned to what he now called Operation Rio San Juan with lifted spirits. He found that he was greatly excited and took much pride in building the Boquis cattle herd. The only problem he experienced in this was the conflict in his mind about his youthful plans to own a cattle ranch and what he was doing in his present occupation. Throughout his studies in animal husbandry at BYU, he had dreamed of developing a successful ranch. After a few minutes spent in this dream, he would just shrug it off and think that there was no way he would ever have enough money to buy a ranch.

He also enjoyed working with El Cinco, helping them gain armaments. But more than either of those factors, he knew that he was falling in love with Katia Solano.

As soon as Pablo saw John, he told him of the attempts on Katia's life while he had been in Limón. John thoughtfully replied, "Thanks Pablo. I'm really worried about her, and yet she really believes she will always win. I've talked to Valderas, and he seems to think that she will always win too. So I want to move her activities as much as possible to Costa Rica. I think she'd be safer there. If we did that, I could watch her in Costa Rica, and one or the other of us would be with her in Nicaragua."

Pablo readily agreed to this strategy.

In his next meeting with Hardesty in Puerto Limón, John said, "You know, Lee, the Rio San Juan is a huge weaponry conduit for the Sandinistas. One thing we should do is cut off the flow of some of that weaponry."

"And you think—are you getting mixed up in what your purpose down here is? You know that we are not actually fighting the Sandinistas. All we're supposed to do is get information back to the powers that make decisions—you know that, don't you?"

John said, "Yes, I do. But I think I can buy an old fishing trawler, and use it to go up and down the river."

Hardesty thought for a moment. "I don't—what purpose would that serve and how would it help you in getting the information that you want?"

At least one purpose was to keep Katia with him more of the time, but he said to Lee, "Well, I think that would separate me more from the El Cinco group. It makes me so that anyone, a supporter of El Cinco, a Contra, or a Sandinista, could approach me more freely without worrying that I'm connected to any organization."

Hardesty thought for a bit. "You know the Company won't pay for any part of it?"

"Yeah, I know."

"Then you have my approval. Just be sure that you're getting the information we need."

John bought the trawler, thinking it would help keep Katia close to him, and together they rebuilt it for his and Katia's use along the river. They named it *La Gaviota,* the *Sea Gull.* Katia worked closely enough with him to become known to Hardesty, not as Dama Mariposa, but by her own name, Katia Solano.

* * *

John continued making reports every two weeks to Leon Hardesty, always with a strong recommendation that the U.S. begin immediate funding for El Cinco. But aside from the thousand dollars a month that was available to John, not one dime ever made its way from the United States to his newly formed partnership.

The work with the Boquis herds required frequent trips to Managua for the bull auctions and picking up mineral blocks or medicines for the cattle. He drove the road from San Carlos to Managua often enough that it became unusual for patrols along the road to stop him to examine his papers.

John talked Katia into accompanying him on these trips, and they stayed at the Hotel Intercontinental Managua, a beautiful building shaped like a Mayan pyramid. They became known to the staff. The food served in the hotel was good, and in the evenings a small ensemble often played music for the diners.

One evening Katia asked John to dance with her.

John protested. "I'd make you look terrible on the dance floor."

Katia's laughter sprinkled over him like refreshing rain. "Chohnee! It's impossible for anyone to make me look bad. I will make *you* look good."

She stood and pulled John to the dance floor. "Now, feel the beat!"

She moved lithely, shifting her weight from foot to foot. She ordered, "Feel the beat, Chohnee! One, two, one, two, two. One, two . . ."

Gradually she moved away in smooth turns, then encircling him, her eyes never leaving his. He knew it was true. Katia was making him look good.

As they danced in the intimate space reserved by the band, Katia paused, laughed, and then pointed. "The big table in the back corner. About ten or twelve people."

John looked and nodded.

"Do you know the two at the end of the table?"

"The uniformed one is General Ortega. The other is his brother, self-appointed President Ortega." He couldn't see anything to laugh about and said so to Katia.

She buried her face in his shoulder and said, "It really isn't funny. If they knew who we were, what we stand for—we would both be in El Chipote in an hour to rot away the rest of our lives."

Still, Katia seemed to take perverse pleasure in making their headquarters in the Hotel Intercontinental Managua, just four blocks from Ortega's presidential palace and overlooking the Guardia headquarters.

* * *

Boquis regularly deposited money into an account in John's name in the Banco Managua. John never drew from the account, and the amount was becoming sizable, even by American standards. The only clouds on the horizon were the continued and intensified attempts on Katia's life. Like a cat, however, she always seemed to land on her feet.

Since he felt sure she was safer in Costa Rica than in Nicaragua, he persuaded Katia that she could centralize her activities in Costa Rica and still be effective for El Cinco. The only argument they had was when John suggested that while in Costa Rica she keep hidden her identity as Dama Mariposa. Katia finally agreed, but insisted that she would always do what she thought best. She spent a good portion of time in Nicaragua, and so John worried, because even though both he and Pablo tried to be with her, she was often alone.

There was a branch of the LDS Church in Limón that John attended when he could, and he became acquainted with the branch president. He knew that his work with the CIA prevented him from fully participating in the Church. At first he rationalized that he could take a few months, even a year or two off from Church activity and association. In the past he had successfully told himself that sometime the Church would be an integral part of his life, especially if he was ever successful in realizing his dream of a ranch. And always, he thought about life with Katia. He knew that she had to be converted if she were ever to become a permanent part of his life.

At his next meeting with Hardesty, he decided he would try to get Katia to go to church with him. John made arrangements at the Hotel Las Olas for a separate room for Katia.

After meeting with Hardesty, John contacted the branch president and told him that he was going to bring someone to the Sunday meeting and wondered if he could arrange for one of the speakers to tell the Joseph Smith story. He also contacted the missionaries and obtained a copy of the Book of Mormon.

Katia was received with warmth and friendliness by the members. One of the missionaries spoke. He was from Panama. He told of how, when he was fourteen years old and part of a youth gang in Panama City, he had heard a story that almost seemed a fairy tale: the story told of how our Heavenly Father and Jesus Christ had appeared to the boy named Joseph Smith, who was no older than he was. Young Joseph was promised that if he was faithful he would be instrumental in the restoration of the true Church.

The young elder testified that by diligently seeking for the truth, he had changed his life. He would never have to return to the destructive life for which he had been headed in the poor sections of Panama City.

John watched Katia closely to see how she reacted to the story. Though she listened, John could not decide what impact the testimony had on her. After the meetings, John spent the afternoon telling her about his beliefs. He started by reminding Katia that she had questioned if he had really been a missionary. He explained that the young man who had spoken in church that day was a missionary and that he himself had been a part of a force of thirty thousand young men and women teaching the gospel throughout the world when he was in Honduras. He continued telling Katia about God. He was disappointed because she did not ask any questions.

Sensing his disappointment, she said, "Chohnee, I believe in God, but for me, God and religion are different things. I was impressed by the young man's story—but—but before that story can have any effect on the lives of Nicaraguans, they have to have freedom. I—I don't see the need for religion right now— that is, for me—I always planned that someday I would go to church—probably the Catholic Church. But it seems to me that for now, at least, freedom for Nicaragua is all I have energy to think about. Please don't be too disappointed."

John didn't say so, but he was very disappointed. Nevertheless, he gave her the copy of the Book of Mormon that he had obtained, with the words, "I'll try to understand your feelings about the revolution. But in the meantime, I want you to read this book with a prayerful heart."

Katia examined the book. "Does it tell the rules of your church?"

"No. Just like the Bible is a testament of Jesus Christ, the Book of Mormon is another testament of Him. It tells about God's dealings with the ancient people of the Americas. There is one part in . . ." He stopped and thumbed through the book until he came to Alma. "Right here in this part. It tells about a man named Moroni who fought against people who wanted to destroy the freedoms of his people. You might find his story especially interesting."

Katia took the book with hesitation. "I'm not making any promises."

John said, "The only promise that I want from you is that whenever you read it, you remember this assurance . . ."

He flipped to the book of Moroni and pointed to the words marked by the missionaries. "And when ye shall receive these things, I would exhort you that ye would ask God, the Eternal Father, in the name of Christ, if these things are not true; and if ye shall ask with a sincere heart, with real intent, having faith in Christ, he will manifest the truth of it unto you, by the power of the Holy Ghost."

Katia was still hesitant. "I don't have much time to read."

John grinned at her. "I know, but make a little time for me. Okay?"

"All right. I'll try."

"And Katia, I want you to know that I know with all my heart that this book is the word of God and has the power to change the lives of people who follow its precepts."

"Chohnee, I don't want to get your hopes up to think I might become a Mormon. But I do have one question, and if you promise to answer it—matter of fact, if you can answer it in exactly sixty seconds and not preach anything to me, I'll ask it."

"Okay. I promise."

"If this book tells about God's dealings with the ancient people of America, how did the Mormons get it?"

"It's a pretty big question to answer in sixty seconds. But I did promise—so . . . A man, named Mormon, who lived four hundred years after Christ, I think somewhere in ancient Mexico, or Guatemala, started an abridgement of the records of his people. He wrote on golden plates. His son Moroni finished the abridgement and buried the gold plates before he died. After Joseph Smith received his first revelation from God, Moroni appeared to him and told him where the plates were buried. Joseph Smith translated the records which we have today in the form of the Book of Mormon. Is that short enough for you?"

Katia smiled. "You made it in thirty seconds—and that young missionary was right. It does sound like a fairy tale."

"Then with my other thirty seconds I'll just say that you should remember that the young man also said that seeking the truth of that story changed his life—just as mine has changed. And yours can too."

* * *

The National Security Council was in full attendance. The president gave Morgan a warm introduction. "Andrew Morgan has carried out many special assignments for me. As each of you know, we have received strong recommendations to assist a small group in place along the San Juan River in Nicaragua. I have asked Mr. Morgan to discuss this with you."

Without fanfare, the president turned the time to Mr. Morgan.

Morgan said, "I'm aware of the group called El Cinco. I met with their principals a few months ago. The group's not only small, but ineffective, and there is the logistical problem . . ."

A former congressman from Florida interrupted. "But El Cinco does have the advantage of already being in place in

Nicaragua, where the Contras have to make an invasion to be successful."

Morgan paused for just the right amount of time to assure the group that he was being properly thoughtful. It was not a good idea to let the council know that his contacts were with the Contras and that he would not be able to sell a dime's worth of weaponry to El Cinco.

"The brave freedom fighters deserve our total committed support. We must wipe out every trace of communism in Central America. As for this El Cinco group, they are small and insignificant. But more importantly, my sources indicate they are just as communist as the Sandinistas. They only want to place themselves in power instead of the Ortega brothers."

It was not an easy sale, as many of the council refused to accept Morgan's statements without hard evidence. But in the end, Morgan prevailed, and the council voted to refuse any support to the small group of insurgents.

* * *

John was summoned to meet with Leon Hardesty. Katia was in San Carlos, and John hoped Pablo was with her. Hardesty gave John the bad news in the restaurant of the Hotel Las Olas. While they waited for the food, they watched the restless Caribbean Sea ebb and flow under the supporting pilings. When they had eaten, Hardesty said, "We have orders to close Operation Rio San Juan. You have one week to put your organization away and bury any evidence that it ever existed."

John sat in speechless silence for a moment. Then he said, "Are they crazy? Haven't they read my reports?"

"Of course. But your reports aren't their only source of information. They have solid evidence that most of the El Cinco principals are communists."

John spluttered angrily, "That's ridiculous!" Yet, he knew he had no evidence except his own feelings for the people he had come to know. "We aren't going to give up trying to get rid of the Ortega brothers are we?"

"No. That remains a priority."

"What are we—*they* going to do about it?"

"Redouble our efforts to support the Contras."

John's words were angry. "Bermudez is a Somocista!"

"That has no bearing on his ability to rule Nicaragua."

"Lee, can't you see? That's a mistake! Most Nicaraguans would fight to their last breath to prevent the return of Bermudez! Backing the Contras is backing another generation of revolution in Nicaragua!"

"John, I don't agree with your assessment. More important, the powers that be don't agree. The Sandinistas were communist supported and directed from the first. You have anything to say that's not already in your reports?"

John viciously chopped at the leftover food on his plate with a table knife. Finally he said, "No. I've reported everything I've found out."

"Then the matter's ended. You will close Operation Rio San Juan. I'm being moved to San Jose. I recommended you to take over the Limón office one week from today. That will make you assistant chief of station in Costa Rica. I hope I haven't made a mistake. I'll meet you here next week to acquaint you with your duties. Should you not accept the assignment, I'll have to suggest your transfer to another assignment."

* * *

John traveled up the Rio San Juan. He did not follow Hardesty's orders. He simply told the people that the operation would be closed for a while. His last stop was Hacienda Medina. He said nothing to Valderas of his problems. Valderas told him that Katia was coming back from San Carlos and would be there in an hour. John borrowed a horse from Valderas and rode along the trail to San Carlos. There was a clearing overlooking the Rio San Juan. This was the place where he would tell Katia of his decision.

John tied his horse out of sight and waited. He didn't hear the approach of the Appaloosa pony, but he was warned by the way his own mount's ears pricked up. John stood at the edge of the clearing and watched along the trail. Suddenly he felt a hard object poking him in the back. He felt the hair on the back of his neck rise and was tensing to try a belated defensive move when Katia's wind-chime laughter washed over him with some mockery.

"Chohnee, you never learn! What are you doing waiting along the trail to San Carlos?"

"Jehosaphat, Katia! *I* never learn? What if I had taken that .38 from you and hurt you!"

Katia laughed again. "You think you could do that? Turn around and we'll try it again."

John did turn around and Katia gently pushed the gun against his back. He dropped quickly to the ground causing her to fall slightly forward. He clasped a hand around the arm that held the gun and flipped her over his thigh. Then he caught her in his arms and gently let her drop to the ground. He pushed the arm that still held the gun over her head. He kissed her long and hard on the lips. At first she seemed too surprised to resist and then she returned the kiss for a moment.

Pulling her lips from his, she said breathlessly, "That wasn't fair, Chohnee. You knew I wouldn't pull the trigger. Now let me up."

John's carefully reasoned speech fled his mind. "Not yet, Katia. I love you. I love you and I want you to marry . . ."

Katia broke into his words, "I've told you that I can't . . ."

"I know. You say, 'Not till the revolution is over.' But I want you to marry me now, Katia. Now! Not sometime in the distant future. Not sometime when this war that will never end is over.

Now. We'll get married in Costa Rica, and then I want you to come to the United States with me."

Katia finally pulled an arm free and placed her fingers over his lips. John could feel the trembling of her body under his. He gently pried her hand from covering his lips. "I love you, Katia. And I know you love me."

Tears welled in her eyes and spilled over her cheeks. Her eyes were the tawniest of browns. "It is true, Chohnee. I do love you. Since the second day I ever knew you. And someday . . ."

Her words stopped. John again placed his lips against hers. She kissed him long and warmly. Finally John opened his eyes to see a stream of tears pouring from those beautiful eyes. He whispered, "Not someday. Now, Katia. I want you to marry me now."

"You're not making it easy for me. Someday. I promise. I can feel it. Soon freedom will . . ."

The full impact of Katia's words finally penetrated. Freedom for Nicaragua was more important to her than his love, even worse, than her own happiness was to herself. He abruptly stood up. His mind and heart felt empty and cold.

Katia tried to place her hand in his. "Can't you understand, Chohnee, that I . . ."

"No, and even if I could, it wouldn't hurt any less."

After a time of silence, Katia asked, "What—why did you come to Hacienda Medina today? Did you come only to ask . . ."

John's words were a whisper. "No. The Company is closing Operation Rio San Juan. I'm supposed to go to the office in Limón."

"What do you mean supposed to go? What will you do if . . ."

"I'm fed up. I'm going home."

Katia said urgently, "You can't do that! I need you to stay."

Her words brought a momentary surge of hope, and then that hope was dashed as she said, "Nicaragua needs you to stay. Central America needs you to stay."

John didn't answer.

Finally Katia said, "I—I know after I have said I won't marry you, I have no right to ask, but Chohnee, please don't go home. Take the job in Costa Rica. If not for me, then for the people of Nicaragua."

When John still did not respond, it seemed to dawn on Katia that John was telling her more than that he was being transferred to Limón.

She asked, "What happens to the plans that El Cinco would get help from the United States?"

John slowly shook his head. "It—it won't happen."

"They're willing to accept the Ortegas after all this time?"

"No. The U.S. won't accept a communist government in Central America."

"Then what? I don't understand."

John whispered, "They'll only give support to the Contras."

Katia's stunned words raised to a shrill cry. "Are your people crazy? After all our struggle, all the death and destruction! And the United States wants to start it all over again!"

She began to pound on his chest with doubled fists. Tears streamed from her eyes. "Chohnee! You can't go home to your peaceful country and leave us to struggle alone! Go to Limón. Tell your leaders our story. Make them *help* us, not destroy us!"

John caught her fists. "You ask too much of me, Katia! You demand my future. My life! And you offer me nothing in return! And I've tried to tell Nicaragua's story. I'm a peon . . . a reporter whose information is used to make decisions. I'm tired of a fight that isn't mine. I—I'm sorry, Katia."

John took the watch from his pocket. He flipped the lid open and said in a whisper to the music, "I believe in yesterday." He snapped the lid shut and handed it to Katia. "Next time you get lonely, play that, and know that I will never, ever forget you."

John walked to his horse and swung into the saddle.

Katia stood clutching the watch and looking up at him. Tears streaming from her eyes, she whispered, "Don't go home, Chohnee."

"I won't make any promises. But if I stay, you can reach me at the Hotel Las Olas in Limón. *Vaya con Dios,* Katia."

He let the horse make its way slowly down the trail. A cold, hard lump in his chest made breathing difficult. John had come to regard Valderas as a close friend. He didn't know what explanation he would make to him.

As he rode the horse to Hacienda Medina, Valderas waited for him. Valderas took the reins of the horse as John dismounted and said, "I can tell from the look on your face that it's bad news. What's going on, Chohnee?"

In all of the nine months that John had worked with El Cinco, neither he nor Katia had ever told anyone of his role with the CIA. John knew he could not explain that role now. In a moment of inspired deception, he merely mumbled, "I guess it's best described as a lovers' quarrel."

Valderas nodded sympathetically. "I could have told you that no man will ever put a net around Dama Mariposa. She is one beautiful butterfly whose heart will never be captured."

John could easily relate to those words, for he knew they were true. He nodded his head in agreement. "I'm going to go to Costa Rica for a while."

"Where in Costa Rica?"

"Limón. I told Katia how she could reach me if she changes her mind."

Valderas laid a heavy arm over John's shoulders. "I don't want to discourage you any more than you already are, Chohnee, but it won't do any good to wait around for her to change her mind."

"I guess you're right."

Valderas stuck out his big hand. "Good luck, Chohnee. You've helped us. Maybe someday . . ." His words drifted off.

John knew there was little else to be said. His mind was bleak. Maybe someday. But probably not. Aloud he said, "Thanks, Valderas, for everything. *Hasta una dia mejor*—until a better day."

It was nearly as hard for John to abandon his work with Boquis as it was to part with El Cinco. He could not face Ernesto Boquis and tell him he was leaving his job only partly done. The first of the new breeding stock was due to be calved in a couple of months. He had paid for the pensión in San Carlos for another three months. He would write to Ernesto and explain things and go to Limón without seeing anyone at Boquis.

* * *

It was a crisp fall day. Morgan would soon have to close his mountaintop home for the winter. The fire was burning brightly, sending off slight wisps of tangy piñion pine smoke. The *whuff-whuff* of helicopter blades intruded on the quiet. He glanced at his watch. Right on time.

Paul Gentry was defensive. "The one you asked about is called Dama Mariposa. She's a tough one to put a net over, and Dama Mariposa is a truly descriptive name for her. She's the slipperiest I've ever known. It doesn't help that she's loved by the people who know her. They regard her as some kind of goddess. There is one of our own who works with her—and protects her."

"One of our own should be easy to eliminate." The order for John Tanner's death was given without any sign of thought, let alone regret.

"Why not just transfer him to some other theater of operations?"

Morgan's voice was hard and his jaw set. "I thought I made myself clear. I want him eliminated."

"Do I understand you correctly, sir? You are ordering one of our own operators killed?"

"Do you have a problem with that?"

"I have a big problem with that, sir. I won't do it!"

Morgan turned to the fire for a moment, then turned back casually. "If the order comes from Chandler, will that make a difference to you?"

"I've never refused to carry out an order from my superior officer. But Senator Chandler will never . . ."

Morgan's words were gentle. "You will do it for two reasons, Mr. Gentry. First, because Chandler's instructions *will* be on your desk in the morning, and second, and perhaps more importantly, because I know your wife has not known of your woman—your—ah—Da Nang indiscretion."

Gentry walked stiffly toward the patio door and the waiting helicopter. Morgan's words stopped him at the door. "I want a positive report in no more than two weeks. Do I make myself clear?"

Paul Gentry turned, his countenance not showing his inner turmoil. He felt great shame at succumbing to blackmail. He wondered how Morgan had found out about Da Nang and why he had never told Anne. For just the briefest moment his eyes locked with the eyes of the elegantly handsome, well-groomed man who stood by the crackling fire. Then he lowered his eyes. "Ultimately clear, *sir*." He gave a smart salute and stepped out the door.

CHAPTER SIX

JOHN RETURNED FROM HIS TRIP to Hacienda Medina a few days early. Leon Hardesty was in San Jose, and there was little John could do in the office until the change of command actually took place. He was still trying to decide whether or not to accept the Limón assignment. John told Francesca, the Company office secretary, that he would spend the time in R & R and that if anything came up she should leave a message at the Hotel Las Olas.

On Sunday he went to the block of meetings at the branch in Limón. Though the members were friendly and even curious about him, he felt unsatisfied because he had to keep his life confidential from them.

He spent the next two days wandering along the beach north of Hotel Las Olas. He missed Katia so much, he wasn't sure he could stand it. They had been apart for several days in times past. But it was not the same, because this time he felt sure he would not see her again. As he walked, he watched a storm develop over the Caribbean Sea.

Normally a storm would come up, bluster a bit, throw a few strikes of lightning and thunder, clean the air, water the greenery, and go its way. This storm was different. It started in the early afternoon and was accompanied by driving rain, flashes of lightning, and crashes of thunder. He returned to the hotel and sat looking out the sliding glass door in his room. He watched immense waves build and then force huge breakers to come crashing in white, foaming torrents of force against the beach. His mood was a perfect match for the harsh display of nature. The storm loomed larger and larger, just like the troubles that plagued the people of Central America.

When he returned, he paced the room that he sometimes thought of as home. The thought of home in the States brought Juliana Brown's warm smile and dancing eyes to his mind. For a moment he compared Juliana and Katia. Katia's smile was exciting and sometimes mocking. The dance in Katia's eyes, depending on her mood, was fiery, tumultuous, or cold. Juliana was warmth and home, and Katia was excitement and turmoil and emotion. How different the two women were and how alike in a strange way. Katia would settle down when the demands of the revolution had been met, and Juliana would settle down when her great adventure was over. He stood abruptly and thought, *Admit it! Juliana has never been more than a dream of a dream—dreamed first when you were a boy in Mexico. The only thing that's made me happy down here is Katia Solano, and now—* He could not complete that thought, but spoke the next aloud. "Maybe I've been in Central America, in the Company, too long."

In sudden anger at himself, he opened the door. Again he spoke aloud. "I'm just hungry!"

Restless waves crashed under the floor of the hotel and then pounded up against the rocky beach. John walked along the covered corridor connecting the hotel and restaurant. The storm continued in a constant drumroll of thunder and in flickering tongues of lightning. Some bursts crashed down to the sea in brilliant flashes of light and rending blasts of sound.

The restaurant was empty. John took a table where he could look down and see the water breaking over the first rocks of the shoreline. The waiter had served John off and on for nearly a year and knew him by name.

"*Buenas tardes,* Señor Tanner."

"Hola, Marti. Bring me what you think's best on the menu for the day."

"The usual to drink?"

John nodded his head and stared moodily out over the sea. Tropical greenery grew down to water's edge in both directions as far as could be seen. An occasional palm was outlined as it thrust bending, twisting fronds and danced to the drumbeats of thunder and flaring blasts of lightning.

John thought how fitting the music coming from the intercom in building crescendos was. It was from Wagner's *Flying Dutchman.*

Shortly, Marti brought a carbonated orange drink, hard rolls, butter, and a salad. He commented idly, "Strange weather."

John answered, "Yeah, it is. You know the story of the music?"

"On the intercom? No."

"A Dutch sea captain is under a spell. His ship is lost from home, and he can't find his way back. The only way he can be released from his bewitchment is for a faithful woman to declare, then prove, her love for him."

Marti smiled. "That Dutchman, he might have a long wait to find a faithful woman."

John concurred. "Isn't that the truth."

Marti excused himself, and John sat thinking that he was as bound in the enchantment woven by Katia as was the Flying Dutchman in his spell. Marti brought a steaming plate of a spicy barbecued beef, fried *platanos,* and a colorful bowl of fruit.

John had nearly finished the meal when Marti brought a telephone to him. Katia Solano had never been able to make an American *J* sound. His name always came off her tantalizing lips as "Chohnee," and that was the voice and sound that greeted his, *"Mande."*

"Hello, Chohnee. I had a hard time finding you."

His heart leaped. "I've been out of the hotel most of the day."

Katia spoke casually as if nothing had happened between them. "I'll be on *La Gaviota*. Can you get a crew together and be backup for me tonight?"

"What's happening?"

"Can't talk over the telephone. Will you meet me in half an hour?"

"Where?"

Katia's voice lifted the darkness of depression from his mind almost as if she had waved a magical wand over his head.

* * *

John focused the eyepiece of the binoculars. One moment only the small, seemingly empty wharf was visible in the humid night air, and in the blink of an eye, a sleek white boat seemed to materialize. The heavily laden craft, its deck strewn with large stalks of green bananas, sat low in the gently rolling waves. The smoothly lined fiberglass boat was wide, the three graceful ridges of its cathedral hull designed for speed.

The long rainstorm drizzled to a stop. John glanced at his watch. Someone on the deck signaled his presence by bringing a match to his face to light a cigarette. The glow of the ember brightened occasionally as the man passed time in silent watch.

The boat bore the name *Triunfo*. John spoke quietly into the mouthpiece of a short-band radio. "We've got a customer— made up to look like a banana dealer. But I think we've got your *pistoleros!*"

The portable radio squawked briefly. "Do you recognize the boat?"

"The marking says *Triunfo*. Isn't that Julio Kamba's?"

"Si. Where are they?"

"They're tied up at that little wharf three kilometers inland."

"Just tied up—anchored?"

"Yes." There was silence for a minute. John said, "Okay, Katia, you're calling the shots. What do you want me to do?"

Katia's uneasiness sounded in her voice. "I don't know, Chohnee. The word I received said the exchange is to take place within a mile of the confluence of the Rios Chiripo and Colorado, and the whole thing should have gone down by now. So why are they tied up fifteen kilometers away?"

John waited for her to say more. He was becoming impatient. "Who knows? You want me to pull off?"

"No. Just keep your eye on the boat. If they get company or start to move, let me know immediately."

"Okay, Katia. Ten-four."

The morning sun turned the still slightly clouded sky into a golden, orange-yellow postcard. The ripples of the water turned a brilliant red. Something in the fiery sunrise lifted John's spirits as the long, wet night finally passed.

The colorful sunrise was replaced with a brilliant white morning sun. John was idly following the progress of a huge *zomposo,* or red ant, when a second figure emerged on the boat. The newcomer stretched, did a few quick bends touching his hands to the deck, then breathed the sultry morning air in deeply.

John adjusted the focus on the binoculars, and a feeling of vague familiarity stirred in his thoughts. He recognized the gray slacks and mauve-colored guayabera shirt, the dapper trademark of Julio Kamba, but the walk and movements were feminine.

Another figure appeared on the deck. John noted his closely cropped hair and grizzled beard. He wore a shirt that had been white a long, long time ago. John had a moment of queasiness in his stomach that he recognized as a bad premonition. There was no doubt that the flat face with its smashed crooked nose belonged to Fiero Rinskin.

Julio said something to the watchman, who then leaped on to the small wharf, untied the mooring rope, and tossed the rope to Julio. Julio secured it with a couple of quick flips around a cleat. Then he shook the shoulder of a person curled up on the cushions of the pilot's seat. The man sat up, stretched, and touched the controls. The immediate rumbling hum testified to the constant care the powerful engine received.

Before John Tanner could scramble out of his jungle cover, the boat, despite its heavy burden, leaped out and away from the wharf. In a muffled roar, the boat left a wide foaming wake and raced inland.

John immediately called Katia on the short-band radio. "Julio's on his way! I'll be right behind. You set, *mi amiga?*"

With an edge of excitement, Katia said, "Ready and waiting, Chohnee."

Without a signal from John, his men were already roaring toward him. He stood at the water's edge, waiting for the boat to glide close enough that he could leap aboard. The pilot didn't wait for him to be seated, but spun back out into the mainstream. The action threw John toward the only vacant seat. Two pairs of ready hands reached out and guided him into place between his companions.

The airboat was wide and flat bottomed, designed to navigate marshy streams and swamps. The noisy aircraft engine was hooked directly to the propeller and encased in a protective cage.

They made their way up the stream of a river located at the base of a deep chasm created by tall green trees. The airboat zoomed along the winding river and slowed briefly so they could look up the Bravo Channel. There was no sign of the *Triunfo* along the first five kilometers, and John signaled his pilot to continue along the Rio Colorado. At a bend in the river, John spotted the boat of Julio Kamba. It had slowed down and was just barely making headway against the sluggish stream. John signaled for the pilot of his own boat to slow down. They were approaching the fork of the Chiripo and Colorado Rivers, where

Katia and her crew waited behind a midstream island for the boatload of weaponry.

John and Katia's plan was simple. They would trap the boat between them. There was a quad-mounted .50-caliber machine gun on the heavier boat that Katia and her crew operated. There was no way that Katia's boat could keep up with Julio's, but it wouldn't have to. The firepower of the gun's six hundred rounds per minute would cut the fiberglass-hulled *Triunfo* in two pieces with a steady burst of fire.

The ancient fishing trawler *La Gaviota* moved away from the island's jungle edge and into the mainstream of the joined rivers. The smooth sound of the engine put the lie to the bedraggled appearance of the stodgy craft.

Julio didn't alter his course to the left or the right, but continued to run aggressively upstream, heading straight for *La Gaviota*.

A burst of fire from the .50-caliber churned into the water in front of the *Triunfo*. Using a handheld voice amplifier, Katia demanded, "Stop right there!"

The *Triunfo* stopped its forward movement and began drifting in the current, turning broadside to Katia's crew. Julio had not noticed the airboat. John nudged one of his men. "Tonio, give him a taste of a .22 rifle. No blood. Just a warning."

A half dozen long-rifle .22-caliber bullets ripped into a stalk of bananas still lying on the deck. Julio jumped and turned toward John's approaching craft. Katia chose this moment to let loose another blast. Three bullets ripped into the hull just below the deck line. In a crouching crawl, Julio moved behind the cabin to peer at *La Gaviota*.

Katia handled the .50-caliber with the featheriest of touches, allowing only three bullets into the meter-long barrel in one third of a second. It took great skill to place those bullets exactly at the deck line, where they would attract the most attention and do the least damage to boat and cargo.

The bullhorn squawked as Katia called, "Julio! Come on deck! And get everyone else topside with their hands on their head!"

Julio hesitated in compliance. The machine gun coughed again, and a second group of three holes appeared in the hull, making a pattern of punctuating colons. Julio ordered his men on deck.

In less than a minute, five men stood, obviously nervous, with their hands on their heads. Julio stood facing Katia with his hands on his hips.

Once again, the automatic weapon spit out a series of bullets. Katia called, "Next time, your boat goes down, Julio! Get the others on deck before I count to ten. *Uno, dos . . .*"

Without waiting for an order from Julio, the men below deck scrambled to line up with the first five. Katia's voice again came blasting from the bullhorn. "Now, one at a time, swim to this boat. Right now, muchachos!"

John added emphasis to Katia's words as he nudged Tonio, who fired another burst into the stalk of bananas. The two men closest to the riddled stalk of bananas immediately jumped overboard and began splashing toward *La Gaviota* to be pulled aboard by Katia's crew members.

The whump of a rocket launcher startled John. The missile exploded harmlessly in the water in the triangle formed by the three boats. John turned to see one of the heavily armored boats the Costa Rican Coast Guard used to patrol not only the coast around the mouth of the San Juan River, but also the numerous inland waterways of the Tortuguero National Park.

Katia's voice came crackling over John's radio. "Chohnee, get your boat out of my line of fire!"

"Negative, Katia! That's a coast guard cutter. Don't fire on it!"

The discussion was interrupted by a command from the coast guard vessel.

"This is Captain Morales of the CG 720! You in the airboat! Put your weapons down, then haul about and tie up alongside."

John placed his .22 rifle back in the canvas case and instructed his men to do the same. Then he spoke to his pilot. "Do as he says."

John's airboat circled around to approach the coast guard cutter from the rear. No sooner had he moved behind the government boat than another missile lobbed up and exploded just in front of the old trawler. The captain shouted, "You onboard *La Gaviota!* Come on deck with your hands in the air!"

Katia's voice rang out defiantly. "What about Julio Kamba? He's carrying weaponry for the communist Sandinistas!"

The captain called, "Is that Dama Mariposa who speaks so insolently? My next shot will blow you out of the water! Surrender! Now!"

"When I see Julio Kamba standing on your deck—handcuffed!"

John Tanner came aboard the CG 720 and looked up in anger as he saw Leon Hardesty wearing his ever-present tropical suit. His tall, lank frame was huddled over the captain. Hardesty was saying, "Don't argue anymore. Blow that wooden junk pile to kingdom come!"

John grabbed the microphone from the hands of the captain and spoke urgently. "Katia! This is Johnnie. Come out on deck—and your crew also."

When a minute passed with no sign of action on *La Gaviota,* Hardesty said, "Captain—"

John cut him off. "Katia, please! We've got what we wanted. Whatever Julio's carrying won't get passed to the commies. Come out on deck!"

Slowly the heavy makeshift boilerplate cover protecting the operator of the .50-caliber lifted up, and Katia stepped out in the clear. She wore her usual uniform of camouflage fatigues, her curly, shiny black hair stirring slightly in the breeze. She unbuckled her sidearm and tossed it to a deckhand. Then she stood, hands on her hips.

John's anger boiled up. "What the devil's going on?"

Hardesty shouted, his words angry, "I don't know if you knew that Katia is Dama Mariposa, Tanner, but your explanation better be good!"

"What makes you think Katia is Dama Mariposa?"

"It depends on which side of the fence she's operating, whether she's Lady Butterfly or Katia Solano. In this operation, she's Dama Mariposa."

"What operation? We just heard that a shipment of guns was—"

Hardesty interrupted. "Hold on, Tanner." Then speaking to the captain, "Pick up the butterfly lady on the airboat. Bring her aboard. Tell your people to keep a close eye on her crew. I don't want them escaping!"

Turning back to John, Hardesty continued. "Now, what do you mean *we* heard about a shipment of guns?"

"Katia got the information from friends in Nicaragua . . ."

"Yes. *Her* friends. Our enemies."

"That's a serious charge, Lee. You'll need evidence!"

Hardesty shouted, "I've got all the evidence I need to prove she's gone back to the Sandinistas!"

"She would as soon join the devil!"

"If that's true, she'll have a chance to prove it."

There was a sinking feeling in John's chest. He had on a couple of occasions, most recently this morning, wondered where Katia was getting her information. He muttered, "Katia will have a logical explanation."

He could not bring himself to argue further with Hardesty. He watched as Katia's crew was tied to the rail of *La Gaviota* and as Katia, aboard the airboat, was brought to the coast guard cutter. When she came aboard, her head was held high in haughty disdain. She was led to Hardesty. Then the airboat was sent to bring Julio Kamba to the coast guard vessel.

Katia stood defiantly. "Hola, Señor Hardesty. Am I supposed to have done something wrong?"

Hardesty said, "Perhaps we could start with you explaining why you attacked the *Triunfo*."

She tossed her head and said angrily, "Why would you think? Keeping guns and ammunition out of the hands of the communists."

"But how did you know about the shipment?"

"Señor Hardesty, excuse me for saying it, but that's a dumb question. Did you think I served the Sandinistas for five years without finding loyal friends?"

"Those friends are what is beginning to concern me, Katia, or should I say, Dama Mariposa? The only information about this shipment of arms was leaked to a known communist. In other words, I set a trap, and you took the bait."

There was contempt in Katia's eyes and voice. A cynical smile played on her lips. "What is this? *Dia de inocentes?* April Fool's Day? If it weren't so stupid, I would laugh! If the communists knew a load of arms was coming in, protected only by Julio and his little boys, would they let *me* take them?"

John noted the return of the airboat with Julio Kamba and Fiero Rinskin and was puzzled why Rinskin had been brought to the coast guard vessel with Julio. He watched the arrival of the diminutive Julio Kamba. He had never met him in person. As Julio approached, John couldn't avoid the thought that there was something feminine about the walk of the man. As Julio came close, the first thing John noticed was the clarity of the facial skin. No razor had ever touched that face, and the skin was as clear as if a light shown through it. The finely molded features of the face were familiar. Suddenly, John did a double take as recognition came to him. His heart beat faster for a moment. This was surely not Julio Kamba! This petite person with the beautiful liquid brown eyes, despite the slacks, guayabera, and Afro hairdo, was Juliana Brown!

Hardesty took immediate charge. With a gesture at Katia Solano, he asked, "Brown, do you know this woman?"

Juliana barely glanced at Katia. "She's Dama Mariposa."

Hardesty demanded, "Be sure. I don't want any mistake!"

Juliana said seriously, "I'm sure. This is Dama Mariposa. I saw her just two weeks ago in Granada, Nicaragua, talking to Colonel Efrain Montenegro. She was identified to me then by people who know her. I would swear to her identity in court."

John had not known of a trip that Katia had taken to Granada. He argued with himself, *You couldn't possibly know all her movements.*

Hardesty didn't say anything but arched his eyebrows at Katia.

She matched his stare for a time. "So. I was seen talking to Montenegro. I admit that I was talking to him and at the time she said. As for that, this Julio, or Brown, is speaking the truth. But because someone *says* I'm someone I'm not—what does that prove? Or for that matter does it prove that Dama Mariposa is a bad person?"

"It doesn't *prove* anything. But it's mighty suspicious. We know that Montenegro's communist and that he's a prime receiver of weaponry for the Sandinistas!"

Katia said matter-of-factly, "You're wrong. He's not communist. So release my crew, and we'll go on our business."

"Sorry, Dama, your word's not sufficient. Your pilot can bring *La Gaviota* to the guard station at the canal. Then I'll detain you and your crew."

Katia's words were bitter. "At least the communist Sandinistas no longer profess to be champions of freedom. So, I'm under arrest?" She stared at him until he became uncomfortable and dropped his eyes.

There was a long silence.

Finally, Hardesty said quietly, "I'm waiting to hear your defense."

Katia turned to John. "This is an example of *Yanqui* justice? I thought I was innocent till proven guilty, Chohnee."

John averted his eyes. "I don't know what to say . . ."

Katia interrupted, sparks flying from her expressive eyes. She suddenly switched from speaking Spanish to a broken kind of English. "Is okay. I know how to say! And I say in English to be sure you understand!"

She turned to face Leon Hardesty, and holding up a fist, she extended her fingers one at a time as she spoke the names. "I offer my defense the name Ramon Quintana, Sergio Mercado— Sandinistas. Jorge Caño, Humberto Royo—communists. As you know, all taken in Costa Rica by *my* people!"

Her voice quivered in anger. "Is not enough? I offer my defense ten thousand round ammunition, two hundred Belgian FAL automatic rifle, ten case Portuguese 81-millimeter mortar shell, more than hundred Chinese rocket grenade, and thirty case your own United State grenade. As you know, all capture from communist on Rio San Juan by *my* people! I offer my defense twelve successful raid for *you* on Sandinistas!"

She spun on her heel and lashed back, her hands trembling with fury. "It hard to believe—you suppose to be smart man! You think the communist Sandinistas tell me these things so I capture them and be your—your best agent in Costa Rica? What are you people? *Tontos—poco luzes . . .*"

She breathed deeply, then said in Spanish, "The first time in my life since I was a small child that I trust anyone, and I am surrounded by—by—imbecilic gringos!" With these words she lapsed into angry silence.

John was so enwrapped in Katia's fiery defense that he had paid no attention to Fiero Rinskin. He did notice when Rinskin moved from the railing toward the cabin of the small ship. Suddenly, an alarm rang in John's mind. Rinskin pulled a .38-caliber pistol from under his dirty shirt. Not sure whom Fiero was aiming at, he launched himself as a missile, collided with Rinskin, and shoved his arm up just as he fired.

The struggle did not last long, but only because he had taken the powerful Rinskin by surprise. Rinskin began an irresistible movement of his arm to pull the weapon back to where he could fire into John's midsection. John could not compete with the strength of the ugly man and so he rolled with the pull of Rinskin's arm and twisted under it—a standard move he'd learned in training. He pulled forward and used his body as a fulcrum. For just the briefest moment, it was as if he were pulling against an immovable object. Then that object lurched forward, and Rinskin went flying over his shoulder.

Rinskin's shoulders thumped heavily against the thick metal wall of the ship's cabin, and his grizzled head spun back in centrifugal movement and crashed against the heavy steel, knocking him senseless.

The gun fell to the deck after the lone bullet had been fired. John grabbed the gun and turned to the captain. "Lock that man up! Don't dare let him get away!"

He turned back to see Leon Hardesty slump to his knees and slowly pitch forward on his face. A spreading patch of red blood began to stain his white seersucker jacket.

Then John saw Katia standing alone. Her eyes caught John's for just the briefest of moments, and he wondered if the smile was bitter or pitying. It did not matter, for John was ashamed for not coming to Katia's defense with Leon Hardesty's first words. Katia turned. In three quick steps she cleared the rail of the ship and in a graceful dive splashed into the clear water of the river. A few strong swimming strokes brought her alongside the airboat. She grasped the edge of the boat and, kicking powerfully, raised her body out of the water. For just a moment, her wet camouflage uniform shimmered in the morning sun. Then in a neat tuck she rolled over into the boat.

In a fluid motion, she pulled a jungle knife from a holster hidden under the cloth of her fatigue pants and strapped it to her calf. She slashed through the rope that moored the airboat to the coast guard cutter and moved to the controls. Katia looked up and again caught John's eye. She gave a mocking half salute and called, "So long, Chohnee! Vaya con Dios!"

She pushed the starter button. The engine fired immediately and the boat roared off, heading up the waters of the Rio Colorado. John raised the pistol, and aiming wide of the fleeing boat, fired the remaining bullets from the gun.

He whispered, "Vaya con Dios, Katia Solano."

He watched for a few more seconds while the fleeting vision became blurry in his tearing eyes. Then he turned to see Juliana examining the wounded Hardesty. She said, "It looks like a bad wound."

The boat captain, having had Rinskin dragged away to be locked up, came running back and said, "He needs medical attention, and first aid won't do the job. I'll have to make a run to Puerto Limón."

"Where should we put him?"

The captain didn't hesitate. He called to one of his deckhands, "Bring first aid and a stretcher!"

John watched as the captain, with an expertise that demonstrated much experience, ripped open Hardesty's shirt, exposing the bleeding, black-centered puncture hole. A sailor dashed to his side with a stretcher and first-aid kit. The captain opened a pad, wiped the blood away, sprinkled sulfa on the wound, and taped another pad in place over the raw edges of the torn flesh. "Get him onto the stretcher. We'll put him in my quarters."

As he was put on the stretcher, Hardesty asked John, "Did you get her?"

"No. I was concerned about you and didn't think about her till it was too late."

Captain Morales summoned more help, and they moved Hardesty to his cabin. When Hardesty was lying on the captain's bunk, he spoke fiercely. "I want Dama Mariposa! Which way did she head out?"

Juliana answered, "Upstream on the Colorado."

Hardesty demanded of Captain Morales, "Get underway immediately. We've got to capture that woman!"

Captain Morales shook his head. "No. I draw too much water. I wouldn't make another ten kilometers up the river."

Hardesty turned to Juliana and said, "Brown, the *Triunfo*—"

John interrupted. "I'll get her. I know the likely spots where she might try to hole up or cut through to another stream."

Hardesty's next words were just as fierce. "No you won't!" He partially raised up. "Captain, put this man under arrest!"

The captain looked warily at John. It was clear that he did not relish the task of trying to arrest the man who had just tossed Fiero Rinskin around like a stalk of bananas. "Do you want him in a cell?"

John said, "That won't be necessary. If Mr. Hardesty wants me arrested, I won't try to get away."

The captain looked to Hardesty for direction. Hardesty said, "It's okay, captain. If he says he won't try to escape, he won't." He coughed and then slumped back on to the bed. "Brown, you get back on the *Triunfo* and head up river as quickly as you can."

Juliana looked at John and then spoke hesitantly. "All right, Mr. Hardesty. I—"

There was fierceness in Hardesty's voice again. "Get moving! Every minute puts her farther away." Then he spoke urgently to the captain. "Get on the radio and have the pilot of the *Triunfo* bring it alongside!"

Hardesty closed his eyes.

John asked, "Permission to accompany Brown to the rail of the ship, Mr. Hardesty?"

Hardesty waved his hand tiredly. As they reached the door, he spoke, his voice an angry whisper. "Brown, I want Dama Mariposa, dead or alive!"

Juliana paused and spoke quietly, but surely. "If I can find her and it's possible, I'll arrest her. But I won't just out and out shoot her. If that's what you want, Mr. Hardesty, you'd better send someone else."

Hardesty moved his hand slightly. It was taken as a dismissal.

While Juliana and John waited at the rail for the *Triunfo* to come alongside, John said, "It's been a long time, Juliana."

"I've often wondered how it would be to see you again. I supposed it would be a chance meeting like this with not a minute . . ." Her voice trailed off.

John said, "It's been three years."

Her eyes met his. "Three years next month."

John wondered that she had kept track of time that closely.

The slight flush that came to her cheeks with her words brought memories both painful and sweet. He had forgotten how much he had loved her.

The *Triunfo* came rumbling up to the side of the coast guard cutter. Juliana said, "I've changed . . ."

Neither knowing what to say next, they stopped talking.

One of the crew on the *Triunfo* stood with arm outstretched to help Juliana aboard. She turned to John. "I guess duty calls."

John took her hand and detained her for a moment. "What are you doing posing as Julio Kamba? And how did you come by his boat?"

"He was arrested—the Company commandeered his boat. Mr. Hardesty is convinced that Katia is Dama Mariposa and is—has turned communist—he wants her pretty bad. I didn't know you and she . . ."

"That's a long story. Before you go after her—she's not—not what Hardesty thinks. I don't have all the answers, but I know she hasn't gone back to the Sandinistas. And you're on a wild goose chase. She has too many tricks up her sleeve. You'll never find her. She'll head on up the Rio San Juan—and even if you did find her, you'd never take her . . ."

Juliana interrupted. "Mr. Hardesty captured her."

John's words were strained. "No. If I hadn't told her to surrender, she'd have gotten away. So don't look too long—it's dangerous."

"Don't worry. I've been trained to take care of myself."

She jumped lithely across the rail and onto the deck of the *Triunfo*. She moved to the cabin and took command of the *Triunfo*.

As the *Triunfo* rumbled out of sight, the CG 720 headed back down the river toward the coast of the Caribbean. John decided that he owed Katia Solano, at the least, some words of defense. He returned to the cabin, where Leon Hardesty was lying with his eyes open.

John asked, "You okay, Mr. Hardesty?"

Hardesty looked at him for a moment. "The captain gave me some pills. So. It's 'Mr. Hardesty' now."

The quarters were cramped and stale and stuffy. John paced the full length of the room in two steps, and then whirled, nearly tripping over a little table that had a map of the region laminated to its surface. John asked, "What was Rinskin doing onboard a boat with Brown in command?"

Hardesty's response let John know that he would get no answer. "Classified. It's stuffy—see if you can open that porthole. Isn't there something to sit on? You're making me nervous."

John pushed open the tiny window and pulled the only chair in the room from under the table, placed it to the side of the bunk, and sat down.

Hardesty sighed and said, "That doesn't let any air in. I suppose you intend to defend Katia Solano."

"Mr. Hardesty, I want . . ."

"Will you knock off the Mr. Hardesty routine!"

"Not as long as I'm under arrest, sir!"

"Look! You fire a consistent two hundred on the range. You *let* her get away! Leopards don't change their spots. Katia Solano, alias Dama Mariposa, is a Sandinista through and through."

John sat for a moment. Finally he said, "You're right about leopards not changing their spots. Katia hasn't changed hers. In that respect, she *is* a Sandinista through and through. As a matter of fact, she regards herself as a Sandinista—hecho y derecho."

Hardesty asked in exasperation, "Then how can you defend her?"

"Because she's the same as she was. It's the Sandinistas who've changed. Let me tell you some things about Katia Solano that you most likely don't know."

Hardesty's words were sarcastic. "Do I have any choice? I can't go anywhere."

"True. But you could tell the captain to throw me in the brig."

"If I start to hurt again, I might do that. Matter of fact, you tell me any lies, and I *will* have you locked up."

"You ever know a Mormon boy to lie to you, Mr. Hardesty?"

Hardesty answered slowly. "I *used* to think that you never lied to me." He moved his shoulder in a testing way and settled a little deeper into the pillow. "Well, let me hear what defense you can offer—what details you managed to leave off the Dama Mariposa dossier."

John Tanner stood and paced the small room briefly. The indictment of the lies he told Hardesty hurt, but, John thought, the lies had been necessary. "Katia is not communist." He wiped the beaded sweat from his forehead, his tanned olive skin a stark contrast to the white handkerchief. John ran his hand over his straight black hair and said, "It was my first assignment for you in Central America. You sent me to San Carlos in Nicaragua."

CHAPTER SEVEN

JOHN ENDED HIS NARRATIVE for the wounded Leon Hardesty with the details of his talk with Katia at Hotel Las Olas. He stared out the tiny porthole at the glittering swells of the restless Caribbean Sea. The small ship approached the docks of Puerto Limón.

After a moment, Hardesty said, "Except for the romantic details, Tanner, you haven't told me anything not already in Dama Mariposa's file."

John turned slowly to face Hardesty, who was now propped up in the captain's bunk. He spoke flatly and without emotion. "If you can say that honestly, Mr. Hardesty, I haven't told her story very well."

Hardesty lay in silence for a time. Then he spoke emphatically. "John, you're way out on a limb. You think back. You don't have one piece of solid evidence that she wasn't a communist from day one. You admit her brother was communist, and speaking of her brother, don't you know what became of him?"

"No. I didn't want to hurt Katia by asking."

"Well, I'll tell you what happened to him. Nothing! Not one blasted thing. He's working for the communists in Managua."

"Well—that doesn't prove anything. He was her *brother.*"

"Yet you told her that her brother would bring the Sandinistas down on her neck if she let him go—and they never arrived!"

The captain entered the cabin. "We'll shift you to a hospital boat in five minutes."

Hardesty nodded to the captain but spoke to John. "Tanner, the discussion about Solano is closed, at least until you can think objectively about the evidence."

"Mr. Hardesty, you're twisting facts!"

"I'm twisting nothing! You're not to leave Limón!"

John turned back to the porthole. His voice was strained with anger. "You're the boss. What do you want me to do in Limón?"

"Nothing. Not one blasted thing! Sit in your room at the hotel or in the office."

John stood staring out the porthole.

Hardesty roared, "Well, are you going to do what I say, or do I need to have Captain Morales turn you over to port authorities?"

John had no intention of following these instructions, so without turning around, he said, "I already told you—you're the boss."

John turned to the captain. "Have you heard anything from the *Triunfo?*"

The captain shook his head in the negative. "Not a word."

John had wondered many times that morning why Hardesty had not pursued the question of who Fiero Rinskin was shooting at. He said to the captain, "You'll be sure that Rinskin gets locked up with the others?"

"Of course."

No further words were spoken while the sling was rigged to transfer Hardesty to the small hospital ambulance motorboat. John accompanied them to the hospital.

John said to Hardesty, "With permission, I'll go to the office to check on the *Triunfo*. I'll see you at the hospital later. Is that okay?"

Hardesty nodded his head and waved his hand in dismissal.

John watched as Hardesty was rushed into the small hospital. Then he hailed a taxi to take him along the dirt road to where the office was located. The Company operated a business that ostensibly served the needs of the rich who chartered fishing boats for their sporting pleasure. The Company maintained three boats for charter and one that, though rigged as a fishing boat, was kept exclusively for Company business.

The office was located in a rambling yellow stucco building with a red-tile roof. Surrounded by drooping palms and tropical greenery, it was nestled down by the sparkling blue waters of the restless Caribbean. A pile of fluffy white cumulus clouds tumbled up behind the building.

As the taxi approached the building, John noted that only the Company boat, the *Delfin,* was tied up at the dock, but there were just two vehicles in the rocky, unpaved parking lot. One was the Company Wagoneer, an all-terrain vehicle. *The other must belong to a charter,* John thought. He also noticed a girl tending a flourishing bed of colorful flowers growing in profusion in front of the stucco building.

Large prints advertising various Caribbean tourist activities covered the walls of the office. Leather chairs lined one wall. A military desk with a couple of telephones and a computer terminal occupied one corner. The only concession to creature comfort was a ceiling fan, slowly stirring the humid tropical air with a gentle swishing sound.

John pushed open the door labeled *HOMBRES,* stepped inside, and stood in front of a full-length mirror. He touched a switch on the wall, and a light turned on overhead. After a moment, the light went out; he heard a latch click, and the framed mirror moved toward him slightly. He grasped the edge of the mirror and pulled it forward to enter a plush, air-conditioned office. Carpet covered the tile floor. Soft, golden, smoothly finished slabs of guanacaste wood covered the walls. Two colorfully bold posterlike copies of Matisse paintings were the focal point of the room. A gleaming walnut desk occupied the side of the room facing the paintings.

A petite woman looked up and greeted John with a warm smile. Francesca had sufficient Company trust that she operated both sides of the door—legitimate charter business or Company business.

"Hola, Chohnee. How was your boat ride?"

"Hola, Francesca." How had she known he had been on a raid? Katia had told him of her acquaintance with Francesca, but she had never said whether Francesca ever worked with El Cinco. "It was a lousy trip. You alone?"

She pointed to the radio room with her head. "Except for Omar."

John came and sat on the edge of her desk. He quickly recounted for Francesca the events of the morning.

She said confidently, "You don't have to worry about Katia. She can take care of herself. Is Mr. Hardesty badly hurt?"

"I don't know for sure. I'm mostly worried about Agent Brown."

Francesca nodded. "I don't know her. This is her first assignment in Costa Rica."

"I'm going to check the radio log to see if we've had any report of her pursuit of Katia. I want to find out if she's started back to Limón. While I check, would you see what you can find on Fiero Rinskin?"

Francesca's face clouded briefly. "Rinskin? He's in a classified—still, you are to take over the station."

John was relieved. Clearly Hardesty had not been able to warn the Company office that he was *persona non grata*.

"Thanks, Francesca." John entered the radio room.

A stockily built, curly haired young man wearing radio earphones glanced up as John walked into the room. He smiled in recognition of John.

John said, "Hey, Omar. Anything from Brown on the *Triunfo?*"

"*Triunfo?* I got a garbled call at 1100 hours."

"Let me hear it."

"Be my guest and good luck. You'd have to have ESP to understand it."

Omar punched a few buttons. High-pitched squealing and crackles of static drowned out most of the words. "She repeated her call three times. Apparently, she didn't get my response, so she sent the rest of this."

John listened to the taped message. "I can't make heads or tails of it. I'll be in the file room. Make a hard copy of this, please."

When he returned to the main office, the section of wall that contained the two Matisse paintings had been moved aside. Two slips of paper with entry codes were on the typing stand by the terminal.

When he punched in the file code, the following appeared on the screen:

CLASSIFIED—FIERO RINSKIN

He quickly scanned the Rinskin file. It provided no new information. He took the second slip of paper and wondered why Francesca had placed it in a manner so obvious as to draw his attention. Nevertheless, he punched in the file code. The screen was filled with the words:

TOP SECRET

THE GENTRY DIRECTIVE

RE: FEMALE LEADER OF EL CINCO

The directive contained alleged evidence against Katia Solano. The first statements were true and identified Katia Solano as Dama Mariposa. There was a charge that she was active with the Sandinistas. He hoped it was false. Some charges he knew to be false. What troubled him was that he had wondered about some of the information himself. And there was something about seeing the charges all neatly labeled and spelled out that seemed particularly hard to dismiss casually.

Though the directive was from Paul Gentry, the information had been submitted by Senator Chandler. He wondered why Senator Chandler of the National Security Council had as much influence over the affairs of the CIA as the agency head himself. He closed the files.

Francesca said, "You look worried, Chohnee."

"I am. Nothing about this day makes sense. Rinskin shoots Hardesty, and Hardesty doesn't say anything about putting him away. I did that on my own. And only garbled word from Julia—Agent Brown."

"Do you know her from before?"

"Yes. And that's a long story. As soon as Omar gets me a copy of that transmission from Brown, I'm going over to the hospital . . ."

John's words were interrupted by a buzzing from Francesca's desk. She pushed a button and Omar walked in with a paper in his hand. He said, "It doesn't make any more sense written out than when you listen to it."

John reached for the paper.

Omar continued. "The asterisks show the garbling between understandable words."

John read the message then slipped the paper in his pocket. "Can you work on the transmission to see if we can break through the static?"

"I got a friend who specializes in that. I'll get him to work on it."

"Thanks, Omar." To Francesca he said, "I'm going over to the hospital to see Mr. Hardesty." As he reached the door, he turned and said, "Hold the *Delfin* for me. I want to use it later today. I'll be gone for a couple of days and need some cash, maybe a hundred fifty thousand colones."

Francesca was hesitant, then said, "I guess it should be all right. I'll have it ready for you when you take the *Delfin*."

"Gracias, Francesca. I'm going to use the Wagoneer. I'll be back by four. Oh, and see if you can put a crew together who are loyal to Katia."

"Pablo's in Limón on business for Valderas. Will his crew be okay?"

Her answer bothered him. *How does she know Pablo?* But he said, "I couldn't ask better than Pablo."

John arrived at Leon Hardesty's room just as he was being wheeled out the door. He asked an attendant, "What's going on?"

The attendant ignored John and continued to push the cart along the hallway of the small Puerto Limón hospital. Hardesty opened his eyes and looked up at John. "The X-rays show that the bullet's in a bad place. They're flying me to the Clinica Biblica in San Jose. Funny. It's just a dull ache." He abruptly changed the subject. "Now, I don't want you going off half-cocked on this Mariposa thing. You're relieved as assistant chief of station and restricted to Limón. You got that?"

John made no reference to Katia Solano. It was also clear that this was not the time to talk about Senator Chandler. He said, "I'm worried about Brown, Mr. Hardesty. We received one garbled message, and now we can't raise her."

"Brown will be okay. I want your word on the Mariposa thing."

"I'm not giving my word on anything relating to Katia Solano!"

The attendant said urgently, "You're holding up the flight, sir!"

Hardesty ignored the attendant and said heatedly to John, "You're being insubordinate!"

"You can't charge me with insubordination just because we have a difference of opinion about Katia Solano!"

The attendant finally began to wheel the stretcher toward the waiting ambulance. Hardesty called, "You're not to make further contact with Dama Mariposa, and you're not to leave Limón!"

John was sure that further argument would not be good for Hardesty. And there was no way he would not try to make immediate contact with Katia. As far as being fired as assistant chief of station, that was a relief. He could act freely. The attendant transferred Hardesty to the ambulance.

John gave a half salute at the closing ambulance door and drove to the police station. The man at the desk glanced up. When John asked permission to interrogate Rinskin, the sergeant replied that he had been released.

John was dumbfounded. "Released? On whose authority?"

"I don't know. When a call comes from Senator Chandler, we don't argue."

"You just turned a killer loose on the basis of a phone call?"

"He wasn't charged with murder. And anyway, nobody in this department argues with Senator Chandler."

There was nothing he could do. It was nearly four o'clock, so he called the station. Francesca answered his phone call. He said, "Tanner here . . ."

Before he could say more, she interrupted. "Mr. Tanner? I have a message from Senator Chandler. You are to return the *Delfin* immediately."

What was Francesca saying? She knew very well that he wasn't calling from the *Delfin*. It was still tied up at the Company dock. He said, "I received a tip about a shipment of weaponry from Panama. I'm sailing from Punta Cahuita. Give me the message."

"I can't over the air. I'll give it to you when you return to port. What's your ETA?"

John was puzzled. He could be back to the office in ten minutes, and Francesca knew it. What was she trying to tell him?

"I need to make a stop at Tuba Creek. I can be in port by 1900 hours."

There was urgency in Francesca's response. "A direct order from Senator Chandler requires that you be in port no later than 1700 hours."

Bewildered, John concluded his call. "Wilco. Over and out."

Ten minutes later he pulled into the parking lot of the office, braking in a swirl of dust. Francesca was standing in the lot waiting for him. She jerked the door of the Wagoneer open. "Thank goodness you understood."

"What's this all about?" John demanded.

Francesca grabbed his arm and pulled him toward the dock. "No time! I've written it all down." She thrust an envelope into his hand. "The money's in there. After you've read what I typed, burn it."

Francesca pulled him toward the dock, where the *Delfin's* engines were already idling. "Where am I supposed to be going, Francesca?"

"Wherever you were planning when you told me to get a crew together. You read the file on Katia, didn't you?"

"Yes. And it infuriates me!"

Their pounding feet echoed a staccato rhythm from the planks of the wharf. At the end of the dock, the *Delfin* rode lightly in the water. Omar held the mooring rope loosely with one wrap still around the post.

John stopped and demanded, "But what's all the rush?"

"No time for discussion. All operators in Costa Rica are under orders to arrest you or Katia. If you resist, you're to be shot. So get going."

"Shoot me? What kind of nonsense is that?"

"I wish it were nonsense, Chohnee. The Gentry Directive charges you with defection and being an accomplice to the communist Katia Solano. It's doubly reinforced with Senator Chandler's signature."

"What about you and Omar? You could be in real trouble."

"This will protect us when you sign it." She shoved a sign-out form for the *Delfin* and a receipt for the one hundred fifty thousand colones at him. "You can see the sign-out time for the *Delfin* is 1528 hours. Omar patched your telephone call through the radio, and we taped it so we have evidence that you were told to report back to the dock by 1700 hours."

John looked at both of them and said, "You're both great! Thank you."

Omar said, "Only one more thing, Chohnee. My electronic expert said the interference on the transmission from the *Triunfo* was deliberate. There's no way we can find out what that message really said."

As Omar moved to release the last coil of rope, John jumped aboard and turned and spoke urgently, "Wait! What if—how can I communicate—"

Omar called, "The paper Francesca gave you explains. Good luck, Chohnee!" He unwrapped the last coil of the rope and tossed it to John. As if that had been a signal, the *Delfin* leaped away from the dock in a roar and headed out to sea in a swirling mist of white foaming wake.

John moved immediately to the control deck of the fast-moving boat.

Pablo's snapping black eyes laughed up at John. "Hola, Chohnee. Where do you want me to take this boat?"

The small-statured Pablo wore no shirt and only a pair of knee-length, ragged white cotton trousers. The pistol that was holstered around his waist could have been one of Katia's own .38s. A warning bell rang in John's mind as he realized that Pablo was not a regular Company employee.

"Pablo, how come you're so familiar with the *Delfin?*"

Pablo grinned as if the matter were of no importance. "I supposed you knew. Francesca uses me quite often."

Another alarm rang in John's mind. How could Francesca hire people to do Company business and use Company equipment?

Pablo asked, "Where do we go? You want to return to the Tortuguero?"

How had Pablo known he had been in the Tortuguero?

"Head out to sea in a generally southern direction. Later we'll turn back to the Tortuguero. For now, I want to keep our movements hidden."

John regarded the young Nicaraguan for a time. Once more, he tried to force the ugly feelings of deception from his mind. He silently cursed the charges of the Gentry Directive. What if that first raid had been intended to slip through, and he had ruined the whole plan with his harebrained action with the grenades? What if that was the reason that Valderas had so generously offered to repair the damaged boat? What if David Solano had been a prisoner only while he, John Tanner, held a .22-caliber rifle on him and had immediately been released by the generous Valderas? And what if every shipment of arms he had ever intercepted he had simply turned over to what he thought was the opposition to the communist Sandinistas—El Cinco?

These thoughts sent chills coursing up and down his back. What if he'd been played for a prize sucker! A sucker for half the year!

He asked Pablo, "How many men do we have for a crew?"

"It was short notice. We could only get three, plus myself, that we *know* are loyal to Dama Mariposa."

"Do I know the other crew members?"

"Si, I think so. They're below deck. You want to talk to them?"

John said, "In a bit. First, I have some studying to do."

"Okay, Chohnee, but I think this boat is too small to keep going out to sea. Would it be all right to head north to the Tortuguero now?"

"The *Delfín* can easily handle any water in the Caribbean, Pablo, but go ahead—head her north." John then sat in the cushioned seat at the back of the control deck and took the envelope Francesca had given him from his pocket. First he thumbed through the money in different denominations of colones. As he looked at the typed instructions, another uneasy feeling came over him. After all, Francesca, too, was Katia's loyal follower.

The only new information was instruction on how to contact Omar through a call signal to Omar's radio expert friend, thus saving a recorded call through the station. As for Gentry's demand for his and Katia's arrest or death, he would have to depend or Francesca's having told the truth. He tore the paper in small pieces and let them drift in the wind and the waters of the Caribbean.

Pablo turned to him and with a big grin asked, "How about if I get los muchachos up for a briefing?"

John wondered if the pistol around Pablo's waist looked big because Pablo was small or because, as so often was the case, he himself was unarmed. "Good idea."

Pablo's smile had almost become saucy. "Those gringos live soft lives."

John realized, irrelevantly, that Pablo didn't think John was a gringo.

Pablo flicked a switch on the control board of the boat and spoke into the intercom. "Muchachos! Come on deck. Chohnee wants to talk to us." He spoke again to John. "You don't even have to leave the controls to talk to anyone on the boat."

John greeted each man as they came up the gangway of narrow stairs. "Hola, Mario." John nodded. A darn tough fighter and taciturn, Mario wore a pistol as a sidearm and carried a Belgian FAL automatic rifle.

As the next man stepped up, John greeted him with a tip of his chin and murmured his name. "Halcón." Another tough man. He, too, was armed with a Belgian FAL.

John recognized the last man but could not remember his name. Besides packing an M16, he carried a long knife in a holster toward the rear of his left hip.

Pablo grinned and said, "This is La Raspa. You might not know him. He used to live in Managua. Don't let his size fool you. He will loan you his gun and then take it away from you and skin you with his knife."

John proffered his hand and murmured, "Mucho gusto. Glad to know you."

John opened a cabinet and took out deck chairs for the group. As the men sat around him, John felt not only naked with no weapon, but also completely surrounded. The troubling thought that the only one who smiled was Pablo preceded the idea that the one really in charge of the group, if he excluded himself, was Pablo. Strange that a boy of nineteen was directing the activities of hard, perhaps ruthless, men, not a one of whom could be less than fifteen years older than Pablo.

The silence had gone too long for Pablo. "Okay, Chohnee. Tell us what this is all about." It seemed less a request than order.

John sat on the cushion of the seat at the back of the control area. "I don't need to ask if you are all loyal to Dama Mariposa. I remember each of you. Yes, La Raspa, even you a little. I know of your loyalty to her and to the cause she represents." John felt safe in saying this; whether Katia was Sandinista hecho y derecho or communist, there was no doubt of the loyalty of the men hemming him in. He continued. "Just this morning, Dama and I were going to take weapons from a shipment on Julio Kamba's boat, the *Triunfo*. We were arrested . . ."

Pablo interrupted. "That's hard to believe. Dama's never been . . ."

John cut him off smoothly. "I accept responsibility for that. It was my fault."

Pablo nodded to indicate that he could accept at least that part of the statement.

"Dama was taken aboard a coast guard vessel, but she dived overboard and escaped on my airboat. I was arrested and returned to Limón. I'm free now, thanks to Omar and Francesca. I need to find Dama Mariposa. I also have a friend who is missing after starting up the Colorado to help Dama. I want to try, also, to locate her."

He looked at each of the four faces in turn. "Do you have any questions?"

The three men solemnly shook their heads in the negative. Pablo said, "I don't think there's any worry for Dama. She's okay . . ."

John looked at him quickly. "You heard from her today?"

"No, but I know Dama. We'll help you find your girlfriend and then be about our business."

John saw no purpose in continuing the discussion. He was not being challenged. For the first time that evening, he began to feel relaxed. John said, "I was awake all of last night and today. I'm going to stretch out here on the deck and catch a few winks of sleep. Thanks for helping."

A mixed chorus of words, most distinguishable as *"por nada,"* rumbled from the men as they stood and made their way below deck.

John asked Pablo, "Will you recognize the Colorado?"

The saucy grin was back. "With my eyes closed. No problem."

"Then I leave the ship in your command. Wake me when we reach the Colorado, Pablo. I want to bypass the *resguardo* if possible."

* * *

John awakened in a moment of confusion. He glanced at his watch. It was almost midnight. La Raspa moved silently back to a deck chair.

Pablo said, "We're close to the guard station. What do you want to do?"

"Run quietly as possible. Try not to let us be seen."

Pablo silently maneuvered the boat and was successful in getting them past the security station protecting the entrance to the San Juan River system.

John said, "Head silently up the Colorado all the way to the San Juan if we need to. We're looking for either an airboat or Julio Kamba's *Triunfo*."

There were few places where a boat the size of the *Triunfo* could be tied up, but there were hundreds where the airboat could have been located.

Pablo said, "We could travel a lot faster if you let me turn on the spotlight, Chohnee."

"Problem with that is we'd advertise our presence. Better to go slow than to spook anybody and be sorry."

These words were hardly out of John's mouth when they rounded a bend in the wide river and saw the small airboat dancing lightly in the water, tied to a huge tree trunk hanging in an arch over the river. John made a precarious descent to the small boat. A quick check gave no clues at all. The three .22-caliber rifles, including the canvas they had been wrapped in, were gone.

When John came back aboard, he answered Pablo's unasked question with a wave of his hand upriver. "You can open her up now, Pablo. We'll go as far as Hacienda Medina if we have to."

They came to the juncture of the Rios Colorado and San Juan without seeing anything and they continued upstream for an hour. A kilometer from the small river dock at Trinidad, they could see the *Triunfo* ahead.

For a moment John's heart beat faster. Then it plunged. The way the *Triunfo* rode high in the water, it was clear that her cargo was gone. John whispered, "Looks like there's no one aboard. Pablo, bring us alongside. I'll board her."

"Don't be a *tonto*, Chohnee. What you think we come along for? So you can have all the fun? I'll come alongside just like you say. But if I flash the spotlight on all at once, it will blind anybody waiting for us. Then the four of you go aboard with your guns blazing."

John grinned at Pablo. "Amigo, you forget *why* we come. What if Dama Mariposa is onboard and asleep . . . ?"

Pablo responded positively. "Dama's not on that boat. We'd never get this close without having to identify ourselves."

"You're right. But what if my friend is aboard and asleep or worse, tied up. Men, listen up. I'm going aboard. On my signal, Pablo will light up the boat. Pablo, you'll have to stay at the controls to keep the boats together. When you men come aboard, you don't have to come quietly, but do move quickly to a safe position. You'll only fire on my command. Are you ready?"

He received a tight nod from each of the men.

"Okay, Pablo, bring me alongside." He would soon find out if he was a prisoner with this crew. "Let me borrow your pistol, Pablo."

Pablo looked at him for a moment in amazement. "You loco, Chohnee? You come into action like this without a gun?"

John smiled. Pablo's reaction let him know he had no cause for concern, at least with Pablo. "Yeah. It is dumb, isn't it?"

Pablo handed the pistol to John, who slipped it under the belt of his pants. Stomach muscles knotted and adrenalin running, he jumped over the shiny bright railing of the *Delfín* and landed lightly aboard the *Triunfo*. He dropped to his belly and slithered to the galleyway in the center of the boat. John heard no movement below deck and so signaled for the light. As blazing light illuminated every part of the boat, Mario, Halcón, and La Raspa clambered over the rail.

John called, "Ahoy, the hold! Come on deck with your hands in the air!"

After sixty seconds of silence, John motioned for La Raspa. He moved silently to John's side. "I'm going below. Cover me."

La Raspa grinned. "No, this is my specialty." He handed John his M16, pulled the long knife from his holster, and turning the back of the blade against his opened lips, clamped the knife between his teeth.

John placed one hand on La Raspa's shoulder for a moment. La Raspa's glittering brown eyes reflected the searchlight, his lips parted to reveal white teeth clamped on the shining blade, and his wild black hair moved slightly in the breeze. The man would frighten anyone. "No matter what, don't attack a woman."

La Raspa nodded his head in agreement and, weaving as a snake, silently moved down the steps. After a moment he called, "No one down here!"

John called to Pablo, "Move the *Delfín* in close. Halcón will tie us together." Then he moved to the controls of the *Triunfo* and pushed the starter button. The engines fired in a smooth, muffled roar. Next, he turned on the lights and made a cursory examination of the cabin area. He noted six small holes behind the control panel and in the wall of the cabin. His heart sunk briefly. He thought that those holes were probably made by a .22-caliber rifle. He knew that Katia had great disdain for the small weapon, yet it was the only one available to her. He murmured, "Why, Katia? Why?"

Pablo joined him as he stepped up to the radio. John's heart seemed to freeze as he saw a carved silver watch dangling and swaying with the gentle movements of the boat. He reached out and took the watch in an unsteady hand. He flipped the lid open, and each gentle chime of the tune thrust icy stabs of pain deep into his heart.

Pablo said, "Chohnee, for the first time I'm getting worried about Dama. That's her watch and chime box. I saw her playing that tune over and over again with tears in her eyes just two days ago. She wouldn't leave it here unless she were in trouble."

John whispered, "Unless she were leaving a message." His mind was in turmoil as he considered the implications of the watch. Was she leaving it to show her anger at his lack of defense in front of Leon Hardesty? To signify a severance of any possible love she had for him? To declare her independence from all things American and her return to the Sandinistas?

Pablo interrupted John's string of unanswered questions. "Yeah, a message to tell us she's in trouble. I think we better try to raise El Cinco on the radio, Chohnee. Maybe Valderas will know what's happening."

John put the watch in his pocket, picked up the handset, and began to turn the dial of the sending set. A loud scream from the set pierced his ears.

Pablo said, "Mario's an expert on the radio."

John said to Mario, "Use the radio on the *Delfín*." He turned to La Raspa. "Is there anything in the hold?"

La Raspa shook his head and growled, "Not a thing."

Halcón whispered, "Chohnee, look." He pointed to a building at the end of the dock whose sides had been repaired and rerepaired with different kinds of material, including weathered signs. A flickering light shone in a window.

La Raspa was already on the dock, and he moved silently to the door of the ragtag building. A man stepped out of the door. He wore no shirt or shoes and was still buckling his belt. La Raspa grabbed him, and the long knife gleamed in the moonlight. John vaulted over the rail of the *Triunfo* while La Raspa held the knife to his throat. John said, "You will live, amigo, if you remain silent. Do you understand?"

The man nodded his head.

John asked, "Who brought the boat here?"

The man's eyes rolled in agonized fear. "Please, Señor, I don't know. A man gave me a thousand colones to watch it. That's— that's all I know, even if you kill me for it."

"Who were you to report to if someone came for it?"

The man looked genuinely puzzled. "The man, he was a big man, gray mustache, maybe sixty years old. He only told me to watch it."

John told La Raspa to let the man go. "Go back inside, amigo. You would do well to forget you saw us. Go back to sleep."

When John went aboard the *Delfin,* Mario had just finished the radio transmission. His words seemed hard. "Valderas told us to leave the *Delfin* here and take the *Triunfo* to headquarters—and bring you."

Pablo spoke slowly. "The *Delfin* will be safe." After a pause, Pablo said to John, "I think it's time for you to return my pistol, too."

John knew that with all the weaponry in the hands of Pablo's friends, he had but little choice. He handed the pistol to Pablo. "I do want to send a message to Omar telling him that I'm heading on up the San Juan and that they can pick up the *Delfin* here at Trinidad."

Pablo paused and then agreed. "Give Mario the call numbers."

In a short five minutes they were headed up the San Juan. It would be well past dawn when they approached the dock at Hacienda Medina. John stood on the bow, staring sightlessly up the river. He couldn't decide if he was more worried about the disappearance of Juliana Brown or the defection of Katia Solano.

CHAPTER EIGHT

THE *TRIUNFO* APPROACHED the landing dock at Hacienda Medina. Valderas, wearing an old denim jacket and carrying a wide-brimmed straw hat, heaved up the galley stairs of his boat. He jumped heavily to the dock. The .22 rifle strapped across his shoulders was not his usual weapon of choice.

The *Triunfo* bumped against a protective row of old tires. A mooring rope sailed from Halcón's hands. Valderas caught the rope and expertly looped the end around the projecting stump of a worn and splintered piling.

On other visits to Hacienda Medina, Valderas had welcomed him with an *abrazo,* but this morning Valderas was unsmiling and distant, not even extending his hand in friendship. John glanced at the pile of crates stacked on the dock bearing the Senator Chandler symbol, the symbol that identified the bait held out for Katia—bait she had taken.

Pablo called anxiously, "Valderas! Do you know what happened to Dama?"

Valderas answered Pablo's question, but his cold eyes never left John's. "She called me for help yesterday. Said there was a shipment of armaments heading for Campo Azul—brought in by the CIA. I took *La Dorotea* downstream, and we captured the weapons." Valderas turned to John. "So, Chohn Tanner. What brings you to Hacienda Medina?" He seemed full of suspicion.

John could not make himself believe that Katia would betray him. Still, he felt a distinct chill travel the length of his spine as he looked into Valderas's cold black eyes. His gaze did not falter, and he spoke quietly. "I came to talk to Katia."

"She wants to talk to you, too." Valderas unslung the .22 rifle from his shoulder and paused briefly, the stock resting lightly against his hip. The small black muzzle pointed right at John's heart for one breath-stealing moment. Slowly, the barrel turned toward the nearby jungle. Without aiming, Valderas pulled the trigger. John started at the sound of the bullets snapping out and then dying, muffled by the jungle overgrowth. A saddled buckskin horse standing tied to a tree whinnied and reared, nervously sawing its head up and down, pulling against the reins that held it in check.

Valderas threw the gun at John, who reflexively thrust out his hand. The gun smacked into his palm. Valderas nodded his head at the horse still stamping nervously. "Dama told me to show you that the gun worked and to have a horse ready for you. She said you know where to meet her."

John walked to the horse, untied the reins, and held the horse in check, one hand on the horn of the saddle and a foot set in the stirrup.

Valderas barked at him, "Chohn Tanner! In case Dama Mariposa turns soft, you better come down that trail together. You in front!"

John mounted and sat easily in the saddle. Valderas's threat was not lost on him. He nodded his head. "Valderas, I would have thought that you knew by now that I would never do any harm to Katia—neither would I have thought you would just shoot me. Thanks for the warning, though."

He turned the horse along the trail and then turned back. Leaning over the horn of the saddle, his brown eyes steadily engaging the bulky man's gaze, he said, "For the record, Valderas, I've never violated any confidence anyone in El Cinco entrusted to me—and there are two sides to every story." He continued along the trail.

John knew where he would find Katia. He tied the horse along the trail. He would not have been able to give a rational reason for his next action. He breached the chamber of the small weapon and took out the clip of bullets.

He walked along the trail carrying the now useless .22. After a short distance, he moved into the rugged underbrush and walked parallel to the trail. He approached the clearing. Katia was seated, her back against a boulder, and facing the trail. A poncho was spread over her legs. A floppy, broad-brimmed straw hat drooped down over her eyes. A pink, gauzy scarf covered her hair. She sat without moving, and if it were not for the uncomfortable position, she might have been asleep.

John moved quietly until he stood near the boulder, the small, empty rifle held at the ready. He said quietly, "Hola, Katia."

At first she did not move, then her head rose. Her small, black-muzzled .38 materialized as if from nowhere, and she stared straight into his eyes. Katia removed the scarf. John found himself caught in her steely black gaze. She had arranged herself so that it only *looked* like she had been seated facing the trail with her back leaned against the boulder. She had spread the poncho so it looked like it covered her legs, but she faced the back of the clearing. The gauzy scarf allowed her to see, and she had simply awaited his approach.

Neither of them moved for a long moment of silence. Finally, John said, "That was very good, Katia. What's the score now?"

With a significant movement of the .38 and without a smile, she said, "I'm not sure, but I think I'm ahead."

John stood and Katia sat, each facing the other, both with weapons ready for instant action. John had never seen Katia's eyes so coldly black. He thought it would make sense to put the empty .22 down, but some quirk of obstinacy made him hold it steadily, matching the threat of her .38.

"Looks like a Mexican standoff," John said.

Finally Katia asked, "Why have you come?"

"Valderas implied that you expected me."

Katia nodded her head. "I got away from you and Fiero Rinskin and Señor Hardesty, but I guess I didn't really think you'd be dumb enough to come back here."

"Why was raiding the *Triunfo* so important to you?"

"Why did you let Señor Hardesty say those things?"

"You haven't answered my question about the *Triunfo* yet."

Bleakly Katia said, "All right. Question for question. What makes you think I captured the *Triunfo?*"

John took the watch music box from his pocket and let it dangle, glinting in the sunlight.

Katia gave a shrill forced laugh. "That doesn't prove anything. I gave that . . . *trinket* to some guy in Concepción two hours after you gave it to me."

Her words made John wince even though he didn't believe them. "I also noticed the crates of weapons on Hacienda Medina's dock."

"And how do you know the crates came from the *Triunfo?* Unless you were part of, as Mr. Hardesty called it, my trap?"

"The crates are marked with the Senator Chandler symbol. The truth is I don't care about the weapons—or a trap I had nothing to do with."

Katia's words came slowly as if they cost her much effort. "I think maybe this is the first time you ever lied to me, Chohn Tanner."

John's answer came evenly. "I have *never* lied to you, Katia Solano. Not now, not ever! I had nothing to do with Hardesty's trap." After a moment of silent staring, John said, "Tell me what happened to Agent Brown, and I'll leave quietly."

Katia slightly changed the aim of the .38 to point straight at John's heart. "If you are not lying to me, put the .22 on the boulder—and do it very carefully."

The position of John's little machine gun did not waver. "I want to know what happened to Agent Brown."

"I don't know what happened to Brown. And you lie about your trap!"

"The cabin of the *Triunfo* was sprayed with at least one blast from a .22. Do you really deny being onboard?"

Her answer was steady. "No. I just don't know what happened to Brown. Do *you* deny knowing that Fiero Rinskin tried to kill me?"

"I didn't know who he was shooting at. You didn't notice that it was me who took his gun away from him—and threw him against the cabin?"

"I did notice that *you* were shooting at *me* when I took your airboat!"

"I consistently fire darn close to two hundred on the range, Katia. I *hit* what I shoot at."

For just the briefest moment, Katia's eyes flickered to brown, and she ducked her head. Then she raised it back up, her eyes and words filled with contempt. "You are finally getting to where you are a good agent, Chohn Tanner. You lie in a convincing way. I almost believed you for a second."

John regarded her for a moment then lowered the rifle from its aim at Katia. He let the small weapon drop to his side and slowly walked forward. He never let his eyes stray from hers. Finally, his worn cowboy boot scraped against the boulder, and he slowly placed the gun on the large rock. Then he stood and said, "If you think I have ever lied to you, pull the trigger, Katia."

John noticed the slightest mellowing of her black eyes. "I didn't bring a weapon with me. Pablo loaned me a gun when we went in search of the airboat and the *Triunfo*. I gave it back to him at Trinidad." John pointed to the rifle on the rock. "Valderas threw that gun to me and told me to meet you here."

Katia continued to regard him in silence.

"As soon as I was out of Valderas's sight, I unloaded the .22. Check it. You'll find I speak truly."

A slight gasp issued from Katia's throat. Her face first flushed deeply then seemed to drain to an ivory white. The .38 moved wildly for a moment. She started to reach for the .22, then quickly swung her gun back toward John. He didn't move. She stood up, and the poncho dropped to the ground, revealing an FAL rifle at the base of the boulder. Her words were shrill. "Chohnee, you are loco! *My* gun *is* loaded! I might have—I almost shot you! How do you think I'd feel if I shot you and then found out you weren't even armed?"

With a slight smile, he said, "Guilty, I would hope."

Katia waved the handgun in small, almost helpless circles. "Where are we? What—what do we do now?"

"First . . ." He reached out and gingerly turned the mouth of the gun, no longer looking deadly, away from him. "Put your .38 away. And second, we can get some answers to both our questions."

Katia's weapon was back in the holster before John had completed his sentence. She said, "Maybe I'm finally waking up from a long nightmare."

John's thoughts were in turmoil. The accusations in her file boiled in his mind. He wanted to trust her, but he had too many unanswered questions.

"I left the music box on the *Triunfo* to tell you I hated you. I was wrong. Forgive me, Chohnee?"

"I had it coming when I didn't defend you to Hardesty."

"The worst was when I thought you were shooting at me. You said the only thing that could have changed my heart from stone when you reminded me that you always hit what you shoot at. What were you doing?"

"Trying to make Hardesty think I was after you. It didn't work."

"Is he hurt bad?"

"I don't know for sure. He's in the Clinica Biblica in San Jose. They have to take the bullet out. Are you ready to talk about Agent Brown yet?"

"You're in love with her."

"I was—a long, long time ago. How did you know?"

"I watched when you realized she was not Julio Kamba. I saw it in your eyes. I think she's going to take you away from—Central America."

"All you'd have to do—"

Katia stopped his words by placing her fingers over his lips. "Don't say it, Chohnee. Don't start to lie to me now." She turned her back to him. She looked at the sky for a moment and then took a deep breath.

John said, "Somehow I knew, just as Pablo did, that you would be all right."

Katia turned, her eyes were changing to a smoldering black. "Were you coming to look for me or for your Agent Brown?"

John dropped his eyes for a moment and didn't answer.

Katia said, "I see. She must be somebody important to the CIA."

"She isn't. Matter of fact, Hardesty seems quite unconcerned about her. That's why I've got to find out what happened to her." After a pause, he said, "I guess it's your turn for explanations, Katia."

"Will you believe me if I tell you?"

"How many times have you lied to me?"

"Only when I thought it in Nicaragua's best interest."

"How come I have to tell the truth, and you can lie?"

"Because, Chohnee, you're a . . ." She switched briefly to English. "How you say? A straight arrow?"

John could not maintain eye contact. "Yeah. Straight arrow. I guess I used to be. Lately . . ." His words trailed off.

John sensed a sadness in Katia's eyes. "Then it's time for you to go home. The only straight arrow I've ever known is beginning to warp crooked."

John thought, *And you don't know the half of it.* "First I've got to find out what happened to Operative Brown."

A gentle smile played briefly on Katia's lips. "Didn't I hear you call her Chuliana when you first saw her?" Katia had the same trouble with Juliana's name that she did with John's.

John nodded in the affirmative.

"Okay, Chohnee. I rode your airboat up the Colorado for maybe ten minutes before your Chuliana caught up with me. I knew that in the *Triunfo* she could easily swamp me, so I cut through the marsh at Laguna Aqua Zarcas. I knew the *Triunfo* couldn't cross there. Just before I lost sight of the *Triunfo,* it came under attack by two small motorboats. I didn't want the comunistas to get the arms, so I fired on them with your stupid .22. As soon as I opened fire, I knew I was outgunned, and so I went on across the marsh and then back down the Bravo Channel to the resguardo."

"How come?"

"I wanted my automatic rifle—those popguns of yours. But everything had been taken off *La Gaviota.* I used the radio to contact Valderas. He was already on the river, close to Tambor, so we decided to go for the *Triunfo.* At least for the weapons. I moved up the Bravo Channel, and Valderas came down to the Colorado. We intercepted the *Triunfo* while it was still in Costa Rican waters. When Valderas and I boarded the *Triunfo,* your Chuliana was already gone. I didn't know she was important to you . . ."

John probed. "Okay. So what happened after that?"

Katia shrugged. "Not much. I followed Valderas in the *Triunfo* back to Trinidad, where we switched the arms to Valderas's boat. Then we returned to Hacienda Medina in *La Dorotea.*"

"And you don't have any idea what happened to Brown? You didn't question the crew of the *Triunfo?*"

"I didn't. Valderas may have."

"Did he bring any of the communist crew back to headquarters?"

"Yes. The pilot."

John walked to the edge of the small clearing in silence.

Katia came to him and stood by his side. "We've traveled a long road for a long time, Chohnee. But I feel like we've never been further apart."

John looked down into liquid brown pools, the shining sun making small diamonds of the tears held in check in her eyes. A stirring of breeze lifted a lock of glistening black hair and blew it gently. He felt the familiar quickening of pulse and intake of breath, and wondered, *Can I, after all this time, walk away?* The thought brought a churning to his stomach and a feeling of intense emptiness to his heart.

Katia asked, "What are you going to do?"

"I'll talk to the pilot Valderas brought to Hacienda Medina."

"I mean about us. About Nicaragua."

John suddenly didn't care if the surge of bitterness in his thoughts would show through in his words to Katia. "I tried hard, for a long time, to be as loyal as a Nica. I don't know what I'm going to do about Nicaragua. And you—you've never given me reason to think—" He paused and then continued in a very positive manner. "The first thing I have to do is find Juliana. Then I'll decide about other things. When she's safe."

"It sounds like you're making your Chuliana a top priority."

The truth seemed to crystallize in his mind for the first time. Finding Juliana *was* his first priority. He said, "You're right. I am."

Anger clouded Katia's face, and her eyes began to smolder again. "And you say it was a long time ago when you loved her?"

Amazement crept into John's mind. Never in his acquaintance with Katia Solano had he ever thought that she would be capable of jealousy.

Katia whirled around, and without looking at John, she murmured, "Then this is good-bye. Go find your Chuliana, Chohnee."

"Katia, I . . ."

She turned and pointed down the trail. Her cheeks flushed red, and anger sparked from her tear-filled eyes. "Well, go find your Agent Brown!"

"I need you to come with me. Me in front."

Katia didn't answer. She picked up the FAL rifle as well as the .22, walked quickly across the clearing, and started down the trail.

After a few meters, she stepped off the rocky trail, leaned the rifle against a tree, and threw her arms around the neck of her little horse.

She whispered, "At least *you* are a faithful friend." After a moment of caressing the horse's neck and ears, she pushed the FAL into the holster, swung into the saddle, and turned down the trail.

John called, "Hold on, Katia! You'll get me shot yet! Valderas was dead serious when he warned me to be in front when we came down the trail."

Katia didn't answer but pulled up on the reins and let him walk by. He plodded down the trail a few meters. Neither of them spoke. They approached the place where John had tied the horse. Sitting casually in the saddle of the huge, powerfully built bay was Valderas, automatic rifle hung carelessly over his forearm, hat strung by halyard on his back, his curly silver hair stirring in the breeze.

John stared into angry brown eyes, then slowly raised his hands and, lacing his fingers together, set them heavily on his head.

Valderas's words rumbled. "Emptying that gun saved your life, hombre. If you had approached Dama Mariposa with it loaded, you'd have been a dead man before you took two steps into the clearing."

Katia's face flushed in anger. She urged her mount forward and, standing up in the stirrups, bellowed, "Valderas! You stood guard for me? I told you I could handle Chohnee! Why did you interfere?"

"Pretty little butterfly. I didn't interfere. I did nothing but be sure you were safe. *Nada mas.* Just see that you were safe."

Katia's anger was not assuaged. Flushing darkly, she lifted on the reins and lightly raked the flanks of her little pony. Sandinita answered in a scrabbling leap and churned off down the trail, casting dirt and spurts of dust with her pounding hooves.

Valderas turned to John. "So, hombre. You a little loco coming to Hacienda Medina uninvited, unarmed, and with Dama Mariposa angry at you."

Despite the threat in Valderas's words, John would explain nothing to him. He walked slowly to where his horse was tethered. He swung into the saddle and turned the horse down the trail.

The large man clucked and gave an almost imperceptible twitch of the reins. The big bay jumped and blocked the trail. "Hold up, hombre. I tried to find out from Pablo what's going on. He didn't make sense, and Dama wouldn't talk to me all the way back from Trinidad."

John kneed his horse and tried to urge it around Valderas.

With a slight hitch of his shoulder, the FAL swung around and smoothly slipped into the grasp of Valderas's large brown hand. "Neither of us is going anywhere until I get some answers. Do you understand, Señor Gallo?"

Suddenly John felt consumed with anger. He stood forward in the stirrups of his saddle. His finger, pointed at Valderas, shook with rage. "What's with you, Valderas? If you've talked to

Pablo at all, you know that *I* arranged a boat to come up the San Juan to find out what happened to Katia. I didn't even bring a weapon, and you *know* it! And you saw me empty the one you gave me so there would be no possibility of an accident when I talked to her. I've known the location of your headquarters for half a year, and you've never had any reason to question that I've given that information to anyone at any time. I've helped with some dangerous and successful missions. In the past year, I've sent weaponry to you that I could just as easily have sent back down the San Juan. I've fought for El Cinco many times! What does a man have to do to earn your trust? Lie dead somewhere with a bullet in his head?"

After a moment John eased back down in his saddle. He spoke quietly. "Let me by, please. I'd hoped that after all my service to El Cinco I was entitled to a little help in return. I see I was wrong."

Valderas turned slowly in his creaking saddle and pushed the automatic rifle down into the holster attached to the saddlebags. "Okay, Chohnee, mi amigo. Por favor, accept my apology." He clucked to his horse, and the big bay moved sideways along the trail. Valderas continued. "You're free to go, but I'd appreciate it if you would tell me what's happened."

John studied the older man and thought, *I hate always having to lie!* Aloud he said, "Katia called me three days ago. She told me about a shipment of arms coming up the Rio San Juan."

John told Valderas the story of how Katia had thought he was shooting at her when in reality he was trying to help her escape. He could not tell him of his role with the CIA. He concluded by saying, "The captain of the *Triunfo* was a woman masquerading as Julio Kamba. I've known her a long time."

Valderas asked, "She have a name?"

"Juliana. Juliana Moreno." He used the Spanish version of Juliana, spoken *Hooliana,* and he rationalized, *Brown is* Moreno *in Spanish.*

Valderas asked, "Why do you want to contact her?"

"She's disappeared. She's an old friend—and I think maybe Katia is—maybe a little bit jealous about Juliana."

Valderas laughed. "Dama jealous? You flatter yourself, Chohnee." Valderas enjoyed another moment of laughter at what he thought was John's expense. "Let's go down to headquarters. Maybe we can get some information about your Juliana."

Katia was not around when John and Valderas rode into the compound. John supposed she had gone to the little thatched house that she occupied when she was at Hacienda Medina. It was located a hundred meters from the big house.

The man called La Raspa was sprawled in the shade of a huge mahagua tree. John had often seen the paisanos peel the reddish bark from a branch of a targua tree to reveal its blood-red sap. They then dipped a finger in the oozing sap and rubbed it on the gum above a sore tooth to make a toothache go away. This was the activity La Raspa was engaged in.

Valderas called, "La Raspa! We have a man to interrogate."

La Raspa reminded John of a snake uncoiling as he stood up and sauntered toward them. His hair and beard was unkempt. His clothing clearly had not met with soap and water for at least a month. La Raspa casually replaced his knife in its long holster and stuffed the targua branch under his belt.

Valderas ordered, "You come with us too, Chohnee. Maybe you can tell if the comunisto tells any lies."

John followed Valderas and La Raspa toward a small shack at the edge of the jungle compound. The walls were made of palm fronds thatched over a jungle-tree frame. There was no door to the opening of the hut. The man's ankles were clamped in leg irons that were attached by a rusty chain to an iron rod driven deep into the earth, allowing him only five feet of freedom. The man looked feverish, and his lips were chapped and swollen.

Valderas tossed a key to La Raspa and walked to a huge fallen log and sat down. "Bring him out here."

La Raspa removed the lock that kept the leg chains bound to the iron stake. The man moved awkwardly, dragging the chains behind him. Valderas stood up and faced the prisoner. La Raspa grinned hugely and pulled the targua branch from his pocket and peeled a long, thin sliver of bark from the wood. Beads of blood-red sap oozed out and traced behind the razor-sharp knife. John watched the pilot and could feel the growing terror of the man. The pilot clearly believed the beads of blood-red sap could be his own if these men did not get the answers they wanted.

Valderas asked, "What were you doing on Julio Kamba's boat?"

"I'm his pilot."

"How come you were making a run without Julio?"

"A month ago we got arrested down by Panama . . ."

Valderas interrupted. "What were you carrying?"

The man averted his eyes. "I'm only the pilot. I don't know."

Valderas moved his head toward La Raspa. La Raspa stepped toward the pilot, his knife gleaming in the sun.

The pilot's eyes widened in terror. He began talking rapidly. "Cocaine. We were running cocaine to a yacht tied up in *Isla Colon*. One day a guard told me he could get me free if I'd make a run of guns and ammunition up the Rio Colorado in Julio's boat. I agreed to do it."

Valderas asked, "They let Julio out of jail too?"

"No. There was a man who pretended to be Julio. The guy did a good job to imitate Julio, but it wasn't Julio. I think Julio's still in jail."

John asked, "What happened to the person imitating Julio Kamba?"

"He was a queer one . . ."

Valderas nodded his head at La Raspa. That was all the urging the pilot needed. "I don't know exactly. It was confusing. Seemed like we were being attacked from every direction. First a beat-up old trawler, then an airboat. Then the coast guard came along and took Julio—only it wasn't Julio—"

John interrupted impatiently. "I just want to know what happened to the one we'll call *Julio!*"

Valderas raised his arm as if to strike the man.

The prisoner ducked and fell to the ground. He looked frantically between Valderas and John and then at La Raspa, who had stopped whittling and drawing blood from the branch, but was still grinning.

John took Valderas by the arm and turned him toward the log. "Por favor, Valderas. You and La Raspa are scaring the man witless. Both of you go sit on the log for a minute." Then he knelt on the ground by the prisoner. "Listen. You answer my questions without any nonsense, and tell me the truth, and I'll see to it you get water and food. Fair enough?"

"Si, si! Tell me what you want to know."

"I know everything that happened up until the coast guard boat got into the picture. And I know what happened when the airboat and Valderas came back. I just want to know what happened in between and especially where the one called Julio went."

"We came alongside the coast guard boat, and the one called Julio took charge of the boat again. He told me to follow the airboat across a marsh. I started to argue, because the propellers would foul, but he pulled a gun on me. We didn't get five hundred meters into the marsh when we *did* run foul. Then two small boats came alongside and told us to deliver the arms to them. The commander, I think, was called Ramos. Ramos was on board the *Triunfo,* and then the airboat came along and opened fire on us but left immediately. The one called Julio shot Ramos, and I was afraid the people in the boats would kill us all, so I knocked the one called Julio down. I think he hit his head when he fell. They took him and Commander Ramos on one of the small boats. They left two men with us to get the *Triunfo* back to the Rio Colorado saying they would send a bigger boat for the arms. We got the propeller clear and back into the main channel when the airboat came back and—"

John interrupted. "Valderas came along. Did you hear them say where they were going to take the one called Julio?"

"Not exactly. One did say something about how General Ortega would like to talk to the one called Julio. That would mean taking him to Managua, I think."

John stood up. He turned to Valderas. "I found out what I wanted to know. Now, you should feed him and give him some water—and quit treating him so roughly."

Valderas just laughed. "Rough? I was quite gentle with him. But if you insist. La Raspa, put him back in the hut and get him beans and water." He placed his heavy arm on John's shoulder and headed him back toward the compound. "So, Chohnee, what you going to do?"

"I'm not sure. I guess I'll go to Managua."

"Dangerous—and dumb to go without information or help."

"You object to me taking the *Triunfo?*"

Valderas spread his hands. "It's not my boat. When you leaving?"

"Immediately."

"Daytime's not too good a time. How about tonight? Maybe I can get you a crew, or even better, help you make a plan that might do something besides get you killed."

"I'd appreciate some help. Mostly information, I think."

Valderas's expression did not change. "Don't think I'm being altruistic. You know too much about El Cinco for me to take chances on you getting caught by General Ortega. If you think *my* methods of getting information out of someone are primitive, you'd really be impressed by his." Valderas glanced at his watch. "You ride on up to the main house. Get Señora Reyes to fix us something to eat. I'll join you in a little while."

The old house had been built nearly a hundred years ago but was still a handsome yellow stucco home. Graceful arches supported a large front porch. The red tiles of the roof, though ancient and moss covered, were still sound. Vines and flowers grew in profusion around the porch. John knocked on the massive, polished mahogany door. His knock went unanswered, and so he tried the door and found it unlocked. The only sound came from the kitchen.

The spacious kitchen gleamed with copper pots hanging on pegs attached to the swirls of cream-colored stuccoed walls. A huge, old wood-burning stove was kept spotless despite the fact that it was no longer used. Antique oil-burning lamps had been converted to electrical use. Water no longer flowed from the pump located on the ancient yet beautifully tiled counter, but instead it came from gleaming faucets only recently installed in the kitchen.

Señora Reyes was busy scrubbing on copper pots in the sink, her short, sturdy back turned to John. Her long gray hair was coiled in a braid.

John greeted her. "Hola, Mamacita Reyes. Can you spare a tortilla for a hungry stranger?"

Black eyes snapping and a happy smile breaking across the mellow brown parchment of her face, she turned, welcoming John with a warm abrazo. "Chohnee! I always have something for my young friends. How are you?"

"I'm well. You look especially pretty. Is there a dance I can take you to tonight?"

Señora Reyes laughed. "Save your honey-sweet talk for Dama Mariposa. When will you talk some sense into her pretty head and get her to settle down with you to make a bunch of beautiful children?"

"I don't think she can cook. Besides, why would a vaquero dance with a princess, if a beautiful queen will dance with him instead?"

Señora Reyes tipped on to her toes and kissed him on the cheek. "You're a charmer. A flattering charmer." She turned and lit one of the burners of the bottled-gas stove, placed a cast-iron pan on it, went to the refrigerator, and began removing bowls of different kinds of food. All the while she grumbled. "In the old days there would already be a fire in the stove, and it would only take a minute to fix you a burrito."

John laughed. "But then I wouldn't be able to talk to you long enough. By the way, Valderas said he would be in to eat also."

She placed a large glass of juice on the table and gestured for John to sit down. "I remember you don't like beer."

John ignored her invitation to sit and hovered close. "I can hardly wait. No one in the world makes food so delicious, Mamacita Reyes."

She smiled and placed food on a plate. "Here, eat this while I fix another. One could not fill you. I don't know how you stay so thin—"

Valderas interrupted her words by entering the kitchen. He dropped his white sombrero on the shiny floor and sat heavily in a chair. He said to John, "I talked to Montenegro. Soon as he finds out anything, he'll get back to me. How many people you want to take with you?"

"I haven't figured it out yet."

Señora Reyes brought a plate of food for both John and Valderas. Valderas placed a forkful of burrito in his mouth and chewed for a moment. "You might run things by the seat of your pants in Costa Rica, but you'd better have some *good* plans if you tangle with General Ortega in Nicaragua."

John wanted to ask if Valderas had ever figured out how he'd survived six months in Nicaragua and Costa Rica. Instead, he said politely, "I already told you I'd appreciate your help."

"Did you know that Jaime had gone communist? Soon as he knew I had found out, he disappeared. Pablo has replaced him in El Cinco."

"No, I didn't. Pablo's an excellent man."

"Miguel's at Campo Azul. But with Pablo, Dama, and myself, and Colonel Montenegro on tap, we can help you get your Juliana."

They finished the food in silence.

As they left the kitchen, John hugged Señora Reyes and whispered, "Muchas gracias, Mamacita, and don't forget we have a date if there's a dance tonight."

She laughed. "Where were you thirty years ago?"

The maps were just rolled up on a long piece of bamboo, but John was impressed with the detail. Even small cities like Juigalpa and Granada had sections that showed streets and main buildings. "I'm impressed, Valderas." John studied the map briefly. "You think Montenegro can find out where she's jailed?"

"Time will tell."

Valderas glanced at his watch. "Well, Chohnee, you have plans, or are you keeping them secret?"

John's words were hesitant. "I've got a newspaper friend in Managua. Maybe he'll have heard where they've stuck her, and then it's just a case of *mordida,* a little money under the table to get them to let her go."

"Sometimes bribery works, but not always. Let me study this out."

While Valderas studied, John thought, *What a mess.* Even a CIA operator in Managua, dared he approach one, would not know any more than he did.

Promptly at three o'clock, Pablo walked into the room. Valderas looked up and asked, "Where's Dama?"

Pablo said, "I don't know." He looked at John. "What's this about?"

Valderas continued staring at the map. "I'll explain when Dama gets here."

After ten minutes, Katia entered the room. John looked up and did a double take. She had changed out of the camouflage fatigues and wore a fashionable pair of pegged Calvin Klein jeans tucked into brown, white-stitched boots. Her blouse with white piping and gleaming pearl buttons matched the cornflower-blue pants. A jaunty feminine white cowboy hat hung over her shoulders. Her black curly hair sparkled and caught glints of sunlight as if it were filled with jewels. Her face glowed even more than usual.

Katia smiled brightly. Valderas stood up, swept off his hat with a bow, made nervous movements straightening his clothing, and brushed his hair with his hand. John smiled at the thought that Valderas was flustered. Pablo's infatuated eyes were a dead giveaway to his feelings for Dama Mariposa.

Valderas stammered, "Dama, you—you look . . ."

Katia studiously ignored John. She turned to Pablo, held out her hand, and greeted him warmly. "Hello, Pablo. How was your trip to Costa Rica?"

Pablo took her extended hand in both his and was surely not so tongue tied as Valderas. "It's good to see you, Dama. You're a beautiful rose amidst a bramble of weeds." Then he looked suspiciously at John and asked, "Now, Valderas, what's this emergency meeting about?"

Katia said, "I thought you would know, Pablo. We're to get Chohnee's girlfriend out of the clutches of General Ortega. Isn't that true, Valderas?"

Valderas gave her a curt nod, walked to the map, then turned and faced Katia and Pablo. "Chohnee's been a good friend." He seemed to measure Katia for a moment. "You're the one who brought Chohnee to us, Dama. Over the past months, he's earned our help. We can't turn him down."

Katia started to speak, but Valderas ignored her and continued. "I haven't worked out details yet, but this much you need to know—"

Katia succeeded in breaking into Valderas's words. "You know who this Chuliana is, Valderas?" No smile softened her facial expression.

"Chohnee's friend. I don't need to know more. Now pay attention! Montenegro is standing by, and you should know, Dama, he's in support. Matter of fact, he's finding out what prison she's in."

Valderas stopped and cocked his head waiting for Dama to say more.

"All right. I'm listening."

"This Juliana was impersonating Julio Kamba when she was captured—"

The radio crackled, and Valderas moved to stand by the operator's side.

Through crackles of static, they heard Montenegro's voice. "Get me Valderas."

Valderas spoke tersely into the mouthpiece. "Valderas."

"Subject in unit seventeen. They don't know who she is. Rescue doubtful. If you proceed, use bull auction on coming twelfth. Use Intercontinental. Confirm?"

"Positive. Out."

John asked Valderas, "I suppose you understood that?"

Dama spoke to John for the first time. "We can't be on the air too long, so our messages have to be brief and specific. The message says your Chuliana is in prison unit seventeen, that's El Chipote. Montenegro is concerned about the potential for success in getting her out of El Chipote, but if we decide to proceed, the cover we should use is a bull auction that will be held on the twelfth, and we should stay at the Hotel Intercontinental."

Chills ran down John's back as he asked, "How much does her being in El Chipote complicate things?"

Valderas stood in silence for a time before answering. "There are advantages and disadvantages to her being in El Chipote. We can move about Managua easily, but El Chipote is a *mighty* tough installation. We'll never be able to break her out of there. Montenegro will be working on a plan . . ." He smashed a large fist into his other heavy hand and paced for a time. He whirled on John. "How much *does* she know about El Cinco, Chohnee?"

John rubbed his chin in thought. "I don't know. I only talked to her for ten minutes at the most. If she knows anything, it's from a source other than me. Having her show up on Rio San Juan was a surprise to me."

Valderas paced some more and then said, "We can't take a chance. We'll have to get her out one way or another."

John said quietly, "I don't like the way you say 'one way or another.'"

"Don't worry, Chohnee. We can get her out." He looked at Dama and then Pablo. "But people involved have to go voluntarily. I could use you, Pablo."

Pablo asked, "Will you be going, Valderas?"

"Si. In fact, I'd like to buy a bull if I get lucky and can buy at a good price."

Pablo gave a big grin. "I've never been to Managua. I wouldn't mind seeing the sights."

Valderas turned to John. "You look right good on a horse, Chohnee. You know anything about bulls?"

"I used to tend Herefords, but I can tell a good Brahma if I see one."

"We'll need a hacienda for you to bid for."

John only paused for a moment before he said, "Boquis good enough?"

Valderas looked at him speculatively. "Boquis? That'll do—if they don't already have someone at the auction."

"Even if they have someone, I can fit in."

Valderas next directed a questioning look at Katia.

She said, "I've been to Managua. I'm not sure I want to go this time."

Turning to John, Valderas asked, "Would she add or detract from your cover?"

Before John answered, he thought about how many times Katia's life had been threatened in the past months. No matter what, he did not want to leave her alone along the Rio San Juan.

"If she's going to help, she's got the most devious mind of any person I know. She'd be an asset. I'd like her along."

Valderas turned a few of the maps on the bamboo roller, pausing at a large map of the city of Managua. John didn't need him to point out prison unit seventeen. It was labeled on the map. His gaze was drawn to the grouping of names. He'd known it all before, but somehow seeing all those names in such a tight cluster made the task seem that much more formidable. Within a single kilometer radius was the army field hospital, Guardia headquarters, First Battalion headquarters, and, if that wasn't enough, the president's palace. Not too far away was prison unit seventeen. El Chipote.

With a sinking feeling in the pit of his stomach, John pointed at prison unit seventeen. His questioning eyes engaged Valderas.

With a hard smile, Valderas said, "Si. That's the place."

"You sure you want to commit El Cinco? I think I could go in there and get her out. It would be less noticeable if I went alone."

"It's true that too many people would attract attention," Valderas said, as he turned to Pablo. "You think Mario, Halcón, and La Raspa will go with us?"

Pablo spoke with complete confidence. "If I ask them to."

Valderas counted on his fingers. "We can't count Montenegro, but there's me, Pablo, Chohnee, and the three of them. We need ten maximum. We can pick up four—"

Katia interrupted. "Only three. I'm coming along."

Valderas mused, "I can take my boat to Granada. We'd need some way to get the bull from Managua to Granada . . ." He lapsed into silence. Then he said, "All right. But we can't go in a large group." He studied John. "You're the only one I worry about, Chohnee. How good is your cover, really?"

"Good enough. I have a pickup truck and cattle trailer in San Carlos."

Valderas said, "Good. You and Dama check into the Intercontinental late tomorrow. A husband and wife team . . ."

Katia interrupted, "Not husband and wife—we've already established ourselves . . ."

As her words faltered, John laughed and said, "What Katia means, Valderas, is we've been at the hotel before. They'll think we're from Boquis."

Valderas accepted that. "Okay. I'll take Mario and Halcón with me on *La Dorotea*. Pablo, you and La Raspa—clean him up before you leave here tonight—we'll let you off by Santa Lucia so you can get a bus into Managua. I want everyone in place by tomorrow night."

Valderas looked at each person for a moment. "There's a place on the promenade at Lago de Tiscapa. Dancing, food. It's called Mama Sanchez's. Be there between seven and nine. Casual. There'll be a lot of people, and no one'll look out of place. I need to know everyone arrived okay. Questions?"

John asked in surprise, "Such a public place?"

Valderas smiled. "You never heard? Hide in plain sight. By the way, every hotel phone and half the others in Managua are tapped by Ortega's secret police. Another thing. Keep your eyes open for the secret police. Ortega wants to know what every stranger in town is doing."

Pablo asked, "What about weapons?"

"Except for La Raspa's knife—he wouldn't go if you tried to take that away from him—we'll pick up what we need in Managua."

John asked, "Will you take us to San Carlos in *La Dorotea?*"

Katia interrupted. "It's not too long a horse ride, and there'll be a full moon. Chohnee and I can be in San Carlos in time. I don't want to leave Sandinita here alone."

John said, "Okay. I need to keep Omar posted. Can I use your radio, Valderas?"

"Sure." Then he said to Pablo, "Get your men ready. We'll leave today. You can all rest on the boat."

With a final look at each person, Valderas said, "Okay, let's go!"

CHAPTER NINE

KATIA HAD CHANGED into her camouflage uniform and saddled Sandinita in silence. John quietly saddled Valderas's big bay. Katia led out in a brisk trot. In spite of the full moon, John's black mood made the morning dark. He asked himself, *Why are* you *going to Managua? Juliana's not your responsibility.* He answered, *She is because Hardesty isn't concerned about her.* He didn't try to keep up with Katia.

John rode, his thoughts in turmoil, and watched the sky lighten. At the ridge where the trail began the descent to San Carlos, he saw Sandinita tied to the branch of a tree and Katia seated on a gray, barkless log. As John approached, she said, "Señora Reyes fixed food for us."

John tied the reins of the bay to a low-hanging branch. Katia unrolled a cloth that held four stuffed tortillas. They ate in silence.

Finally John said, "You're not very talkative this morning."

"I'm sad, I guess—like I've come to the end of something." After a pause she said, "Maybe you should tell me more about Chuliana."

"She was born in the Colonies in Mexico . . ."

Katia interrupted. "Colonies?"

"In the late eighteen hundreds, a group of Mormons settled in Northern Mexico. They built homes and irrigation systems, farmed, and planted orchards. They called their towns by names like *Colonia Juarez* and *Colonia Dublan*. These towns came to be known as the Mormon Colonies."

Katia nodded her head slowly.

"Juliana Brown's great-grandfather was one of the first settlers. I was born in Dublan, Mexico, a year after Dad went to work for Juliana's father."

Katia rolled up the cloth. "We can talk while we ride."

"Dad worked with the campesinos. I did chores and herded cattle with them. My parents spoke English in our home, but I mostly spoke Spanish. I went to a village school in Dublan till I turned twelve, when Dad started me in the Juarez Academy, a school owned by the Mormons. I felt more Mexican than Anglo. I didn't fit into the Academy very well.

"I was in eighth grade. Juliana had long auburn hair, brown eyes. She was the smartest in every class. Reading, math. She made better reports, wrote better poetry and stories. It wasn't just in schoolwork. Whatever the kids did, she was the best. She could swim better, catch balls better, ride better. I fell in love with her. In tenth grade I played basketball for the Academy. I felt a little more important. I asked her to go to the graduation dance, and she agreed. I was on top of the world. A friend of hers came down from the States for the summer. At the dance, she introduced me as one of her father's hired hands. How do you think that made me feel?"

Katia said, "It's hard for me to think of you as someone with self-doubts, someone who needs to be made to feel important."

John continued, "Mother died soon after that, and Dad moved back to Utah. He bought a small feedlot near a town called Payson. When I came home from my mission in Honduras, I went to school at BYU. That's a church school. I was over Juliana. I earned a bachelor's degree and then went on for a master's. Then I saw Juliana at the school. She was taking the same program, and we were in a lot of the same classes.

"It was the first time since I had known Juliana that I did better than she did. I got better grades and graduated in a higher class standing. We were both recruited during our last year by the CIA."

Katia abruptly pulled up on the reins. Her words were shrill. "We're going to Managua to rescue a CIA agent? We're risking everything that El Cinco has built for a CIA agent? It's crazy! Does Valderas know?"

John turned the horse and faced Katia. "No. But I didn't ask for El Cinco's help. I wanted to go alone, but Valderas is afraid she knows too much. I think he doesn't care if she's rescued or not, just so she can't talk to General Ortega. Valderas would be happy to have her dead."

Katia asked, "Well, how much *does* she know?"

"Who knows?"

"You're destroying El Cinco for a stupid love affair! I've got to talk to Valderas about this." She spurred Sandinita, and the little pony jumped forward on the trail.

John slashed at the bay's side with the end of the reins and kicked the horse in the flanks. The startled horse jumped across the trail, and John grabbed Sandinita's reins. "Katia, I want you to listen to me!"

Her eyes flashed in anger. "Let go of my horse's reins! I understand!"

"No, you don't! When I told you I was going after Juliana and you got jealous—"

"Jealous, Chohnee? Don't be silly. Why would I be—"

"Whether you want to admit it or not, you were jealous. The point is I don't *know* why I have to help Juliana. But it hasn't got anything to do with love. I fell in love with you when I first met you. Whatever else happens, that won't change. I love *you,* and I always will."

Katia sat on the little pony and stared at John, lips trembling and tears in her eyes. She asked, "Is it true, Chohnee? You love me? And you will love me no matter what? You won't leave me? You'll always love me?"

John made the long reach across the saddle and pulled Katia as close as he could in the awkward position. Katia's eager lips met and lingered on his.

After a time she whispered, "Move your foot from the stirrup."

She swung up behind the cantle of John's saddle. Placing both hands around his waist and leaning against his back, she said, "Let's get on to San Carlos. But don't ride too fast. It won't take all day to drive to Managua."

* * *

In San Carlos, John called Ernesto and told him he would be at the auction. Ernesto asked him to help his son, Ruel, pick out a good bull. John hooked up the cattle trailer and drove to the old Solano homestead. Katia changed into the cornflower-blue jeans of the previous evening and handed John a small suitcase, which he stowed by his own bag behind the seat of the pickup.

The trail-like road out of San Carlos was slow going, but in San Miguelito the road changed to pot-holed pavement. A half dozen soldiers played cards in the shade of a rudely built wood and galvanized iron port.

John slowed to a stop, and one of the men detached himself from the card game and strolled toward the pickup. John held a leatherette paper holder up to be seen. Katia leaned across John with a dazzling smile.

"Want a ride to Managua, soldier?" She patted the seat, "We've plenty of room."

The soldier glanced at John and, seeing his frown, laughed, and waved John through. He said, "Thanks, beautiful. Maybe next time."

As they pulled back onto the road, John muttered, "You're nuts! What would you've done if he'd accepted your invitation?"

"But he didn't. He didn't even look at your papers, and if he had come with us, we'd have breezed all the way to Managua without worry."

John mumbled, "Unless he figured out who we are."

Katia just laughed good-naturedly. "You worry too much."

It was clear that the soldiers at Juigalpa recognized the pickup and didn't want to leave the shade to check John's papers. They were waved on.

They began the slow descent through green- and sparkling-leaved coffee plantations and sugarcane fields to the junction of the road at San Benito. A soldier stood by the roadside and waved John over. A ways down the road, John noted a troop of at least thirty soldiers lounging in the shade of a huge grayish green eucalyptus tree.

With a racing heart, John drove the pickup to the side of the road and handed the leatherette packet to the unsmiling man. The round black hole at the end of the automatic rifle stared unblinkingly into John's eyes as the soldier leaned over to accept the packet.

"Where you heading?"

John answered as smoothly as his dry mouth would allow. "Managua."

The soldier glanced at the papers briefly. "What's your business in Managua, Señor Tanner?"

Katia leaned across the seat and smiled into the man's face. John noted that the soldier's eyes strayed appreciatively, almost caressing her trim body. She asked, "You a good dancer, soldier?"

The man seemed startled. "What did you say?"

"I like to dance, and *mi viejo* spends all his time looking after his cattle business. You know a good place to dance?"

"Uhh . . . I've heard you can usually find a dance at Lago de Tiscapa."

"If you come and *gordito* here is off looking at bulls, maybe we can dance and have a drink. What do you think, handsome?"

The soldier held the packet in one hand and tapped it against the open palm of the other hand. For just the briefest moment his eyes met the laughing eyes of the beautiful girl. "If I can make it." He handed the packet to John and waved them through the checkpoint.

Katia leaned out the window and waved.

John muttered, "Katia, there's one thing . . ."

Katia's gentle laughter mocked John for a moment. "I know, Chohnee. I have to quit flirting with the soldiers."

"I just think it's dangerous to call attention to ourselves."

"I'm not *calling* attention. I'm *distracting* attention. When I flirt with them, they forget they're soldiers. They might remember what I look like, but I doubt it, and they sure won't remember you or if you were driving a car or a pickup truck or even a tractor."

Finally they were driving parallel to the railroad tracks that encircled Lago de Managua. Passing the Sandino Airport, the road took them around the old part of Managua. The massive gray stones of the Guardia headquarters, surrounded by brick walls and iron gates, seemed to loom ominously. As John drove by the building, butterflies began to dance in his stomach.

A Mayan motif was carried throughout the Hotel Intercontinental Managua. There were paintings of ancient Mayan noblemen standing by their temples and castings of indecipherable Mayan glyphs adorning the walls.

John tipped the bellboy. Katia stood at the door to her room. "See you at seven, Chohnee?"

"I have to arrange to get the truck and trailer to the auction grounds."

Katia said, "Knock when you're dressed."

* * *

Katia promptly opened the door. Her black curly hair sparkled with bits of glitter. Her body moved seductively under the pale blue outer-chiffon dress that covered a shimmering body sheath. The spiked heels of her fashionable blue shoes added to her height. She breezed out the door and responded to John's appreciative whistle with a graceful pirouette.

John had dressed in gray slacks, shiny boots, and a blue, four-pocketed, finely pleated guayabera. He asked, "Do—do I need to dress more formally?"

"No, Chohnee. You look very nice."

"You're dressed so chicly, I'm afraid I'll make you look bad."

"I've told you before that you can't make me look bad. I'll make you look good." She linked her arm through his.

John asked, "What's the occasion?"

She pouted. "You think I've overdone it?"

"Just my usual concern. Attracting too much attention."

"What if I see my soldier friend? I'd want to impress him."

John frowned. "If your soldier friend comes around, I'm likely to bust a knuckle on his teeth."

Katia said, "Have you never thought how I hate being out in the country and never having reason to dress in anything but my camouflage uniform? You think I really *like* how I look in that uniform?"

"Why always wear it then?"

Katia was serious. "You saw how Valderas and Pablo acted when I dressed up yesterday at Hacienda Medina. I wear the uniform to keep the men's minds where they belong. On the revolution."

In the lobby, John's attention was drawn to a dark-complexioned man seated in one of the soft leather chairs. He paid no attention to Katia and John.

They stepped out of the air-conditioned freshness of the hotel, and the fragrance of jasmine drifted with the warm breeze of the tropical night. The attendant whistled for a taxi, and John helped Katia in the back door and then walked around to the other side. He paused for a moment, placed his foot on the rear bumper of the automobile, and dusted at his very shiny boot with a handkerchief. The dark-complexioned man stepped out the doors of the hotel. The man held up his hand in signal for a taxi of his own.

John got in the car, and the driver turned to inquire where they were to be taken. "There's a night club out by Lago de Managua. Turtle House, or something like that."

The driver looked startled, glanced at Katia, then nodded. "Si. Tortuga Morada."

"Yeah. That's the place. Take us there."

Katia looked at John, started to speak, then settled into her seat. The driver pulled away, followed by the taxi carrying the man John had noticed in the hotel.

The driver headed north on the four-laned Avenida Central at a leisurely pace. John took ten dollars' worth of córdobas from his wallet and leaned forward. "I think somebody's following us. Can you find out?"

The driver accelerated quickly, changed to the left lane, passed five cars, and abruptly moved back into the right lane, slowing down as he did so. John watched the pursuing actions of the taxi behind them.

"Okay. I got 'em. It's the green taxi, two cars behind us."

John thought, *Good. He's an alert driver.* "Can you lose him?"

The driver spoke cautiously. "You're not running from la Guardia?"

"We're not running from anyone. I just don't want him to know where my woman and I are going. It's worth fifteen hundred córdobas if you lose him."

The driver immediately began to accelerate.

"I don't think you can just outrun him. Continue on down Avenida Central. When you come to Calle Six A, speed up and circle that block, and we'll jump out in the block behind Club Managua. Are we on?"

"For fifteen hundred córdobas, why not?"

John gave him part of the money. "The rest just before we get out at Club Managua." Then as insurance in case the dark-complexioned man should somehow question the driver, John said, "I'm staying at the Hotel Intercontinental, and if we have an uninterrupted evening, you've got another fifteen hundred córdobas tomorrow."

The driver grinned and said, "Sounds like a good deal to me."

John sat back in his seat and said to Katia, "When our driver stops, I want us out of the taxi and him on the way in less than ten seconds. You'll have to take off those fancy shoes."

"If I ruin my stockings, Chohnee, I'll be upset." She handed her shoes to John. "Don't lose them, or I'll *really* be upset."

As they passed the old city hall building, John leaned forward to warn the driver.

The driver nodded his head. "I know. But I got a better plan. I'll drop you behind Club Managua but quicker and easier."

At John's look of doubt, the driver said, "Trust me. By chance, you got the best driver in Managua."

John hesitated for just an instant and then in quick decision handed the driver the remaining córdobas. "How are you called, friend?"

The driver's eyes held with John's in the rearview mirror for an instant. He grinned and said, "I am Diego."

Diego slowed down as if searching for an address, and as the traffic light was changing, the taxi leaped forward and crossed Calle Six A in a burst of speed. The pursuing taxi could not enter the coming traffic.

John saw the flashing lighted sign and marquee of the Club Managua, and then in a sudden lurch, Diego turned into an alleyway between the tall concrete walls of buildings lining the downtown portion of Avenida Central. Katia was thrown against John, and they had barely righted themselves when the taxi made another lurching turn in the alley and jammed to a stop. "There's a light over their back door."

John said, "Muchas gracias, amigo." Then he ordered, "Go, Katia!" But her door was already open. John slammed his door, and the taxi lurched forward in a squealing of tires and a small cloud of blue smoke.

They dashed into the back door of the club. A man, John thought the chief cook, was standing at a long, hardwood table. He was chopping at meat and rolling it in some kind of salsa. As John and Katia burst into the room, he looked up in questioning.

Katia took her shoes from John. Standing first on one foot and then the other, she dusted the bottom of her feet and replaced the shoes. She stepped up to the wooden table, ran her fingers along it, looked at her fingers, and then rubbed her hands, as if the counter was distastefully dirty.

The cook still had not spoken. Katia said in an officious voice, "I'm from the department of health and sanitation. We have a complaint about your ladies restroom. Where is it?"

The cook hesitantly pointed with the large knife, and before he could say a word, Katia headed in the direction he pointed. She called back, "See you at the front door in three minutes, Chohnee?"

The cook looked expectantly at John. John made his voice as officious as Katia's had been. "I'll check the tables in front." He followed Katia through the doorway where busboys rushed by, loaded with trays of food and dirty dishes. John smiled. The cook had not spoken a single word.

John made his way through the crowded noisy club to the rhythm of a Latin tune. Katia came toward John, picking up the beat of the music, and danced to where he waited for her. Then she danced him to the front of the Club Managua. A taxi, delivering a foursome of well-dressed Nicaraguans, drove up as they stepped outside.

Entering the taxi, John said, "Paseo de Tiscapa, please." Katia settled back in the seat. "What was that all about?"

"You didn't notice the fellow in the lobby of the Intercontinental?"

She shook her head. "The first that I suspected anything was when you told Diego to take us to Tortuga Morada. How did you pick up on the man at the hotel?"

"He just seemed out of place."

"He was probably a Sandinista secret policeman." Then Katia started to giggle. "How did you come to pick the Purple Turtle?"

"I just saw it once, and it looked interesting."

"It's more interesting than you'd think. Sometime we'll stop by there. But I bet a straight arrow like you won't go in."

Shortly, the taxi driver pulled up by a park, and they got out. Katia linked her arm in John's, and they strolled across the plaza. A pond occupied the center of the plaza. Lined with a kaleidoscope of red, yellow, and purple flowers, walkways flared out in a half circle leading down to the sparkling blue waters of the lagoon.

Katia led John on a walkway by the lagoon and, pointing to the lighting poles standing empty of bulbs, said, "The Ortega brothers don't waste money on public service."

Different melodies of more than one band echoed distantly. A terrace with tables and a roof of thatched palm fronds provided backdrop for a fire burning in a barrel.

The smell of barbecuing beef wafted through the air along with the sounds of a band. Katia said, "Just follow the smell of the barbecuing meat and the sounds of music. That'll be Mama Sanchez's."

They walked through a grove of trees to a large palm-thatched pavilion built over a jagged stone wall. Kerosene lanterns hanging from peeled ceiling logs gave mellow romantic light to the area under the roof. A girl's clear soprano voice sang the plaintive melody of "Guantanamera."

Colorful cloths covered the tables. The tantalizing aroma of barbecue drifted in the tropical evening air from charcoal embers glowing in three metal drum burners. An ice-filled iron tub contained soft drinks and beer.

People were eating at tables. Some were dancing to the rhythms of the small group of musicians. John and Katia watched to see Valderas kiss a gray-haired woman on both cheeks, render a gallant bow, and return her to her table, where an older gentleman—tall, thin, and well dressed—stood and helped her to a seat. Waving a bottle to the music, Valderas moved to another table, where he plopped into a wicker chair.

John saw Mario at a table. Mario's boots, denim pants, and guayabera fit as naturally as a work-worn glove to the palm of a hand. John felt a knot of concern in his stomach as Valderas continued waving the bottle and singing. He said, "I thought Valderas would have better judgment."

Katia just smiled at him. "He gets as tired of country life as me."

Pablo and Halcón were enjoying the flirtations of a pretty girl at another table toward the back of the bowery. For a moment, John did not recognize La Raspa sitting alone. He had shaved and wore clean denims and a guayabera. John watched as La Raspa cut his steak in chunky pieces with his huge knife. Juicy meat peeled cleanly off the sharp blade only to be speared with the knife and placed in his mouth. He broke off a piece of bread from a tapered, hard-crusted loaf and spread refried black beans on it with the knife. The food was washed down with guzzles from a brown bottle.

A waitress approached. Katia ordered for them. "Barbecued beef and two Cokes, please." She smiled at John. "They won't have orange soda."

The small four-member band started to play. Katia stood and moved seductively to the music. "You going to dance with me, Chohnee? Or do I have to go looking for my soldier friend?"

John took her into his arms. The music was a fast-moving rumba, and Katia broke the embrace. She moved lightly away and then returned in enchanting, graceful movements. The song ended, and John walked her slowly to the table. The waitress brought two plates with wooden spears loaded with small bits of barbecued meat, a bowl of mashed black beans, and a loaf of bread. John had only taken a few mouthfuls of the savory meat when the band began to play again.

Pablo was suddenly at the table asking Katia to dance. John could not quell the pangs of jealousy he felt as Katia danced a rumba around Pablo and made him seem as dashing as John felt when he danced with her. The dance had barely ended, and Valderas bowed precariously to Katia. She curtsied in response and proceeded to make Valderas look to be as good a dancer as Pablo or John.

When Mario asked Katia to dance, a surge of anger welled up in John's chest. He now ate food that was definitely no longer as savory as it had been with the first bites.

When Valderas waited for another turn around the small concrete floor with Katia, John attacked the spears of *carne asada* and the loaf of bread. He looked at La Raspa sitting alone. His steak was gone, and he tore a chunk of bread from the loaf, wiped the last remnant of meaty juice from the platter, and popped it into his mouth. Then he carefully wiped the long, sharp knife blade on the checkered tablecloth, sighted along the blade, and ran his finger down its keen edge. Next he carefully polished the handle on the tablecloth, his handling of the knife almost a caress. He finally deftly tucked the knife in the holster hidden under the guayabera.

The music ended, and Katia laughingly and breathlessly waved the waiting Pablo away. She breezed over to the table where John sat. She stood, brown eyes sparkling, one arm akimbo, and drank from the glass of cola. John did not even glance at her.

She laughed merrily, placed the glass on the table, and reached down and turned John's face toward her. "Jealousy is painful. Right, Chohnee?"

"Don't be silly! Who's jealous?"

"I wonder. But if you're not . . ." She turned as if she would find someone else to dance with.

John grabbed her hand and said, "Sit down, Katia. Please!"

Katia did sit down. Reaching across the table and taking John's hand in hers, she said, "Chohnee, if I have no reason to be jealous of your Chuliana, then you have no reason to be jealous of the men who danced with me."

John's gaze held in Katia's liquid brown eyes. "I'll try to believe you. It's just that I hate to see you making other men look as good as me when you dance with them."

The band's next choice of music could not have better suited John. The plaintive melody of "Spanish Eyes" gently reached for the ears and hearts of the listeners. The soprano sang, and the tropical night air gave special significance to the song.

John wished the feeling and the dance would never end. It was so good to hold Katia in his arms—to inhale her perfumed fragrance, to sense the sweetness of her breath.

The singer's last words hung in the night air. "You and your Spanish eyes will wait for me . . ." The last strumming notes of the guitars faded. They stayed in a close embrace for a moment. Katia finally pulled away and led John to their table.

As they sat, John noticed Mario and Pablo just walking out of the circle of flickering light cast by the lanterns. Valderas walked to their table, leaned over, and kissed Katia on both cheeks. "Buenas noches, lady most beautiful. Thank you for dancing with me."

Valderas then gave John a huge abrazo. His voice was loud and words slurred. "Thanks for sharing the most beautiful woman in the world for a few dances with me."

John braced for the beer-smelling Latin hug, but only noticed a slight lingering trace of Valderas's aftershave lotion. He thought, *I'll be darned. He hasn't even tasted that beer he's been waving around.*

Valderas lurched to the table where Halcón still sat and nodded at him. Halcón stood, and he and the girl also left the pavilion. Finally, Valderas moved in the same direction as the others had. When he reached the limits of encircling light, he called back, "Adios, amigos, adios." He continued his unstable way, singing in a deep bass voice. "*Vamos. Vamos. Vamos a pistear! Vamos . . .*"

John said, "I thought we were to get information, do some planning."

"I talked to Valderas, Pablo, and Mario while I danced with them and you sulked at the table. And though I hate to have to ask you to think of your Chuliana, you're to come up with a way for her to know a message comes from you. Valderas will talk to you later by the main plaza in the park. In the meantime, I'm going to make it difficult for you to think of Chuliana."

John nodded his head toward La Raspa, who was still seated at the table and drinking beer. "He sticking around as bodyguard?"

Katia shrugged her lack of knowledge. "I don't know. But for now, the music is just for you and me, Chohnee."

She slipped into his arms, and they danced for half an hour. John's apprehensions had mellowed, when, in a slow turn, he saw a tall man, smartly dressed in slacks and guayabera, walk into the circle of light. A pretty, dark-haired woman hung on his arm.

Katia must have felt his sudden intensity. "What's happened, Chohnee? What do you see now?"

John finished the turn and asked, "Isn't that man your brother?"

Her answer was quietly strained. "Let's get out of here. Pay for our food. I'll slip out behind the wall. Meet me at that first pavilion."

"Katia, I'm not leaving you at night and alone—"

"Chohnee! Next you will forbid me to go on jungle trails unless you're along to protect me!" Her order allowed no argument. "Pretend you don't know me!" She spun around and walked toward the back of the building.

But they were too late. Solano called, "Katia! Wait!"

The dark, petite girl with Solano looked on in curiosity. John felt a welling of anger toward David Solano, whom he had last seen in the custody of Valderas and whom Leon Hardesty had told him was working for the Sandinistas here in Managua.

Katia hesitated, then turned, "Hola, David. How are you?"

John used the opportunity of distraction, paid the waitress, and walked out of the light of the pavilion. Then he turned to watch what happened.

His curiosity evident, David asked, "What brings you to Managua?"

Katia said casually, "I came to dance."

David's glance quickly encircled the pavilion. "Dance? Who with?"

"It doesn't concern you, David. I'd like to say it's good to see you. But I can't. Good-bye." She strolled to where La Raspa sat at his table.

La Raspa's face bore a stupefied expression as Katia leaned over and kissed him lightly on the cheek. She said, "Come on, viejo, I'm tired. Take me back to the hotel."

La Raspa nearly knocked his chair over as he stood up. He made an awkward bow to Katia. It was clear that he had not faked the amount of beer he had consumed. He tried to stand with dignity.

Katia said to him, "You should pay Mama Sanchez, dear."

La Raspa, fumbling, took a couple of crumpled bills from his pocket, held them under the light of the lantern to be sure of the denomination, and then in careful movements, flattened them and placed them under a glass.

Katia took his arm and headed him toward the plaza. After a few steps, La Raspa caught the rhythm and walked, almost straight, at the side of Katia. John marveled that Katia could make even the ungraceful La Raspa look good. She turned a mischievous grin toward David, who was watching, perplexed. With a slight wave of her hand, she called "Adios, David."

John could not decide which expression was the most humorous—La Raspa's when Katia kissed him on the cheek, or David's when Katia actually walked away with the ungraceful and unappealing man.

At the plaza, a small group of people stood in a cluster at the road's edge. John watched as lights materialized into a noisy bus that came clattering along the road. It wheezed to a stop, and one at a time, the team from El Cinco trooped aboard the bus, including even La Raspa. As the last person reached for the polished chrome bar and heaved up the high step, the engine roared a stuttering complaint, the gears clanged, and the door creaked shut. In a cloud of black, sooty smoke, the bus grumbled along the road.

John started back toward the plaza and counted in his mind. All were gone except himself, Katia, and Valderas. He walked along the walkway in the darkness. A fire still burned in the barrel by the first thatch-roofed pavilion that he and Katia had passed earlier. In that flickering light, he saw the unmistakably bulky figure of Valderas and another person seated on a bench.

When John reached the back thatched wall of the pavilion, the two were no longer visible. John walked around the building. Katia sat on a discarded wooden box near where Valderas sat on his heels, idly scratching in the dirt with a stick.

As John walked quietly to them, Katia murmured, "I'll keep lookout while you and Valderas talk." Then she stood and moved to the edge of the building.

Valderas said, "Katia says you had to shake off one of Ortega's men earlier. Good work."

John nodded in acknowledgment of the compliment. "Everything under control?" He took Katia's recently vacated place on the wooden box.

Valderas nodded. "Si. No problems."

"You were going to recruit more people in Managua. You get them yet?"

"The older man, and the woman I danced with when you and Katia arrived. The girl with Halcón is a nurse. The older man is Doctor Fuentes. He and his wife run a small medical clinic."

"You got everything figured out?"

"Your Juliana has to come down with an infectious disease so her jailers will send her out to a hospital. Fuentes says the best disease for her to get is dengue fever . . ."

The unexpectedness of the strategy caused John to forget caution. "Dengue fever! You're planning to deliberately expose her to dengue fever?"

Katia turned and snapped, "Quiet, Chohnee! You talk too loud. And it's clear you know nothing of El Chipote. I saw you watching La Raspa tonight. What you don't know is that part of what La Raspa *is* comes from two years in El Chipote. It's a dark, underground dungeon. No lights, except when they're being fed, and the half-spoiled beans that only a desperately hungry person would eat are snatched away before you can force them down. The toilet facility is a faucet on the wall and a hole in the floor. There's a bed hanging from the ceiling by rusting chains. Every day your Chuliana spends in that place is a day in hell! I don't like your Chuliana, but I *don't* want her to spend five more minutes in El Chipote than she has to. I—in a place like that—I would die in a week!"

Her flood of words stopped. The intensity of her emotion was evident in the tears that sprang to her eyes. She turned and with clenched fists resumed her post.

Valderas's words were nearly as harsh as Katia's. "Katia tells it like it is in El Chipote. But we're not going to infect your

Juliana with the dengue virus. We *are* going to make her sick. Doctor Fuentes says there's a medicine. I think he said methotrexate, a treatment for cancer. If she takes six or eight pills, an hour later she'll have all the symptoms of dengue fever. Vomiting, and it'll give her diarrhea, chills, fever, blurred vision. The whole works. And if she also takes some niacin, she'll get flushed. Like I said, all the symptoms of dengue fever.

"She'll look so bad the guard will report her conditions promptly. They got a lot of political prisoners in El Chipote—they don't want 'em free, but they sure don't want them dead from a dengue epidemic! Doctor Fuentes treats the prisoners from El Chipote. They'll take her to his clinic. We'll meet at a park near Mercado Oriental before we hit the clinic. You satisfied, Chohnee?"

"How sick will she actually be?"

"Pretty sick. It'll last a day or two, but there's no real danger and no long-term effects. She'll be back to normal in a week."

"You sure there's no other way to get her out of there?"

Valderas leaned back against the wall. "Nobody ever broke out of there yet."

"How you going to get the capsules to her?"

"I've got my ways . . . I can get a message or the pills into El Chipote. I can't get anybody *out*." His words seemed very final.

After pacing back and forth, John said, "All right. I guess there's no choice. What do you want from me?"

"Juliana has to take the capsules at the right time so she'll be sick when the guard turns on the light to bring her food. She probably wouldn't consider taking that much medication unless told to by someone she trusts. Katia was supposed to tell you to figure out—"

"She did but I—I'll have to think for a minute."

John paced and Valderas continued talking. "There's a showing of bulls tomorrow at the Tres Naciones auction grounds. I'll be there first thing in the morning. You plan to inspect the bulls at nine yourself. Bring Katia.

"By the way, tomorrow let your surveillance follow you around until we get ready for the final action at the Fuentes' clinic. We'll both just be a couple of cattlemen looking at the stock. You're from a ranch with a lot more money than me."

John snapped his fingers. "That's it! Give her the instructions and tell her Nate Brown's hired hand believes that she needs to follow them to the letter if she's going to make it to the Juarez Academy reunion next summer."

Valderas said, "Okay, Chohnee. Nate Brown's hired hand and Juarez Academy reunion. Got it. See you tomorrow."

John took Katia by the arm and led the way back toward the main plaza.

CHAPTER TEN

JOHN AND KATIA STROLLED into the hotel restaurant at seven o'clock. John said, "I don't see our Sandinista friend."

As John held the chair for Katia to sit, she murmured, "He might be gone, but his replacement is here."

John nodded toward a man dressed in casual slacks and a yellow guayabera, a newspaper was tucked under his arm, and he was just seating himself at a table across the room. "Yellow shirt. That's who you've got picked out as the replacement?"

"Si. I'd bet a dinner on it."

"No bet." John smiled at the waitress wearing a flowery embroidered Mayan dress as she placed a woven basket full of crispy *bolillo* rolls on the table. John ordered steak, eggs, and fruit of the season for both of them.

Katia asked, "Do I go to the auction grounds with you this morning?"

"You aren't getting out of my sight from now on."

John ate heartily. Katia, however, did not touch the steak, left part of the eggs on her plate and then picked at the fruit while John finished his plate of food. John said, "Better eat. It might be a long day."

She murmured, "It's not bad enough seeing David last night. It takes my appetite away at how lavishly the rich can eat and know how little food the poor people can get."

John called for his bill and said philosophically, "That's what we're fighting for, and you won't be a better soldier by starving yourself."

He watched as the yellow-shirted man left his table at the same time they did and followed them at a respectable distance across the lobby and to the front of the hotel.

The sun was bright, with just a few white cumulus clouds tumbling up into the deep blue sky. The doorman greeted them cheerfully, but his words were interrupted by a shout from across the street. "Hey, Chohnee!"

John looked up. It took a moment, but then he recognized the man. He said to Katia, "That's Diego, our driver from last night, here to collect the money I promised him."

Katia asked, "Where'd you get the money you've been throwing around the last couple of days?"

"It's Company money. I got it while I was in Limón after I dropped Hardesty off at the hospital."

Katia laughed. "Good. I don't mind giving your gringo money to the campesinos. Matter of fact, the more the better!"

John ignored Katia's comment and said to the doorman, "We'll use the driver across the street."

They walked across the street, and the slender Diego held the door for them to get in. "You and Miss Katia have a pleasant evening last night, Señor Chohnee?"

"Magnificent. Thanks, Diego. How do you know our names?"

Diego got into the driver's seat. "I told you, you got the best driver in Managua. No mystery. I just listen to people. Where do you want to go?"

"The cattle auction grounds. Tres Naciones." John leaned forward over the back of the front seat and looked closely at the pictured taxi permit. The driver's name was Diego Rivera, and his license number was 19210. John committed the number to memory. He handed him fifteen hundred córdobas. "Here's the money I promised."

Diego murmured his thanks and, making a hard left turn, tires squealing on the pavement, headed west on Avenida Bolivar. A taxi of the same green color that had followed them the previous night moved smoothly out into the stream of traffic two cars behind. Diego adjusted the rearview mirror, downshifted, revved the engine, and quickly passed a couple of cars. He made an abrupt left turn past the Pasa España then slowed, dropping behind a car moving in front of them. Diego engaged John's eyes briefly. "You picked up a tail again. You want me to lose him?"

John didn't even look around. "I appreciate your alertness, Diego. But no, we don't mind him following us—for now."

Diego, glancing in the rearview mirror, turned onto the freeway Pista de la Risistencia. The green taxi was never more than three car lengths behind. After ten minutes, Diego exited the freeway and moved with the ebb and flow of traffic as he continued along the highway to Granada.

Business buildings gave way to homes barricaded behind tall, ornately decorated, spiked steel fences. Soon there were only a few scattered shacks in the nearby fields. Besides Diego's, the only vehicles left on the road were a pickup truck and the green taxi. Diego slowed and turned onto a dirt road. They bumped over a rusting railroad track, and the small procession paralleled the tracks for another kilometer.

Finally Diego guided his taxi to a hard-packed dirt parking lot. John glanced around and saw his pickup and trailer parked on a patch of weed-covered ground at the end of the parking lot. The green taxi pulled in fifty meters from where Diego had parked. Diego turned in his seat and said, "It will be hard for you to get a taxi back to town from here, Chohnee."

John held up another fifteen hundred córdobas and asked, "Will this make it worth your time to wait for us? I think at most a couple of hours."

"More than enough. I'll be waiting in the coffee shop over there." He jerked his head in the direction of the cluster of old, weathered buildings at the end of the dirt yard.

John helped Katia from the taxi and then watched Diego make his way to the coffee shop, the only one of the buildings with windows—large expanses of dirty glass that reflected the glaring sunlight. Yellow Shirt talked to his driver briefly then followed them into the stockyards.

The hot and humid morning air seemed to trap the dust and odors of the stockyards in a clinging layer of unpleasantness. Katia wrinkled her nose and picked her way carefully through the small piles of manure that were scattered all along the way. A couple of men stood talking by a tumble of weathered, gray boards that formed a four-layered bleacher of sorts—a stand from which potential buyers could view and bid on the animals to be auctioned.

Two young men, clad only in dirty white peasant pants and boots, were working to clean the area in front of the bull pens. A sheen of sweat showed rippling muscles on their brown backs as they went about their task. One of the men spread water on the dusty ground by the simple expedient of dipping his hand in a bucket of water. He then threw water in a rainbowed semicircle of sparkling droplets that were quickly soaked up by the dusty ground. The other man swept straw and bits of garbage into a pile. A rumble of bellowing came from a few head of tan and gray Brahman cattle in the holding areas. A bull would occasionally bawl out its indignation at being confined to the small pens and would give accent with the crashing of hooves against the heavy boards that formed the lower walls.

Katia tugged on John's arm and pointed. In front of the pen, Valderas was talking to a man nearly equal in height. John said, "Yeah. I saw him. The man Valderas is talking to is Ruel Boquis."

Ruel looked up and, recognizing John, gave a big smile and waved for John to join him. As John and Katia walked up, Ruel said, "Juan, this is Señor Hector Valderas from the Hacienda Medina."

John held out his hand and shook Valderas's hand. "Glad to know you."

John smiled when Valderas, in response to his introduction of Katia, bent over in a smooth bow, sweeping off his ever-present white sombrero. "It is my pleasure to meet you, Señorita Solano."

Ruel said, "Señor Valderas operates a hacienda along the basin of the Rio San Juan. I was telling him how you've helped us, and he was wondering if you'd give him some tips on which are the best bulls at the auction."

John said, "Surely. Perhaps while we look at the bulls you could go to the offices and see if they have papers on the bulls to be auctioned."

Ruel said cheerfully, "But of course. I'll rejoin you shortly."

John reassured him, "There'll be time a little later for us to discuss the bull Boquis might want to acquire."

When Ruel was out of earshot, Valderas motioned for them to move toward the closest pen, where a wide-eyed bull leaned into two stout tethering ropes. The bull was snuffing and whuffing and pawing the ground, his horns waving in menace to anyone who should dare approach him. A handwritten cardboard sign identified the bull as Magnanimo de Prodigo.

John asked quietly, "How are plans proceeding?"

"Chuliana will take the methotrexate and niacin with the morning meal so she'll be sickest at the noon meal. Everything's ready at Doctor Fuentes's clinic. Right now the big concern is to get Chuliana and the rest of us safely out of Managua after we take her from the clinic. We'll keep it as quiet as we can, and as secret as we can, but sooner or later they're going to know she's free. That's when our troubles could start."

"So we go right after the auction today?"

Valderas rubbed a hand over his mustache. "Yes, but we need a way to divert attention from us traveling down Lago de Nicaragua . . ."

Katia's countenance lit up. "What we need, Valderas, is to *attract* attention to the fact you're hauling the bull down the lake."

"I suppose there's a reason for attracting attention to what we do?"

"Of course. We call attention to the fact that we're hauling a bull on the boat. Nobody even thinks to look closely at the crew! And Chuliana does a good job of impersonating a man. She goes on the boat as a crew member."

"But she'll be sick!" Valderas argued.

"So she'll be a sick crew member!"

John said, "Sounds good to me." He looked in the direction Ruel had taken and noticed Yellow Shirt sitting on the rickety bleachers, watching them from fifty meters away. He noticed Ruel just entering the offices and had a sudden thought. "How about we haul the bull you buy and the one Boquis buys to Granada in my trailer and then take both bulls on the boat. That ought to stir up enough interest to keep people's attention on the bulls. And let Ruel drive the pickup back to San Carlos. Maybe we can find a girl to ride with him to make it look like Katia and me driving back to San Carlos."

Valderas mused. "That means we'd need another driver. But maybe that's a good idea—split us up, make us less noticeable. Have Mario drive down with Ruel in your truck." Looking around, his eye fell on the man seated on the viewing stand. He nodded toward him and said, "The guy in the yellow shirt. He following you?"

"He's our Sandinista secret policeman."

Magnanimo gave a bellow, and Valderas turned and glared at the bull. The bull was not intimidated and raised its head, shook his horns, and let out an even louder bellow. Valderas muttered, "Be silent, you dumb beast."

John looked at the bull. "If you're going to buy a bull, you could do a lot worse than this one. Maybe you ought to stay on the good side of Magnanimo, especially if he's as good as his name."

Stroking his heavy mustache, Valderas turned a disgusted look on John. "You making dumb jokes?"

Before John could respond, Valderas said, "Here comes your friend Ruel. Looks like he got the papers. You really know about cattle, Chohnee?"

"That answer will be arriving over the next few months with the first crop of calves, born from the changes I've made in Boquis's breeding stock."

Valderas said, "You show Ruel around and talk to him about the bulls. Keep your eye out for a good bull for me. I've got some business to do."

"How much you willing to pay for a bull?"

"I couldn't go much over one hundred thousand córdobas."

"So you going to bid on a bull?"

"Si. You tell me which is a good bull. It doesn't have to be the best. Tell me how much is too much, and don't bid against me." Valderas started to walk away and then turned back to add, "I've got to arrange for a girl to ride with Ruel and a driver we can trust . . ."

John interrupted. "I've got a driver I'm confident about."

Valderas looked at him speculatively. "We've got a lot at stake."

John thought about Diego. He believed he could trust him. The problem was how much at risk Diego would be. John said, "I feel pretty sure about him. His name is Diego Rivera, and his permit number is 19210."

"All right. You line him up, but don't tell him too much. If he doesn't check out, I'll get someone else." Valderas pulled a stubby pencil from his pocket and jotted the name and number down.

This time Valderas did walk away. Ruel waved at Valderas as they crossed paths directly in front of Yellow Shirt.

John studied the papers while he and Ruel examined each bull. He had already bought three good bulls for Boquis and decided that he would try to help Valderas buy the best bull at this auction—and that looked like Magnanimo de Prodigo.

Yellow Shirt walked casually along, well within earshot, examining the bulls and not paying any obvious attention to Katia, Ruel, and John.

When they had looked at all the bulls, John asked, "Which bull do *you* think is best, Ruel?"

"I think the one over there called Brutus would be my choice."

Looking only at the animals themselves and accepting the history of the breeding of each of the bulls, John agreed with Ruel's selection. He would, however, choose Magnanimo de Prodigo for Valderas on the basis of the good qualities of the animal itself, coupled with the pedigree of the bull. He said, "I think Brutus is a good choice, if the bidding doesn't go too high. Do you have instructions on how much to spend?"

"My father said not to go over two hundred thousand córdobas. Did you make any recommendation to Señor Valderas?"

"He seemed quite taken with Magnanimo de Prodigo. I agreed with him."

Ruel seemed concerned. "You think Magnanimo would be better?"

John put his worrying to rest. "Magnanimo's a good bull, but not worth over one hundred thousand, and Señor Valderas can't afford to pay what Brutus will go for. I think Brutus is the best choice for Boquis." John paused and said, "You know, Ruel, your father wanted you to make the final choice and do the bidding."

Ruel beamed that John had clarified his role.

John was keenly aware of Yellow Shirt, who was never very far away. "Do you think you could haul a load of mineral blocks to Hacienda Boquis?"

Ruel hesitated. "How would I get the bull to the hacienda?"

"I took the liberty to talk to Señor Valderas. He's going to take his bull by boat down Rio San Juan. It wouldn't be out of the way for him to stop at San Carlos—that is, of course, if you think it's a good idea, Ruel."

"It's a very good idea." Then Ruel took Katia's hand. "I would look forward to you visiting Hacienda Boquis. We often have fiestas and dancing."

Katia's mellow brown eyes held with Ruel's. "I love dancing. Contact me at Papa's home for the next one."

"It's a promise. Adios, Katia."

When he was out of earshot, John asked, "Don't you ever feel guilty at breaking hearts, Katia?"

She smiled. "You getting jealous again, Chohnee? Besides, look who's talking." She mimicked John's words. "That is, of course, if you think it's a good idea, Ruel."

John chuckled and glanced at his watch. "Shall we wander over to the coffee shop and get Diego to take us back to town?"

"I thought we would just stay here for the auction."

John looked up into the sky. "It's going to rain. And besides, I have some business I want to conduct with Diego."

They drove back toward downtown Managua. The green taxi stayed within easy sight of them. John asked, "You have a family, Diego?"

"A boy, ten, and a girl, six." He steered with one hand and reached into his pocket and, extracting his wallet, flipped it open to a picture of himself, an attractive woman, and two children.

John, leaning over the seat, looked at the picture. He held the photo up and said, "Katia, look at Diego's lovely family."

Katia glanced at the picture. "Si, they are handsome . . ." She took the picture from John and studied it more closely. She breathed, "Carla?" She turned toward Diego in some excitement. "Is this Carla Salguero?"

"Now she's Carla Salguero de Rivera, my wife. You know her?"

"I don't know *her*. But I knew Carlos Salguero, I think her twin brother."

"Really? You knew Carlos? He was killed four—five years . . ."

"In the Matagalpa campaign. He was an officer of Commander Cero's."

"Did you know him well?"

"Very well. I was with him when he died."

Diego's head jerked around, "*You* were with Carlos—how did that come about?"

"In a way I was responsible for his death. I was ordnance officer for Commander Cero, and I had personally approved the shipment of weapons, one of which killed Carlos. A gun blew up in his face."

"Don't blame yourself! Carlos would not have blamed you. It was the times. Many died . . ." he said in scarcely more than a husky whisper. "Many died in the revolution, and their lives were wasted because the Ortega brothers turned the revolution to their own gain."

Katia clasped Diego's shoulder. Her words were as husky as his had been. "It is up to every loyal Nicaraguan to prevent those lives from having been wasted, Diego. Each must fight the disloyalty of the Ortegas in his own way. Every Nica must be a Sandinista, hecho y derecho!"

"Si, it's true. If we only knew how. But we have no leaders."

Katia's words were positive and definite. "We *have* some leaders, and we are developing others. Be patient, Diego—and be ready. One day, El Cinco will ask for your support. When they ask, give it, and give freely with your whole heart. Then beautiful Nicaragua will be for all Nicaraguans."

There was hope in Diego's words. "I've heard of El Cinco. I've wondered if it isn't just some kind of rumor."

"It's no rumor. Real people work very hard for freedom for Nicaragua."

John made his decision. He would tell Diego of his need, warn him of possible consequences, and use him to drive if he was willing.

A sudden drenching downpour of rain nearly hid the road from view. John glanced through the back window. Yellow Shirt in the green taxi was directly behind them. "Diego, take us someplace relating to cattle. I want to talk to you about a job this afternoon, but I don't want to hire you until you know what you're getting into. And I don't want Yellow Shirt back there to think we're just driving around talking."

"There's an experimental cattle breeding ranch five kilometers along the road to Granada. Want to visit that?"

"Sounds just fine."

"Okay. I'm listening, Chohnee."

"First of all, when I asked you to lose our tail last night, I kind of lied to you. Katia and I are not what I tried to make you think."

Diego just laughed. "Don't try to fool me, Chohnee. You might not be sleeping together, but I've seen the signs. You love each other."

John flushed and said, "What I meant is . . ."

"I know. You meant the man following you is one of General Ortega's men, not Katia's husband."

"Yeah. Anyway, I'm not going to tell you much about our business this afternoon, because whether you drive for us or not, I'd rather have you innocent of what we do in case things go badly for either us or you. General Ortega would not approve of what we do, to say the least."

"So how do I fit into your plan?"

"Right after the bull I buy is loaded, I want you to take myself, Katia, and perhaps one or two others to a location not too far away from the Mercado Oriental in old Managua and wait for us. Depending on circumstances, we might want you to drive us to Granada. Or if things don't work right, go about your business, and forget you ever met us."

Diego turned off the freeway onto a side road. In just a few minutes, Diego slowed down and pointed to a pasture enclosed by wire fencing. A small herd of cattle grazed contentedly in a spectacularly green field.

John said, "Perfect. Pull over, and I'll study the cattle for a minute."

John rolled down the window. He did not want to go out into the hard driving rain. The driver of the green taxi drove to the entrance of the experimental farm, where he turned in and parked. John gazed at the cattle for a few minutes, then said, "Okay. Take us back to the auction grounds."

Diego made a U-turn and headed back toward the freeway. John asked, "Well, amigo. What do you think?"

Diego's brown eyes locked on John's for a moment. "Is the thing you do associated with El Cinco?"

Katia leaned forward on the backrest. "Yes and no, Diego. Yes, because El Cinco does the job. But no, because the job has nothing to do with El Cinco, and we don't want you or your family in trouble in any way."

Diego smiled broadly. "I think you just recruited the best driver in Managua. And don't worry about me. Whatever happens, my story will be that you pulled a gun on me and forced me to drive you."

John took some bills from his wallet. "Will ten thousand córdobas be enough for what we've outlined?"

Diego looked at the money and said, "No, Chohnee. You already paid me enough so I could afford to take next week off. You don't owe me any more."

Katia took the money from John, folded it and reaching over the seat, stuffed it into the pocket of Diego's shirt. "Buy Carla some flowers. Take her for dinner and dancing. Better yet, buy her a dress and some new shoes."

"But I want to show my support for El Cinco . . ."

Katia said firmly, "Then drive us safely, and don't talk to anyone about what we do. We won't use you if you won't be paid."

CHAPTER ELEVEN

THE RAIN HAD CLEANED the dust off the leaves of the trees, making them scintillate in the brilliant sun. The small patches of manure were gone. Even the windows of the coffee shop had been washed. The atmosphere was one of friendly festivity.

The bulls were on display in the corral, all held securely in place with stout ropes attached to iron stakes imbedded in concrete buried in the ground. Each of the bulls had been scrubbed and curried until they fairly glistened in the sun. Most of the bulls stood in haughty disdain of the inquisitive humans. Magnanimo de Prodigo, however, kept his head moving angrily up and down. An extra pair of ropes had been thrown over his horns. His muscles rippled smoothly under his gleaming coat. His angry eyes glared at the curious people, and he pawed the ground in furious stabs with his heavy hooves. An occasional bellow expressed his indignation.

John saw Valderas standing, one foot on the bottom pole of the corral, stroking his mustache. John paused a few feet away. Hardly looking up, Valderas asked, "You sure that angry beast is the one I should bid on?"

"He's a good bull. He just doesn't like being on display, and people seem to bother him. He won't be on parade at Hacienda Medina. Besides, his angry antics work to your advantage. Everyone is just as concerned in trying to handle him as you are. That'll keep the bidding low."

Valderas said, "They're probably selling him because he has such a mean temper." He looked at Brutus standing in quiet dignity. "That bull looks pretty good to me—and a whole lot tamer."

"He is a good bull, but the best bull is that angry beast. He'd calm down a whole heap if they'd take those ropes off his horns. But it's your money, so buy what you want." After a pause, John asked, "Everything ready?"

"Si. How about you?"

Before John could answer, a murmur of noise swept the crowd. The auctioneer walked into the pole corral. He carried a handheld voice amplifier, and his voice blared out, "Ladies and gentlemen, if you intend to bid on the bulls, you are invited to take your seats in the stands."

John looked directly at Valderas for the first time in their conversation. "Good luck on buying a bull. See you later."

People began making their way to the rickety stands. Ruel stopped John and introduced him to a pretty girl whom he called Elena.

The first bull went quickly for just over fifty thousand córdobas. The second bull took some handling, but after a few balky moves and being jabbed with an electric prod, it finally stood looking in disinterest at the people in the stands. The bidding for this bull was more interesting. Valderas made two bids, first for twenty thousand córdobas and then sixty. He became silent as the bid moved quickly to ninety thousand córdobas.

Several bulls were sold, and Valderas bid on each unsuccessfully, as in each case the bid went over his hundred thousand córdoba limit. John glanced at his watch. The selling of the bulls had taken a full hour. As each bull was sold, it was led away by professional bull handlers riding flashy horses.

Brutus was brought before the cattle buyers. A buyer from a hacienda near Matagalpa had already bought two bulls and seemed intent on obtaining one more. The bidding started at forty thousand córdobas. Valderas bid fifty thousand, but the bid quickly went to ninety thousand córdobas. Valderas exceeded his self-imposed limit by bidding one hundred ten thousand córdobas, where it stayed long enough that John thought Valderas would get the bull.

Magnanimo chose just this moment to let out a thunderous bellow. The sound seemed to have an electric effect, as though the bidders realized if they didn't take the placid Brutus, they might be stuck with the angry Magnanimo. The bid quickly went to one hundred fifty thousand córdobas. Then the man from the hacienda at Matagalpa bid one hundred eighty thousand, and Ruel bid one hundred eighty thousand one hundred. The bidding stuttered up until it reached two hundred twenty thousand by the man from Matagalpa. Ruel looked to John for advice, but John refused to meet his eyes as he struggled with his conscience. Valderas wanted a bull, and if John signaled for Ruel to stop bidding, Ruel would probably buy Magnanimo. Then Ruel saved John from making a decision. He stood up, glaring at the rancher from Matagalpa. His voice broke slightly, and he bid two hundred and twenty-five thousand córdobas.

The man grinned at him. "He's your bull, amigo."

A great cheer went up from the crowd. They clapped and roared their approval and began to chant, *"Toro! Toro! Toro!"*

Ruel flashed a triumphant grin at John, then marched down and personally took charge of the operation of leading Brutus to the cattle trailer.

The crowd was still having a good time, and occasionally the chanting would break out again. The man with the bullhorn finally got everyone to settle down so they could start the bidding on the final bull, Magnanimo de Prodigo. Clearly the bull's handlers would not take a chance. They brought in two extra horses. Magnanimo strained against the ropes slung over his chest and attached to the stakes. The handlers tried to urge the bull to move backward. Magnanimo would not move in any direction but planted all four feet and bawled out his indignation. One of the men punched on the bull's shoulder with an electric cattle prod. The bull roared and, lowering his horns, charged forward, nearly pulling all four horses from their feet. The crowd roared its approval, clearly enjoying the show as much as a bullfight.

Even with the magnification of the bullhorn, the auctioneer could barely be heard over the uproar. "We'll auction him where he is!"

The handlers were all too happy to comply.

"Do I have a bid on the magnificent bull appropriately named Magnanimo de Prodigo?" the auctioneer called from his bullhorn.

There was silence. No one wanted to deal with this angry animal.

The auctioneer pleaded, "A fine bull! Strong pedigree! From the best stock in the country! Do I hear a bid of fifty thousand córdobas?"

Valderas finally stood and tentatively bid, "Thirty thousand córdobas!"

The crowd laughed.

The man from Matagalpa called, "Thirty-five thousand córdobas—maybe he'd be good for breeding a new strain of fighting bulls!"

The crowd roared.

The auctioneer begged for a higher bid. "An excellent bull! His sire has made over two thousand calves. Magnanimo'll make a lot of strong beefy calves! Do I hear forty thousand córdobas?"

Finally Valderas called, "Forty thousand!"

Magnanimo took this moment to make another charge at the horses holding him in place. He ended the lunge in a furious bellow.

This final charge seemed to make the decision for the man from Matagalpa. He called to Valderas, the only other man brave or crazy enough to have bid on the bull, "I hope you have some way to get that loco beast to your hacienda. Good luck, my friend." He made his way down the stands.

The auctioneer seemed to decide he was lucky to get that much money and declared Valderas the successful bidder.

Again the crowd roared and began to chant, "*Toro! Toro! Toro!*"

John looked down at Valderas. The previous successful bidders had looked happy, even Ruel, who must have known he had paid too much for his bull. But Valderas watched the bull handlers struggling to keep the huge Brahma in check between their horses. The iron peg that had held him secure to this point had bent, and the concrete block had cracked through the surface of the ground. The five ropes were all stretched to the breaking point.

Valderas took off his white sombrero and stood with his head slightly bowed. With sad eyes he looked toward the chafing bull.

John jumped lightly down the few steps of the wooden stands and clapped Valderas on the shoulder. "You got a fantastic buy! You'll see."

Valderas looked at John in disgust. "I just wasted forty thousand córdobas. He's so mean and tough, he won't even make good barbecued beef. We won't be able to load him on the trailer! And if we get him to Granada, he'll tear up the boat. I'll have to shoot him to get him to Hacienda Medina!"

John laughed. "We'll just bring the trailer over here."

Valderas growled, "Well, hurry up before I have to shoot him in the head."

John trotted across the stockyard and explained to Mario, who was just shutting the gate to the double trailer, how they would load the other bull.

Ruel walked up, and John said, "Mario is good with cattle, so he's going with you to Granada. He'll load the bulls on

Valderas's boat. Then he'll come back here and get the mineral blocks, and we'll meet you in San Carlos."

Ruel, partly in statement and partly in request, said, "I'm going to take Elena with me to San Carlos."

John nodded his approval and then drove the pickup and trailer through the open corral gate to where Magnanimo still pawed the ground. John took immediate charge. He scooped a large handful of grain from a trough in the back of the trailer and then walked slowly toward the bull with his outstretched hands full of grain. He called softly to the riders, "Ease forward. Don't try to force the bull to move—let him walk toward me and the grain. Don't give him too much slack, though."

John stopped walking but continued to tempt the bull with his calm words and the grain. Finally, the bull stepped tentatively toward John. The riders expertly allowed just enough slack for the forward movement of the bull.

Magnanimo eased toward John until he was able to lick up a mouthful of the grain. Magnanimo moved forward again, and John retreated up the ramp. When the bull had both front hooves on the ramp, John backed into the trailer and emptied the grain into the trough at the front of the compartment. All the time he kept up a steady patter of soothing words. "Easy, Magnanimo. Take it easy. Good bull. Have some more grain." Soon Magnanimo had moved up the ramp and began to nose into the grain trough.

John began to loosen the ropes that were tied around the bull's horns. One of the riders called, "Don't take those ropes off his horns! That's the only way we can control the crazy beast!"

John ignored the order and tossed both ropes off to the side. In a monotone, he said, "That's what's making him so mean. Those ropes pulling on his horns give him a headache." John's voice continued in a soothing tone, though louder. "Mario. Soon as I take the ropes off his body, be ready to shut the back gate—but don't slam it."

"Bueno, Chohnee. I gotcha."

One of the riders was muttering, "I never saw anything like that before. Only an *idioto* or *torero* would approach an angry bull on foot."

John flashed a grin. "Magnanimo and I speak the same language, amigo." Then with an even bigger grin at Valderas, John confidently said, "I told you. You got a good buy!"

Valderas didn't look quite as convinced. "You gave a great performance. But who does that when you're not around to talk to the angry beast?"

"I'll teach *you* his language."

Valderas asked, "You see any signs of General Ortega's secret police?"

John shook his head. He glanced at his watch. In less than two hours, they needed to be in place at the park near Mercado Oriental. He handed the keys of the pickup to Mario and said, "Katia and Valderas will ride over to the coffee shop with you. I'll just trot over."

At the coffee shop, John leaned through the open pickup window. "Now, Mario, when you load Magnanimo on the boat, keep two things in mind. It's plain stupid to throw a rope over those horns of his. If you need to, get a head harness. And second, don't touch him with a cattle prod. I'll tell Ruel you're ready to go."

Valderas asked John, "Your driver close by?"

John nodded toward the taxi with the driver dozing in the front seat. The front door of the car projected out past the dilapidated wooden building. Diego had placed a cardboard OCCUPIED sign in the front window of the taxi.

John asked, "Where's La Raspa?"

"He should already be with my driver. We've got the ambulance all lined up and stocked with weapons. I couldn't find a .22 for you."

John smiled. "That's no problem." He held his hands in a mock karate stance. "I've got my hands."

Valderas gave him a crooked smile. "I pray that's all you'll need." He stuck out his big hand, took a deep breath, and continued. "Okay, Chohnee. See you in an hour at the park. I hope everything goes as smoothly at the clinic as here at the auction and that we are as successful."

"That's for sure. Adios, amigo. See you shortly."

They gripped hands briefly, and Valderas turned and walked away.

The big man lumbered across the unpaved parking lot, carrying his white sombrero by its wide brim. His gray hair lifted slightly in the afternoon breeze. Each of the heavy steps of the worn cowboy boots stirred up little puffs of dust. John felt waves of tension building in his stomach.

The parking lot, which had been so full when they had arrived, now had only a dozen cars still parked in it. Diego followed a car out onto the dirt road. Three other cars were churning up clouds of dust immediately behind them. John watched in apprehension as all of them followed Diego's taxi onto the freeway.

John leaned forward on the seat rest, and Diego said, "I think it's the gray Ford—and I think it's the same guy who followed us the first night with a different driver. I'll pull over and check my tires."

As Diego slowed and pulled to the right side of the road, the gray Ford passed by. John's heart beat faster as he recognized the dark-complexioned man. "I guess your work's cut out for you, Diego."

Diego flashed a confident smile at John. "Don't worry. It's actually easier on the freeway." He jumped out, walked to the left rear of the car, kicked at the tire, and then got back in. The gray Ford slowed down and moved to the right lane. Diego accelerated quickly and steered to the left lane. The gray Ford had no choice but to match Diego's speed or be left far behind.

After five kilometers, Diego said grimly, "All right. Hold on. I'm taking the next off-ramp, and it's going to be tight."

Diego watched through his rearview mirror and manipulated the speeds of the cars expertly. The tailing driver was forced to stay in the right lane. There was one car between them and the secret service man's car and two cars immediately behind that.

Suddenly the sign for the next exit flashed into John's vision. Diego snapped, "Hold tight!"

He whipped the taxi to the right and into the space between the pursuing car and the one in front. The startled driver stabbed at his brake but, at the angry blast of horns from the cars following, had to release quickly or be smashed from behind. He spun his wheel and turned to the open lane at his left. Diego's taxi zipped on through the opening and with squealing tires, it dashed onto the off-ramp with only centimeters to spare.

John watched as the secret service car moved on down the freeway. He released a breath of held air. "That was pretty fancy driving, amigo. Another coat of paint on your taxi would have ruined everything."

Katia laughed tightly. "That's more fun than a carnival ride, Diego."

Diego flashed a quick thumbs up and said, "We're not home free yet. We got to cross Managua. If your friend takes the next off-ramp, he can find us before we make it."

Diego got back on the freeway and approached the clinic from the other side of Managua.

While he drove, John fumbled in the small bag he had carried with him and handed a blonde wig, along with a makeup kit, to Katia. He again reached into the bag and pulled out a gray wig with a mustache and beard for himself.

The blonde wig covered Katia's curly black hair. She painted her eyes with dark blue circles of eye shadow, rouged her cheeks, and painted her lips a fiery orange-red.

John pasted his beard in place, and Katia tucked in a few strands of John's hair. She said, "I guess you'll do."

John said, "Okay, Diego, drop us at the park, then stay where you can see us. Got any questions?"

Diego pulled up at the southern end of the park and kept his engine idling. "I'm familiar with the Fuentes Clinic. There's an alleyway out the back if I have to use it."

"Keep out of sight, Diego, and pick us up within two minutes of when we step out on the street across from the monument." John pointed to a bronze statue of a woman caught forever bending over an infant.

Diego gave a mock military salute and quietly drove away. John noted a once-blue Chevrolet parked on the road at the eastern side of the park. There were spots of brown metal primer where the car was being prepared for a paint job. John presumed the driver was a man lying in the shade of a tree.

Katia nodded in the direction of a large, older gentleman with a white sombrero by his side. He sat on an iron bench under a gnarled umbrella-shaped tree. The old man's head was swathed in white bandages, and his right arm was cradled in a sling.

John indicated his recognition of Valderas and led Katia to a very uncomfortable bench. The back was too short, and the scrolls of the ironwork dug into John's spine. John said, "Sweat's running down my back. It must be a hundred degrees in the shade."

Katia smiled. "It never gets over ninety in Managua. You're nervous."

John agreed. "As usual." He scratched at the skin under his false beard. He came to immediate attention as he noted a greenish brown ambulance moving rapidly along the street.

As it passed, Katia breathed. "Wrong one. No red banner at the back."

They continued to follow its progress until it had passed the Fuentes Clinic. John looked around but could not see Diego's taxi in the vicinity. Another ambulance came along the road, this time, a white and orange vehicle. Once again, the vehicle lacked a red banner.

John glanced at his watch. After half an hour, another military ambulance moved along the road. Camouflage patterns splotched it from front to rear. As it passed by, a red bandanna fluttered its white floral pattern gaily in the breeze.

John glanced to see Valderas moving toward the spotted car. He got in the front seat, the arm in the sling no hindrance at all, and drove down the street and into the entrance of the parking lot behind the clinic.

John and Katia quickly walked to the statue. They waited two minutes in impatience. Where was he? John's hands were sweaty, and his stomach was doing its usual dance of jitters in anticipation of the coming action.

At just that moment, Diego drove up. John opened the door and let Katia get in first. His words were short and angry. "Where've you been?"

"I was going to pick you up when I saw your secret service friend. He's got someone with him—tall guy. I was parked deep in an alley and just held back till he left the area. Sorry, Chohnee."

"No, you did the right thing, Diego. Excuse my irritation."

"No problem. Do I just drive into the parking lot?"

"Yes—and with our secret service man cruising the streets, the quicker the better."

A white sign with black lettering identified the white-stuccoed building as the Fuentes Clinic. Diego drove by and then pulled into the parking lot at the rear of the building. The back door of the building was labeled as an emergency entrance, and a white-striped area indicated a no-parking zone.

The open back doors of the ambulance provided John a quick look at its interior. The front doors of the vehicle hung open, and music came from a radio in the ambulance. The driver leaned against the building, smoking a cigarette. Two soldiers, rifles hung carelessly on their backs, stood in the shade, casually talking with the driver.

The soldiers came to a condition of semialertness as the taxi pulled into the parking lot. When none of the occupants got out, one of the soldiers ambled toward the car and leaned in the window to talk to Diego. Katia rolled her window down and smiled saucily at the soldier. He immediately lost interest in Diego and changed his position to lean in the back window. He asked, "What's going on, amiga?"

She leaned forward seductively. "My boyfriend got hurt in a fight." Then she inclined her head toward John, whose fake gray beard and hair made him look much older. "The old man and I are waiting for him to get here in the ambulance."

The soldier said solicitously, "I hope it wasn't serious."

Katia opened her door, and when it was apparent that she would get out of the taxi, he helped her. She clung to the soldier's arm. "It's too hot to sit in the taxi." She smiled into his eyes. "I don't know how bad my boyfriend got hurt . . ." Her words trailed off as she moved to the beat of the music. "But nothing's too serious when the music's good."

Katia's wig and garish makeup made her look like a tramp. John thought Katia was, as usual, attracting too much attention. Yet not one of the soldiers paid attention to anything but Katia. He glanced at his watch. Suddenly he hoped the song would not end. Katia would keep the soldiers distracted when El Cinco's ambulance arrived.

John got out of the taxi and walked behind the parked ambulance. He heard a vehicle approaching from the street and looked to where Katia was still amusing the soldiers. The vehicle was an ambulance. The driver's face was disfigured by a nylon stocking pulled over his head. A metal hawk fastened to his fatigue hat identified the man as Halcón. He pulled up and parked. The three soldiers were still totally engrossed with Katia.

Halcón eased the driver's door open. Pablo pushed open the back door of the ambulance. He also had a stocking pulled over his face. A hole had been cut around his mouth so he could speak. Pablo handed John a pistol, which he quickly jammed under his loose-fitting guayabera.

The stocking over La Raspa's head pulled his long features into a grotesque caricature of a human face. John joined Halcón. Pablo and La Raspa walked quietly at his side. Their appearance in front of the soldiers was sudden, and the surprise complete. The soldiers made no move. Pablo asked one of the men, "How many soldiers inside?"

The man's face took on a hard, stubborn look. "I don't know." He spat at Pablo.

"That was dumb, amigo. We didn't intend to hurt anyone." Pablo stepped behind the man, jabbed his rifle at his back, and nodded at La Raspa. "Find out how many soldiers are inside."

La Raspa's ugly, sinister features became devilish with a horrible smile. His knife moved smoothly from its holster. With the rifle in his back, the soldier could not back away from the knife. La Raspa did not say a threatening word, but reached out, and in a caressingly gentle movement, traced the knife carefully down the man's cheek. The razor edge just broke the skin, and a red line followed the gleaming blade. La Raspa's voice grated. "How many?"

The man's hand stabbed up, and he wiped over his cheek and held it out to see the blood.

"I won't ask again, and if you lie to me, you won't see the sun go down today."

La Raspa's voice, almost like fingernails scratching across a slate board, caused chills to race up and down John's back. He knew, he *really* knew, that La Raspa meant what he said, and so did the soldier.

The soldier's eyes had grown very wide, and he whispered, "Two. Only two—one carries a FAL like yours. The other only a pistol."

They disarmed the soldiers, and Pablo said to Halcón, "Get the handcuffs."

Pablo waved his rifle in an unmistakable demand for the soldiers to get in their own ambulance. Halcón then handcuffed them to the racks that held a stretcher in place. When the men were secure, Halcón jumped lightly to the ground and pushed one of the doors closed.

Pablo pointed to Halcón and La Raspa. "You two stay on guard out here. If any one of them shouts or stirs, shoot him." He spoke loud enough to be clearly heard by the men in the back of the ambulance.

Halcón growled his agreement. "With pleasure!"

Pablo shoved a pistol at Katia and said, "Hide this pistol in your clothes." He grinned at her. "If you can find a place."

Katia took the pistol, smiled, and slipped the pistol under her waistband.

Pablo quickly glanced at each of the others. "You all know the plan, compas. Are you ready?"

John nodded and walked into the clinic. He made his walk the shuffle of an older man. His heart was beating rapidly, and he wondered that others didn't hear its thunder. They entered a long hallway. There were doors on both sides, all closed. At the end of the hall he could see benches on one side of a room that widened out. A pair of worn cowboy boots stuck out of a pair of tan whipcord pants. That would be Valderas. On the other side of Valderas, one foot, shod in shiny military boots, tapped a bored rhythm against the chromed metal stand of an ashtray. John shuffled down the hallway.

As his scraping steps approached, the shiny boot disappeared, and then a soldier stepped into the hallway. He held an automatic rifle pointed at John and ordered, "Hold it, old man. What do you want?"

John continued his shuffling walk toward the soldier. He held a hand up to his ear. His voice cracked with age. "Ehhh? What say, soldier?"

The soldier waggled the barrel of the gun menacingly. "I said, stop right there!"

John kept walking. He held out a shaky hand, the shaking not entirely an act, his voice irascible with age. "I must see El Doctor Fuentes."

There was an ominous click from the rifle as the soldier prepared to fire. Katia stepped from behind John and said, "Please, my father is just sick and needs to see the doctor. He can't hear anything you say."

The rifle wavered and then dropped to the soldier's side. Raising his voice to a shout he beckoned to the old man. "All right. You can check in at the desk."

John continued his infirm walk, placed his hand behind his ear, and in a quavering voice said, "What say?"

Katia placed her lips to John's ear and shouted, "Go check in at the front desk, Papa!" She pointed in the general direction of the waiting room.

The soldier, not completely convinced, backed toward the bench where Valderas sat, his head still bandaged and his arm still in a sling. The soldier held the rifle by the barrel and let the stock rest on the floor. Katia walked up to him and stood very close. "He's just a harmless old man. What's a soldier doing in the clinic?"

The soldier tried to back up farther. It was clear that he didn't regard the garishly made up woman as a threat. His words were sarcastic. "Not that it's any of your business, *bruja*, but I guard a prisoner."

Katia's fingers formed a spear that jabbed suddenly and buried itself in the inverted V of the man's rib cage; a spot unprotected by muscles. The man gagged in pain and doubled over. Her hand flashed again, and this time her stiffened fingers jabbed up toward his neck and buried themselves just under his chin. He weakly struggled to bring up his gun, but Valderas's hand flashed out of the sling and in a quick jerk pulled the gun away from the soldier who sagged back on the bench, an attempted shout coming from his throat in a hoarse whisper.

Katia thrust her face very close to the soldier's face. She said, "I hate to be called witch. It makes me very angry."

John, no longer a feeble old man, dashed quickly to the front desk and thrust a pistol in the face of the frightened white-uniformed receptionist. He ordered her to precede him to where Valderas and Katia stood guard over the soldier, who was bent over, gagging and desperately trying to catch his breath.

Pablo moved along the hallway and stood with two rifles. Valderas nodded at him and said, "Keep an eye on the hallway—and that door." He pointed to a closed door halfway down the hall. Then he opened a door into one of the other rooms. He returned in a moment with a roll of white adhesive bandaging tape. The white-uniformed woman shrank back from him.

"If you don't make too much fuss, lady, you won't be hurt."

She looked at Valderas in wide-eyed terror. He ripped a long piece of tape from the roll and proceeded to bind the hands, feet, and mouth of the soldier, and then those of the receptionist. He picked up the soldier as he would have a bag of grain and thrust him into the room where he had obtained the tape.

Valderas then grabbed the rifle he had taken from the soldier and pointed to the door he had told Pablo to watch. "She's in there."

He looked at both John and Pablo briefly. "The guard in the room is armed only with a pistol. Whoever . . ."

Katia interrupted. "Better let the viejo and the bruja lead the way."

"Okay then. Are you ready?"

She nodded her head tightly. "Ready."

John pushed open the door and shambled into the room. His voice cracking with age, he demanded, "Where's the doctor? I can't wait any longer. I demand to see Doctor Fuentes!"

Katia followed him into the room, saying, "Papa! Papa, you have to wait. You can't go barging all around the clinic!"

Doctor Fuentes was drawing medication into a hypodermic needle. He looked up in anger. "Get those people out of here!"

The patient, thrashing around and being held down on the examination table by the nurse, was Juliana Brown. She was still clothed in the gray slacks and mauve-colored guayabera she'd worn on the boat. She had looked so dapper then. Now her clothes were soiled and wet with sweat from the methotrexate-induced fever. Her hair was matted down on her head, her face was flushed, and sweat beaded on her skin. She looked up with frightened and feverish eyes. But her eyes passed over the old man without a flicker of recognition.

The soldier, leaning casually against the wall and looking out a window, came to immediate attention. He drew the pistol from his holster and moved toward the intruders.

Doctor Fuentes snapped, "Fool! Put the gun away before you hurt someone! He's a harmless old man. Just get them out of here!"

The soldier obediently returned the gun to its holster and grasped the old man by the arm. John spun his body, grasping the soldier's hand in an iron grip. He rolled the unsuspecting soldier's body toward him and lashed back with his elbow and smashed into the man's soft belly. The soldier gasped and doubled over in pain. John swung his outstretched, stiffened hand down as an axe across the back of the man's neck. The soldier collapsed in an unconscious heap on the floor.

Valderas dashed into the room, the roll of tape in his hand. He turned the soldier over, bound his arms behind his back, and then pulled the man's legs up and strapped them to his hands. He dragged the man to the hallway and told Pablo to place him in the room with the other soldier.

Valderas demanded, "Is the patient ready to travel?"

"As soon as I give her this shot." The nurse held Juliana's arm still and swabbed a spot on the soft flesh of the forearm.

"Does the nurse know how to treat her?"

"Yes. If she doesn't return to normal in forty-eight hours, you should see a doctor. You remember what medication the patient received initially?" Doctor Fuentes asked.

Valderas said, "Methotrexate and niacin."

"Good. Then you should be on your way. I tried to cancel all appointments for the afternoon, but . . ." His eyes twinkled as he looked at John. "Sometimes patients come to the clinic as impatient as the viejo was."

"I hate to treat you roughly." Valderas looked apologetic. "Don't you think if I tape your hands together and lock you in this room, that would do?"

Doctor Fuentes gripped Valderas's hand briefly. He held up a key from his ring. "Don't tape me too tightly." He pointed with his chin toward a telephone on the wall. "You'd better pull the phone out by the cord."

As Valderas wrapped the doctor's wrists with tape, he said, "We can only give you our greatest thanks. I pray you will find no trouble from helping us." He turned to the nurse. "Can the patient walk?"

"I don't think so. Not yet."

John walked to the table and murmured, "She seems so sick." Then he bent down, saying, "She's so small. I can carry her." He picked her up easily, and Juliana's arm slipped around his neck. The action seemed natural to John as he bent his head forward and kissed her still-damp forehead.

Valderas asked the nurse if she had the medication she needed. In reply she held up a black medical bag. "The men's clothes I was told I needed are in the bag also."

Valderas ordered, "Change and be in the parking lot in two minutes!"

The girl moved without hesitation to a restroom in the hallway.

Valderas grabbed the telephone cord and gave it a jerk and then pulled the door shut and locked it from the hallway.

Doctor Fuentes's words followed them into the hall. "Vaya con Dios, amigos."

Valderas motioned to Pablo, who was standing guard near the waiting room. "All right. Check to be sure it's all clear."

Katia and Pablo passed each other in the hallway, and Katia took the extra rifle that Pablo carried. Pablo headed to the back of the clinic.

Valderas first looked quickly in the room where they had placed the two soldiers, then he locked the door. John followed Valderas down the hall, noticing that Katia did not follow behind him. He turned around and looked at her. There was anger in every line of her face.

John recognized the anger signals and turned to speak to her. He realized that this was neither the time nor the place to try to deal with jealousy. He gave a slight shrug of his burdened shoulders and walked behind Valderas toward the back of the clinic. Just then, the nurse came out of the restroom wearing pants and a tan work shirt. She carried the medical bag and followed John out the back door of the clinic.

John hurried across the parking lot, and when Diego saw him carrying the girl, he jumped out of the taxi and held the rear door open for John. John carefully placed Juliana in the back seat. The nurse dropped her black bag on the floor of the taxi, got in, and grasped Juliana's wrist to check her pulse. John wondered why Katia had not gotten into the taxi with him.

Valderas walked to the ambulance, which now imprisoned the soldiers, and slammed the door shut. He jerked his head at La Raspa, ordering him into the other ambulance. Wrapping wire around the handles of the door, he shouted, "Let's go!"

Halcón took a final look down the driveway, trotted to the El Cinco ambulance, and got in the driver's seat. Katia was standing by Pablo, who had taken her arm to help her up into the vehicle. John dashed up and shouted at Katia, "What's going on? You were to come with me!"

Pablo jumped lithely into the ambulance and turned and held out a hand to Katia. She ignored John and reached up and grasped Pablo's outstretched hand. John grabbed her arm and shouted, "What are you doing?"

Despite her gut feelings not to, she responded in tight and angry words. "I changed my mind. I'm not going back with you."

John stood in perplexity. "Why are you going with Valderas?"

Katia wiped angrily at a tear starting to trace down her gaudily made-up cheek and wiped it away. Her words were harsh. "Because I don't want to interfere with your tender, loving reunion!"

Valderas spun John around, slammed the ambulance door and growled, "Get going, Chohnee. This is no time to try to solve a lovers' quarrel."

John stood looking at the closed door of the ambulance. Valderas looked at his watch and snapped harshly, "I said get going! We've only got a few minutes leeway!" His words softened a little. He put his heavy arm briefly on John's shoulder and started him toward the waiting Diego. "I once told you no one would ever put a net over that beautiful butterfly. I was wrong. You did. Now go, Chohnee. I'll get her to Granada, and you can straighten things out as we travel down Lago de Nicaragua. See you in a couple of hours."

John stood, undecided. Finally Valderas thundered, "Fool! Go! Now!"

John turned and trotted to the taxi and got in the front seat by Diego. "Okay. Let's get out of here! Take the route out through the alley."

Diego hesitated. "What about Katia?"

"Change in plans. She's making the trip with the others." John took off the itching beard and wig and sat in the front seat of the taxi, brooding and not paying attention to the route Diego followed.

The paved road followed along at the base of a range of hills that separated the lakes Managua and Nicaragua from the Pacific Ocean, and passed through mile after mile of fields that alternated between tobacco and sugarcane. The taxi climbed low hills and dropped down into Masaya. The nurse opened the windows to let in humid but fresh air.

Juliana, who had not stirred during the drive from Managua, seemed to revive a little. Her cheeks were still flushed red. She looked around in confusion. "Where am I?" Then, eyes darting wildly around the car, she saw John in the front seat of the taxi. "John? Johnnie. Is it really you?"

He turned and held out his hand to her. "Yes, it's me, Julie. You're safe now. In a matter of hours you'll be in Costa Rica."

Juliana grasped his hand in both of hers and began to sob. "Oh, it was horrible! John, you can't believe how bad it was!"

The nurse gently pried her hands from John's and forced her to lean back in the seat. She began to pat on her shoulder. "Shhh. You have to stay quiet. Shhh." Soon she was asleep again.

As they crested a hill, they reached a place where the road overlooked the placid blue waters of Lago de Nicaragua. Then the road dropped down in elevation until the lake was no longer visible. Two kilometers from the old colonial town of Granada, Diego turned off the main road at a sign that indicated a dockyard. As they rounded another bend, the sparkling blue lake spread out before them. Boats of all sizes and colors were tied up to a dock that extended out into the water. A row of dilapidated old buildings, warehouses, and offices of various kinds lined the edge of the lake for a couple of blocks.

Diego pulled into a sandy parking lot a hundred meters from the row of buildings. The pickup and trailer were parked nearby. Just then, Mario walked from the wooden docks toward the row of buildings. John got out of the taxi and called, "Hey, Mario!"

Mario's features lit up, and he jogged over to the taxi. "How did things go?"

"Smooth as silk. Valderas had to ditch the ambulance, but they should be right behind us. Did you have any trouble loading the bulls?"

Mario laughed. "None. That Brutus is so placid; I feel sorry for the cows at Hacienda Boquis. And I treated Magnanimo just like you told me."

Then Ruel and the girl came out of the restaurant. They got in the pickup, and Ruel called, "See you when you unload the bull."

John waved and said, "Adios, Ruel."

John said to Mario, "Let's get Juliana on the boat. We need to be ready to take off as soon as the others get here."

John leaned in Diego's window and gripped his hand. "We'd never have been able to do our job without your help. Thank you, Diego."

Diego handed John a scrap of paper. "If you're ever in Managua and need the best driver available, there's the number to call. Tell me where and when you want me. I'll be there. So long, Chohnee. Vaya con Dios."

John put the scrap of paper in his wallet. He wanted to say more but could think of nothing appropriate. "I pray that God will be with you, my friend."

* * *

Katia stood, dressed in the awful blonde wig, her lips a grotesque slash of color across her mouth and her cheeks rouged like a clown, and watched John pick the limp girl up and kiss her on the forehead. She tried to argue her anger away. *They grew up together. He's been worried about her. You bet he's been worried! Enough to risk his life and all of El Cinco for her! Katia, Katia, don't be silly. He told you on the way to Managua that he loves you. Then why did he* kiss *her? I don't know. Why* did *you kiss her, Chohnee? Why?* She angrily dashed her tears away.

Now he stands in the hallway with the girl in his arms and looks at me and says nothing. What do you want him to say? He could say, "Don't worry, Katia. I love only you." And what did *he say? Nothing. Not one thing.*

She followed him down the hall of that awful clinic where they had all risked so much. *And for what? So he could rescue his wilting little flower! That's for what! Well, the devil with him! I'll go back to Hacienda Medina with Valderas where I belong, and I'll be the soldier God intends me to be.* She glared at his back as he carried the hated girl. *And you'll* never ever *be the father of my brave sons and beautiful daughters, Chohnee! Never! Never!*

Tears welled again in her brown eyes, and she stormed into the ambulance. John just stood at the door and asked her what she was doing.

She pleaded silently, *Chohnee, I love you so much. Please tell me you don't love that girl. Tell me that you love* me.

And all he could think to say was, "Why are you going with Valderas?"

The ambulance lurched out of the driveway and turned to the left. They traveled for no more than three minutes when she heard the blast of a horn and felt a lurch to the right. Then she felt a heavy, crunching impact that caused the ambulance to roll up on two wheels and dangle precariously for a moment before it crashed over on to its side.

Katia felt herself spinning like a blonde-wigged rag doll across the ambulance and a terrible pain surged through her head as she crashed against the side wall of the vehicle. Flares of red and orange and yellow seared across her vision. She struggled with consciousness for a minute and tried to get up. She could hear someone pounding and wrenching at the back door of the ambulance. She felt a slight rush of air and the late afternoon sun shone in her eyes for a moment. She could hear a sharp pounding by the side of the ambulance.

Finally she realized the sound was gunfire. David's face came hazily into her vision. She had to get her rifle. Where was it? As she moved, David's face spun crazily, and the brilliant yellow of the sun changed to a fiery orange. She closed her eyes, and the color evolved into crimson red and then folded softly into deep purple and finally into solid, impenetrable black.

She did not know how many hours had passed nor where she was. She held up her hand and could not see it. She reached out with the other hand and felt for the first. It was there, and it was solid. Sharp stabs of pain throbbed in her head as she touched the large sore lump at her temple. She was lying on a bare, dirty, smelly mattress. She reached up and felt chains. Damp, rusty chains supported the bed frame! In panic, she remembered La Raspa telling of the bed he had slept on for two long, miserable years.

Recognition churned in her mind. *El Chipote!*

She screamed silently, *No!*

She looked around. The only break in the darkness was from a line of muted gray some distance over her head. Another picture generated by La Raspa demanded, *El Chipote!* She screamed out loud this time, "No!"

She swung her feet over the side of the bed and felt gritty, cold, damp concrete. An insect scrambled away. Her feet shrank back from the floor. She touched herself on the legs and then on her shoulders. They had not removed her clothing. Then why had they taken her boots? She patted the bed from one end to the other and then reached down and traced along under the bunk. Her hands touched something and again she shrunk back in fear.

This time La Raspa's grating voice spoke in her mind. *El Chipote!*

She screamed again, "No! It can't be El Chipote!"

She touched the object under the bed again. *My boots!* Someone had put them under the bed. What comfort filled her mind in just finding her boots.

And then the gurgling sound of rushing water penetrated her mind. The gurgle of water was followed by the rank, fetid smell of sewage. La Raspa had said, "The worst thing about El Chipote was the hole in the floor for a toilet and the gurgle of water every hour to wash the waste away." She remembered the repugnance on his face as he said, "And the smell. I'll never forget the foul air in El Chipote!"

She screamed again, "I can't live in El Chipote!"

A voice came floating up as from nowhere. She looked around. There was nothing but blackness. Blackness and that single small bar of muted gray above her head. The voice spoke again, "Just remember the flowers." The words became soothing and loving. "Think of the green-forested mountains. Think of children's faces. Think of anything you love." The words took on a bit of harshness. "Keep your mind tough. You'll survive."

Katia pleaded, "Where are you?"

"Next door. The holes in the floor are bad, but they let us talk to each other."

"What time is it?"

"Time means nothing in El Chipote."

"How long have I been here?"

There was silence for a moment. "I'm not sure. One feeding I think. You've been here maybe eight hours. It's probably night-time outside."

The voice had calmed Katia. "I—I'll make it. Thank you."

She lay back on the bed. She thought of the words the voice had spoken. "Think of anything you love." She closed her eyes and willed the image of Chohnee's face to come into her mind. At first it appeared—but with that woman. She pounded on the bare mattress and rejected that vision. She willed his image into her mind again. This time he came to her with a bit of red cloth tied around his neck. His dashing face was smiling, and his eyes were filled with tender love for her. She whispered to him, "Chohnee. I'm sorry I doubted you. Chohnee, I love you. I'm in a horrible place, and I can't stay alive if you leave me here. Come and get me, Chohnee. Come and get me out of El Chipote."

Chohnee smiled at her and said soothingly, "Hang on, Katia. Hang on. I love you—and I'll get you out. I'll be there as soon as I can."

Katia turned on the foul-smelling bed and prayed, "*O Dios*, let it be true. Don't let it be a hopeless dream. Let him come for me."

CHAPTER TWELVE

JOHN AND MARIO SAT in a shabby restaurant overlooking the northern port of Granada. The colorful prints on the walls and red-checkered plastic table coverings brightened the drab room somewhat. Staring out the dirty window, John watched boats coming and going. He glanced at his watch.

Mario said, "That's the fourth time you've looked at your watch in the last five minutes, Chohnee. You worried?"

He stood and looked out at the restless movement of the water ebbing and flowing along a stretch of beach where children played in the sand. "If they don't get here in the next quarter hour, I *will* be worried. It's already taken them an hour more to make the trip than it did my driver."

John left the restaurant and paced the dock from one end to the other, walking up and down in front of the group of rag-tag buildings. He walked down to the parking lot and even out to the junction of the road and main highway.

He rejoined Mario in the small café. Mario drained the glass in his hand. He asked, "Anything happen in Managua to make you worry?"

"No. It's just taking them too long."

The waitress wiped the shining surface of the table next to them and asked if they wanted anything more. John answered, "No. Is there someplace to use a telephone close by?"

"There's an office by the parking lot. They'll place telephone calls for you for a few córdobas."

John stood and nodded for Mario to follow him. He was not sure what, but he knew he had to do something. He asked, "Do you know how Valderas contacts his people in Managua?"

Before Mario could answer, a car entered the parking lot. The car was a once-blue Chevrolet bearing splotches of rust-brown primer.

Mario said, "See, I told you—you didn't need to worry."

John headed toward the parking lot. As he passed the office the waitress had spoken of, he noticed the door was still open. He looked into the windows of the approaching car. A churning knot began to tighten in his stomach, and a sinking feeling filled his heart. He called, "Where's Katia?"

Valderas's normally brown skin was a milky coffee color. John shouted, "Where's Katia?"

Pablo growled, "Quiet, Chohnee. We'll get Valderas to the boat, then I'll tell you about it."

Valderas looked ten years older than when John had last spoken to him three hours ago. John asked quietly, "How bad are you hurt, amigo?"

Valderas's words were barely a whisper. His lips quivered. "I'll live, but I—I lost Katia." He choked briefly and said, "I lost Katia. I lost her."

John looked frantically at Pablo. "Is she—she . . ."

Pablo shrugged, his facial expression hard. "I don't know. Right after we left the clinic, a truck rammed the ambulance, and she was taken away."

John's first impulse was to grab Valderas and demand that he tell him what had happened. But he forced his mind to deal with the most immediate problem first. He asked Mario, "Do we need . . ." He paused. He knew a hospital was out of the question. "Do we need a stretcher?"

Valderas opened the door of the car. "Just give me a couple of shoulders to lean on. I can get to the boat."

Pablo supported one shoulder and Halcón the other. Valderas painfully hopped between them on his left foot. As they passed the office, John made a sudden decision. He would try a telephone call to Roberto Rusol of Press International in Managua. He called to Pablo, "Get Valderas settled on *La Dorotea* and have the nurse look at him. I'll be there in a few minutes."

It seemed a small miracle to John when his call went through within a minute and Roberto himself was on the line. John broke through the normal pattern of meaningless greetings that politeness required of friends who had not seen nor talked to each other for a few weeks.

"Berto, I've got a serious problem and need some immediate help."

"Sure, Johnnie. You know I'll help if I can—and it's legal."

"A friend disappeared in Managua today. I need to know what happened to her."

"Ahhh. That kind of friend. I don't do a gossip column, but—"

John's words were curt. "I don't have time for joking around; my problem is dead serious, Berto."

"Sorry. Give me a name and tell me what you know. I'll find out what I can."

John paused. He was remembering Valderas's first rule for the trip to Managua. *No telephones.* He asked, "Is this line clean?"

It was Roberto Rusol's turn to pause. "I've never had reason to think otherwise. You—you sure this request for help won't get me in trouble with the Ortega brothers?"

John's breath came a little faster as he knew he must lie. "There's no problem at all. The name is Katia Solano. She might have been arrested this afternoon." John paused, took a breath, and continued, "A case of mistaken identity—I think."

Roberto Rusol exhibited no sign of suspicion. "Do you know who your friend might have been mistaken for?"

"No. Not for sure. Maybe Dama Mariposa."

Roberto whistled. His words now reflected some suspicion. "That's a pretty bad case of mistaken identity. I'm not at all sure . . ."

John's words took on an edge of hardness. "I've never asked a favor before, Roberto." His use of the formal *Roberto* was a clear signal. "I need help, or I wouldn't ask now. It's a legitimate news story. I'm not asking you to break any law, just find out where Katia Solano is. There's a sidewalk café on Calle Once de Julio near Mercado Oriental. I'll eat breakfast there about eight in the morning. Take a table near me."

His words were met with silence. John spoke angrily, "Can I count on you or not?"

Finally Roberto said, "Si, Johnnie. You can count on me."

"While you're at it, see what you can find about a Fiero Rinskin." John thought for a moment about the first night when Katia's brother had seen her at Mama Sanchez's. He said, "Katia has a brother, David Solano. I'd like to know what his line of work is."

Roberto's response was quick. "I'll check on Rinskin. David Solano is a second or third assistant in Ortega's secret police."

"I saw him with a pretty girl. Tall and dark. Know her?"

"He has a girl who fits that description. Nita Delgado. You need more than that?"

"Not on David Solano. See you tomorrow."

On the boat, Valderas was in his own quarters. The nurse felt the injured leg through the rough fiber of Valderas's pants. "I think it's broken. You'll have to go to a doctor."

Valderas said, "The only doctor I'd dare go to is Fuentes, and I can't make it back to Managua. So you just fix it up the best you can, little lady."

She said, "I'll do what I can, but I'll have to cut your pant leg."

Valderas said impatiently, "So cut it!"

The nurse took scissors from the black bag and neatly slit the pant leg. "I can't tell how bad the break is. It needs an X-ray."

"Can't you just wrap it with a splint?"

She shrugged helplessly. "I don't have a splint."

Valderas hollered, "Halcón! Get some sticks so she can make a splint!"

Halcón stepped inside the small room. He held up two flat pieces of wood. "I started looking for a splint a while ago. These do?"

Valderas grinned at the nurse. "Will that make you happy now?"

She spoke stiffly. "As long as you know I don't recommend it."

Valderas turned to John and took a deep breath. "While she's working on my leg, I'll tell you what happened."

John pulled a stool to Valderas's side and sat down.

Valderas spoke in a monotone. "I guess the truth is, I don't know exactly what happened. We were going to dump the ambulance and switch to a car. We were heading along Avenida Trece when all of a sudden this big truck roared out of a side street, plowed into us, and turned us over on our side. That was when I busted my leg. Halcón fell on top of me—I didn't bust my leg from Halcón falling on me but . . ."

John nodded, trying to be patient. "I know what you mean."

"I was cursing the crazy truck driver when somebody started thumping against the back of the ambulance. I figured they were trying to help. Halcón rolled the window down and climbed out. Somebody started shooting—"

John interrupted. "You find out who was doing the shooting?"

"I was telling you. Halcón hollered at me for a rifle. My leg felt like it was going to bust open. When I got my rifle out the window to him, I saw a guy by a gray—"

John whispered, "A gray Ford."

"Yeah. How'd you know?"

John just said, "Go on."

"Halcón scrambled behind the ambulance. There was this tall guy. I've seen him somewhere before. He pulled Katia out of the ambulance and shoved her in the Ford and tore off screeching around the ambulance. They went roaring down Avenida Trece, and that was the last we saw of them. Pablo and La Raspa had been in back with Katia, and they were out cold. I guess I was hurt the worst. Unless Katia . . ." His words faded, and he bowed his head for a moment and shut his eyes tightly.

John asked, "This tall fellow that you think you've seen before. Was he about fifty? Ugly and heavy set? Gray . . ."

"No. He was young. I'd call him handsome. Six two. Really thin. Dark hair. Matter of fact, come to think of it, he looked kinda like Katia."

John sat in silence, watching the big man for some time. Finally he asked, "Do you remember the first operation I worked on with you, Valderas?"

"Sure. What's that got to do with . . ."

John asked, "Do you remember the prisoner that I turned over to you?"

Valderas's big hand hit the table with such impact that the roll of gauze the nurse was using to wrap around his leg fell to the floor. She jumped in surprise. "That's where I saw him before!"

John asked quietly, "Why did you let him go that first time?"

"Because he promised not to have any more dealings with the communists. That and because . . ." His voice dropped. "That, and because for some reason he reminded me of Katia."

John said, "He reminds you of Katia because he's her brother."

His big face lit up in a grin. "Brother? Then she's all right!" He began to frown. "But if he's her brother, why'd he haul her off like that?"

The nurse had completed wrapping Valderas's leg with the makeshift splint. She said, "I don't suppose it will do any good to tell you to stay off that leg, but you should."

Valderas said, "Thank you. And if it'll make you feel better, I will *try* to stay off my leg. It's a bad time for me to bust a leg, though."

The nurse gathered up her equipment and left the cramped quarters.

John asked, "How come it took so long to get here after the accident?"

Valderas tugged on his mustache. "We looked everywhere we could think of to find Katia. Finally Pablo insisted we get to Granada to get me fixed up. He hasn't said anything, but I think he'll be going back to Managua as soon as—I'd go myself, but with this busted leg, I'd be in the way."

John asked, "Can you contact Montenegro for information about Katia?"

Valderas glanced at his watch. "I was going to do exactly that at nine o'clock. Now get out of here and let me rest a little."

John left Valderas's quarters and began to pace the deck of the small boat. He would not go back to Hacienda Medina without Katia.

The nurse came out of one of the small cabins below deck and walked up the gangway, calling softly to him, "Chohnee, Juliana wants to talk to you."

He stepped inside the cramped quarters of the cabin. Juliana was sitting up. Her matted hair had been brushed. Much of the flush was gone from her cheeks. Her eyes seemed focused, and she seemed quite rational.

She looked up at him with a bright smile. He tried unsuccessfully to return that smile. Her gaze met his for a moment, then dropped to study her hands, which were folded on her lap. "I'd ask you to sit down, but there's no place to sit." After a pause, she said, "I've put you through a bad time, John. And not just in the past few days, either."

He held back an impulsive answer and said, "I'm just glad you're safe. You'll be in Limón before you know it."

"I—I just want you to know how much . . ." She stopped talking as if she realized that her words were a hollow expression of gratitude. She spoke hesitantly. "You say *I'll* be in Limón. Aren't you coming with me?"

"Not right now. I've unfinished business in Managua. I'll be back there tomorrow. But you're in good hands. You'll get to Limón safely."

There was a moment of awkward silence. Finally John said, "I'm glad to see you looking better. I was pretty scared when I saw you at the clinic."

"I was pretty scared myself when I realized how sick those pills made me. But I *am* feeling better."

There was much John wanted to say, but this was not the time. Suddenly, he knew that the reason he had felt impelled to get Juliana out of prison was to close and seal off the early days of his life that had centered around her. "Well, I've got some things to do before tomorrow."

She held out her hand to John. He hesitated and then took it in his own. "Before you go—I don't know how to say what I—while I lay in that dark dungeon, I had a lot of time to think. I guess the only way to say it is that I've behaved badly. I'm sorry I hurt you in times past." She was silent for a moment. "When that guard gave me those pills from Nate Brown's—it struck me at the time as a cruel way to let me know you sent the message. But it did make me realize that I have never been fair to Nate Brown's hired hand, and I'll never be able to repay him what I owe him—especially now."

She turned her face down again. John watched tears well in her eyes and then trace down her cheeks. She said, "As soon as I can, I'm going home. My—my big adventure is over. Except for you, it might have ended in that abominable place. I really would have preferred to die than stay there—even another day."

John still held her hand.

She murmured, "I guess it's over for us, isn't it?"

John stood in an uncomfortable silence then kissed her on the cheek. As he left the small room, he said, "May happiness find you quickly, Julie."

She seemed to know he was walking from her life and whispered, "God be with you, Johnnie."

There was no one around the bull pens, so John went there. He closed his eyes and began to plead, "Dear Father, please protect Katia. I know I—my life in the past months hasn't been what it should be—but I promise, I'll try to do better . . . please take care of her and let her know . . . let her mind be comforted. Please . . . Father . . . help me to know what to do to save her. Please help me, Father."

He went to the crew's quarters and stretched out on an uncomfortable bunk. He dozed off into a fitful sleep. He didn't know how long he had slept when Katia spoke to him from a deep enveloping darkness. Her voice was different. She spoke again, and he knew the difference in her voice was fear. She was trying hard to control her sobs. She said, "Chohnee. Come and get me, Chohnee. Come and get me out of El Chipote."

John sat up in his bunk. His heart was thudding in his chest, Katia's words echoing in his mind. He lay back down and tried to calm his mind. He repeated over and over that he had just had a bad dream inspired by his conversation with Juliana. But his heart would not calm nor would his mind. Gradually he came to think that at least a part of his prayer was being answered. He was being told where Katia was imprisoned.

He finally got up and walked out onto the deck of the boat, trying to shake the feeling of oppressiveness that had fallen on his mind like a dark blanket. The moon that had been full when he and Katia had started this journey was now fading into a half moon. Still, the night was bright.

A flash of gleaming metal by the bull pens startled him. He made his way quietly to see who was on deck. Suddenly he froze as he felt the pressure of sharp metal held against his throat.

As suddenly as the blade of the knife had been pressed upon him, it was released. Then the grating of La Raspa's words sounded in his ear. "Sorry, Chohnee. I thought someone was messing with the bulls."

"La Raspa! You scared me out of ten years. What are you doing wandering around the deck this time of night?"

La Raspa's words were hesitant. "I—ah. I can't sleep."

John remembered that Katia had told him La Raspa had spent two years in El Chipote. He should be a good source of information. "I can't sleep either, worrying about Katia. I wonder where she is."

La Raspa idly peeled long, thin strips from a piece of wood with the razor-sharp knife. Finally he grated, "You'll think I'm crazy, but I was sleeping, and Dama Mariposa talked to me."

His words brought a coursing flood of chills rushing up and down John's back. "She talked to you? You mean you *dreamed* she spoke to you."

La Raspa's dissonant voice growled, "Dreamed—I guess. But it was a powerful dream. Her words came out of darkness. Awful, scared words. And Dama doesn't scare easy."

"You say she spoke? What did she say?"

"She was hollering, 'El Chipote! No!'"

Once again, John felt chills racing up and down his back as La Raspa gave confirmation of his own experience.

La Raspa's face reflected the mental pain he felt. "I think Dama's in El Chipote. And nothing could scare you more, unless you spent a night with the devil."

John's heart started its thudding again. "How can I get into El Chipote?"

"If you got a little money, gettin' in is easy. Gettin' out— that's the hard part."

John grasped La Raspa's arm. He felt like his legs would collapse under him. He slowly sagged down to the deck. La Raspa sat on his heels at John's side. John said, "Katia spoke to me also. Either I had a terribly real and bad dream too, or she *is* in El Chipote. I've got to go for her. Tell me in careful detail everything I must know and do to get her out of there."

La Raspa's glittering eyes regarded him in silence. His voice grated as if over stones. "You love her enough to go down to face the devil to save her?"

At first John didn't answer, then he felt tears rush to his eyes. "Yes. That much."

La Raspa's eyes glittered even more brightly in the moonlight. "I won't have to tell you about El Chipote. I'll go with you."

John looked at La Raspa in wonderment. "Why would you . . ." His words died on his lips, for suddenly he knew the answer. He had seen it in La Raspa's eyes a dozen times; he'd just not recognized it. His next words were not a question, but a statement. With a catch in his voice, he said, "You, also, love her that much. That you would *return* to save her!"

La Raspa said, "Si." Then he hastened to say, "I don't know if I love—I'd do anything—nobody ever was as good to me as Dama Mariposa. I'd go back to El Chipote for *her* but not for nobody else."

John sat on the deck, staring at La Raspa, listening to his declaration of love or allegiance, whichever it was. "What kind of help can we put together? Valderas said Pablo is planning—"

La Raspa quickly shook his head. "No! Me and you, we can get into El Chipote—and maybe come back out with Dama, but more than us is impossible."

John stood up and said, "All right. But I must talk to Valderas."

La Raspa sat on his heels, looking up at John for a time in silence. Then he said, "But Valderas only."

As John turned toward the companionway to move below deck, La Raspa spoke hesitantly. "We could go into El Chipote and maybe come out if we're really lucky. But we need some things."

"Some things? Like what?"

"Money, for one."

"How much?"

"Couple hundred thousand—probably more—córdobas."

John stood in silence. He still had a hundred fifty thousand Nicaraguan córdobas and a little more than a hundred thousand Costa Rican colones in cash. And there was two hundred fifty thousand available to him in Company funds in Banco Managua unless the last orders pertaining to him at Limón had canceled the account. He could also use the money he had been accumulating from Boquis. He asked, "Is that all?"

"We need official-looking papers saying why we're there and pistols with silencers. Can you get what we need?"

"Pistols, no problem. I'll ask Valderas about silencers. That much money in cash and papers will take more effort, but I think I can do it."

Valderas was awake. He said, "I talked to Montenegro an hour ago. I was going to tell you in the morning. Montenegro said he talked to David Solano, and David said that he happened by just as the truck ran into our ambulance. The back door of the ambulance sprung open by the impact of the crash, and he saw Katia lying there unconscious. He was going to rush her to the hospital, but on the way, she regained consciousness and insisted that she would not go to a hospital. He took her to some of her friends in Managua. David said she was going to return to San Carlos by autobus early next week. Solano gave Montenegro his word that Katia is safe."

John stood looking down at the big man. "And you believe that story?"

"Not for a minute, but Montenegro said he would check it out tomorrow."

Valderas waved at his splinted leg. "And there's nothing I can do about it myself. Pablo will . . ."

John decided he would say nothing of his and La Raspa's dreams, or whatever they were. He interrupted. "Valderas, listen to me. La Raspa and I are going back to Managua. We—"

"Not La Raspa. He's too unstable—"

"Hear me out! I have a friend at Press International who can get me information. Montenegro can also help locate Katia. If we have to, we'll lean on David Solano. La Raspa and I will leave early this morning by autobus."

Valderas lay on the bunk, pulling on his gray mustache. Finally he said, "Okay. But I want Pablo along . . ."

John was sure it would do no good to argue the point. "If you say so, but it seems to me you're weakening El Cinco at a critical time. You're laid up for a few weeks. Miguel—and you might get angry at me for saying it—but I've heard reports that Miguel's deserted El Cinco. You need Pablo close at hand in case something comes up. You need Halcón and Mario as well. That leaves it up to La Raspa and myself with all the help we can get from Montenegro. Am I right or wrong?"

Valderas studied John's words for a time. Finally he said, "But what if—I hardly dare say it. What if Dama's in El Chipote?"

"Then we all want her out as soon as possible. And who better to help get her out than the man who spent two years there?"

Valderas thumped the bed in frustration. "By thunder, *I'll* go!" He grunted as he swung his splinted leg over the side of the bed. When his leg hit the deck, he grimaced in pain and motioned for John to help him. He muttered, "I'd be dead-weight. What's your plan?"

John looked grim. While he carefully lifted the crudely splinted leg back onto the bunk, he said, "It's not any better than it was when you asked for my plan at Hacienda Medina to rescue Juliana. I'm going to Managua and playing it by ear. I'm going to get Katia back safe or . . ." His words died on his tongue. "I need a couple of things. Official-looking papers and two silencers for pistols. You wouldn't happen to . . ."

Valderas interrupted. "Pistols I got, but no silencers. There's a pad and pen in that table. I'll give you a name and address in Managua. An introduction also."

In the small drawer under the tabletop, he found a pen and clipboard with paper. He handed the items to Valderas.

The big man wrote on the paper for a moment and handed the paper and clipboard back to John. "That's a tool store. There's a man looks a little like La Raspa. His name's Lopez. Give him this note, and tell him what you want. It might take a couple hours. You better have the pistols with you so he can fit the silencers to them. He can handle the papers you want, too. Oh, and you'd better have cash. He doesn't take credit cards."

John fervently hoped his numbers for the account at Banco Managua would still work. He said, "Thanks, Valderas. I'll get Pablo, Halcón, and Mario up here so you can tell them to head on down to Hacienda Medina with you. Maybe one of them will take Juliana to Limón."

Valderas fumed. "*Chihuahua!* What a time to get busted up!"

When Pablo came down, he argued with Valderas for several minutes. Finally, Valderas gritted his teeth, pushed himself up on one arm, and looked Pablo straight in the eyes. He spoke fiercely. "Pablo, I need you! So I'm giving you a direct order. You're to remain with me." He paused and grimaced in pain, sinking back down on the bunk. "I hope you won't refuse to obey my direct order."

Pablo was clearly torn between loyalty to Valderas and his feelings for Katia. He turned to John, anger and resolve evident in his grim expression. "You got three days. If you haven't got her safe by then, I'm going to tear Managua apart!"

John's level gaze met with the youthful revolutionary's. With a curt nod of his head, he agreed. "Three days. And in three days, if she's not free, I'll help you tear the place apart myself."

Pablo paced the small room for a moment, then he whirled on Valderas, saying fiercely, "I'll take you to Hacienda Medina, then I want your boat to come back for Dama—and La Raspa and Chohnee."

Valderas suddenly thumped on the bed with his huge fist. "No. We're doing this all wrong!"

Pablo started to argue, but Valderas was clearly back in command. "That's enough, Pablo. You'll do as you're told. It was Dama's plan to use the bulls as masquerade to travel down Lago de Nicaragua. We'll still do exactly that!" He turned to John. "You've got three days, all right. But in that three days, you get Dama to Puerto Tres Madres on the north end of the lake. We'll stay tied up here tomorrow and wait at Tres Madres for two days. If you're not there, I promise, they'll think a cyclone hit General Ortega's command headquarters!" He stopped talking. Tears welled in his eyes. "Just be there by this time in three days, Chohnee! Be there with Dama."

* * *

La Raspa could easily pass for an unkempt and slightly ugly country man. John took some pains to be sure that the shirt he wore himself was not too clean nor too well ironed and that the pants he wore were slightly soiled dungarees. His worn boots and the old cowboy hat were perfect to complete the picture of a taller-than-average farmer on his way to market. He hid the two pistols in his underclothing, which he carried along with an extra shirt and toiletries in a typical mesh bag.

La Raspa took the window seat and placed his knees against the seat in front of him. In this position, he promptly went to sleep, his head lolling against the dirty glass. The old, rusting second-class bus chugged along the road, stopping frequently to pick up people burdened with baskets of produce to be sold in the market. There were potatoes and green beans and beets and carrots as big around as an arm. There were baskets of platanos and bananas and mangoes and papayas. There was a basket of live chickens and another of small pigs. And the closer they got to Managua, the more crowded the bus became.

John's mind raced with plan after discarded plan. He was sure in his heart that Katia was in El Chipote, but it would be foolhardy to go into El Chipote with no more evidence than the bad dreams he and La Raspa had both experienced. Right now he wasn't sure the dreams were an answer to prayer.

He nudged La Raspa until he opened a bleary eye and without saying a word indicated he was listening. John said, "If I can find out where David Solano lives, we could go to his place first thing. You, with your knife as persuader, could force him to tell us what he did with Katia."

La Raspa grunted and closed his eyes again. His voice was even more gravelly than usual. "You'll have to come up with a better idea than that."

"What's wrong with forcing the man who took Katia to tell us where . . . ?"

La Raspa heaved a great sigh. He didn't look at John as he talked. "Number one, we don't know where Solano lives, and it would be as hard to find that out as to find out where Dama is. Number two, I could persuade him to talk. But after he's talked, you think he'll sit quiet while we rescue her? And I'd as soon kill him as look at him, but not without Dama telling me to. I heard you tell Valderas he's her brother. You get a *good* idea, let me know." He closed his eyes and let his head loll against the glass again.

John's ears burned slightly in embarrassment as he thought of Valderas saying La Raspa was unstable. *He's more stable than I am.* Still, he felt they had to have a plan of action. "Okay, you're right. So what do we do when we get to Managua?"

La Raspa said, "I'm pretty sure where Dama Mariposa is, so I'll talk to some people from when I was there. Believe it or not, I got friends . . ." He paused and added, "enemies, too, who work at El Chipote. But I sure as death don't want to go in to El Chipote if Dama's not there. So we find out for sure. We need to have a driver and a reliable car so we can get out of Managua safe. You'll have to arrange that, too. Just be careful who you talk to and how. We meet somewhere tonight. We tell each other what we found out—and we make plans. Now I need sleep."

John studied him in silence for a moment. His own stomach was churning. How could the man calmly go to sleep? John said, "Okay. Where do we meet?"

"Close by the bus station. Let's say the Hotel Sultana. By the way, I should have maybe a hundred thousand córdobas now."

John gave him the money. "What room and what time?"

La Raspa casually tucked the money into his shirt pocket. "Nine o'clock. Don't worry about what room. I'll find you. And when we get off the bus at Mercado Oriental, we don't know each other." He let his head droop back against the seat for a moment and then suddenly sat up as if he'd had a frightening thought. His glittering eyes drilled in to John's eyes. "I don't know if I need to tell you to stay away from the fancy places you been used to staying at. That's where you'll pick up one of Ortega's secret service pups."

It was good advice, even though the thought had already occurred to John. He said calmly, "Thanks for the advice. By the way, I notice you've been referring to Katia as Dama Mariposa. That's a death warrant for her in Managua."

La Raspa gave an ugly but sincere grin. "Thanks. Makes us even. I think we'll be good partners."

John decided to accept the words as a compliment.

John and La Raspa got off the bus at the market. John followed the basket of chickens off the bus. A large group of people began squabbling to buy the chickens, which were gone before the crowd dispersed, as were the pigs.

John walked through the market. There was an air of excitement and anticipation as the farmers displayed their baskets of produce. John noted that the things such dried beans and rice and manufactured goods such as soap and lightbulbs were missing.

John made his way toward the perimeter of the market, timing his arrival at the sidewalk café a little before eight AM. A white and red-striped awning provided protection from the morning sun and the frequent showers of rain that fell on Managua's streets. John sat at a table. A pretty girl brought a small basket of bread rolls. John asked for orange juice and *huevos rancheros*. He nibbled on one of the hard-surfaced rolls.

Promptly at eight, a man, newspaper folded under his arm, paused at the sidewalk café and then sat at the table next to John. He absorbed himself in reading the morning edition of the official Sandinista newspaper, *Barricada*. The waitress arrived, and without looking up from the paper, the man ordered coffee and a plate of the fruit of the season.

The headlines of an article in the paper caught John's attention: CHAMORRO DEMANDS ESTABLISHMENT OF CIVIL RIGHTS COMMISSION.

The waitress brought John's order of eggs, poached in a spicy tomato salsa, at the same time she brought coffee and fruit for the man reading the newspaper. With the arrival of his food, the man folded the newspaper neatly, tossed it on the table, and looked at John. He greeted him with a nod of his head and a formal, "Buenos dias."

John nodded back in greeting. Each man ate in silence for a time. The man tapped a finger at the paper. He spoke as if he were continuing a conversation from before. "Nothing on Rinskin. And there's nothing about a woman being arrested or attacked yesterday in the whole of Managua. There was, however, a rumor that came from two separate and usually reliable sources. A male prisoner was being treated for dengue fever at a clinic and was nearly captured by unidentified rebel forces, but the man, masquerading as a woman, was quickly retaken by Ortega's secret police and returned to El Chipote. You have to understand, that's just a rumor."

There was enough truth to the rumors that he did not doubt their authenticity.

Roberto said, "From the look on your face, I've brought you bad news. I'm sorry, mi amigo. I wish, really, I wish I could help in some way."

"Thanks." John signaled for the waitress. He paid her and stood up. Without looking at Roberto, he said, "You're right, it is bad news, though news I already suspected but had not wanted to accept. I know I can count on you. Adios, Roberto."

John walked from the sidewalk café, his shoulders slightly hunched as if he carried too heavy a burden. He took the paper that Valderas had given him from his wallet and glanced at the address of the tool shop. It was not far from the Mercado Oriental. He was sure he would pass a branch of the Banco Managua. And if he passed a telephone center, he would call Diego.

Many buildings lining the narrow street were unoccupied and still evidenced unrepaired damage from the Sandinista revolution. There was no parking strip. The narrow sidewalk directly abutted tall walls that lined both sides of the street. Many of the solid, double wooden doors that had formerly allowed automobile access through the walls hung crazily broken.

He turned the corner, and at a short distance, he saw the sign of a branch of the Banco Managua. He glanced at his watch. It would be an hour before the bank opened.

He continued walking until he came to the address of the tool shop. Lopez was cooperative but expensive. John gave him a deposit of the remaining córdobas he had with him.

He walked into the bank shortly after ten o'clock. With a rapidly beating heart, he placed his identification on the desk.

The cashier looked John up and down, John's peasant clothing a contrast to the furnishings of the bank as well as to the well-dressed employees. The cashier handed a slip of paper to John. "You need to sign here, please."

Despite a shaky beginning, the signature came out just fine. The cashier stood up, taking the signature and identification with him. "Just a moment, Señor Tanner. The amount you ask for is large, especially for a cash withdrawal. I will have to get this approved."

Fifteen minutes passed, and John stood up tensely and edged toward the lobby of the bank building. Just then, a man walked from a door behind the cashier's desk accompanied by the cashier. The cashier had to raise his voice. "Oh, there you are, Señor Tanner. Allow me to present the manager of this branch of the bank, Señor Cruz."

Cruz smiled and extended a hand in friendly greeting. "Two hundred fifty thousand córdobas is a large sum of currency. Would a cashier's check not do?"

"Thank you, no. I must have the money in cash."

Cruz was clearly reluctant, but he said, "You realize the bank cannot—"

John interrupted. "Don't worry. I will only have it for a very short time." He smiled. "I'm dressed like this so no one will suspect I carry a large amount of money with me."

In a few minutes, the cashier counted out the money to John and asked for another signature to verify receipt of the money.

John returned to the tool shop and found the silencers to the pistols ready. Lopez showed him how they attached to the end of the pistols and then handed him an official-looking green leatherette folder. John opened the folder and examined the letter of authorization to conduct an inspection of civil rights violations at all federal prisons in Nicaragua. The letter was written on official letterhead, bore the official seal of the Nicaraguan government, and had been signed by President Ortega himself.

John said, "Looks official to me. Will it look okay to the guards at the prison?"

Lopez answered grimly, "Just don't present it at the front gate, or President Ortega will be contacted immediately. Good luck to you, amigo. Where you are going, you will need it."

John said, "There is one more thing I need. A money belt."

"You need go no further than this shop."

John found another branch of the bank and, because he did not want to raise questions by closing the account, withdrew half the money that had been deposited in his name by Boquis Cattle Ranch. The transaction went smoothly and without incident.

John wrapped the stuffed money belt securely under the waistband of his pants. Then he went to an open-air restaurant not far from the bus station. He passed the afternoon away in a slow-paced agonizing over the fate of Katia. Prayers for her safety and success for himself and La Raspa were never far from his mind.

At eight o'clock that evening, John stood looking at the outside of the Hotel Sultana in distaste. It had probably been a hundred years since it was built, and even then it had not been designed for more than the poorest of travelers. Whatever material had been used in its construction had been hidden under a gray coating of stucco that was streaked in long, jagged stains of dirty black. Smudgy windows overlooking the traffic-filled street had gray wooden frames with checking and peeling paint.

When John stepped inside, his feeling of distaste changed to repugnance. The odor of Pine Sol, not used for cleaning, but rather for masking the dirt it should have cleansed away, filled the air. The man at the desk hardly even looked up. He was clearly used to the derelicts who frequented the hotel. "Two hundred córdobas—in advance."

John took the money from his wallet. Even at the official exchange rate, that was just more than a dollar for the night's lodging. The clerk took the money and dropped it in a drawer.

"Room 210." He nodded toward the stairs at the back of the foyer. There was not even the formality of signing a register. John asked for a key.

"There's no key. You can latch the door from inside."

John walked to the stairs muttering to himself at the indignity of having to stay in such a place. Then he grunted, "La Raspa's right. There's no chance I'll pick up one of Ortega's secret service pups here."

He walked passed the toilet facilities that were shared by all the rooms of the second floor. He entered room 210 and looked around. The clerk was right. The door could be latched from the inside. He smiled grimly. The latch would keep an intruder out for all of ten seconds. He decided not to even bother with it. There was a rusted iron bed with a dirty cover over, he presumed, an even dirtier mattress. By the window was a rickety old kitchen chair.

He went to the window and forced it to slide open. Then he lay with his head close to the open window, the silenced pistol in his right hand.

It was just a few minutes after nine when the door was pushed open. The space in the open door was empty. John jumped off the bed, his pistol ready to fire. Then La Raspa's grinning face appeared unexpectedly near floor level. "Hold your fire, Chohnee." He stood up carrying a mesh bag.

John expelled his breath in a noisy sigh. "Whoa! You scared me. You're right on time. How'd it go?"

La Raspa wasted no time on frivolities. "We go into El Chipote with a load of dry beans in the morning between eight and nine. We come out with the garbage at eleven o'clock. The driver of the garbage truck will delay for a time if he has to, but at twelve he leaves with or without us. Your driver needs to pick us up behind the Hotel Camino Real sometime after eleven. The garbage truck stops there after El Chipote."

John said dryly, "You make it sound like we'll just be waiting for the bus."

La Raspa said grimly, "It won't be an afternoon tea. Tell your driver he should take off if we don't show up by one o'clock. You get the papers?"

John handed La Raspa the green leatherette folder. "This do the job?"

La Raspa casually glanced at the paper. "It looks okay to me—but I don't count. It has to look okay to the guards in El Chipote."

"Okay. I better talk to my driver. I'll be back in ten minutes."

When he returned, the first question John asked La Raspa was, "After we get into El Chipote, how do we find Katia?"

La Raspa didn't answer for a moment. He turned to the door and thrust the flimsy bolt into the small receptacle. He looked at it for a moment in disgust and then grabbed the chair and tipped it up to lean against the door. He adjusted the chair until he had wedged a leg against a wide crack in a broken floor tile, and the back of the chair under the doorknob. It occurred to John that some previous occupant, desiring more safety than the small bolt allowed, had broken the floor tile in just that place.

La Raspa turned to John. "A man, Martanza, who used to put the screws to me, is head honcho. His office is soundproof. I heard he still tortures prisoners there. I'll put some questions to him. I give you odds he'll send for the prisoner we want."

John felt frustrated at having to drag every detail of the plan from La Raspa. He asked, "And how do we get around inside the prison?"

It was clear La Raspa sensed John's frustration. He picked up the mesh bag and handed a uniform to John. "I had to guess at your size."

The uniform was neatly pressed. La Raspa also pulled out two shiny brown leather holsters for the pistols. John took off his dirty dungaree pants and slipped the camouflage patterned pants of the uniform on. Though they were a little short, they would do. The shirt and cap had a colonel's insignia attached. He put the shirt on.

La Raspa said apologetically, "I couldn't find any boots. But yours look shiny enough." His head hung down a little more, and he said, "And I'm sorry, Chohnee. I can't tell you exactly what will happen when we get in El Chipote. I—I get all tense inside, and I can't think too straight when I think about going back in there." La Raspa's words came out between suppressed gulps of air. "And when I try to think of anything about El Chipote, my mind about goes crazy, and I can't hardly even think about a plan. I think we're lucky I even got as much a plan as I do. All I can think is that I don't want Dama to have to spend one more night in that place even if I have to die—" A huge sob interrupted his words.

With a rush of contrition, John said, "You've done a great job, La Raspa. We'll come up with something."

"I nearly forgot. We need a hundred thousand córdobas for the guy who takes us in, and a hundred thousand for the driver of the garbage truck, and fifty thousand for a guard at the prison. You got that much cash with you?"

"Yes. We're all set."

La Raspa picked up the mesh bag.

John asked, "Where you going?"

"I got to clean up. I got to look like an officer tomorrow."

When La Raspa returned, the only difference John noticed was that he had shaved off the three days' stubble of beard. La Raspa replaced the chair as security to prevent an unexpected entry into the room and lay with his back against the tilted leg of the chair.

John argued, "You can't get much sleep on the floor."

La Raspa grinned. "I sleep on the floor most of the time. Besides, if anyone tries to get in, he can't do it without waking me."

John lay fully dressed on the dirty bed cover, the mesh bag his pillow, and his mind in turmoil. The picture of La Raspa's gleaming knife tracing over the soldier's face just the day before came into John's mind. A cold chill traced down his back as he thought what might happen if Martanza should resist bringing Katia to them.

"La Raspa, I've been thinking—I—ah—I can't approve of torture tomorrow."

La Raspa's voice grated at John. "You want Dama out, or not? We have maybe a half hour at most to get Martanza to bring her to us. No time to ask him nice. Believe it or not, Chohnee, I don't want to torture him." He paused, and then the grating words continued. "I guess if I'm honest—I really would like to—to leave my marks on him. But I think he isn't very brave. So you don't have to worry."

Lying on the smelly mattress, John prayed, *Heavenly Father, I have to get Katia out of El Chipote, but I don't want to do anything wrong either. Help me to know what to do.*

The picture of General Moroni writing on his coat to make the title of liberty and then threatening the followers of Amalickiah with death came into his mind. He wondered if he, like Moroni, would be justified.

Then he thought about La Raspa's willingness to go back to prison for Katia. He thought how his work with the Company had begun to have a less than good effect on him. He thought about his words to Leon Hardesty just a week ago, about not lying, and how often and how easily lies now came to his lips. His thoughts churned around and around. Finally he decided that no matter what, he *would* get out of the CIA. He thought, *As if you'll have any choice. If you get out of El Chipote, you have to face Leon Hardesty, and after this past week, you'll be lucky not to end up in an American jail!*

La Raspa spoke from the darkness of the room. "Chohnee?"

"Yeah?"

"Someday when you and Dama are old and sitting in your rocking chairs and you think back on these days—I—will you do something for me?"

"What makes you think Katia will be spending her old age with me?"

"I've seen how she looks at you." There was a moment of silence. Then the rasping voice continued. "Someday I want her to know . . ." His words dropped off to a whisper, then a deep sigh. "Ah, never mind."

John's breathing was restricted by a lump in his throat. His words were husky. "If we survive, she'll know, La Raspa. I promise, she'll know."

John admitted to himself that he was very frightened at the prospects of the next day's action. The only thing that strengthened his resolve was thinking of Katia lying on a mattress even dirtier and smellier than the one on which he lay.

CHAPTER THIRTEEN

L A RASPA PUT THE UNIFORM in his mesh bag. It was just six o'clock. Both men still wore the clothing of the previous day. La Raspa asked, "Well, Chohnee. Are you ready?"

"*Si, listo.*" He followed La Raspa out of the dingy halls of Hotel Sultana to the busy streets of Managua. La Raspa pulled a loaf of bread from his bag. "This is all we'll get to eat till we get out of El Chipote."

John wasn't hungry, and it would take effort to stuff the bread down his already dry throat. Nevertheless, he thanked La Raspa and ate the bread.

The morning air was fresh and cool. After a time they came to a loading dock at what was obviously the bean warehouse. The truck was nearly loaded when John and La Raspa arrived. La Raspa went immediately to talk to the man who supervised the loading and said to John, "This is the man you pay."

John counted out one hundred thousand córdobas and handed the money to the driver, who jammed the money in his pants pocket. Then he pointed to a small space between the bags of beans and said, "We'll stop a few blocks from El Chipote, and you'll hide in the space there. While the men unload the truck, you change to the uniforms." He pointed at the mesh bags. "You can't take that stuff with you."

John took the uniform and a clipboard with paper on it from the mesh bag and handed a pistol and silencer to La Raspa.

La Raspa stepped to the door of the van and looked toward the morning sun that was beginning to fill the city with its heat. After a moment, La Raspa heaved a sigh and turned to the driver. "When we get inside, we'll help unload the beans so we can look around. Let's go."

It was a wild ride, but finally the van pulled to a squeaky stop, and the driver opened the doors. His two helpers joined him, and without a word, he nodded toward the limited space between the bean bags. Both men slipped into the cramped space. Two layers of bags of beans were placed over planking. John immediately felt a claustrophobic inability to breathe. Sweat poured from his body. In a moment, the van lurched off down the street.

When the van stopped again, John knew they had arrived at El Chipote. A voice asked, "What do you want?"

The driver responded, "We got a load of beans."

John could hear the man's steps as he walked toward the back of the van. The door swung open. John could see the probing beams of a light down around the sacks of beans. The guard grunted as he moved some of the top sacks slightly and peered under them. Finally the guard called, "Nothing in here! Only sacks of beans!"

The door of the van slammed shut, and the guard called to the driver, "Go ahead."

The engine of the truck roared, and the van lurched forward. John muttered, "They didn't make a very thorough inspection of the truck."

La Raspa snorted. "Why should they? No one in their right mind wants to get into El Chipote."

When the truck stopped again, the driver jerked the back door open. In a moment, the bags of beans that had been suffocating John were lifted off. John jumped out of the truck. They were in a kind of center square surrounded by tall, dirty gray stone walls on all four sides. Heavy iron doors opened onto stone landings. Barred windows stared out like blank, unseeing eyes.

The driver pointed to the larger of the two iron doors. "I'll be in the kitchen. When the beans are unloaded, let me know."

John, outwardly calm, kept his eyes in constant motion, trying to memorize every detail of the stark bare plaza. He wanted to be prepared for the trip out of El Chipote.

John asked, "Where does the garbage truck load?"

La Raspa said, "Right here. There's a bin inside where they throw garbage. A couple times a week the garbage is hauled out and loaded onto a truck. You'll smell it when we get inside."

Just then, the heavy iron door next to where the driver had disappeared slowly creaked open. A guard poked his head out. He carried an automatic rifle in one hand and beckoned with the other for them to begin to unload the truck of beans. The guard walked back into the building, uninterested in what the laborers did. He leaned his gun carelessly against the wall of the corridor into the prison, sat on a stool, and pulled a magazine from under his shirt.

Carrying his first sack of beans, John looked around and saw the large bin that La Raspa had mentioned. It was overflowing with garbage. There was a gate at the interior end of the hall.

La Raspa said, "Beyond that gate is a corridor that goes to Martanza's office. Also, there are stairs that go down to *la mazmorra,* the dungeon. This outside door will still be open for the garbage removal. We've got to get that interior gate open when we come out. One good thing is the bolts on all the gates are electronically operated. By Martanza's office there's a control box that can lock or unlock most doors in the prison."

As the last sack of beans was carried from the van, La Raspa pointed to the empty bags to be used in case of a broken sack, hanging on the wall of the van. He said, "We can clean up a little before we put on the uniforms."

As they wiped themselves on the bags, John asked, "What's next?"

"The driver closes the door but doesn't latch it outside. When he stops for them to open the iron gate to the west, we get out. Have the money ready to pay the guard at that gate, and we go inside. Martanza's office is straight to the front of where the kitchen is."

One of the helpers closed the back door of the van and said, "Tell the driver we're ready to go."

La Raspa was already struggling into his uniform. He snapped, "Hurry and get changed, Chohnee. We only have a minute."

La Raspa strapped the holster in place around his waist. The uniform fit sharply and actually improved his appearance. He looked every bit a professional. La Raspa stuffed their sweaty clothing down between the walls of the van. John handed the clipboard to La Raspa, who rapped on the back panel of the van with the butt of the pistol. The truck began to move.

La Raspa held the unlatched door. The extra gravel in his voice was the only indication of his nervousness. He said, "Get your money ready, Chohnee."

"It's ready." He handed a pen to La Raspa. "Our authorization is an inspection tour, so write on the paper whatever and whenever I tell you."

The truck stopped, and the gate was dragged open. The two men jumped out, and La Raspa pushed the van's door shut and latched the bar in place.

John and La Raspa ran toward the iron door just inside of the arched stone tunnel. A soldier stepped forward and raised his automatic weapon, the deadly, round black mouth threatening both men. John shoved the fifty thousand córdobas toward the soldier. The gun dropped to the man's side. His hand flashed out, and he jammed the money into his pants pocket. With an urgent nod of his head toward the door, he shut the gate as the truck passed through.

Three bare lightbulbs spaced at twenty-meter intervals sent feeble glimmers of light into the long stretch of dark hallway. Suddenly, the light behind them died, and the heavy iron door clanged shut with an echoing and final-sounding ring.

John spun around. There was another echoing chunk of metal sliding on metal and clicking into place as the door's locking mechanism engaged. John felt a sudden panic. Chills raced up and down his back. He had a terrifying thought that he would never see the natural light of the sun again. He felt suddenly, fully, and finally imprisoned. Whether it was his fear or the clammy air of the prison, sweat poured from his face. John sagged against the heavy door.

He started in a new moment of terror as he felt a hand on his shoulder. La Raspa's voice grated, "It almost scares the life out of you, doesn't it? We better get moving."

John took several deep breaths. He whispered, "Sorry, La Raspa. When that door slammed—I don't know what I expected, but . . ." Taking a deep breath, he moved away from the door. "Okay. Vamos."

He mentally counted off the numbers on each of the doors—271—270—269. He wondered if they'd walked past the cell that held Katia imprisoned. Their footsteps rang loudly on the cold concrete floor.

At the end of the corridor, under the harsh glare of a bare bulb, they turned to the left. A soldier stepped from an alcove, his automatic weapon held in a position of readiness. He ordered, "Halt!"

John only paused in his stride. He glanced at his watch. He demanded, "Step aside, soldier! Commander Martanza doesn't like to be kept waiting."

The soldier stammered, "Sorry, Colonel . . ." He paused. It was clear he hesitated to ask the high-ranking officer and his aide for identification. "I must see your authorization papers."

John was condescending. "Good soldier. Show him our papers, Lieutenant."

La Raspa flipped the leatherette folder open for the soldier. As the soldier glanced at the papers, John said, "I've been looking for a conscientious man." John pursed his lips and clapped his hand on the man's shoulder. "What's your name?"

It was evident the soldier would do almost anything for the chance to get away from duty at El Chipote. He snapped to attention and said, "Sergeant Pedro Carazo, at your orders, Colonel."

John patted him on the back. "Good man." John pointed down the corridor. "Where the light shines more brightly, I will find Commander Martanza? True?"

"*Exactamente*. His office is to the right."

John and La Raspa walked down the dimly lit corridor in measured treads that were a stark contrast to John's raging pulse. They came to an intersection in the hallway. John glanced at a large door. There was no guard in evidence on this side of the door. They continued to walk from the comparative darkness of the long passageway into the growing light that was their destination. Two soldiers stood talking casually.

As John stepped fully into the light, the first soldier obviously got a look at the insignia on John's cap. He nudged the other soldier and whipped smartly to attention and rendered a snappy salute. The second soldier gave an equally respectful salute, which was casually returned by John.

The first soldier asked politely, "May I see your papers, please?"

John nodded at La Raspa, who whipped out the green leatherette packet and flashed it at the solder, refolded it, and started to return it to the clipboard.

The soldier, still polite, said, "I didn't see the paper clearly. I need to look at it so I can read it."

La Raspa handed the soldier the paper, which he read carefully. He looked up at John and asked, "Your letter seems to be in order. But why weren't you cleared through the front gate of the prison?"

John's words barked out, "What's your name, soldier?"

The man was not intimidated. His eyes locked fiercely with John's. "Sergeant Acosta . . ." There was a long enough pause to let the colonel know that the sergeant was sure of his ground and that he wasn't backing up, even to a colonel. "Sir!"

La Raspa was already scribbling on the paper attached to the clipboard. Nevertheless, John snapped at him, "Lieutenant! Get that name down!"

La Raspa's chilling voice grated, "Got it, sir!"

John wanted to congratulate La Raspa. He was filling his role admirably. John spoke to the cocky soldier, his voice sarcastic. "You read well, Sergeant Acosta?"

"Very well, sir." The man was still not ready to back off.

The second soldier was clearly bewildered, but he continued standing at attention, his weapon ready to assist whoever won the exchange.

John spoke each word clearly and with careful enunciation. "If you read well, then you have noted that the lieutenant and I are in El Chipote on a civil rights inspection tour—an inspection mandated by President Ortega himself." John leaned forward and spoke calmly. His words had a note of kindness in them. "Tell me, Sergeant Acosta. Would I find any violations if I were announced through the front gate of the prison?"

Sergeant Acosta looked as if someone had unexpectedly pulled the rug from under him.

John stood his tallest and asked sternly, "How many violations would I find?"

Sergeant Acosta swallowed. John was sure that this soldier as well as all who worked in this prison had at one time or another been disturbed by the thought of the way they violated the rights of the prisoners they guarded. Acosta took a deep breath. "Civil rights—I'm sorry, Colonel. I didn't—I've never heard of a civil rights inspection. It's the first time anyone has ever entered the prison without being checked in before." He took a couple more deep breaths and asked, "How can I be of service, sir?"

John's words were kind again. "I was told that Commander Martanza is in his office. This is his office and he is in. Correct?"

"Sí. That is correct."

"Does he have anyone in the office with him?"

Acosta hesitated a moment. "No, ah, I don't think so." The sergeant swallowed. "I could check by the intercom."

John said, "I think it would be better if we entered Martanza's office as unexpectedly as we've entered El Chipote." He looked directly into the soldier's eyes. "Arrange that, please."

Acosta stammered. "That's—that's not possible, Colonel. The door locks electrically from the inside."

John turned to La Raspa. "Lieutenant. How many violations so far?"

La Raspa thumbed through the pages. He muttered as he counted, "Ten—fifteen." He flipped to the last page of the clipboard. "Eighteen, sir."

"And the office is the place we are likely to find the greatest violations." John suspected that every man in El Chipote knew what really went on in that office. He turned to the now frightened soldier. "You don't want to appear on the report as accessory. Do you?"

Acosta could not speak. He merely shook his head negatively.

John said, "I know there's an electrical override to the office door." His words were commanding. "Unlock that door!"

Acosta turned to the electrical panel on the wall, his hands shaking as he took from his pocket a key and inserted it into the lock to the panel. John said, "Do not disturb us while we talk to Commander Martanza."

John hesitated a moment and asked, "Perhaps you would like to accompany us while we interview the commander?"

Acosta protested. "No, no, Colonel. I wouldn't think of it!"

Briefly John wondered if the sergeant would be checking on their letter of authorization. Then he thought, *I hope La Raspa can make Martanza cave in quickly.*

The locking mechanism buzzed quietly. John and La Raspa went through the door rapidly. Surprised anger registered on Commander Martanza's face. He was seated in a swivel chair, his feet sprawled over the top of his desk, reading the morning edition of the Sandinista paper.

John quickly surveyed the room. The walls were covered with some kind of thick, white cushiony material. Then it dawned on him. The material was foam insulation. La Raspa had said the room was soundproofed. John's eyes next fell on the uniformed man at the desk, his sidearm hanging harmlessly over the back of a heavy wooden chair in the corner of the room to the right of the desk. As John glanced at the wooden chair, chills raced along his spine. It was securely anchored in place to the floor. The arms of the chair had two sets of chains hanging down the sides of the chair. On the outside of the arm was a hook. The chains would hold a person secure.

John pushed the door, also padded with the white material, shut, with his back. He screwed the silencer onto the end of his pistol, his eyes never leaving Martanza's face.

Martanza swung his legs off his desk. He started to rise, bellowing, "What's the meaning of . . ."

In three smooth strides La Raspa was standing by the man, his knife pressed against his neck. Martanza's eyes darted between the gun held in John's steady hand and the knife pressing against his throat. He sank back into the swivel chair.

John watched Martanza's eyes flicker toward the intercom. It was out of his reach.

La Raspa flicked his knife at the box. "You want me to permanently disconnect the intercom?"

"No. We'll need it when Martanza's ready to help us."

Martanza was beginning to recover from his first surprise and shock. He asked in a slightly shaky voice, "What do you want?"

La Raspa, with the slightest twitch of his hand, drew a bead of blood from the man's neck. His voice washed over the gravel in his throat. "I want you to refuse to do as this man tells you so I have the pleasure of slicing you up a little at a time."

Martanza blanched and drew back from the knife then blustered, "You're insane! You can't come into El Chipote and assault me!"

La Raspa gave a high-pitched laugh. "I *am* crazy! And you're the one who made me that way!" His wrist twitched, and a drop of blood beaded up on Martanza's throat.

John's own gaze was riveted on La Raspa's insanely glittering eyes. La Raspa's lips were drawn into thin lines across his face, exposing his teeth in a devilish mockery of a smile. John remembered Valderas's words: "La Raspa is too unstable."

Martanza suddenly pushed hard against the desk with his feet. The chair scooted backward, and Martanza struck upward at La Raspa as he tried to scramble out of the swivel chair. But La Raspa stepped back smoothly. The pistol in John's hand bucked slightly. With a muffled spitting sound, a bullet tore through the padding in the wall right beside Martanza's hand. Martanza's eyes rolled, and his gaze switched uncomprehendingly to John.

Martanza screamed shrilly, "Acosta! Get in here!"

La Raspa laughed again. "You think I had forgotten? The room is soundproofed by your own instruction. Into that chair."

John jumped and grabbed the holstered pistol from the back of the chair.

Martanza seemed rooted to the swivel chair. He did not move.

John's pistol coughed another bullet. John warned, "Do as he says!"

With a terrified screech, Martanza jumped toward the chair. La Raspa shoved him hard and he fell backward into the wooden arms of the tightly anchored chair. La Raspa snapped the chains into place, slipping a link of the chain into the hook. The metal of the chains bit into the man's arms.

Martanza's eyes searched the wild eyes of his captor with the gravelly voice. His question was shrill. "Who are you?"

There was disappointment in La Raspa's voice. "You've had so many people in this chair that you've forgotten me?"

Martanza's voice was desperate. "I've never seen you before in my life!"

John decided that La Raspa had instilled as much fear in the man as could be inflicted without doing real physical damage. He said, "Cooperate, and your ordeal will quickly be over, and you'll be alive. Our wants are simple. The woman who was brought here between four and six PM, day before yesterday. Have her brought to this office."

Martanza seemed genuinely puzzled. "There are no women . . ." Understanding lighted his face. "The man who masqueraded as a woman. Wore a blonde wig and heavy makeup? The one recaptured by Captain Solano?"

"The description you give makes me think it is the very one we want."

There seemed to be relief and puzzlement on the face of Martanza. "When Captain Solano returned the prisoner, he said it was just to teach him a lesson, that he was no one of importance . . ." His voice faded. It was clear he realized the person must be of more significance than he had assumed.

Martanza said, "I'll send for the prisoner you want." He rolled his eyes. "Though no matter what, I can't protect you after you leave this room."

"That problem is ours. Getting the prisoner in here alone is yours."

John stepped to the desk and reached for the intercom.

La Raspa said, "Momento, Colonel." He flicked the knife in front of Martanza's face. An insane light danced in his eyes. "I feel cheated after the many hours I spent in that chair. Guess what will happen if I even *think* you've given warning when you speak on the intercom or if the wrong person walks through that door?"

Martanza's voice broke. "I told you, the prisoner's of no consequence. But I have no way to know if the person I send for will be the one you seek."

John said, "Then you play Russian roulette—and if it takes more than three minutes for them to get the prisoner here, he operates." He held the speaker portion of the intercom in front of Martanza. "Control your voice and words. Tell Sergeant Acosta to send for the prisoner. And Acosta is to bring the prisoner into this room alone." John flicked his head at La Raspa. "He means what he says. This could be your last minute on this earth. Got that?"

Martanza nodded his head up and down desperately.

John said, "When you're ready."

It took a moment, but then Martanza nodded his head at John. La Raspa leaned forward with the knife just pricking against the sweating chest of the terrified man. John said, "I start timing now." He flicked the switch on.

Acosta's voice came through the intercom. "Si, Commander?"

Martanza's voice quavered slightly. "Bring the prisoner from cell 113 in the dungeon to my office in three minutes. Bring him in to my office alone. Do it now!"

There was no hesitation. "Very good, sir."

John stood with his pistol aimed directly at Martanza's chest and tossed La Raspa a handkerchief. "Clean the blood from his neck and get him out of that chair. If he rolls his eyes wrong, kill him."

La Raspa grated, "With pleasure, Colonel!"

In a moment, John said, "Now, Commander, back to your desk."

John sat casually on the desk, facing both the door and Martanza without having to move his head. He put Martanza's pistol on the desk to give the appearance of normalcy in the office.

He folded his left arm over his right hand, which held the silenced pistol, continuing its aim at Martanza. La Raspa stood behind him, the knife hidden, just pricking into Martanza's back.

John kept close track of time. Within the three-minute limit, the intercom buzzed. John nodded at La Raspa, who twitched the blade slightly in Martanza's back as a warning.

John asked, "You ready, Commander?"

The frightened man nodded his head in the affirmative.

John flicked the switch of the intercom. Martanza told Acosta to bring the prisoner in. Acosta opened the door and looked quickly around the room. Clearly he saw nothing amiss, for he turned back and pulled a handcuffed prisoner into the room. The slight figure was dressed in small cowboy boots, denim pants, and a dirty shirt-blouse that hung outside the pants. John's heart leaped in elation as Katia Solano looked up and then swayed unsteadily.

John barked, "Sergeant! Have you not understood the purpose of our inspection of this facility? What do you think the prisoner could do unarmed and surrounded by guards? Remove the handcuffs immediately!"

Acosta looked stricken. "I'm sorry, sir. It's prison rules. I . . ." His words died. It was clear he supposed this would be interpreted as another infraction of civil rights. Without a further word, he reached in his pocket, extracted a key, and took the handcuffs off the prisoner.

John said, "Thank you, Sergeant. If we need you, we'll call."

The sergeant left the room quickly and shut the door.

John motioned with the gun at La Raspa. "Put him back in the chair."

The fight had deserted Martanza. He stood without prodding and walked to the chair and sat down. La Raspa clamped the chains over his arms.

Then Katia turned to John. He could see her lower lip tremble. He nodded his head to signal, *Not yet.* He motioned for

La Raspa. "We need something to gag Martanza so he can't call out when we leave the room."

In unison, La Raspa and Katia said, "You're not going to leave him alive!"

John left no room for question as he responded, "I don't intend that we sink lower than we already have. He stays alive."

La Raspa said, "Then leave me with him. You two get out. To leave him alive is to sign our death warrants!"

John said calmly, partly for Martanza's ears. "No. We go out the front gate together as planned. Now we need a gag."

John was relieved as Katia responded, "Cut a strip of cloth from his shirt!"

Katia took the strip of cloth from La Raspa and jerked it over Martanza's head, pulling it tightly over his mouth and cinching the ends at the back of his head.

John warned, "Careful. You get it too tight, he might suffocate!"

Katia jerked the band of cloth tighter and snapped, "Good idea!"

As an afterthought, John said, "Cut a couple more strips and tie his feet to the chair's legs."

John handed Martanza's holstered pistol to Katia. "You'll need this."

She took the pistol out of the holster and slipped it under the band of her pants. She left the shirt hanging out to cover the slight bulge.

John said to La Raspa, "Don't forget the clipboard." He glanced at his watch. They were fifteen minutes into the grace period. "I'll open the door from the desk. You two go on out the door and wait for me. I'll be right behind you."

La Raspa and Katia stepped through the door as it opened. John spoke to the empty desk. "Thank you, Commander Martanza. You've been cooperative. That will count in your favor. *Buen dia.*" John stepped through the door and pulled it shut.

Acosta looked up in curiosity. John said, "Commander Martanza is quite upset at our charges. Give him some time to pull himself together. He'll call you when he wants to talk to you about it." John clapped an arm over Acosta's shoulder in a friendly gesture. "I'm sure that with your continued cooperation there will be no charges brought against you. After all, you have only been acting on instructions. This prisoner . . ." John nodded at Katia, "has mentioned conditions in the dungeon of the prison that we must look into. Also, is it true that prisoners sometimes work in the kitchens?"

"Si. Most of the time."

"Then I must also check them." He paused in thought. His face lighting as he came to a solution. "In the interest of security, you will only have to unlock the gate just past the stairs to the lower levels. Give me five minutes in the kitchens, and then we will move on down to the lower levels, where the guards can open the cells I want to inspect."

Acosta hesitated. "Perhaps one of us should go with—"

John said, "Thank you, but no. I don't want guards or prisoners alerted about the purpose of our inspection."

Acosta said nervously, "I only wanted to be helpful, Colonel. I will do exactly as you require."

"Very well. We shall return the prisoner to you when we have completed the tour of the dungeon."

John turned and nodded his head curtly at La Raspa, who then led the way to the corner corridor and turned to the right. The hallway was only lightened by a bare bulb that exposed the stairs leading to the lower levels of the prison. Just as they walked past those stairs, the distant jangling of a telephone seemed to crash through the silence. John's heart jumped to a raging beat. There was a guard standing at attention as they approached the gate. It was slightly ajar. The guard watched the three people who approached him. At just that moment a small red light began to flash above the gate.

In one smooth movement, the butt of La Raspa's pistol crashed across the head of the unsuspecting guard. John caught his falling body, kicked his weapon through the opening, and dragged the unconscious body through the gate. Then he slammed the gate shut. He gasped at La Raspa, "We'll put him in the trash bin."

As the guard dropped with a heavy thud into the bottom of the metal bin, John could see that the outside metal door was still open, and daylight was streaming through it. Then the light was blocked as a guard came through the door, his weapon slung over his shoulder. When he saw the three people coming at a dead run down the hallway, he dropped to one knee to bring the weapon into firing position. Before he could fire, John drove his booted foot into the man's neck. The man fell in an unconscious heap to the dirty floor as the three people raced out the door. John pushed the door shut behind him. It took a moment to adjust to the brightness of the outside light.

The garbage truck had a metal bed and sidewalls with bent wooden hoops over the top. A dirty brown canvas was tied to the hoops. John dashed to the man standing at the door of the garbage truck, one foot on the step into the truck. John brought out the money he had already counted and thrust it into the hand of the driver. He looked quickly around. "Where—?"

The driver jerked his head toward the front of the truck. "We left a cavity under those boxes next to the cab. The front hoop is loose. Climb in there and quickly! If we get stopped before we get out of here, I won't try to protect you!"

La Raspa was already in the truck, holding the wooden hoop and canvas up with his back to provide opening for Katia and John. He held a hand out to pull first Katia then John inside. The driver pulled the canvas and hoop down and tied it. He started the engine, and the truck drove to the iron gate at the west end of the compound.

The guard at the gate swung up onto the step of the cab and peered inside. There were only the driver and his two helpers. He waved them on.

The big truck grumbled through the gate. John sank down, protected from the foul-smelling garbage only by a couple of thicknesses of cardboard. In spite of the odorous mess in which they seemed buried, he uttered a brief prayer of thanksgiving. Within a couple of blocks from the prison, the raucous cry of the prison alarm system began to fill the air with its noise.

John cried, "We'll have to get off this truck!" He struggled to raise the hoop. It was tied too tightly. La Raspa pushed him to the side, and his sharp knife slit through the canvas and made room for his arm to cut the rope binding the hoop in place. The canvas, anchored to the wooden hoop, now caught the wind and raised easily. John poked his head out the side of the truck and then waved until the driver looked in the rearview mirror.

The truck slowed, and the driver gave a couple of quick blasts of his horn. John came off the truck first, his legs churning to keep up with his body's momentum. Even so, he stumbled to the ground and came back on his feet in a roll. Then he ran along-side the truck. Katia scrambled over the side and stood on the metal ledge of the truck and balanced for a moment and then jumped. She hit the tarmac running, her arms flailing to gain balance. La Raspa came off last, and they bounded toward the stony walls that were the shell of an old building.

They had no sooner gotten inside the building than they heard the wailing of an approaching siren. John peeked through a hole in the wall that had at one time been a window and watched a military vehicle speeding by.

La Raspa panted. "That was close!" With these words, another vehicle, siren screeching, whizzed down the road in front of the ruined buildings.

La Raspa slid down the wall and sat, looking up through the broken roof at the cloud-studded blue sky. A bright beam of sunlight shone down on his widely grinning face. John could not understand what he would find to smile about in the circumstances.

Katia whispered, a sparkling mist of tears in her eyes, "I knew you would come, Chohn Tanner. I knew you would come. Thank you."

John caught her hand and squeezed it. "La Raspa has the most thanks coming. And we're a long way from being out of this mess."

La Raspa was still sprawled out on the floor of the ramshackle building. His face still had a big, unfaded grin on it. John growled, "Just what do you find so funny?"

The grin widened. "Last night in Hotel Sultana I was sure I would go into El Chipote and never come out. Never feel the sun shining on my face again. And look at me! I'm sitting free in the sunshine!"

"We're a long way from free!"

La Raspa just continued smiling at John. "Don't spoil the moment, Chohnee. We just did something nobody ever did before. Nobody! Nobody ever broke out of El Chipote in all its history. But *we* did it!"

John finally gave a grudging smile. "Okay. You have one minute, then we have to get moving! We have to decide what to do, and we can't walk around Managua in these foul-smelling uniforms."

John moved to the back of the ruined building and stared down an alleyway filled with debris. He muttered, "I wonder where we are."

La Raspa stood up and moved to his side. "This is the old *barrio*. It was ruined in an earthquake several years ago and was never rebuilt."

"Then we'd better get out of here. If I were looking for escaped prisoners, this is the first place I'd look." He glanced along the rubble-filled alley and then waved at Katia and La Raspa. "Let's go!"

CHAPTER FOURTEEN

DIEGO RIVERA, THE BEST TAXI DRIVER in Managua, did not sleep well. As he tossed and turned in his bed, he wondered again and again at the thing he had committed to do. He argued with himself. It was one thing to help Chohnee and Katia the first time. He was lucky, but to do it again? What would happen to Carla and the kids if he got caught? He moved fitfully for an hour before the answer came. He briefly relived the conversation with Katia. He had said, "Many died in the revolution, and their lives were wasted because the Ortega brothers turned the revolution to their own gain."

She had answered, "Every Nica must be a Sandinista, hecho y derecho."

He repeated Katia's words in a whisper. "One day, El Cinco will ask for your support. When they ask, give it freely with your whole heart."

His wife tossed and sleepily asked, "What did you say, querido?"

"I love you, Carla. Go back to sleep."

But Diego could not sleep until he had worked out in his mind what he would do. He would not drive his own taxi tomorrow. He would borrow a car from his friend Franco and tell him to report it stolen as protection to Franco. His plans made, and his conscience at ease, he slept.

Franco had not pressed for details and had been only a little hesitant. The car's engine ran smoothly and the tires were good. As a precaution, he placed three twenty-five-liter metal containers filled with gasoline in the trunk of the car. He could take Chohnee and Katia where they wanted to go.

Diego drove along the alley behind the Hotel Camino Real. There was time to be sure of the territory. On a second slow trip through the alley, he noticed paper and trash lying against sagging wooden doors of a garage, indicating the doors had not been opened for a time. From here he could see any movement behind the Hotel Camino Real and make a quick retreat if needed.

At twelve thirty, a large garbage truck drove into the alley and pulled up by the bin of trash against the back wall of the hotel. The driver and his two helpers released the ropes that tied the wooden hoops supporting a covering canvas. At that moment, a military vehicle entered the service area. Three men carrying automatic weapons got out.

When Diego saw the soldiers, he started the engine of Franco's car. He sat, engine idling smoothly, and watched. The soldiers stationed themselves around the garbage truck. Then the two helpers lifted the top off and leaned it against the building. One of the soldiers jumped up on the metal ledge around the walls of the truck. He told the two helpers to stand clear and then in three distinct volleys, sprayed the full clip of bullets from his automatic rifle into the garbage that filled the truck. In a few places, bulges appeared on the side of the metal bed where bullets, primarily spent in the path through the garbage, finally pounded against the heavy iron sidewalls. He watched for a moment, then jumped to the ground and casually motioned for the garbage men to continue with their task.

At the crashing volleys of bullets into the metal bin of the truck, Diego's fingers clutched the steering wheel of the car more tightly. He thought, *What a terrible way to die, entombed in a mass of garbage!* He felt anger building in his chest. Despite his fury, he drove slowly and deliberately out of the driveway and around the block to the front of the Hotel Camino Real.

Diego parked on the Panamerican Highway in front of the hotel, his anger rising at the calloused destruction of the enemies of the Sandinista state. After a few minutes, the truck nosed out of the alley and headed down the highway toward a waste disposal site a few miles south of the Sandino Airport. Diego drove along the highway in front of the garbage truck. Watching carefully, he saw the military vehicle with its complement of three soldiers pull out on to the highway and follow the truck.

It occurred to Diego that the soldiers were going to the dump site to be sure there were bodies in the mass of garbage. He decided it would be foolish to risk arrest by following the truck to the dump. As he was ready to turn off the highway, he noticed the front of the canvas-hooped top on the truck lifting slightly in the breeze generated by the movement of the speeding vehicle. As the truck roared past, he realized that the canvas was not torn but cut! The rope, too, had been cut, not frayed through!

He did not know if it was irrational hope, or genuine possibility, that Chohnee and Katia had escaped before the episode behind the hotel. In impulse action, he turned off the highway and began to cast in his mind as to what route the garbage truck would have followed after leaving the prison.

The tumble of buildings ruined in the earthquake came into his mind. The old buildings were on a direct route from El Chipote to the Panamerican Highway. Just in sight of the jumble of buildings, he saw a military vehicle blocking traffic. The soldiers, armed with automatic weapons, were sufficient reason to turn into a neighborhood nearby that had survived the intense earthquake of 1972.

Diego realized that the soldiers were also pursuing the possibility that Chohnee and Katia might be in the old neighborhood.

After a few minutes of observation, he drove by side streets to the opposite end of the ruin of buildings. Another military vehicle blocked traffic at that point. A jeep came into view and drove slowly by, two armed soldiers in the back. He decided to drive to the market.

* * *

John led the way through a narrow alley that looked like the aftermath of an ancient war. Building after shattered building now formed heaps of rubble overgrown with tropical vegetation. After stumbling over piles of stones and bits of brick and tile and broken slabs of concrete and crossing from one rubbish-blocked alley to another, Katia asked, "Where are we going?"

John said, "I don't know. We planned to get to the Hotel Camino Real. I don't even know where we are."

La Raspa said, "I lived here before the earthquake, and in the new section of houses after. I know the alleys and roads. If we can get to Rio Tipitapa, we can borrow a boat to get to Tres Madres."

John said decisively. "Good! Then we follow you, but first we have to get out of these uniforms." He pulled off the shirt he wore.

La Raspa removed his shirt and, taking John's discarded shirt, raised a broken slab of concrete, stuffed the clothing beneath it, and let the concrete fall back into place. "We just keep going the way you were headed."

They continued through the rubble and soon arrived at the last gutted old building. John looked through an opening in the wall. A hundred meters away an olive drab military vehicle was parked, blocking the intersection of the street. Four armed soldiers stood by the vehicle to stop traffic.

John peered through the opening and whispered, "We're trapped!"

Katia came to his side.

John breathed, "I'll shoot out a tire of the jeep. At the same time, La Raspa shoots at that little shed with the corrugated metal roof."

"What do you have in mind?"

"Distraction. With both pistols silenced, nobody will know where the shooting is coming from. While they're looking to see what's going on, I cross the street. I make another distraction, and you and La Raspa cross."

La Raspa said, "Let me do it. There's an alley, just past the jeep, by Calle Tamarindo. If I can get into that alley, I can get us all the help we need to make the soldiers think the devil himself broke loose."

Katia said, "It'll work, Chohnee!" She handed Martanza's pistol to La Raspa. "Trade me this pistol for your silenced one."

La Raspa handed her the pistol and said, "After two minutes, start shooting, then it will take three minutes till I'm ready to cross the other street. After that, in maybe fifteen minutes at the most, you be ready to cross. I'll be waiting for you in the alley. Don't make any move till you hear a disturbance from over there." He pointed toward the metal shack.

La Raspa started toward the back of the ruined building then turned back. He pulled his knife from the leather case at his back and cut the uniform pant legs in jagged strips just below the knees. He then scooped up hands full of dirt, made white by remnants of plaster, and rubbed dirt all over his pants. Suddenly the short-legged pants he wore bore no resemblance to a uniform. He was changed from a uniformed soldier back to a ragged campesino. He handed the knife to John with a questioning look.

John took the knife and imitated La Raspa's actions.

Again La Raspa headed back out of the broken and ruined building.

Katia murmured, "Go with care, my friend."

John glanced at his watch and then positioned himself at the window where he could see the jeep. Katia moved to another break in the exterior wall and stretched out in the prone position.

John said, "We don't have a lot of ammunition, so maybe five rounds maximum. Space 'em out a little."

Katia nodded her agreement.

The two minutes lapsed. John took careful aim at the tire. He whispered, "When you're ready, Katia."

The quiet neighborhood air was suddenly broken by a sound that was hard to identify. There was no cracking as of the firing of bullets. The sound was more like rocks being hurled with great force at the metal-roofed shed. Then there was a loud report as John's bullet found its mark, and the air from the right front tire of the jeep was suddenly released. The effect on the soldiers was electric. The two soldiers near the tire dropped to the ground and immediately began to return what they believed had been fire from the shed. The other two soldiers took defensive positions behind the jeep. Once again, the shed began to vibrate with sound as the soldier's bullets tore into it. John fired one more shot, this time aimed at the windshield of the jeep. The glass shattered, and the soldiers crouched down and looked in vain for a target at which to fire.

John whispered, "Two minutes to reload and find another target."

Katia crawled to his side, and both reloaded their weapons with the bullets from the small leather clips on John's belt.

Katia said, "We better pick our target carefully. I didn't think that the soldiers would just start to shoot not even knowing what they're shooting at. I don't want anybody hurt unless it's one of those simpleminded Sandinistas hiding behind the jeep."

John pointed to a stucco building not too far from the metal-roofed shed. The building had two windows to the front. One had no glass, and the other had broken, triangular shards of glass hanging from its frame. "What do you think about that?"

"It looks empty. How much time?"

"Less than a minute."

It was as if the silence of the night had fallen on the area. There was not even the buzz of an insect.

"Now, Katia. Break some more of that window."

Suddenly the remaining splinters of glass in the old building began to explode. John's bullet found another tire, which burst with a sound almost as loud as rifle fire. Another of John's bullets ricocheted with a whine off the front fender of the vehicle, causing the closest soldier to drop to the ground and seek protection under the jeep. Once again, the soldiers returned the fire in a withering blast. Chunks of tile broke and scattered in clumps of orange smoke. A huge piece of stucco dropped from a wall in a cloud of white dust.

As John and Katia stopped shooting, quiet again dropped down as a blanket onto the area. Without having to speak any words, they both moved toward the alley that was across from Calle Tamarindo. At the alley, John dropped to his belly and wriggled out to where he could see the soldiers at the intersection. The soldiers seemed totally absorbed in watching what happened up the street from them. Suddenly, the command of the sergeant in charge of the soldiers reached John's ears. "Keep watch along the street back there! I'll call for reinforcements."

Katia huddled behind a chunk of broken wall. "How much time?"

"Eight minutes. If the distraction starts on time."

The minutes dragged slowly by. The dirt that had caked John's sweat-covered body dried and began to itch. He felt terribly unclean, first from the rancid garbage in which they had buried themselves and then from crawling around in the rubble of the old buildings.

John sat, his head resting on his knees. He started to whisper a prayer. "Dear Father in Heaven. We need Thy help so much . . ."

Katia scooted over to be near him. She put her hand in his and said, "Say our prayer out loud, Chohnee."

John continued the prayer in a whisper, asking for help and protection for themselves as well as for La Raspa.

The distraction started almost unnoticed. A few rocks fell from the nearby rooftops. Then the sergeant's voice was heard clearly from the corner jeep. "They are reporting that three men have taken a child hostage!"

John peered out into the street and saw that the soldier guarding the intersection was intently watching the action now escalating up the street. The shouting was increasing, and demands were being made for the soldiers to quit being cowards and pursue the people who had taken the child hostage. Then rocks and bits of brick began to fly, and the soldiers moved into a defensive position behind the jeep. John motioned for Katia to make a run for it across the street. He stood, pistol aimed at the backs of the soldiers on the corner. When Katia was across the street, she stood with her pistol at the ready, and John made his dash across Calle Tamarindo. No soldier from the jeep even looked their way.

As John and Katia ran down the alleyway, the din from the street receded. It was only a short distance when they saw the grinning, ugly face of La Raspa. He began to run in front of them and called, "Follow me!"

They followed the slight body of La Raspa on a dead run through the debris-filled alley. They dodged around paper boxes and barrels that overflowed with trash. The alley made a sharp turn and abruptly joined the street. La Raspa motioned for them to wait. He cautiously peered out and down the street.

The noise from the unseen crowd had increased in volume. Even more rocks were pelting down on the soldiers. It seemed clear that the people of the new neighborhood were happy with the opportunity to vent their anger on the soldiers of the hated Sandinista oppressors. John had a fleeting thought that these

Sandinista soldiers were certainly not considered Los Muchachos—our boys—by the people of this neighborhood.

La Raspa motioned for John to stand guard for a moment. He and Katia ran across the street. Then La Raspa waved at John to cross the street while he stood ready to fire at the soldiers. It was an unnecessary precaution, as the soldiers were fully occupied with dodging the rocks being thrown at them.

The catcalls and epithets were increasing in intensity.

"Sandinistas! Communists! Assassins!"

"Communists are worse than Somocistas!"

"Filthy communists! You come to our neighborhood and shoot up our buildings for no reason! We'll teach you!"

Suddenly, the sergeant shouted to his men, "If they don't stop throwing rocks, shoot them!"

As if on some magical signal, the rain of stones and shouting stopped. The sergeant looked around almost in bewilderment. He called, "Where were the men who took the child hostage?"

A voice bellowed from the area of the metal-roofed shed. "Three blocks down the street toward El Chipote!"

Clearly the sergeant hesitated taking action because of the blown tires of the jeep. Finally he ordered his men to move out at double time toward the area specified.

La Raspa grinned and motioned for Katia and John to follow him. They ran quickly along the alleys and through the tiniest of backyard plots. They scrambled over fences put together with rocks and bricks and mortar. When they would come to a dead end, a door would open, and they would be motioned through the interior of homes that were often nearly devoid of furnishings. The beds were most often a collection of rags or piles of straw scattered on the bare concrete floor. Sometimes there were tables, often just slabs of wood attached to wooden legs made of peeled pole logs, and chairs that alternated between wooden boxes and woven cane stools. The unpainted plaster walls had darkened nearly to black from years of collecting soot produced by the stoves that were no more than a wood fire and a round iron pan supported on iron legs. On nearly every wall hung a revered crucifix of the Savior. That carved image on the wall was the only hope against the grinding poverty that plagued the lives of these destitute Nicaraguans.

And John's heart welled within him, for also in every house, or in every yard, and along every alleyway, a brown face flashed them a grin of hope for their success. These people, for no apparent reason other than their respect for the ugly man called La Raspa, risked arrest, punishment, even being shot, to help total strangers!

At last they stumbled over a roughly made fence and into a cramped space between buildings that opened into a clear but narrow street. John gasped, "How much farther?"

"A couple of blocks. That's where the market is."

After traveling another block, La Raspa said, "Except for our shoes, you and I could fool anybody. And Katia needs a dress of some kind."

La Raspa led them into another alleyway and called a stop. He stood breathing heavily for a moment, then said, "Give me some money, Chohnee. I can get what we want in the market without drawing attention. Stay here till I get back." He slipped the holstered gun and belt from around his waist and handed them to John. "We ought to get rid of the holsters. Load the guns."

John gave La Raspa some córdobas. "Try to get me a shirt, too."

La Raspa ran on down the alleyway.

John, still struggling for breath, sat in the dirt. He was sweating heavily. Katia looked around for a moment, then brushed dirt from the step of the last door that entered the alleyway. She sat on the concrete stoop and leaned back against the door. Her face was streaked with sweat. Smears of dirt marred her forehead and cheeks. John removed the cartridge belt from around his waist and began filling the chambers of their weapons.

They sat in silence as their breathing began to return to normal. Katia leaned forward and said, "It was my fault that we—you and La Raspa . . ."

"No recriminations. Just thank Heavenly Father that you're out of El Chipote, and pray we can get out of Managua."

"Yes, thank the Lord. But thanks to you, too."

"La Raspa risked as much, with less cause. Be sure to thank him, too."

"I promise he'll know. Someway, I'll be sure he knows."

At that moment, La Raspa came running back. He was breathing hard. "Soldiers are blocking off the roads by the market. I heard someone say that they've already searched the ruins of the old neighborhood and are ready to start on this one. We've got to get out of here!"

La Raspa had already discarded his boots and wore a pair of sandals made of leather straps attached to soles cut from old tires. He tossed a pair of similarly made sandals, wrapped in a shirt, to John.

He handed a bundle of clothing rolled in a shawl to Katia. "They argue whether it was three men or two men and a woman who escaped from El Chipote. There's even talk it might have been Dama Mariposa. We have to make you look like an old lady, Dama."

The men turned their backs while Katia changed into the loose-fitting white blouse and the long brown skirt. The sandals were neatly tooled leather *huaraches* and were the only things that fit well. She picked up the clothing she had worn, and La Raspa merely nodded at a box of garbage that was nearby.

John, with a slight feeling of sorrow at losing the well-worn pair of cowboy boots, tossed them into the box with Katia's clothing. La Raspa tossed the cartridge belt that still had bullets in it into the box. He and John put their pistols in their waistbands.

Katia picked the cartridge belt up and slipped the belt and holster around her waist. "La Raspa, trade back pistols. The silencer makes it too long to fit the holster." The blouse covered the weapon.

La Raspa pointed to a door deeper in the alley and said, "We can get to the street east of here through that house."

La Raspa pushed the door open without knocking. A young mother held a baby in her arms and with wide eyes pointed to the door at the back of the small hovel. The fugitives ran through the nearly barren two rooms and out onto the street.

Without words, La Raspa pointed to the east and sprinted in that direction. He pulled up abruptly as two soldiers started to cross the street that joined the marketplace. He pushed John and Katia into a slight area of depression that was the entrance into another cluster of houses.

La Raspa said, "There's another alley half a block to the west. I'm not sure where it comes out."

Katia said, "It won't matter. We can't stay here!"

La Raspa pointed. "Across the street, just past that house with the iron railing in front. One at a time. You first, Chohnee! But don't run."

John moved out onto the street, trying to make his walk appear casual. After what seemed an endless walk, John stepped into the alley. From the darkness of the alley he saw that Katia was just moving past the iron railing in imitation of an old lady's shuffle.

John and Katia stood and watched as La Raspa started to cross the street. The sound of approaching footsteps clattered from the alley. John took the silenced pistol from his waistband and whirled around.

The man raised his hands and whispered urgently, "Hold your fire, Chohnee! It's me! Diego!"

John dropped his arm as he recognized the man. "Diego! How'd you get here. How'd you know . . . ?"

"No time! I've got a car at the end of the alley. They're closing off this whole end of town!"

La Raspa appeared in the alleyway and stopped short. He was just going for his weapon when John's words cut his action short. "Hold it, La Raspa! This is the driver I hired to get us out of Managua."

Diego was already leading the way down the alley. He called, "My car's at the end of the alley. If we get there in time, maybe we can avoid the roadblock!"

The vehicle was just visible out of a narrow opening where it could quickly move out to the street. They all piled into the car, Katia and John in back, La Raspa in front with Diego. As they headed out of the alley, La Raspa asked, "If they're closing off the roads, where will you go?"

"I was going to take you to Tres Madres, but now I'm just hoping to make the new road to Tipitapa before the soldiers set up a roadblock."

La Raspa said with some enthusiasm, "From Tipitapa, we can get a boat down the river."

At just that moment, a military vehicle, siren wailing, flashed across an intersection of a street paralleling where Diego drove. He muttered, "Chihuahua! Too late! That's where that bunch of soldiers is headed."

La Raspa said, "It's okay. I know a better way. Keep going straight on this street. You know where the old road used to cut through . . ."

Diego argued, "But that's closed. We can't get through there."

La Raspa said grimly, "I know a way. Just keep going straight."

They drove in silence for a time. Diego made a sudden lurching turn to the right. La Raspa growled, "Not that way. It's straight ahead."

Diego said, "We're on the same team, amigo. There's a good place for a roadblock where that street crosses Calle Tamarindo."

As they drove slowly by, the flashing lights of the barricade were clearly visible a block away. La Raspa gave Diego a grudging smile. "I won't say any more till we get to where we join the old road."

"How do we get around the metal barricade across the road?"

"There's a mechanic's shop partway along the block. We go in there. He's got a back door we can drive out of onto the old road."

Even the mellow, late afternoon sun could not make this section of Old Managua look any better. It had never been much more than a slum at best. Most of the houses had been abandoned and then reclaimed by squatters. The owners of the buildings had given up hope of renting them because of the poverty that marked the end of the revolution.

La Raspa directed Diego to stop. He walked through a door by the side of dilapidated double doors that hung with a padlock over a sagging hasp.

They waited in apprehension, the minutes slowly passing by. Finally Diego muttered, "We better get off this street."

Before his words could translate into action, a man dressed in ragged greasy pants came back through the small door that La Raspa had entered and unlocked the padlock on the double doors. He dragged one door open and waved the car through. The door was pulled shut behind them, and the interior of the building was very dark. Diego flicked on the lights of the car. La Raspa was dragging a long greasy table filled with tools and parts of engines, which barred a door at the rear of the room. John leaped out of the car and helped La Raspa move the table.

The mechanic pushed on the back door, and it creaked open to expose a weed- and garbage-filled roadway. La Raspa asked John to give the mechanic ten thousand córdobas. This done, they both jumped into the car. The mechanic pulled the door closed as Diego drove slowly down the road.

La Raspa said, "Diego, seven kilometers down this road we can get a boat. You'll leave us there, and you can drive back to the garage. If you are questioned, the mechanic will say you were at his garage getting your car fixed ever since this morning."

The road was no more than a rough pathway following along the course of a sluggardly stream of water. Occasional traffic kept the bushes, which would have choked off passage, trimmed to axle height. Huge trees grew along the banks of the stream, and limbs stretched out and joined with others spanning both sides of the water.

Diego drove slowly without lights along the rutted road and explained how he had come to be in the alley when the three people needed him the most. As he told of watching the soldier jump up into the garbage truck and empty his rifle into the pile of trash in the truck, tears filled his eyes. "I thought that your efforts at freedom were as wasted as all efforts seem to be to get rid of the Ortega brothers. The fact that you got away gives me hope that freedom can still come to Nicaragua—if we just don't give up!"

The narrow road came to an abrupt end at the Tipitapa River. At one time a bridge, now ruined by an earthquake, had spanned the river. A shriveled old man sat smoking a cigarette. He kept watch over the half dozen *cayucos,* native boats made by hollowing out a log. The boats, tugged by the waters of the stream, were held in place by ropes that tethered them to twisted and rusting steel spans.

La Raspa said to Diego, "This is as far as a car can go."

Diego pulled his car to a stop and got out. He and La Raspa shook hands without exchanging any words. Then La Raspa addressed the old man. "Hola, Padre Paracin. We need to borrow a boat to go to Tres Madres."

The man stared at La Raspa with rheumy eyes. A cigarette dangled from his lips, smoke curling up over his face. Then in a quavering voice he asked, "If you take my boat to Tres Madres, how will it be returned to me?"

La Raspa hesitated. "We would tie it up for you. You could get someone to take you to Tres Madres tomorrow."

The man stared down the river. "I have no gasoline for the engine."

La Raspa said, "Maybe I'd better go over to the village to see if someone there . . ."

Diego interrupted La Raspa. Speaking to the old man, he said, "I have seventy-five liters in the trunk of my car. That's more than it would take to get to Tres Madres. If you lend them your boat, you can have the gasoline."

The man's eyes lighted briefly. "That's good." He spoke to La Raspa. "For you, Guillermo, I will let them take my boat."

Katia looked at La Raspa with a questioning smile. "Guillermo?"

La Raspa lowered his eyes for moment. "The name given me by my father."

Diego went to the trunk of the car and brought the three cans of gasoline to the old man, who handed one can to La Raspa. "Fill the tank. And take good care of my boat."

Katia put her arms around Diego. "Thank you for risking so much. Thank you. We owe you. Someday . . ."

Diego said, "No. The people of Nicaragua owe you, all of you who fight against the Ortega brothers. But, as you say, someday . . ." He turned to John and gave him an abrazo. Then he got back in the car and started the engine. He gave a quick thumbs-up gesture and called out the window as he turned around, "Vaya con Dios, my friends!"

Both John and Katia waved at Diego as his car moved bumpily along the rough road. "God be with you, Diego," Katia said.

John handed Padre Paracin ten thousand córdobas. The old man protested, "No. The gasoline is payment enough."

Katia took the money from John's hand and put it in the old man's shirt pocket behind a crumpled package of cigarettes. "Take the money, Padre Paracin. And if soldiers come by and question you, tell them the boat drifted away or was stolen in the night."

CHAPTER FIFTEEN

THE SMALL, FIVE-HORSEPOWER engine putted quietly and, adding its push to the current, hastened its occupants down the placid Rio Tipitapa. The long, narrow cayuco easily carried the burden of the three fugitives. They sat in single file, with John in front and La Raspa operating the boat from the rear. The heavy craft moved smoothly through the water in the darkening cloudy night. There was the beginning of a misting rain. There was much John wanted to say to Katia, but he contented himself with watching the smooth beauty of her face and the lithe movements of her body. He had a contented feeling in his heart. He had several times mouthed a prayer of thanksgiving to God.

Villages along the Rio Tipitapa passed as if they were drawings unrolling on a screen. The villages seemed the same, and yet each had its own distinctness with a large, thatched structure in the center around which the huts clustered. People sat on benches surrounding fires that burned in pits in the center of the thatched buildings. They were protected from the weeping skies by the crude roofs.

Katia suddenly dropped down behind the rough-hewn sides of the boat. Her urgent voice commanded, "Quiet! Get down, Chohnee! La Raspa, cut the engine. Let the cayuco drift to the bank!"

La Raspa turned off the engine and dropped low in the boat. The night seemed ominously quiet. There was a slight raucousness of laughter from the villagers they had just passed. The engine hissed quietly from droplets of water that fell on its hot casing, and there was the gentle sound of water lapping against the side of the boat. There was no foreign or obtrusive sound.

La Raspa whispered, "The current keeps us from drifting to the bank."

Katia demanded, "Use the oars!"

The sound of the oars dipping into the water and of La Raspa's exertions could be heard over the quiet waves of water lapping against the boat's sides.

John removed the pistol from his waistband and peered cautiously over the side of the cayuco. He could only see the mass of greenery that grew down to the edge and even into the water of the river.

Katia whispered, "Grab a branch and pull us next to the bank."

John caught hold of a branch, and La Raspa paddled against the water. In a moment, they were hidden under the enveloping limbs of a huge-leaved guanacaste tree, whose branches occasionally dipped down into the river.

After a moment Katia said, "It was like somebody stuck a live electric wire in my stomach. Usually a feeling like that means someone is trying to—to do harm to me."

John was puzzled that Katia would have such a feeling when his own feelings had been so relaxed. "You're—you're sure about your feelings?"

"Sometimes they don't mean anything, but the last time was when I got in the ambulance instead of going with you in Managua—I thought it was just jealousy—and look what happened when I ignored it."

John said, "Then we better get off the river! We—" He stopped talking. Just beginning to register over the normal quiet sounds of a night along the river was a pulsing in the distance.

Katia cried, "There's a boat coming down the river! Let's go!"

John objected. "I think we ought to get off the river. Isn't there a trail or road we can take to Tres Madres?"

La Raspa had already turned on the electrical switch and was pulling on the rope to start the engine. "Not from here! Jungle's too thick. A kilometer downriver there's a dock. We can get off the river there."

With La Raspa's next pull, the little engine sputtered into life and the cayuco lumbered out from under the branches of the tree and downriver.

Katia cried, "Open it up all the way!"

La Raspa fiddled with the controls. "I think this is all she's got."

The quiet pulsing, which at first had been barely noticeable, increased. John grabbed the oars and fitted them to the oarlocks and began to pull with all his strength to help move the heavy wooden boat more rapidly through the water. Katia, pistol in hand, watched the western approach intently.

After a few minutes, La Raspa said, "The dock I was telling you about is right around this bend."

John whispered between pulls on the oars, "How far to Tres Madres?"

"By river about an hour. Over the trail and on foot, maybe three hours."

At that moment the boat rounded a distant bend. An oval of light, originating from a searchlight on the bow, swept across the darkly gleaming and rippled surface of the water.

Katia called, "Chohnee! Can you shoot the light out from here?"

"I don't want to call attention to ourselves."

La Raspa called, "Chohnee! Comin' into the dock. You ready?"

John stood in the narrow boat. As it eased against the pilings, John grabbed the rope fastened to the bow of the craft and leaped onto the platform. After a couple of swift hitches around a projecting post, he reached down to help Katia onto the dock. La Raspa scrambled up behind them as the boat came into view. The cayuco was first illumined by the beam of light. Then the shaft of light moved up and stabbed toward where they ran along the wooden decking. For a brief moment, all three of them cast dark shadows on the wall of jungle trees and bushes.

There was a chattering roar of rifle fire, and then leaves around them began to disintegrate. John jerked on Katia's arm and pulled her to the ground and out of the circle of light. La Raspa crawled behind them in a desperate scrabble for the covering of ferns and shrubbery that was the beginning of the jungle.

John whispered, "Where's the trail?"

La Raspa pointed silently to a space some ten meters to the south and beyond the end of the dock.

They could not get past the brilliant beam of light, moving rapidly back and forth along the wall of greenery, without being seen. John said, "We've got to get rid of that light. They've seen us anyway."

John sprawled out in the prone position. The pistol's sight traced smoothly across the lighted orb. He whispered, "Be ready to head for the trail when the light goes out."

The searchlight reached the zenith of its rise, and as it descended, it dropped into the range of the pistol sight. The light shattered in explosion. Under the cover of the sudden darkness, John urged, "La Raspa, you know the way! Lead out!"

They had not proceeded along the trail for more than twenty meters when Katia suddenly called, "Chohnee! La Raspa! Stop! Look!"

The jungle at the side of the trail was mashed and broken. In the faint light of the moon, the tracks of a wheeled vehicle could be seen. It seemed obvious that a jeep or similar vehicle had turned around in that spot. Freshly broken and bruised jungle plants evidenced that the vehicle had forced its way along the path very recently.

The sounds of a boat being moored came from the dock. Then a voice spoke in command. "Sergeant, you stay and guard the boat. The rest of you come with me!" Heavy steps clumped across the wooden dock. In another moment, the voice said, "They must have headed out on that trail."

Katia said, "We've got to find a place to take them by surprise."

John answered tersely, "I don't know how many there are, but I *can* tell that there are too many for us to attack them."

Katia argued, "We can't expect to outrun them for three hours, especially when the jungle gives way to an open road."

At that point there was a slight natural opening of the jungle at the side of the trail. The light of the moon filtered down into a small, nearly circular area that had a floor of heavy ferns.

Katia said, "I'm not going to try to outrun them. I'll fight if I have to!"

Without another word, Katia dropped to the ground and began to force herself backward into the opening between two large trees. In a moment there was no sight of Katia from the trail. John dropped to the ground and felt the bushes and thorns digging into his skin. La Raspa backed into the same area, brushing over the disturbed ground with a branch he had cut.

John's pistol was ready and aimed at the trail. Grimy sweat poured from his face. He wondered if it was possible for anyone to pass by in the quiet of the surrounding jungle without hearing the thundering beating of his heart.

Not more than two minutes had passed when the trail was filled with pursuers. First came Commander Martanza, fierce anger written all over his face, armed only with a pistol. He was followed closely by six uniformed soldiers, all armed with repeating rifles.

Martanza pointed to the small clearing and ordered, "One of you search to see if they've hidden in there! The rest of you hurry up!"

One soldier stomped around the little clearing and briefly looked behind a couple of huge trees, then headed, on a trot, along the main trail.

Katia scrambled from her hiding place and whispered, "Back to the boat! There's only one man on guard."

At the dock, John peered out of the jungle to see a soldier in the pilot's seat, foot propped casually on the control board, rifle close at hand.

John said, "We need to get him out from behind that windscreen. It could be bulletproof."

La Raspa said, "No. I'll go in the river and come up behind the boat. Bring my shoes, por favor."

Then he was a fleeting shadow along the wall of jungle. John did not see or hear when La Raspa entered the water, but suddenly his ugly face, revealed in a gleam of moonlight, appeared above the railing, quietly dripping water. The guard must have heard something, for he rose partway up from his seat, but one foot tangled briefly with the steering wheel of the small boat. La Raspa came over the railing in a gliding movement. His bare feet had not struck the deck when the knife leaped into his hand. The knife glittered briefly in the pale moonlight. John was relieved when La Raspa only used the knife handle as a club. The man fell in a senseless heap to the deck.

Katia clambered aboard the boat. She and La Raspa dumped the unconscious soldier on the dock.

John ran to the control panel and called, "La Raspa, cast off the mooring rope and let her drift into the river!" And pointing to the soldier's rifle that had fallen to the deck, he shouted, "Katia, keep an eye on the trail!"

Glancing at the panel, he muttered, "No key. I'll have to hot-wire it."

John lay on his back and looked under the panel. He began tracing the wires, trying to feel where the wires led from the keyed ignition slot. "La Raspa, let me borrow your knife."

He thought he would have preferred that the knife not be, at least for him, so cumbersome. He raised up and pointed to the chromed starter button. "Hold that down, and if the engine starts, let it loose."

John cut two wires and touched the bared ends together. There was a brief spark, and the lights on the sides and bow of the boat turned on. John grunted his disappointment and cut another wire.

Katia shouted, "They're coming back, Chohnee!"

Then the quiet of the night was shattered by a cracking blast from the rifle that Katia fired.

The boat had barely drifted a few feet from the dock. John called, "Katia get over here behind the windscreen, I think it's bulletproof!"

John fumbled to peel the insulation back from the wire he had just cut and touched the wires together again. The starter motor turned over, and John's heart leaped in an all too brief moment of gratitude.

A bullet ricocheted off the hardened plastic windshield. Katia answered with two shots of her own. John called to La Raspa, "Help Katia keep them pinned down."

John twisted the two wires together and then stood up and touched the starter button. The starter turned over in a grumbling moment of fright. He tried the starter again, and after another heart-stopping moment of silence, it ground out a few more slow turns, the last of which caused the engine to give a couple of coughs of blue smoke.

Katia crawled to his side and asked, "What's the matter?"

John said, "Nearly dead battery."

"You sure you hooked—"

A burst of rifle fire interrupted her words. The bullets again caromed harmlessly off the windscreen across the river and into the jungle. Katia rose up and fired a blistering round of bullets, which sent the soldiers running to the jungle for cover. John murmured a brief prayer, held his breath, and pushed the starter button once more. Two hesitant cranks answered his push, and just as he was going to release the button, another surge of electrical power entered the starter motor, cranking it around again. The engine coughed. As it coughed, it spun a little more freely. The motor cranked more rapidly, and suddenly the engine was running roughly in a hesitant backfiring cloud of blue smoke. With a final backfire, the engine sound smoothed out, and John shoved the gear into reverse.

From the edge of the jungle, Martanza raised a pistol and emptied its chamber of bullets, firing ineffectively at the people in the boat.

John shouted, "Keep down!"

When the boat was clear of the dock, John pushed the gear to a forward position and revved the engine.

Martanza dashed out onto the dock. Seeing the boat heading down river, he shouted to his troops, "We'll take the jeep parked out by the road!"

The boat moved out into the mainstream of the river. John glanced back at the dock and asked La Raspa, "How long will it take them to get to Tres Madres in a jeep?"

"I'm not sure. It'll be close. Open this thing up all the way!"

"Look around the boat and see if you can find any ammunition for that rifle." He handed Katia his pistol. "You should reload all the pistols."

A crash of breaking glass came from below the deck. In a minute, La Raspa poked his head out of the galley way. He carried two rifles and some small boxes in his hand. "We're in luck! There are rifles in a gun cabinet below, and here's a couple boxes of bullets."

John pointed to clusters of huts. "We getting close to the town?"

La Raspa answered, "Maybe fifteen minutes."

Katia said, "I still have the feeling that we're not safe by a long ways. I don't know if that means anything or not."

John throttled back on the engines. The roar dropped to a muffled rumble. "What's Tres Madres like, La Raspa? How big a town? Where do you suppose Valderas will have tied up his boat?"

"It's not really a town. There's only one street. *La Dorotea* draws too much water to get up the river. There's a big hacienda a few kilometers to the south by the lake. That's where I'm thinking Valderas will be tied up."

He paused for a moment and finished loading bullets in the last of the rifles. "If we have trouble, it will most likely be right as we go through the town. There are lots of places along the river to attack from."

Katia asked, "Do you think we could make the boat go on down the river without you guiding it, Chohnee?"

"I could tie the wheel. The throttle would stay where it's set."

La Raspa said in some excitement, "Around the next bend, the river straightens out and makes a straight shot to the lake. See that clump of trees? We could get off the boat there. If I remember right, there's some sugarcane fields that come almost down to the river by the trees."

John said, "Okay. How far to where you think Valderas will be?"

La Raspa hesitated. "Maybe six or eight kilometers."

John steered toward the clump of trees. "We'll have to have something to tie the wheel with."

Without hesitation La Raspa cut the rope that was used to anchor the boat to its moorings. The boat idled up to a tree trunk that hung in a low, saddle-like curve over the water. John handed La Raspa his pistol and kicked off the sandals he wore. "Cut this rope in half, and then you and Katia get the rifles to the shore."

Katia pulled the back, bottom hem of her rough brown skirt up between her legs and tucked it around and under the ammunition belt. Then, with her lithe brown legs bare to just above her knees, she jumped up on the tree trunk. Holding a branch, she reached down and took John's sandals and the rifles from La Raspa. As soon as La Raspa was on the tree trunk, John backed the boat away from the tree and guided it around the branches and into the mainstream of the river.

John cut the engine to idle while he tied the wheel. Then he shoved the throttle forward to half speed and ran to the back of the boat, poised for a moment, and dived over the railing into the river. With powerful strokes, John swam the hundred meters to the tree. La Raspa reached down with one hand to help him onto the trunk of the tree. John pulled himself up to sit in the cradle of the tree. He looked down the river and saw the boat they had used for less than an hour heading straight and true down the river. It was just approaching the first of the painted wooden buildings that lined the east side of the river.

Suddenly the boat was surrounded in a brilliant circle of light and seemed to sprout holes all along the side. A staccato roar of blasting rifle fire reached his ears. A huge plume of water erupted by the side of the boat, followed by the thunder of some larger weapon. Then the boat disintegrated in a shower of splintering wood. A flare of orange flame dimmed the light of the spotlight as the supply of gasoline in the boat added its roar of exploding sound to the night. Chills played along John's back as he watched the quiet water of the river fill with ripples made by the falling chunks of debris.

He and La Raspa clambered down the trunk of the tree. La Raspa handed a rifle to John and one to Katia, which they slung over their shoulders.

John said quietly to Katia, "But for the grace of God and a live electric wire in your stomach, that would have been the end of our story, Katia."

La Raspa was already leading the way along a slight break in the greenery that grew along the bank of the river. This narrow pathway opened into a sugarcane field, the long leaves drying in preparation of harvest. La Raspa called, "It's dangerous here because we have to go along the main road. We better hurry."

They raced along furrows at the edge of the field.

John's brief swim had refreshed him slightly. Now, running through several acres of browning sugarcane, and with sweat beginning to pour again from his body, he was collecting another load of grime.

La Raspa struggled for breath. "Stay along the edge of the road. If you see lights or hear an engine, get off the road!"

John's feet pounded the hard gravel surface. He glanced up and saw that La Raspa was pointing to his right. There was a road that intersected with the one they traveled along. La Raspa disappeared around a turn. John paused, a stitching pain grabbing at his side, waiting for Katia to catch up to him. He did not want to get too far down the intersecting road without her knowing where they had gone. He stood, head bowed, dragging in heavy, painful breaths of air. Katia had slowed nearly to a walk. She was breathing in ragged gasps and had come within a few meters of John when suddenly an engine roared along the road and the twin beams of a car's headlights pierced the night and impaled them both in their brilliant light. The vehicle slammed to a stop.

John was just ready to jump to the edge of the road to bury himself in the weeds, when a voice called, "Stop right there!" As if to emphasize the command, a burst of automatic rifle fire sent sprays of bullets kicking up puffs of dirt at their feet. "Throw down the rifles!"

John's mind demanded that he try to escape, but his tired body would not respond to his commands. He unslung the rifle and let it drop to the ground. He slowly placed his hands on his head and stood in slumped resignation.

The voice ordered, "Kick the rifle farther away from you!"

John gave the rifle a kick so that it lay a couple of meters away, nearly in a depression at the side of the road.

Katia did not respond to the demand to put down her weapon, and another burst of bullets hit the ground and flung shattered, biting pieces of gravel at both John and Katia. She stood, breathing heavily, but defiance radiated from her being. Another burst of bullets came even closer. "The next shots will kill you, Dama Mariposa! Throw the rifle toward the jeep!" Finally she dropped the rifle a short distance from her feet.

The man that walked into the circle of light was David Solano. He wore the uniform of a Sandinista army officer and held a pistol in his hand. "Well, Katia. I was just returning to Managua. I grieved because I supposed you had been killed in the destruction of the boat in Tres Madres. I'm glad to see you're still alive."

She looked at him in contempt. "So it has come to this, Judas! Thank you for the visit to El Chipote!"

David flushed in anger. "I did it for your own good! I did it to let you know what faces you if you don't stop fighting the Sandinistas!"

"Oh, then thank you! My friend and I will leave now." She turned to walk away.

"Katia, don't make me hurt you! Come peacefully. I promise—"

She spun back. "You promise what? No more than two years in Hades? I promise you, David *Judas* Solano—free me now, or you are a dead man!"

John noted movement on the road and outside the circle of light from the jeep. La Raspa crawled along the depression at the side of the road. Beads of sweat along his bare back glistened in the pale moonlight. With Katia's words, John knew that La Raspa had Katia's permission to do what he had only hesitated doing before. John gauged how far his rifle lay from his feet. It was too far away. But he still had the pistol in the waistband of his pants.

David Solano turned slightly toward the lights of the jeep and called, "Sergeant, come over here and search them for weapons."

As the sergeant got out of the jeep, La Raspa opened fire. The bullets clanged and ricocheted around the interior of the engine block of the jeep. The headlights of the jeep flickered out. Suddenly, a person in the front seat of the jeep jumped out and started to run, screaming, "What's happening, David? I only came—"

The soldier by the jeep opened fire with his automatic rifle. The bullets from his rifle struck the figure that ran from the jeep. The figure jerked and moved spastically for a moment and then collapsed in a heap at the soldier's feet. Without even looking at the body, the soldier continued his fire at Katia.

In almost simultaneous motion, John dove for the roadside, and Katia for her rifle. Katia, in a neat tuck, rolled over her rifle, clutched it in one hand, and rolled on over to the side of the road. John continued his roll into a prone position by his rifle.

But before either of them could fire, the last of the bullets in La Raspa's rifle found a mark, and the soldier spun and smashed against the side of the jeep. His body dropped, slumping and landing awkwardly, motionless in the dust of the road.

Solano stood in motionless fear. La Raspa charged, knife gleaming in his right hand, hair flying wildly, eyes lighted in demoniacal anger.

Katia screamed, "No, La Raspa! No!"

But La Raspa did not hear her words. Solano began firing his pistol at him. He was hit. And hit again. But he did not stop his forward movement. His legs drove him forward, and he seemed to only hesitate momentarily each time another bullet smashed into his small body. Sheer willpower drove him forward until his arms wrapped around the startled and frightened David Solano. Almost within the circle of the grasp of La Raspa's arms, Solano fired his pistol into the chest of the attacking man. The knife gleamed in a slash revealed by the pale light of the moon. It took less than a second for the sharp knife to do its horrible work.

The small but mighty La Raspa died at the same time David Solano did. With their arms still wrapped in deadly embrace, both men slumped and then twisted and spun to the ground in a grotesque flourish. Upon impact with the hard, graveled road, La Raspa's arm flung free, and he rolled away from the unmoving body of David Solano. La Raspa's arms stretched outward on the ground. One hand still held the bloody knife. One foot was tucked neatly over the other as in relaxed repose, and his sightless eyes stared unblinkingly at the waning moon.

John and Katia cautiously stood then walked to the unmoving bodies by the jeep. John rolled the body of the soldier over, and then he pushed at the body of the person who had sat in the jeep until the last moment.

John realized that the person was the once-beautiful Nita Delgado. A churning, acrid burning filled his throat and he retched.

Katia dropped to her knees by David's body. Her body shook with her sobs. Tears streamed from her eyes. She knelt by his side, motionless except for her sobbing. Finally the crying ebbed, and she brushed her hands over her brother's hair. Her words were just a murmur. "I would not have killed you, David. I would not have killed you."

Once again she stroked his hair and touched his silent face. She murmured, "He looks like . . . like an angel again . . . just as he did as a young boy." She burst into tears again and sat weeping by the unmoving body.

John bent and touched her shoulder. He wondered what to do. They had to get away from this terrible spot. And yet how could he—what could he do?

After a moment, Katia looked up at John. There was pleading in her eyes. "I loved him—and I hated him. No, I hated that he would not understand how important freedom is for Nicaragua." She sobbed for another moment. "How will I tell Papa? Oh, David, how will I tell Papa?"

"I'm sorry, Katia, but we have to—we have to get away from here."

Then Katia rose and looked at La Raspa, stroked his wild hair back, and pushed the lids of his eyes closed. "Such unnecessary death. How can—he—he was a patriot of Nicaragua. He gave his life for freedom." She looked up at John, and beginning to sob again, she said, "And he died without me ever telling him how much I appreciated him helping get me out of El Chipote."

As John lifted her from her kneeling position to force her away from the terrible scene, he wondered, *Is that what patriotism is? Have all men who have died for their countries all over the world done so as La Raspa? Died with only a half-formed idea of freedom? Died because of loyalty not so much to a cause as to the people who lead them in that cause?* He did not speak his thoughts aloud. *La Raspa died because he was totally loyal and dedicated to you, Katia. He would have followed you into the devil's throat, and done that willingly, but I don't know if he knew what freedom was all about.*

Aloud, he said with a catch in his voice, "We owe our lives to him, Katia. He was, in his way, a great man." Then he whispered, "I salute you, *Guillermo*, whoever you were. I salute you and commend you to God." John then bowed his head and continued in a slightly louder whisper, "Heavenly Father, please accept this very brave man, and give rest to his soul."

A crackle from the jeep's radio interrupted his prayer. The noise galvanized them both into action. John dashed to the radio and flicked the switch. "Go ahead."

"This is Martanza. Get Solano on the radio."

"Captain Solano can't talk right now. Can I give him a message?"

"There are no signs of bodies anywhere around the wreckage of the boat. It looks like the wheel was tied in place, and the boat empty." Martanza paused and then said, "Solano reported he was on the way—who's this on the radio? Give me your location. Who speaks?"

John flicked the switch, turning the radio off, and called, "Get in, Katia! We've got to get out of here!" He turned the ignition key, and there wasn't even a click.

He jumped out and thrust up the hood of the jeep. The bullets that La Raspa had fired had done the damage. Katia dashed to his side and stared at the interior of the engine space. Wires had been severed and the distributor cap had been smashed to bits.

"We'll head down the road La Raspa started on!"

He had barely started running when an idea occurred to him. He turned and ran back to where the soldier lay at the side of the jeep. "Go ahead, Katia. Run! I'll be with you in a minute!"

"What are you doing?"

"Please, Katia, head down the road for a little ways and wait for me."

John stripped off the shirt, pants and boots of the soldier. Then he took off the ragged pants he wore and struggled into the too-small pants he had taken from the soldier's body. Next, he put his ragged pants on the dead soldier and dragged the body to place it close to the body of La Raspa.

The soldier's boots were too small for him, so he dropped them to the ground by the dead soldier's feet. They spoiled the effect for which he tried, but he could never walk, let alone run, along the graveled road without something to protect his feet. He picked up the body of Nita Delgado and placed it not too far from that of the soldier and La Raspa. He looked at the arrangement for a moment, picked up the boots of the soldier, and ran down the road to catch up with Katia.

They ran for ten minutes, and John panted. "I've got to rest."

They stumbled to the side of the road and flopped down in the depression. The rumble of an internal combustion engine forced John to sit up and look for a place to hide. The road at this point passed by a large field of coffee bean trees. They staggered into the trees and again dropped to the ground to rest.

Several minutes passed, and it was clear from the slow approach of the headlights that whoever drove was not in a hurry. Soon they could see the headlights of a battered old pickup truck. There were two people in the back of the truck. Both carried rifles. The light was poor, and it was hard to see. But as the truck drove slowly by, the driver poked his head out the window. Just the slightest flash of moonlight on an emblem worn on the man's cap caught John's eye. The emblem was a chromed hawk.

John scrambled up from his cover and ran to the road, shouting, "Halcón! Halcón! It's us!" Then he recognized Mario staring and raising his rifle to fire. Pablo scrambled to the side of the pickup at the same time. "Mario! Pablo! Don't shoot! It's me, Juan Tanner!"

Katia ran from the coffee trees, and Pablo jumped out the back of the truck before it came to a squeaking stop. He caught Katia in a swooping embrace. He spun her around. "You made it! You made it!" He allowed Katia's feet to return to the ground, and his eyes dropped in some embarrassment. He stepped back for a moment and then looked up and asked anxiously, "Where's La Raspa?"

Tears welled in Katia's eyes. "La Raspa didn't make it, Pablo."

"You didn't—did he get out of El Chipote?"

"Yes. He—he made it to just about here. He saved Chohnee and me."

Tears formed in Pablo's eyes. "As long as you didn't leave him in that awful place. He didn't ever—he told me once he would cut his own throat before they could ever drag him back there."

Katia asked, "How did you know—"

Pablo interrupted. "We didn't *know* anything. We were just going to investigate a big explosion in the village of Tres Madres."

* * *

Commander Martanza got out of the jeep. He looked at the scene of destruction and at the two men in cut-off uniform pants. He walked to the jeep and came back with the ends of two pairs of uniform pant legs. He stood over the body of La Raspa for a moment and then dropped the ragged cloth on the bare legs. He stared at him and then felt the spot on his neck that still stung when sweat beaded up on his skin. The position of the nearly naked body, dotted with bloody wounds, lying on the white gravel, bothered him. He kicked the body. It seemed that La Raspa stubbornly refused to part with his knife. A chill traveled along Martanza's back. There was something frightening about the stubborn defiance of the little man, even in death. He did not look at the man again.

Next he stood and stared in puzzlement at the other body wearing ragged pants, clearly too big for him and with no shoes or boots. After a time, he bent down to examine the body of the woman with the severely damaged face. He realized the woman was Nita Delgado.

He walked back to his jeep and said to the driver, "Go back to Tres Madres and tell them we need a truck to haul these bodies back to Managua."

The driver asked, "Why drive back? I could call on the radio—"

Martanza pulled out his pistol and thundered, "I gave you an order! You going to obey, or do I shoot you on the spot?"

The driver with shaky voice said, "Yes, sir!" Hands shaking, he started the engine and turned around and headed back to Tres Madres.

As soon as the jeep was out of sight, Martanza picked up a handful of dirt and rubbed it all over the feet of the soldier. He searched through the clothing of the dead girl, removing anything that might provide identification. He removed a pair of rings from the pierced ears. She wore a ring on her finger, which he removed. Then he looked in distaste at the dead girl's unrecogniz-able face. Next he walked to the disabled jeep and found a small hand-clutch purse that clearly belonged to Nita Delgado. He put the purse in his pocket and tried the radio. It still worked. He spoke to his headquarters. "This is Commander Martanza. I'm calling to report that I have just found the people who escaped from El Chipote. All three of them are dead, apparently killed by Captain Solano, who also died in the action. One of the prisoners is female, and I am sure she is the notorious Dama Mariposa. The search can be called off. My record is still clear. No one has ever escaped from El Chipote alive. Over and out."

He surveyed his work for a moment. If he could get the body of Nita Delgado disposed of quickly enough, it was prob-able that no one would question that these bodies were those he said they were. There was no doubt who the little one was. The body still bore the scars that he himself had inflicted.

* * *

On the boat, Valderas, despite having his leg in splints, jumped up and hugged Katia. He gave orders for the boat to head to San Carlos.

He said of La Raspa, "He was a true patriot."

There seemed to John something terribly unfair in the casual dismissal of the loss of this small man in his own quest for honor in life.

Valderas called for a celebration. "Chohnee, you can either drink wine or water. There's no orange soda."

Montenegro's message came an hour out of the port near Tres Madres. He said it was reported that in an attempt to free Dama Mariposa from El Chipote, three members of an El Cinco assault team had been killed. One was unknown, but one was the criminal often called La Raspa, and the other was the infamous Dama Mariposa.

Valderas hesitated about telling Montenegro the truth, worried that the radio conversation might be intercepted. He could think of no way to let Montenegro know that the report was two-thirds false. Montenegro would have to suffer in ignorance until he could be told the truth.

Montenegro said, "I heard that Miguel has given up on the revolution and is doing other things—I'm thinking maybe he's gone into the arms business. As a matter of fact, he was inquiring into how to get in touch with Adnan Ahman recently. Anyway, with you injured and Dama gone, we'll suspend operations for a while."

Valderas said, "Things aren't as bleak as you paint them. I—"

Montenegro interrupted. "Three months minimum! Over and out."

The news dampened the celebration. Valderas led them all in a toast. "To freedom for Nicaragua."

After the toast, he said, "My leg hurts. Soon as I get to Hacienda Medina, I'll take my boat to Limón and get a doctor to look at it."

John said, "I've got some business in Limón, myself. Can I . . ."

"Si. Matter of fact, Chohnee, you should take Katia with you. It'd be a good idea for both of you to stay out of Nicaragua for a while."

Valderas concluded the evening by hugging Katia again and saying, "I'm glad I didn't have to hear Montenegro's report before you got here. If it had been true . . ." he bowed his head briefly, "I'd have died myself. Good night, mi hija." He called Katia his daughter.

CHAPTER SIXTEEN

PAUL GENTRY HAD AT FIRST refused to send the directive, even with Senator Chandler's instructions. He had been the first to pull the file on John Tanner. Tanner's eyes seemed to peer out of the identification photo with an intense concentration that stirred deeply in Gentry's soul. The information on John Tanner could have been duplicated in the files of thousands of other men who were in the service of the United States of America. Tanner was sharp, a college graduate, a dedicated citizen who had served a couple of years in the army after Vietnam. He was an above-average operator and had recently been recommended to take over the Costa Rica Station. So what had he done wrong? What thing had earned him the enmity of William Andrew Morgan, one of the most powerful behind-the-scenes figures in Washington, D.C.? Tanner's only fault seemed to have been that he had refused to cooperate in the destruction of one of his own agents.

Finally, Gentry capitulated. But he insisted the directive have Chandler's signature as well as his own. And he would not order Tanner's death, except in the circumstance that he resisted arrest.

Receipt of the Gentry directive at the station in Costa Rica seemed to have been the electrical impulse that set off a keg of explosive activity. Hardesty had been shot trying to capture the elusive Dama Mariposa. A newly assigned operator by the name of Brown had disappeared. Tanner had been placed under house arrest by the wounded Hardesty. The station secretary had given Tanner a large amount of Company money. Tanner had escaped in a Company boat, which he then abandoned on the Rio San Juan.

It had been seven days and nights since the directive was sent, and Gentry found his concentration often interrupted in thinking of its consequences. Gentry had not slept for more than snatches in all those seven nights. If he did sleep, the penetrating eyes of John Tanner accused him. He had found John Tanner guilty on the basis of accusations alone and without a trial.

During one sleepless night, he discovered a man, in a frozen moment of time, etched into the pattern of the skip-troweled plaster ceiling of his bedroom. The man was running. Not just running, but stretched out in the desperate, gasping strides of a man fleeing death. His swollen tongue hung out of his mouth in his final effort at escape.

By the seventh night, the man in the ceiling had become John Tanner. Gentry finally realized that Tanner would not let him rest until he had rescinded the directive sent to the Costa Rica Station. And if he rescinded the directive, Morgan would reveal his Da Nang indiscretion. And though fellow officers might snicker, the only one who would really be hurt was Anne.

Anne lay quietly asleep. He rose up on his side and watched her. She breathed gently, one arm curled back over her pillow, her dark hair framing her strong face. She had always kept her emotions in strict control. He had never doubted her fidelity to him. They had never discussed loyalty, but he had always known he could depend on her. And, except for Da Nang, he had never given her cause to question his loyalty in return. He wondered what she would do when she found out. Would she, keeping tight rein on her emotions, just walk away?

He got out of bed, plush carpeting enveloping his bare feet, and walked to the drapery that cascaded down, covering the window. He pulled the heavy cloth to the side and stared into the quiet Virginia night. The half-moon and the stars made the night bright. Jagged, five-fingered leaves of huge Norwegian maple trees danced quietly in the night breeze. Some, colored in brilliant oranges and reds, danced a final pirouette to the ground.

He did not hear Anne approach and started slightly as she placed her arms around him. She asked, "Can you talk about it?"

"In all my military and professional life, I've tried to act in the best interests of the country, never doing things for personal reasons."

He felt her head nod in affirmation against his back. "It must be serious to keep you awake for seven nights."

"I'm sorry. I didn't know I was disturbing you." He took her hand and led her back to the bed. She lay quietly on his arm, her hand idly tracing the ridges of a scar on his chest. "Have you ever noticed the man staring at us from the ceiling?"

She smiled. "Sometimes I get tired just watching him struggle across that hurdle with his tongue hanging out and gasping for breath."

"If you've seen him too, you've had a few sleepless nights of your own."

"Only when you are in some dangerous part of the world doing heaven only knows what."

Paul took another deep breath. "His name is John Tanner— and I've violated my personal code of ethics—done him a great disservice."

"And that disservice has kept you awake for the past week?"

"Yes. I'm going to Costa Rica to try to set things right. I'm not proud of what I did and am ashamed of why I did it—and when I straighten it out . . ." Paul held her close for a moment. "I've always loved only you—but when I was in Da Nang— there was . . ."

"I know about Da Nang, at least all I want to know about it."

"How do you know about Da Nang?"

Her hand again traced the ridges of the scar. "You never told me about this scar on your chest, and I didn't ever want to know because I know all I *need* to know from your nightmares." She leaned up on an elbow and looked into his eyes. "Did you think I wouldn't sense your withdrawal in the letters that came to me from Da Nang? But then you came back, and I knew you loved me—only me. It would make as much sense to open this scar on your chest as to open the wound in either of our hearts. Vietnam was a terrible part of your life that happened ten, no, a million years ago. I couldn't share then and see no reason to share now, unless for some reason it should fester and need to be opened to drain." Her words were spoken slowly and with emphasis. "I don't need to know anything more about Da Nang. So if what you need to do in Costa Rica is affected in any way by me knowing about Da Nang, you *do* what you *must* do."

This was one of very few times in Paul Gentry's adult memory that tears came into his eyes. He whispered, "Forgive me."

"For Da Nang? I . . ."

"No. I can tell you forgave me for Da Nang years ago. Forgive me for not trusting your loyalty to me."

She placed her hands on his face and kissed him long and gently. After a time she said, "Mother could stay with the kids for a few days. Would it be dangerous for me to go to Costa Rica with you?"

He only hesitated for a moment. "Not the part I'm—we're going to. Costa Rica is a beautiful country. You'll like it."

* * *

Two hours out of the port near Tres Madres, a Soviet-made helicopter equipped with a searchlight dropped out of the dark skies. The bull, Magnanimo, bellowed and shook his horns angrily. Mario, sleeping on the deck, dashed to the makeshift pen and talked in soothing tones to the bull. After a couple of minutes, the observers in the helicopter were apparently satisfied, for the searchlights turned off, plunging the boat into darkness.

In San Carlos, Katia accompanied John to transact his Boquis business, and then they drove to Katia's parents' home. Katia told them of the death of their son, David. She spoke as if she had heard a secondhand report.

Eduardo Solano took the news stoically. "David died when he joined the communist Sandinistas. I'm sorry he got caught up in their godless thinking."

"What about—about his burial service, Papa?"

Despite the tears in Eduardo Solano's eyes, his words were hard. "It will be a communist military affair. Conducted without God, and without me."

Then he crossed himself and said, "I will talk to Father Gallego and see if we can have a small and private service to try to remember what a good—how much we loved him when he was small."

Señora Solano crossed herself and wept.

"I know this is a bad time for you and Mama, but I have to go to Costa Rica. I can't explain . . ."

Eduardo Solano placed his arms around his daughter. "You don't have to explain, my daughter. It's not something we've needed to discuss, but I have known, and approve, of what you do." He paused and looked briefly at John. "If Chohnee is—I think he is a good man." He paused again. "I've never interfered in your life and won't now. God's blessings go with you."

Señora Solano said with tears streaming down her face, "If Papa won't say what should be said, I will. Katia, it is time for you to leave the revolution to others. I'm presumptuous—I know. Nevertheless, Chohnee is a good and honorable man. You should get . . ."

Eduardo Solano interrupted. "No, Mama. We have both said too much now. Katia will do what she knows she must do. Adios, mi hija."

Katia blushed deeply. Then she kissed her parents and told them she would see them as soon as it seemed safe for her to return to Nicaragua.

Downriver they unloaded Magnanimo at Hacienda Medina. John had decided he did not want an arrest warrant hanging over the rest of his life. He contacted Omar by the call signal he had given him. He told Omar they would arrive at Limón around ten o'clock that night. Omar said that Hardesty was better, and, though he was not back on full-time duty, he was in Limón. The Wagoneer would be available for John's use.

"Please call the Hotel Las Olas and see if you can get a couple of rooms for Katia Solano and me." John still felt a nagging concern for Katia's safety. This would make it easier to protect her.

Omar said that Hardesty would be in the office the next morning at nine. Someone important had arrived from the States. Omar didn't seem to want to talk about it, and John wasn't sure who it was.

In Limón, Valderas told Pablo to stay on the boat, but Pablo would not leave Katia in John's care. He said, "I'll get a room at the same hotel."

"It's too late to get a room. And I need you—"

"Halcón will stay with you. If I have to camp out at the hotel, I'll do it. I'm not leaving Dama—"

Valderas thundered, "Pablo, I'm giving you an order, and you better get it through your head. I mean it! Dama Mariposa was killed trying to escape from El Chipote." He carefully enunciated each of the next words he spoke. "Dama Mariposa is *dead!* And don't you forget it!"

Pablo did not give way to Valderas's angry attack. "All right. Then I'm not leaving *Katia* alone until I'm sure she's safe, and *you* just as well must get *that* through *your* head!"

"All danger to Katia died with the death of Dama Mariposa!"
But Valderas's bellow was futile. Pablo spun around and left
him spluttering angrily.

* * *

It was after eleven when John and Katia checked into the
Hotel Las Olas. They did get a room for Pablo, who made a
thorough search of the rooms Katia and John would occupy. He
said, "I'll be out here in the hall. You can sleep without concern
tonight, Da—Katia. Buenas noches."

Katia touched him on the arm. "You should just go to bed
too, Pablo. There isn't anything to fear in Costa Rica. I have no
enemies here."

Pablo said firmly, "I'll be right outside your door in the hall,
but lock it anyway." He walked out, shutting the door carefully.

John paused at Katia's door. "There is so much we need to
talk about, Katia. I . . ."

"It's true, Chohnee, but I'm exhausted. I hardly slept in El
Chipote, and but very little since then. We'll talk tomorrow."

Katia kissed him lightly and then looked deeply into his
eyes. "I love you—but I need—I feel that we need—I don't
know how to say it. I've done things to fight the revolution . . .
while I was in El Chipote, I thought a lot about the book you
gave me. I read most of it before—and I—I have many questions, but I'm too tired tonight, Chohnee. And I know it's
important to you for me to belong to your church—but there's
so much I don't know. We'll talk tomorrow. I promise."

"All right. Good night."

"Good night, Chohnee," Katia said with a tired smile.

Despite Katia's assurance to Pablo that she had no enemies in
Costa Rica, she placed the pistol taken from Martanza in El
Chipote under her pillow. Perhaps it was this or perhaps it was
Pablo's persistence in standing guard in the hallway that made John

feel apprehensive. He put his silenced pistol on the nightstand by the lamp, then lay on the bed fully clothed. In John's fragmented dreams, Commander Martanza's face alternated with the grotesque, bullet-pierced crucifix made by La Raspa's unmoving body on the white gravel roadway near Tres Madres. He tossed and dozed and jerked into heart-thudding wakefulness.

On this night, the ebb and flow of the Caribbean Sea under the hotel grated on his nerves. He told himself that with Pablo keeping watch in the hallway, he and Katia were safe. This thought brought him lurching out of the bed, and he jerked open the door leading to the hall. Pablo looked up in questioning surprise, a pistol leaping into his hand. The two men stood facing each other.

Finally John said, "Just checking." Then, lest Pablo take offense, he mumbled, "I—ah—I didn't mean I was checking on you. I meant I was checking . . ." His words died on his lips. There was nothing plausible to say he was checking on.

"I don't mind you checking on me, Chohnee, but you can go to sleep. You keep her safe in the daytime. I'll keep her safe at night. Buenas noches, mi amigo."

John checked Katia's door one last time to make sure it was locked. Then he returned to his room and pulled an upholstered chair close to the bed. He plumped a pillow in the chair and slumped down, his legs stretched out on the bed, pistol in hand.

As he slept, he dreamed that a heavy rope dropped down over the overhanging roof of the hotel and landed on the small balcony open to the sea. A man came sliding down the rope and landed on the balcony. In a spinning kick, the man's foot crashed through the glass of the door that led to the balcony. The breaking of glass reverberated in his dream-filled mind. Even in his sleep, he knew that he must wake up. Yet he felt like his mind and body were drugged. He could not raise his head from the pillow. Finally, in a frenzied, convulsive jerk, he forced himself awake. His heart pounded in heavy beats, and his mind was a confusion of thought. He looked frantically around the room. The drapery stirred slightly from the partially opened window. He heard a thump against the wall next to Katia's room. *This isn't a dream!* John's mind bellowed.

He jerked from the bed and stumbled to his feet, pistol in hand. In three strides he grabbed the sliding door handle and nearly pulled it from its track in opening it. On his balcony he could see that the sliding door to Katia's room was partly open. He made an irrational running leap across the narrow space separating the balconies. Miraculously he landed on his feet in front of the uncurtained sliding glass door—or what was left of it. Shards of glass were spread across the balcony cement and carpet in the room. John dashed into the room and saw Katia lying in an unmoving heap a few feet from her bed. The wooden nightstand was broken. Her gun was in her hand. A stain of bright red blood was beginning to cover the front of her shirt and spread down over her pants. There was a tear in the drapery that billowed out of one section of the shattered patio glass door. A final shard of glass fell to the floor in a brittle shatter.

A sudden sound caused John to twist in defense. A heavy boot swung out and crashed against his hand, sending the gun sailing through the broken patio door to land against the concrete wall of the patio.

John looked into the cold gray eyes of the ugly Fiero Rinskin, who aimed a silenced pistol at John's head. John arched his back against the wall and lashed out in a vicious kick with the point of a cowboy boot at Rinskin's knee. Rinskin's aim was distorted, and John felt a searing burn across his cheek as a silent bullet careened off the floor and smashed into the wall.

Rinskin dropped to one knee and turned the gun to fire again. Flame traced along John's arm. John spun and in another looping kick drove the pistol from the meaty hand. Rinskin charged, outstretched arms ready to encircle and crush his enemy. John dropped on his back to the floor, his legs curled against his body like a spring. As the heavy body lumbered over him, his legs uncoiled and kicked up and over. Rinskin's huge carcass crashed upside down against the masonry division wall, and then the grizzled head dropped to the floor.

The sequence of action was to John a surrealistic dream. The unmoving, red-stained body of Katia floated in his vision. As from a distance, he heard his own desperate voice shouting, "Pablo! Get in here! Pablo!"

John's eyes, frantically searching the room for a means of defense, could only see the gun in the unmoving hand of Katia. He struggled to his feet.

Rinskin rolled across his massive shoulder, down and forward, and got his feet under his body. John had barely taken one step when a huge hand encircled his boot, and he was jerked from his feet. Rinskin, in that same awkward twisting movement, spun around, and his booted foot thumped into John's stomach. John flew back against the wall and slumped forward onto his knees. The room spun dizzily in a red haze. John fought his agonized body for breath. Rinskin lumbered to where Katia still had not moved. He reached down and took the pistol from her hand. He straightened and glanced at John, now struggling to his feet. In slow motion, the pistol was raised and aimed for Katia's head.

Screaming, John launched his body at Rinskin. With driving steps, his body shot out like a spear, driving himself into Rinskin's lower abdomen. John's arms lashed around the large body, and he continued to surge forward. John heard the roar of a pistol, and a burn like a hot knife slashed down his back. Rinskin's feet scrabbled against the carpeted floor as he tried to regain his footing. John continued to drive forward, and he momentarily felt the softness of the drapery covering the patio glass that was still intact. Almost instantly he heard the sound of shattering glass as their two bodies smashed through the patio door. The drapery was ripped from the rings that held it in place and dropped around the two struggling bodies as a shroud.

The pistol roared again, and John felt another slash of pain along the back of a leg. His forward momentum stopped as he jammed the body of Rinskin against the concrete railing. In one final surge of fury, John tried to smash the man against the concrete railing. At just that moment, Rinskin's foot, still churning to gain traction, struck against a chair on the balcony. He pushed back against John's exertions and was lifted slightly. With John's final surge, Rinskin toppled over the balcony, catching the top of the wall with one hand. The maroon-colored drapery slid off Rinskin and drifted to the sea below. One hand, which would have provided leverage to pull himself to the balcony, still held the pistol. The muscles in Rinskin's huge arm bulged as he strained to lift his bulky body above the concrete balcony railing. He shoved the pistol over the balcony edge for just a moment. The roar of the pistol echoed in John's ears. The bullet caromed harmlessly off the masonry division wall. Slowly, the hand slid from the ledge and dropped over the side of the balcony. The body of Fiero Rinskin fell in an arching turn.

John watched the body twist in the air and then drop in a perfect swan dive. In his still surrealistic thought, John supposed it was the only graceful move of the ugly man's life.

John staggered to where Katia lay. He ignored the people who burst in the door and gently took her arm to feel for a pulse. As he did, her eyelids fluttered for a moment, and she murmured weakly, "Chohnee? What happened?"

Pablo, pushing people out of his way, ran across the room and dropped on his knees at John and Katia's side. "Is she all right, Chohnee?"

"I'm not sure—looks like she was hit in the stomach." John looked up and saw the night clerk standing there. "Get an ambulance and call the police! The man who attacked her fell over the balcony. Don't let him get away!"

A vaguely familiar voice called from the hall. "Don't worry. He won't be going anywhere."

Katia struggled to get up. John held her in his arms and murmured, "Don't move, Katia. Please don't move. We'll get an ambulance and take you to the hospital."

Katia struggled weakly. "Listen to me! I don't need an ambulance! I do need to see a doctor. I can move my arms and my legs. It doesn't even hurt bad in my stomach unless I move. You and Pablo can get me to the doctor a lot quicker than waiting around for an ambulance. Please, Chohnee?"

Pablo was already running out the door. He called back, "You need an ambulance, Katia. I'll call for an one right away."

As John and Katia waited for an ambulance, Katia said, "I don't know how he got in the room. I just looked up, and there Rinskin was with that sick smile, pointing his gun at me. I grabbed my gun and rolled out of the bed. His gun was silenced, but I think he shot three or four times, once hitting the bed where I had been lying, once breaking the patio glass. Before I could get turned to fire at him, a bullet hit me in the stomach. I think I crashed against the nightstand, and it knocked me out. The next thing I knew, you were holding me, crying."

John smiled. "I wasn't crying. Grown men don't cry."

Katia squeezed his hand. "They do when someone they love gets hurt."

* * *

John and Pablo waited outside the emergency room of the United Fruit Company Hospital for the doctor to complete his examination. John had asked himself a dozen times how Fiero Rinskin had gotten by Pablo.

Pablo spoke slowly and quietly. "I've been waiting for you to ask me how come I let you and Katia down."

"I don't think you let us down. I figured when you were ready to explain what happened on your end, you would."

"I didn't go to sleep while I was on guard duty, Chohnee. But I might as well have. I was played for a sucker."

John nodded his head. He still would not ask questions of the man whom he knew was fiercely loyal to Katia Solano.

"The night clerk knocked at the room where I was supposed to be staying. I asked him what he wanted. He said there was an urgent phone call from Valderas—"

John interrupted. "He said Valderas? He used Valderas's name?"

"Yes. I thought nobody knew Valderas was in Limón. I figured it was legitimate, so I went to the office. Somebody on the phone said Valderas and Halcón—"

John interrupted again. "They used Halcón's name, too?"

"Yes. Then I heard the first shot—and I knew I'd been had."

"If Rinskin hadn't had to use Katia's gun, you wouldn't have heard any shot. His gun and mine were silenced. Of course, I never got a shot off with mine anyway. It bothers me that he knew the names . . ."

"Maybe it bothers you half as much as it does me, Chohnee. I've been going over in my mind who knew we were coming and where we were staying. There's only one person—Omar. And till now I always trusted him."

John considered briefly that Francesca would also be a possibility. Had Omar told her where they were staying? He told Pablo of his thoughts.

Pablo was definite. "It wasn't Francesca. I think Omar will meet with a little accident in the next couple of days."

"Pablo, I know it looks bad for Omar. But there isn't any proof."

"What kind of proof you need, Chohnee? He's the only one—"

"That's the problem! He's not the only one. I made calls that were not—" Suddenly he thought, *Of course! The only one who had access to all my calls was Omar!*

The expression on John's face seemed to be all the evidence Pablo needed. John hastened to say, "He's still entitled to a hearing. He has the right to face his accuser! If freedom ever comes to Central America—"

"You waste your breath, Chohnee. I promise, he'll get a hearing, and he'll face his accuser. Me! Just before his accident."

"Pablo, you can't . . ." John's words died as he saw that there was no reasoning with Pablo. "I think you will do what you feel you must do whether I approve or not." After a moment he said, "I *would* like to know who he's been passing information to."

The doctor came from the emergency room. He said, "She lost some blood, but the bullet passed through and didn't hit a vital organ. She's young and healthy and can be up tomorrow." He looked more closely at John and traced the track of the bullet across John's face with a finger. Then his eyes dropped to the blood that had dried on the arm of his shirt. "You been in a war zone?"

When John didn't answer, the doctor said, "When they bring the patient to her room, you'd better have the nurse clean those wounds up a bit."

"Thanks. I'll do that."

As the doctor walked away, Pablo asked, "You going to stay with Katia?"

John nodded.

"Don't go out of her room for any reason. You got a gun with you?"

John simply nodded again. He briefly worried about Omar again, and then said, "Think twice about what you do, and be careful, Pablo."

Pablo didn't even look at him as he walked out of the hospital.

* * *

Katia's face lit in a brilliant smile as Valderas, Pablo, and Halcón walked into her hospital room. She was sitting up in the bed. With a big smile, Pablo handed her a huge bouquet of flowers. "The flowers are from all of us—but mostly me."

Katia held her arms up, and Pablo accepted a hug from her.

John watched from the chair in which he had spent the balance of the night.

Valderas did a stumping *zapatiado* around her bed. Standing on one foot, he showed the other encased in a cast. "I got me a new leg. The doc says it's a walking cast."

Katia held her arms out to embrace the older man. Tears were in his eyes, and his voice was husky. "Oh, Katia, Katia, I'm glad to see you're not hurt too bad. I've been crazy to let you do the things you been doing. I won't ever let you . . ."

Katia placed fingers over his lips. "We'll talk about that later, Valderas."

Halcón, with a shy smile, said, "It's good to see you. Uh— I'm glad you're okay."

It seemed clear that he couldn't bring himself to call her Katia, and he would never again be able to call her Dama Mariposa.

She held her arms out to him. He wouldn't step into the circle of her embrace. He caught one of her hands and kissed it. Katia said, "Halcón, I refuse to be addressed as 'hey you' or 'uh.' Practice my name. Say *Katia*."

Halcón gave another shy smile and said, "Thank goodness you're okay, Katia."

Katia said, "Most thanks go to Chohnee."

Valderas said, "Yes. Thanks to Chohnee. And that's why we're here. We trust one man like him to protect you, Katia, but it will take three like us."

To John he said, "Many, many thanks, amigo." With emotion Valderas gripped his hand. "You been up a long time. You need some rest. I already talked to the doctor. He says Katia can probably leave the hospital this afternoon. We'll bring her to the hotel as soon as she can leave the hospital."

John stood up stiffly. He stretched his sore body. "I *am* tired, and I do need some rest. But I have to check in with the police, and there's one other thing I have to do before I can rest. I should be at the hotel by noon—unless I get tossed in jail."

Valderas said angrily, "They toss you in jail, I'll personally blow it up!"

John smiled. "Thanks, mi amigo." He took Katia's hand. "I'll see you later."

Katia said in mock anger. "I have to teach all of you *desparacidos* how to treat a lady?" She touched a finger to her lips. "You may just as well get used to it, Chohn Tanner. You have to kiss me, *every time,* before you go anywhere."

As John stepped out the door of the room, Pablo followed and said, "Omar used to report to somebody called Senator Chandler."

His words brought John to a standstill.

"The name Chandler doesn't mean anything to me. But you remember Miguel, Chohnee?"

"Sure, Montenegro said he wasn't sure if he's with El Cinco any longer."

"And Adnan Ahman. You might not know anything—"

John interrupted. "I know a whole bunch about him."

"Well, Miguel was talking to Omar the other day trying to get information about Adnan. And Omar got interested and asked a whole bunch of questions trying to find out why Miguel wanted to know about Adnan Ahman. Anyway, Omar wants to talk to you and me, and he said that Miguel wants to be with us. What do you think?"

"I think you better set up a time as soon as possible. Do it and let me know."

"I'll do it, Chohnee."

* * *

The police accepted John's report without comment or charges.

John had already decided that the money he had used to free Juliana was legitimately spent Company money. The money he had spent from the Boquis account was rightfully his own. He would return the money he had taken from the Company account in Managua that he had used to free Katia. He would make the transaction with Francesca and then dictate a letter of resignation from the Company. He took money from the belt and counted out enough to equal the Costa Rican colones he had used.

When he stepped into the plush office, he was surprised to find not only Francesca, but also Juliana, Hardesty, and a man whom he had never met but knew was the author of the Gentry directive.

He felt the eyes of each person in the room focused on him. He gave Francesca a tentative smile, which she returned.

She murmured, "Good to see you, Chohnee."

John turned to Juliana and said, "Looks like you survived the trip okay."

She looked at his seared cheek and the bandage around his arm and wrist. "I did, thanks to you and others. But you look like you had a little more excitement than I did." It seemed clear that Juliana still did not know what role to adopt with John. She simply smiled and didn't step forward to greet him further.

John turned to Hardesty, who was seated in a chair apparently brought in to make the recovering man more comfortable. "Glad to see you're up and around, Mr. Hardesty."

Hardesty growled, "If you didn't hear, your arrest order is rescinded."

"All right. In that case, I'm glad to see you, Lee."

"You've been cleared of *almost* all counts of wrongdoing." Hardesty stuck out his hand. "Well, you bullheaded cuss! It's hard for me to get out of this chair."

John crossed the plushly carpeted room and gripped Hardesty's hand.

Hardesty said, "I owe you a big apology. I should have known a straight arrow like you would tell it like it was—as I'm now convinced you did." He nodded his head at Juliana. "She's told me most everything. Thanks, John." He turned to the man seated at the desk. "This is Paul Gentry."

John did not offer his hand. There was bitterness in his words. "I've heard of you. Matter of fact, I read one of your directives." John's words made Gentry flush slightly.

John looked at the two men. "Looks like I've interrupted a meeting. I have some matters to transact with Francesca, and I'll get out of your hair."

He spoke to Francesca. "The money you gave me before I left was all used in freeing one of our own agents. If I have to account for it in detail, I can do so." Then he handed Francesca a pile of córdobas. "There's two hundred fifty thousand córdobas there, just figure the exchange rate for colones. I used the account in Managua to get money to free one of the group that ran into problems while I was getting Brown out. I used Company money, and since that person didn't belong to the Company, I'm returning the money." He paused for a moment and then continued. "And I want a receipt. And I would like—"

Hardesty interrupted. "I don't see why you should return it. It's a legitimate Company expense since the person was indirectly working for us."

Francesca held the money out to John. He didn't even look at it. "I want a receipt. And would you please type a letter for me?"

Francesca looked at Hardesty for permission. "Go ahead, Francesca. I'd be interested in hearing what the letter he's so anxious to get written says." He looked at John. "Provided, of course, you don't mind us hearing it."

"I don't mind at all."

Francesca moved to the computer, pushed some buttons, and said, "I'm ready, Chohnee."

"I'll want four copies please. One will go to the director of the CIA, one to Leon Hardesty, head of the Costa Rica Station, and one, I think, to Mr. Paul Gentry, liaison officer of the National Security Council. The last copy will be for my own files. Use today's date. 'Dear Sirs: I find my position as an employee of the Central Intelligence Agency untenable. When I started with the Company, I had high ideals and hope of accomplishing beneficial things for the people of Central America. I worked very hard in that job. I never refused to carry out any assignment for the Company except one, and that was the murder of a citizen of Nicaragua. Because I refused to carry out that order, I was placed under arrest and threatened with death if I tried to escape that arrest. Normally when an employer finds his employee's work to be unsatisfactory, he fires him—he doesn't order him killed. I find this sufficient reason to terminate my employment with the Company and do so forthwith. John Tanner.'" He paused and then said, "When you have that ready, I'll look at it."

Neither Hardesty or Gentry said anything for a moment. Finally Gentry broke the silence. "I can't argue with your logic. I have to debrief you, though." Then he stood up. "I have other things to do first. Be here at three this afternoon, Tanner."

"Sorry. As soon as she has those copies ready for signature, I sign them. And when I sign them, I'm through. You want to debrief someone, debrief Brown there. She knows about what happened as well as I do."

Paul Gentry spoke softly. "Perhaps you didn't hear that Hardesty said *almost* all charges are dropped. You be here at three this afternoon."

"Perhaps *you* didn't hear that *I* said when I sign those papers, I'm through." John walked to where Gentry sat in the upholstered chair. He leaned over Hardesty's desk and spoke deliberately, emphasizing his words with a pointing finger. "You file your charges! I'd love to defend myself against those charges before a court of inquiry!" His hands were shaking in anger.

Gentry's voice was cold. "Tanner, I came down here to straighten things out. I need some questions answered. You refuse to answer them, the least thing I'll charge you with is insubordination."

The heat had gone from John's anger and had been replaced with cold fury. "Three things, Mr. Gentry!" John held up a single finger. "Number one, *you* can't charge me with insubordination! I have never worked for you! Apparently Hardesty does, but your name or position doesn't appear on any CIA organizational chart I've ever seen!"

He held up a second finger. "Number two, I'm not even slightly afraid of anything you can do about any action I choose to take!"

He shook three fingers at Gentry. "And number three. I can play the blackmail bit myself—if I have to! I know enough about the actions of you and your boss in Central America to embarrass both of you if you really want to play handball with a hand grenade!"

John wasn't sure himself if he was bluffing, but he knew Gentry would not know how much of the bluff was based on provable fact.

Paul Gentry sat unperturbed in the chair and stared at John. After a moment, Gentry said, "You are technically correct with item one. I can't argue with item two—though I suspect you don't really know how badly I *could* hurt you." His face broke into a crooked grin. "And you've really piqued my curiosity with item three. I wonder what you think you know about me. I don't want to know about any dirt on Senator Chandler. But I'm really curious, because I've heard that you're a straight arrow. I can't help but wonder if you'd really use blackmail."

John flushed. "The Company has put a lot of kinks in my arrow. So you better believe, if I'm forced to, I'll make you and Senator Chandler mighty uncomfortable."

"Don't knock Chandler's power too much. You got off easy with the police by interference on the part of Senator Chandler. By the way, the police were really impressed at the way you handled the local hit man Fiero Rinskin. So congratulations."

Then Paul Gentry's grin widened. It irritated John that the grin made him seem so likeable. "Okay, Tanner. I fold. You win. You're one tough poker player. I think Hardesty's between a rock and a hard place with you. You're too good an operator to lose and too straight an arrow to keep."

Since John had said nothing about reporting in at the police station, he was sure that Gentry spoke the truth about invoking Senator Chandler's protection. The fact irritated him. Senator Chandler had an embarrassing amount of power in Costa Rica, and he felt unclean to find that power used on his behalf. "There are a couple of things I—"

Gentry's words sounded like he was asking for a deal. "No, sir. I'm not making any deals!" John said.

"I'm not asking for a deal. I surrendered unconditionally. I just want to make an observation and ask a couple of favors."

John stood, looking at Paul Gentry. He gave a hard, unsmiling nod.

"I understand your anger, but a letter of resignation becomes part of your personnel record. You may never want to return to Company service, but it's stupid to burn any bridges. Someday you might want to return to some other branch of governmental service."

John gave a noncommittal nod.

"Now the favors. Your letter of resignation, without saying so, casts me in a bad, a justifiably bad, light. I know you have no reason to do me any favors, but I'm asking anyway. Hardesty was only following orders and can't respond to your letter, so it would just pass up to me. Please write a standard letter of resignation, one I won't ever be forced to respond to. Second favor, and it's just a hunch, but I think this favor will benefit you someway."

Gentry paused and looked speculatively at Juliana. "Brown reported Dama Mariposa was killed. Without saying why it's important information, or who it's important to, I want independent confirmation of that fact."

John made a mental note that he would have to thank Juliana for the report she had made that she knew was false. It would be especially beneficial to Katia to have it confirmed that Dama Mariposa was dead. Then he thought, *Katia is alive, but I'll do all in my power to keep Dama Mariposa dead.* "I presume by *independent* you mean from someone other than myself or Brown. First I'll tell you how it happened. Then I'll tell you how you can confirm it. Katia Solano, La Raspa, and a few others went with me to Managua to free Agent Brown. As we left Managua with Brown, Katia was captured. The Sandinistas put her in El Chipote. La Raspa, who'd once been a prisoner in El Chipote, and I went into El Chipote, and we broke Katia out—"

Gentry interrupted. "Tanner, I'm regarded as one of the best interrogators in the business, so be glad we're not recording your story. Remember that you're giving the story of Mariposa's death. So get her into the tale as soon as you can."

John stared steadily at Gentry for a moment. He was trying to figure out what game he was playing. He had a strange feeling that maybe Gentry was on his side. "Thanks. I'm not used to making up stories without a little time to keep the plot line straight. Anyway, we were pursued, and the Sandinistas caught up with us near a town called Tres Madres. In a shootout, three people, La Raspa, one other, and Dama Mariposa were killed."

Gentry interrupted again. "That's good enough. Though I would like a detailed account of how you broke out of El Chipote. Nobody's ever broken out of there before."

John thought briefly before he answered. His personal belief was that Martanza had used clues that John himself had planted to report his success to protect himself. It would do no good to dispute that claim. He said, "Maybe I'll give you a written report sometime. But it would be best for you to get a totally separate account. So for independent confirmation, the Sandinista newspaper *La Barricada,* I'm sure, will carry an account, and you could contact Roberto Rusol at Press International. I think he could get you a report on the matter."

John was surprised, but it did seem that Gentry was satisfied. He turned to Francesca. "I guess since I got my anger off my chest, I should mellow my letter of resignation. Will you change it for me?"

She smiled and said, "Sure, Chohnee. Go ahead."

"'Dear Sirs: Please accept my immediate resignation from government service in the CIA. My reasons for resigning are purely personal. Sincerely, etc.' And be sure the time is on the letter." He glanced at his watch, and said, "It's eleven thirty AM."

John turned to Gentry. "That satisfy you?"

"If it's satisfactory to you, it's pleasing to me. Thank you."

John still wanted to know who had hired Fiero Rinskin. He asked Gentry, "I don't suppose you know who hired Rinskin to try to kill Katia, do you?"

"What makes you think he was hired to kill her?"

"*You* called him a local hit man . . ." John paused for a moment, then continued. "I told you I wasn't making any deals, but if you can find out who hired him, I'll give you a complete report on my last week's activities."

Gentry looked at him speculatively. "How complete? You mean names, places? Anything I want to know?"

"Probably not as complete as you'd want, but more than you know now."

"Okay. You have any suspects?"

"All I have are suspicions. I don't have any hard evidence."

Gentry stood up. "Lee, if Tanner will let me, I'm going to take him to his hotel. I'll be back here around three."

CHAPTER SEVENTEEN

GENTRY DROVE HIS RENTED automobile toward the Hotel Las Olas. Finally he broke the silence. "I'm curious to know who you think hired Rinskin."

"Until I met you in person, you were my prime suspect."

"And how did I get off the list?"

"I don't think hiring a hit man is your style. Matter of fact, I have a tough time with that directive. That doesn't seem your style either."

Gentry seemed to consider a response and then said simply, "I'm glad I don't have to prove my innocence to you. Who's still on your list?"

"A couple of locals. But they'd only be acting for someone else. There's Hardesty. Of course I'm not serious about him, though it still seems mighty strange that Rinskin would show up on the *Triunfo*. There's Senator Chandler, but I don't have any evidence, and I can't think of a motive for him. For that matter, I can't think of a reason in the world why anyone outside the Sandinistas would want Katia dead." John realized that mentioning the Sandinistas in conjunction with Katia was another mistake. He said lamely, "It's possible the Sandinistas at one time came to the same conclusion you did, that Katia Solano and Dama Mariposa were one and the same."

Gentry slowed and crossed the roadway to the parking lot of the Hotel Las Olas. "I'm going to ignore the statement about the Sandinistas for now, but I'll tell you this—if you're right about Chandler, you're not any closer than with the two locals you mentioned. Chandler's an errand boy. A dangerous and powerful man, even my boss, but still an errand boy." Gentry paused, then said, "Well, get some rest. I'll be in touch."

John started toward the hotel. Gentry backed up, then stopped and honked the horn. John walked back and leaned down to look in the open window.

Gentry said contritely, "Look, Tanner, I made a mistake. I'm sorry, and I'd like to make amends. My wife is with me, and we've got some free time. The doctor said limited activities would be good for Solano. Would you—do you think Katia would be up to dinner, maybe here at the Hotel Las Olas tomorrow night?"

John stood in indecision for a moment.

Gentry said persuasively, "I'll have some information for you by then, and I'll give it to you free. No strings."

Finally John said, "Okay. You're on—unless for some reason we decide Katia is not safe here in Limón."

"You going to tell me who *we* are?"

John humphed a small laugh. "You don't let much pass by, do you?"

"I guess that's what got me where I am. I'll call you tomorrow to let you know what time for dinner."

* * *

After Katia had been released from the hospital, John, Katia, Valderas, and Pablo gathered in John's room to discuss their plans.

John asked Valderas, "Why are you thinking of taking Katia back to Nicaragua? It seems to me she'd be safer almost anywhere else . . . and do you think she's well enough to travel?"

"The doc thinks it'd be better to give her one more day and that he should check her before we leave. And believe it or not, there isn't anywhere in the world where Katia'd be safer than I can make her at Hacienda Medina."

"I have my doubts. But for now I'll agree to it. Now Mr. Gentry asked if we, Katia and I, would have dinner at the hotel restaurant with him and his wife tomorrow evening. What do you think?"

Valderas asked suspiciously, "Do they have a dining room anywhere but on that balcony?"

John merely shook his head.

The discussion took place in Katia's room. Pablo growled, "Are you nuts, Chohnee?"

Valderas snapped, "And you're worried about taking her back to Hacienda Medina!?"

But Katia was excited. She said, "Valderas, don't be a grump. With Rinskin gone, nobody wants to hurt me anymore. Besides, I want to go back home as soon as the doctor says it's okay. And a party would do me good."

"I hope you're right about Rinskin, but where do you mean—home?"

"I—I wouldn't feel safe at Papa's ranch yet. I meant the hacienda. If you'll let me stay there."

Valderas gleamed. "Let you stay? *Let* you stay? Hija, I would be so happy to have you stay!"

Katia said hesitantly, "Chohnee too? He would have to . . ."

"Of course, Chohnee too. If he wants."

Her eyes sparkled as she said, "Chohnee wants to stay with me wherever I am. I want you to send a message for Mario to get Sandinita and your bay from Papa's ranch and bring them to the hacienda—will that be all right?" Without waiting for an answer, she continued. "Francesca'll buy me a dress for dinner."

Pablo was not sold. His voice expressed his anger. "You are both out of your minds! That place is open to the street and to any boat interested on three sides. There's no way we can keep Katia safe . . ."

Finally Valderas grumbled, "We can protect you for one night, especially if you promise to go back to the hacienda once this is over. I know we can keep you safe there."

Katia grimaced. "You worry too much, my friend. But I'm glad you do."

As John watched Valderas's reaction to Katia's words, he couldn't help but wonder if Valderas would ever be tough enough not to give Katia anything she wanted.

It was also clear to John that Pablo did not really feel good at this final decision. He quickly left the room with the statement, "I gotta take care of some business."

As for Katia, she turned to John with sparkling eyes. "I promise, we'll both look really good for the dinner—and maybe we'll do some dancing?"

* * *

John and Valderas were talking in John's room after Katia had gone to rest in her room when a knock came at the door. John answered it to find a young man who asked quietly, "You Chohn Tanner?"

John nodded.

"Pablo wants you to meet him downstairs."

John thanked him, slipped the boy a small tip, and turned to Valderas. "Do you think if I send Halcón up to help you watch Katia that you'll be all right here on your own?"

Though Valderas seemed a little puzzled, he said, "*Como no? Why not?*"

Pablo met John just outside the door of the small hotel, and as they walked to the meeting place, Pablo said to John, "I thought real careful about what you said about Omar. I talked to him, and when he heard what his actions had done to Katia, he was terribly sorry. So I didn't do anything to him. Maybe it'll turn out to be a good thing. You'll understand when we talk to him."

A short walk brought them to the *Café Negrita*. Omar and Miguel were seated in a dark corner. As John and Pablo approached, Miguel looked up with a hard smile and said, "Hola, Gallo. "

John humphed and shook hands. Then seeing no reason not to get right down to business, John asked, "What's going on, Miguel?"

"I been watching things pretty close here in Limón. I was talking to a guy named Fiero Rinskin the other day."

He looked at John, and his hard smile broadened. "Of course, that's before he crossed with you. And last time I saw Rinskin made me think I was lucky not to have tangled with you that first time we met."

With those words he gave John a full, admiring smile. "Anyway, before he messed with you, me'n Rinskin were trying to figure out a way to make some money. He told me about a guy I already knew—Adnan Ahman. I met him a few months ago at a meeting in El Cinco headquarters—the time when Katia got on his bad side."

Miguel said, "To make it quick, I found out from Rinskin that the guy Adnan Ahman is staying right here in Hotel Las Olas. Fiero was supposed to get a lot of money if he killed Katia. I wasn't about to let that happen, so it kind of messed it up for me. But I did figure that this Fiero could help me make some money. So I followed him real close. That's how come I was there when he fell out the window at the Hotel Las Olas last night. Matter of fact, I was the first one to get to him. He was still partly alive and mumbling something. It was kinda hard to tell what he was saying, something about Adnan Ahman should pay him for Dama . . . and somethin' like, if he can give a newspaper that says she's dead to a bank manager in Managua, he can get a lot of money. Then just before he died, he gave me this."

Miguel handed John a key with a plastic-covered paper attached to it. John read the scribbled words out loud. "Give this key to the manager of El Banco Nicaragua in Managua to receive money."

John handed the key back and said, "What's this got to do with me?"

Omar said impatiently, "What's the matter, Chohnee? Can't you see that this Adnan is the one who wants Dama . . . Katia dead? We have to do something about Adnan! And Miguel just wants to get some ideas from you."

John looked at Miguel, and Miguel nodded in confirmation of what Omar had just said.

John said, "I'll try to get some information from Company files. I don't know what you have in mind—just be sure what you do is . . ." Then, looking at Pablo, he realized that anything he said would make no impression at all. So he asked, "Okay, do you know how to get in touch with Omar or Miguel quickly?"

Pablo nodded. "You betcha."

"Then I'll try to get some information for you."

John immediately went to the manager of the hotel and asked if he had an Adnan Ahman registered at the hotel.

The manager took John to the front desk and showed him the registration book. There was no Adnan registered. "Has he ever been registered here?"

The manager shook his head in the negative. "I've never heard of him or even a name close to that."

"What about that man, Morgan. I guess he's staying here?"

"Oh, yes. He stays with us with some regularity. Actually, several times a year."

For John it was as if an explosion of lightning occurred in his mind as he heard this. He was sure that he knew who was really trying to get Katia killed. But his mind whirled as he tried to think why.

* * *

John chose a white seersucker suit because it allowed him to hide the shoulder holster housing the pistol he had brought from Nicaragua. He and Katia walked along the covered ramp that led to the dining room. The restless sea rolled below the concrete floor. Sweet, cool refreshing air drifted across the decking. Katia wore a dazzling white dress. A slash of scarlet red dropped down and across the bodice to form a sash. Her white shoes had a matching triangle of red across the toe.

Paul Gentry and his wife were already in the dining room, which had a spectacular view of the sea. As Katia and John walked into the room, Gentry moved toward them. John looked around. Most tables were filled with people taking the evening meal. John didn't know if Katia knew who Paul Gentry was or what trouble his directive had made for them both.

Gentry extended his hand to Katia. She took it graciously and was led to a tall woman smiling at them. Long, dark hair and fair, untanned skin made a perfect setting for her expressive eyes. Gentry included John and Katia in his introduction. "My wife, Anne."

John held a chair for Katia so that she was seated next to Anne, then moved a chair so that he was seated next to Katia. This chair also gave him a better overall view of the room and its occupants.

Gentry said, "I've already ordered. How about a drink while we wait?"

At that moment the waiter came to their table. He greeted John warmly. "Hola, Señor Tanner." He bowed to Katia. "And Señorita Solano. *Bienvenido.*"

John smiled. "Buenas tardes, Marti."

Gentry ordered a daiquiri for his wife and a piña colada for himself.

Marti asked, "The usual, Señor Tanner?"

John nodded and looked at Katia.

"Piña colada sounds good, but without rum."

When the drinks were served, Gentry looked at the orange soda and chuckled. "The usual is an orange soda! You really are a straight arrow, Tann—John."

The four people passed a few moments with each of them making stuttering attempts at conversation. Both Gentry and his wife, Anne, spoke excellent Spanish. Then Marti brought a message to Gentry. "You have a telephone call." He pointed toward the bar at the end of the room. "You can take it over there."

John took advantage of the interruption to look around the room. Valderas and a man John didn't know sat at a table not too far away. Pablo and another stranger to John sat at a table that had been selected because it gave a commanding view of the whole busy room. Halcón was not in evidence. John's eyes landed on Gentry as he talked on the phone. Gentry listened and then signaled for John to come to him.

Gentry said, "There are a couple of people from the States who'd like to meet you. You mind if they join us for dinner?"

Sensing John's suspicion, Gentry put the phone on the counter and stepped away from it. He spoke intensely. "You needn't worry. You've got troops on guard *in* the room . . ." He nodded and pointed with his chin to the road that was visible from the open-sided room. "And also those, at least, that I can see in the jeep out there on the road."

John looked in the direction that Gentry pointed. Halcón was seated in the jeep, his automatic rifle not even hidden. With him were three uniformed men. One clearly guarded the road. Halcón and the other man's eyes never strayed from a close scrutiny of the room where Katia Solano now carried on an animated conversation with Anne.

John asked, "Why do they want to meet me?"

"A man named Morgan wants to hear the story of Dama Mariposa's death from your own lips. I'm going to level with you,

Tanner. The number of troops you have on guard here, your own slips of tongue, plus a few other things convince me that if Katia Solano is not Dama Mariposa, then Katia's at least someone of considerable consequence. It looks to me like you've gone to a lot of bother to get Dama Mariposa 'killed in action.' Don't get me wrong. I'm going along with your story—and by the way, I've got confirmation from Nicaragua. The Sandinistas are bragging that Dama Mariposa was killed just like you reported. The two who want to meet you are Senator Halworth Chandler and William Morgan, a powerful man behind the scenes in Washington. Matter of fact, he's the power behind Chandler."

John said, "I've heard about Morgan, and that gives even less reason for them to meet Katia. And I don't see why I should cooperate."

"I'll give you two reasons. First, your source, Roberto Rusol, seemed to hedge on a final identification of Dama Mariposa. He said his reporter's instinct tells him something's fishy with the Mariposa story. The body was disposed of too quickly as well as something about a missing person—Delgado. But he said that the official report was very definite. Now, to Morgan and Chandler, I can make a solid case for Katia Solano having nothing to do with Dama Mariposa. Second, you *will* meet with Morgan and Chandler whether you want to or not, and you're at better advantage if that meeting takes place publicly and with *friends*. And believe it or not, I *am* your friend." A thought seemed to occur to Gentry, and he snapped a finger. "It would be a good idea for Hardesty to be here at the meeting. How about it?"

"I don't know, Paul, I . . ."

"I'll give you a third reason. Morgan's the man who gave me orders about Dama Mariposa. I can't even guess why, but I think if he meets her suddenly and unexpectedly, we might find out. And if we can find out what Katia knows about Morgan, maybe we can make her safe forever, and I think that's important to you."

John's decision was made. His eyes hardened, and his lips closed in a tight line. He wanted to meet Morgan after all, especially if he was the one who had ordered his and Katia's deaths. "You're right on both counts. But don't say anything to Katia about them coming. Let it be a surprise."

Gentry picked up the phone and John heard him ask about Hardesty. When John started to walk away, Gentry put his hand over the receiver and said, "Wait, John. There's another thing before we go back to the table."

John waited while Gentry handed the phone back to the waiter. "It's just as well you agreed to meet with them. They're already in the hotel and will be at our table in five minutes. The other thing is one of your local suspects has been missing for a couple of days. You know anything about it?"

John's mind leaped, but no emotion registered on his face. "Suspects? I don't know what you mean."

"Somehow I find it hard to believe you didn't know that Omar's not around right now."

John just shrugged and continued to look mystified.

Gentry signaled for the waiter and told him to add a table and three chairs to their seating arrangement.

At the table, Anne was laughing. "Did you ever graduate from university?"

"No. Other things interfered. Maybe someday." Katia glanced up at John and asked, "What was that about?"

John felt a twinge of conscience as he ignored Katia's question. "You two sound like you're getting along well."

Anne asked her husband, "Everything all right?"

"Fine." Speaking to his wife and Katia, Gentry said, "Some people from the States are joining us. I hope it's all right." Without waiting for an answer, he sipped the last of his drink and motioned for their waiter. "Bring us another round of drinks."

Quickly, another table and some chairs were added, and the drinks were served. The conversation flowed smoothly.

John asked Katia, "You okay?"

"I'm having a great . . ." A sudden intake of breath interrupted her words, and Katia's fingers dug into the palm of his hand.

Anne leaned forward and asked, "What is it, Katia? You're so pale!"

Katia's eyes darted frantically to where Valderas sat. He showed that he was watching closely, for he stood and was alert for what was happening.

Katia spoke with white face and through tight lips. "It's like a live electric wire is suddenly sparking in my stomach."

John looked to where Halcón waited in the jeep. One of the men still watched the street. Halcón and the other two men had their weapons trained on three men who were just entering the restaurant. Katia's eyes briefly searched each of the men's faces. Hardesty, walking very carefully, entered first. He was followed by a tall man with a heavy, well-coiffed head of hair, wearing a light summer suit. John recognized him as Senator Chandler. The other man was also tall and had smooth, tanned facial features and graying hair. John had seen this man's face in news photos but would not have connected the name of William Andrew Morgan to the man had it not been for Gentry's previous warning that he was going to arrive at the restaurant. Katia's fingernails dug even deeper into the palm of his hand as Morgan entered the room.

At that moment, Gentry stood and walked to greet the newly arrived men.

John whispered, "It's okay, Katia. Relax. Valderas is alerted, and Halcón and his men sit with weapons ready for action."

Anne asked Katia, "Are you okay? Can I get you something?"

"No. I'm fine. I had a stomach pain for a moment, but it's passed."

Gentry and the three men approached the table. The only indication Morgan gave of recognition was a slight break in his stride, and his eyes did not leave Katia.

Gentry said, "You all know Leon Hardesty. This is Senator Chandler and Mr. Morgan." He quickly introduced those who were seated at the table.

Morgan asked Gentry, "Did you find out about Omar?"

The question seemed to John a solid confirmation that Morgan was deeply involved in the affairs of the Limón station. How else would he be aware of a minor figure like Omar being missing?

Gentry said, "No. Actually he's not too important. He just operates radio transmissions for us. He probably just took a couple days off."

Morgan wasted no more time on that matter. "So. Mr. Tanner, I'm told you participated in an action in Nicaragua in which the infamous Dama Mariposa was supposedly killed. Give me the details." His Spanish was fair, but his pronunciation of *Mariposa* came out closer to *Maw-di-posa*. It was obvious that he could not roll his Rs.

John looked up and engaged Morgan's eyes. His words were spoken in carefully controlled tones of indignation. "Perhaps I should set you straight on a couple of matters, Morgan." John's lack of respect was apparent. "Of primary importance, whether Dama Mariposa was famous or infamous depends on your point of view. I happen to think she was a heroine of the first order. And I didn't hear Mr. Gentry introduce you as a boss of mine or me as a bootlick. If I give you any details of the action in Nicaragua, it will be at *my* choosing and only if you say *please*. And then not unless you have legitimate reason to hear my report and I know why you want to hear it."

Morgan's jaw dropped slightly. It was obvious he was not used to people speaking to him in such a manner.

Hardesty hastened to say, "Mr. Morgan, I should have told you about John Tanner. He—uh, he resigned from the Company the other day—uh, and he was warned about the Official Secrets Act and its application to newly released operators who have handled classified information. I'm sure that under the right circumstances, John will be cooperative."

Anger sparking in his eyes, John started to speak but was interrupted by Gentry. "John, both Senator Chandler and Mr. Morgan are cleared to hear classified reports." Then he spoke to Morgan, "But there *are* people at the table not cleared, so I'd suggest a more suitable place to question Tanner."

Morgan ignored Gentry for a moment and then said, "I'm intrigued that you would regard Dama Mariposa as a heroine, Tanner. You knew her well?"

"As well as anyone in the world. Nicaragua lost a *genuine* freedom fighter when she was killed."

Chandler spoke sharply, "And yet I read report after report in which you denied knowing her and even implied she didn't exist!"

John said without heat, "Reading between the lines of my orders, I recognized that whoever wanted information on her wanted it for the wrong reasons. I made the reports in that way to protect her. As it turned out, it was a vain effort because she was killed by the Sandinistas near a town called Tres Madres not more than four days ago."

Morgan said, "So you say." He turned to Katia. "Strange. You very much remind me of Dama Mawdiposa, Miss Solano."

Katia said with some impudence, "I knew Dama before her death, and I shall take your words as a compliment, for she was beautiful and intelligent. I'm curious, Mr. Morgan, would you say mine is a physical resemblance or is it my ready wit?"

Morgan flushed. "I didn't know her. I saw a photograph of her once."

Katia persisted. "I happen to know that no photograph was *ever* taken of her. Something else. I find it strange to note that *you* remind *me* of someone. A weapons dealer, a very dishonest one. He went by the name of Adnan Ahman. On two occasions that I can testify to, he sold weapons in violation of American

KARL GOODMAN

law. In contrast with you, I met him in person, and I can be very specific about how you remind me of him."

Morgan, red with anger, slapped the table. "Gentry, I didn't know when I accepted your invitation to dinner that I would be seated in the presence of an enemy to the government of the United States! Come, Senator . . ."

Katia's laughter peeled gently over the noise of the room. "No need to get up, Adnan. It's too late to leave. I already know who you are, though I admit I don't know why you want to hide your identity." Her eyes never left his face. Then raising her voice slightly, she called, "Valderas!"

In three plaster-cast stumping strides, Valderas was at her side. Valderas's companion was not far behind. John wondered if his actions were spontaneous or rehearsed. He leaned over the table, and as he did, the jacket he wore parted and the huge pistol holstered near his arm pit was revealed to the people at the end of the table. He looked thunderously around and growled, "Which one do you want dead, *queridita?*"

"No one, yet. I just wonder if you remember the man at the end of the table. He was saying that I remind him of . . ." Katia then gave perfect imitation of Morgan's inability to roll a Spanish R: "Dama Mawdiposa."

Valderas looked at Morgan for a moment and then bellowed, "Of course! The weapons dealer, Señor Adnan Ahman. I'm sorry, Adnan, but you come at a bad time. I'm out of the revolution business and . . ." He crossed himself and spoke sadly. "Dama Mariposa is dead."

Pablo and the man with him arrived at the table and watched the scene in silence. Morgan abruptly stood up and said, "I refuse to stay here . . ."

Pablo roughly pushed him to his seat, "You can leave when Valderas gives you permission."

Morgan's angry eyes lighted on Paul Gentry. "You set this up!" He turned to Anne. "Do you know what kind of man you're married to?"

She smiled. "You bet I do! A patriotic American. A dedicated government employee. A loving husband . . ." Her eyes bored into Morgan's eyes. "And we have discussed Da Nang *in full!*"

Katia's laughter again peeled gently over the noise of the room. Morgan looked around. He seemed surprised to be ignored by fellow diners. Katia spoke in English. She seemed to take delight in calling the very important Mr. Morgan by a name he clearly did not want used. "I think, Adnan Ahman, my friend Chohnee say it is Mexican standoff. I agree you live, you agree Dama Mariposa rest quietly in grave? What you think?"

Paul Gentry spoke quietly. "Hold it, Katia. It's not quite so simple as that. There are a couple of things I want to make crystal clear. I have investigated the death of Dama Mariposa and intend to file official reports listing several independent sources to verify the facts surrounding her death. In addition, I'm going to take depositions from as many witnesses as possible, including you, Mr. Valderas, as to the identity of William Andrew Morgan, alias Adnan Ahman. I want to insure that not only will Dama Mariposa lie quietly in her grave, but that you, Katia, can live free from concern. The reports I put together will be made public if there is even the slightest indication that you have met with any kind of harm."

Morgan looked at Gentry with icy eyes. "I presume you know that you have just ruined any chance for your career . . ."

Gentry smiled pleasantly. "I don't think so, Adnan. With all due respect, those depositions could just as easily be made public if my career is tampered with in any way." He paused for a moment and said, "For that matter, I think Leon would like an assignment at Langley. Am I right, Lee?"

Hardesty grinned. "You better believe it!"

Then Morgan blustered, "But what if Seño . . ." His voice would not give away his inability to roll an R. His words died, then he used the English word *miss.* "But what if Miss Solano meets with harm that I have no control over?"

"Then, Adnan . . ."

Morgan said angrily, "Don't call me that!"

Gentry just smiled pleasantly. "Then, Adnan, I would begin to make it a habit to pray for her safety if I were you."

Gentry looked at John and smiled again. Using Katia's pronunciation, he said, "I like Chohnee's description. Mexican standoff."

Morgan stared around the table for a moment. "I prefer the expression used in chess—*stalemate*." He turned to Valderas. "Do I have permission to leave, or do you intend to shoot me on the spot?"

Valderas growled, "I'd be very happy to shoot you on the spot, but I guess it's up to Mr. Gentry." Valderas looked in question at Gentry.

Paul Gentry shrugged and said, "I think our business with William Andrew Morgan, alias Adnan Ahman, is complete."

Morgan stood and looked briefly around the table. He asked, "Hardesty?"

Hardesty grinned and said, "I'm really tired and my injury is starting to hurt a little, but before I leave, I want to set a time for the deposition for Mr. Gentry's report."

Morgan looked at him icily, then turned to Chandler. "And you, Senator?"

Chandler stood and said with just a trace of a grin, "Oh, yes. Yes, indeed. I'm with you, Adnan." Then speaking to Gentry, he said, "If my testimony will help, Paul, let me know."

John couldn't help but wonder if Senator Chandler, in the interchange, had not gained a new lease on life himself.

As Chandler and Morgan started to walk away, Valderas laid a heavy arm over Morgan's shoulder. Valderas rumbled, "A word, Adnan. The last time I saw you, I suggested you not return to this part of the world. This time I *tell* you not to return, because I promise, if you do, you will not live to see the next sunrise." He gave a signal to the men outside the restaurant. All the people at the table, as well as Chandler and Morgan, looked to see who Valderas was giving instructions to. There were four sets of automatic weapons trained on the figures of William Andrew Morgan and Senator Halworth Chandler. It seemed that the men lowered their weapons with great reluctance.

Valderas turned and said to Katia, "You know I'll be right over there." He pointed at his table.

Katia merely nodded her head in affirmation.

John motioned to Pablo, who came quietly to his side. "I've got to stay here with these people. But I want you to find out which room Morgan is staying in and get this information to Omar and Miguel as quickly as you can. Tell them that we just found out that Adnan and Morgan are the same person. We need to get together and decide what we can do. Got it?"

Pablo grinned and said, "Do I ever got it, Chohnee!"

At just this time, their waiter came up, laden with trays of food. He looked in question at the two departing men. Gentry smiled and said, "It's okay. Now that business is over, we'll all enjoy our meal better."

John watched Pablo move to and speak briefly with Valderas and then leave the area. John said hesitantly, "Paul, are you sure we've done the right thing with this Adnan Ahman business?"

Gentry said, "With his money and the lawyers he can buy, we could never convict him. I think to pull his fangs for Katia is all we can expect."

Katia murmured, "And I always thought that everybody got justice in the United States, even the rich ones. If you really want to do the right thing, just tell Valderas or even Pablo that it's all right with you if Adnan gets his justice. I suspect that if you did that, Adnan's plane would never leave the ground."

John took her hand. "Katia, I think Paul's right, and he's handled it the best way possible for us. I don't think Morgan will want the embarrassment. He'll be satisfied with his stalemate."

Katia grinned. "Then let's eat." She pointed to an open balcony where people were dancing. "Then after, we can dance on that balcony!"

John looked at her severely. "There will be no dancing for you for several days, young lady!"

"That's what you think. I bet Valderas will dance with me. Even if he has to stump around on one leg."

John said in exasperation, "No bet. I know he would."

* * *

Senator Chandler followed Morgan from the dining room to the entrance of Morgan's room. Morgan jerked the door open and turned to stare at Chandler in great anger.

Chandler started to speak but was cut off with Morgan's icy words. "You don't know what damage you've done to yourself!"

The smile never left Chandler's face. "Oh, Adnan, I'm not sure . . ."

"You made a huge mistake tonight, Senator! You'll very quickly find how I can cut you in pieces!" With these words he slammed the door, and Chandler walked on along the hallway, whistling quietly, with the grin never diminishing from his face.

Morgan picked up the telephone and told the hotel operator whom he wanted to talk to. While waiting for the response to his call, he began to pace the room. His mind went back to that day in London so long ago when he was returning from the war and decided that if he ever needed an alias, Adnan Ahman would be that alias. The picture of the small-statured, black-haired boy, who identified himself as Adnan Ahman, came to his mind. He muttered, "Well, Adnan, we've done pretty good so far."

At that time the phone rang. It was his pilot. "Where in Hades have you been?!" A brief moment later, he replied, "That's a lousy excuse! Get the plane ready to leave in one hour!" Another moment passed. "I said one hour!" He slammed the phone into the cradle.

* * *

After the meal, Katia led John, Paul, and his wife to the balcony, but after two dances, Katia admitted she was tired. As they parted, Gentry steered John away for some privacy and held his hand out. "You know the Company really needs men of integrity. All you have to do is tear up that letter of resignation, and you can be chief of station here in Costa Rica. I could easily fix . . ."

John interrupted. "Paul, I appreciate that offer, but I'm at a crossroad in my life right now. I'm not sure what I want do. You made a casual remark earlier this evening that really hit me hard."

Gentry's puzzlement was clear on his face. "Oh?"

"You said I was a straight arrow, and you said that just because I usually drink orange soda pop."

Paul's expression revealed an even deeper lack of understanding. "Straight arrow?"

"I've never thought of myself as a straight arrow and hadn't even wanted to. I've only wanted to be able to look my bishop in the eye and say I'm doing my best to keep the standards of the LDS Church. And an orange soda pop just doesn't cut it. I've found myself lying . . ."

Gentry quickly responded, "Hold it, John. I'm not even close to being your bishop. So you can't confess to me. But I think I understand your concerns. Believe it or not, you're not the first Mormon I've met with a similar problem. It seems to come with work in the Company. So here's what I'm going to do. I'm just going to hold on to your letter for a time. I'm putting you on administrative leave, with pay . . ."

"Not with pay, I . . ."

Gentry didn't even pause. " . . . for a month. That's reward for an outstanding job very well done. And we're through talking about it for now. I'll be down here for a couple of weeks. I'm giving my wife a well-deserved vacation. If you need anything, contact me through the Company office in San Jose."

John started to say, "I'm not sure . . ."

Gentry again interrupted and said, "John, please. Just accept it."

John fumbled with words for a moment. "I guess in honesty I'd have to say I'm not sure I want out of the Company. I will say that if I continue to work for the Company, things have got to change enough so I can . . ." He smiled a self-deprecating smile. ". . . Get back on the right track in trying to be a genuine straight arrow."

Paul chuckled, stuck out his hand, which John gripped firmly, and said, "You've got some time to decide what to do, so just say thanks and get out of here!"

John was silent for a moment and then simply said, "All right. Thanks, Paul."

As John and Katia walked out of the dining room, John said, "I wonder where Valderas is."

Katia said, "I don't know. But I'm too tired to look for him tonight."

* * *

The next morning, Valderas knocked on John's door. As John opened the door, Valderas said, "Chohnee, we're about ready to head up to Hacienda Medina. You ready?"

John wondered about Pablo. He had the impression that Valderas had given him some kind of assignment the evening before. He answered, "Pretty much. What time we are planning to leave? By the way—I haven't seen Pablo. Is he down at the boat?"

For just a moment, John thought Valderas was going to hedge on him, but he didn't. "I sent him up to Managua yesterday. He'll be back at the hacienda in a day or two. So I'll see you and Katia at the boat at ten."

* * *

John and Katia, seated on deck chairs, watched the screen of tall green trees as their boat floated by. There was an occasional exposed patch of riverbank spotlighted by the sunlight breaking through the umbrella of dark-green tree leaves. Crocodiles often dozed in the warmth of the sun.

John said, "This is the first time I've traveled this river when I could notice how lovely and serene it is."

Katia responded, "It's probably the most beautiful river in the world when people aren't roaring along shooting at each other." Katia leaned closer to John, murmuring, "What's going to happen with us, Chohnee?"

After a moment of silence, John asked, "What do you mean?"

Still leaning closely to John, Katia spoke just loud enough to be heard above the noises of the boat as it glided over the smooth waters of the river. "I mean—I—I love you, but we're so different. It—it seems to me too big a problem just to say, 'Don't worry, we'll work it out.'"

John was glad Katia had realized that the differences between them should be worked out before marriage, but as he thought how to begin a discussion, Katia continued. "We were raised differently, in different countries and with different religions—and I—I've come to realize that your religion is very important to you. But for me, even when I was young, politics seemed much more important than religion. And although I learned the catechism when I was little, Mama and Papa only went to church on certain feast days or for the end of the year. I don't think either Mama or Papa have ever been to confession. I never have—even though at times I knew I should."

She looked up with questioning eyes. John put his arms around her and held her close, trying hard to think of the right words to say to a problem that had troubled him since he first realized how much he loved Katia. Finally, he said, "What you've said is true. But maybe for now we should just enjoy the trip."

John took Katia by the hand and pulled her to him. "Katia, I love you so very much."

Katia responded, "Maybe, just maybe as much as I love you."

Their loving kiss was interrupted by a cough from Valderas. He said, "Sorry, I didn't mean to interrupt, but I need a break from steerage . . . and I know you can handle the boat, Chohnee. Maybe you could spell me off."

John was puzzled by his own attitude, because although he objected to Valderas's interruption, he was grateful for it. He knew that he still had some things that he needed to decide on about Katia. In his mind he knew that he loved her very much, but he couldn't help but worry about taking up a life down here in Nicaragua—so very far from what he had always thought would be his home, the lovely valleys of Utah.

* * *

At the dock, Mario had Katia's pony and the big bay saddled, as well as a horse for John. When Katia came into sight, the little pony began to dance and whinny. Katia walked to the pony and nuzzled her cheek against the small horse's head. Valderas stumped up to where Katia was talking to Sandinita. He said, "Katia, maybe riding a horse isn't too good an idea for you right now."

"Sandinita would give me the gentlest ride I could ask for." Still she took the bridle and began to walk along the roadway, which was little more than a path, toward the ancient house that stood majestically at the top of the gently rising hill.

For a short distance, Valderas, John, and Katia walked along the road in silence. In a shallow vale, there was a cluster of fifteen tan Brahman cattle. Standing as a monarch surveying his kingdom was the bull Magnanimo. As the three people paused to look at the scene, the bull gave a loud bellow, shook his horns, and switched his tail.

Valderas waved at the bull and shouted, "Hello, you handsome beast!"

The bull shook his horns briefly, snuffled at the grass, and began to pull tender blades into his mouth. Valderas said, "Chihuahua! Maybe I can learn that beast's language on my own. How am I doing, Chohnee?"

John grinned. "Pretty good, I'd say."

Valderas said, "I have something on my mind I been wanting to talk to both of you about. I was going to talk about it tonight, but this seems like a good time and a good place."

Valderas pointed to a grassy spot in the shade of a tall mahagua tree. A couple of huge logs offered makeshift benches to sit on. Valderas dropped the reins of his bay and stumped over to the shade, carefully sitting down on one of the logs. John spread his denim jacket on another log and helped Katia sit on it.

Valderas turned abruptly to John and asked, "What do you want out of life, Chohnee? Surely you want more than just fighting a revolution, don't you?"

John reached to the ground and pulled a blade of grass and chewed on the sweet, tender end for a moment before he answered. "I was born and raised on a big cattle ranch in Northern Mexico, Valderas. I always dreamed that someday I would own a spread of my own. I would raise the best beef cattle in the world. But that's pretty much a forgotten dream. Land costs so much nowa . . ."

Valderas interrupted. "I don't know exactly when I figured that out. I mean that you wanted a ranch—but I did." They sat in silence briefly. The sound of busy insects buzzed in the quiet air. "I don't know if Katia would be surprised for me to tell her that I feel like she's the granddaughter Dorotea and I never did have."

Katia moved to him, put her arms around him, and kissed his cheek. "You know I wouldn't, Valderas. I've always felt like you are mi abuelo."

Valderas turned to John. "And Chohnee, I've been jealous of Señor Boquis ever since I met him at the auction in Managua, and he told me everything you've been doing to help him with his ranch. I kinda hoped you could do the same for me." Valderas quickly wiped at his eyes. Then he glanced around and called to Magnanimo, "Hello, Señor Toro!"

Magnanimo again responded with a snuff and twist of his head and a muted bawl.

John and Katia exchanged puzzled glances. Then Katia placed her hands on his rugged face and said, "Valderas—mi abuelo, I don't understand what you are saying."

Valderas said quietly, "I'm just trying to plant some thoughts for both of you. I feel like Chohnee is the man I'd want to run Hacienda Medina—and sometime, Katia, you could maybe—maybe give me some grandkids that I'd never have any other way. And I'm not trying to rush either of you into anything. But just so you understand, if I didn't make myself clear, if you lived here and did the things I've said, the ranch would sometime belong to both of you. Course I'd need *some* money and a place to stay and work sometimes. See, Chohnee, if you'd manage the ranch, I'd be free to go to Managua to try out some of Katia's new ideas about making Nicaraguan citizens more aware of the need for democracy and freedom. I got an old friend, name of Chamorro. Maybe—but that's off the subject."

John looked at Valderas for a moment and said, "Live here at Hacienda . . . ?"

Valderas grunted, "Help me up, Chohnee. I'm going on up to the house. You don't have to give me an answer right away."

Puzzled, John held out his hand to help Valderas up from the log. The proposal had come so unexpectedly that he didn't know what to say.

"I see I surprised you. Talk about it. Give me an answer in the next couple of days." Despite the cast on his leg, Valderas swung fluidly into the saddle. The one casted leg projected out at an odd angle. He flicked on the reins, and the big bay turned up the road in a smooth lope that Valderas quickly checked to a quiet walk.

John and Katia stood in silence for a long time. Finally Katia said, "Come on. Let's go on up to the house. Can we walk? I think I don't want to ride for a few days."

John caught her hand. "Wait, don't we need to talk about what Valderas said?"

"*I* don't. I can't live in San Carlos now. Hacienda Medina is almost my home, and I'd love Valderas to be the adopted grand-father of my children."

"But even if I stayed here, I couldn't possibly have him *give* us the ranch."

Katia smiled at him. "I don't want to make Valderas's offer seem less generous than it is, because it is very generous, and I'm very grateful. But Hacienda Medina is so far away from towns and supplies and doctors that he'd almost have to give it away to sell it. And when the deeds are recorded, it would just bring it to the attention of the Sandinistas, and then they'd take it away. I've watched you help Boquis make money and build stock. If you manage the ranch and make it profitable for him, Valderas would get more money in the long run from you than if he sold the hacienda to anyone."

They walked quietly to the hacienda, each immersed in their own thoughts.

That evening Valderas presided over a feast in the stately dining room. All of the ranch hands of the hacienda and their wives had been invited. Mama Reyes hurried and scurried and scolded, but she never stopped smiling. It was clear that cooking the food for a fiesta such as this was her greatest delight.

Valderas stood and made an announcement to begin the festivities. "Chohnee and Katia are going to be in charge of the hacienda for a while. It will be my good fortune if it is for a long time."

Mama Reyes beamed and heaped huge piles of food on Valderas's plate. No sooner had he eaten what she had provided than his plate was again laden with savory barbecued beef and cooked platanos and piles of steaming tortillas. She refilled his glass with sweet red wine.

Valderas raised the glass of wine and said to the celebrants, "You better all enjoy the wine tonight, because Katia said there will be new rules when she's running the house. No wine served for any reason." With these words he emptied his glass.

Pablo quietly entered the room. Valderas looked over, and Pablo grinned and nodded. John wondered if the signal meant that Pablo had been successful in some venture.

Later in the evening when Valderas brought the festivities to an end, he asked John and Katia to come with him and Pablo into a large room with desks and file cabinets and huge leather-covered chairs that clearly showed it to be Valderas's office.

Pablo shrugged his shoulders and said, "I don't really know what to say, Valderas, but I'm guessing that somebody finally got to Morgan before I had a chance to even think about what I should do. Anyway, I think this article in the Managua Press tells it all."

He then handed the complete newspaper to Valderas, who glanced at it and showed it to John and Katia. An article on the first page was clearly outlined in a bold red marking.

MANAGUA PRESS INTERNATIONAL
U.S. INDUSTRIALIST'S BODY
FOUND NEAR MANAGUA
Roberto Rusol

The presence of the body of W. Andrew Morgan, found in the wreckage of a military vehicle, along with a cache of U.S. made weaponry near Managua yesterday still has not been explained to the satisfaction of President Ortega. Mr. Morgan, in addition to his industrial interests in the U.S., was a high-ranking cabinet officer and advisor to the president of the United States. President Ortega demands that the U.S. explain what mission Mr. Morgan was performing in Nicaragua as well as detailing Morgan's close relationship with a weapons dealer, Adnan Ahman. President Ortega promises he will not accept less than a full explanation on the part of the United States government.

Reporter Rusol also comments that the death of Mr. Morgan seemed a little suspicious—almost as if he had taken his own life. An investigation will pursue this charge by Rusol.

Valderas said, "That leaves us a lot to talk about tomorrow. I want Katia to move up here to the big house, so, Chohnee, go help her get what she needs for tonight." He spoke directly to Katia. "I want you up here."

She kissed him on the cheek. "Tomorrow will be fine, Valderas. I'm too tired tonight."

Valderas called to Señora Reyes and told her to have one of the girls, Maria, stay the night with Katia. To Pablo he said, "Get someone to watch Katia's place." To John he said, "Walk down with her and stay till Maria gets there, and then come back. We've got a lot to talk about."

John and Katia walked slowly along the path to Katia's little house. The night was warm and the air fragrant with the scents of myriad tropical flowers, the brief moment a tiny fragment of serenity for them. At the door, John held her close in his arms. His lips moved closer and she did not draw back. Their lips touched at first tentatively and then fully and sweetly. When a young girl hesitantly coughed, they pulled apart. His parting words were, "I'll come for you in the morning for breakfast."

She smiled. "Our first breakfast together. It sounds wonderful, Chohnee."

* * *

As John completed his evening prayers, his mind was quiet for the first time in several years. He was sure that Katia would join the Church and that they would be happy together. He knew that he loved Katia deeply, and he felt sure for the first time that Katia could let the problems of her country rest quietly in the hands of others. She could make her life with John be a priority. He finally went to sleep, planning in his mind all of the things about the Church that he could help Katia learn. He was sure that his life was on the right track for the first time since his mission ended.

John still had the problem of what he would do about his role in the CIA. That role in his former life at this time seemed empty and joyless. What had always been exciting and challenging seemed to have lost most of its savor. And if he thought of living without Katia, a spark of life and joy was extinguished from his heart. Still he wondered if Katia would have a desire to learn more about the gospel. Could she gain a testimony of the restored Church? Just thinking about this warmed his heart with hope.

Just before he dropped off to sleep, he thought of the challenges he had to overcome to bring the Hacienda Medina to its greatest potential. He went to sleep thinking of all the things that he knew would improve the cattle stock for Valderas. His final thought was of the joy he had simply by talking Valderas into buying the bull Magnanimo. He smiled to himself in a moment of fairly earned satisfaction.

The next morning he walked to Katia's cabin to bring her to the main house for breakfast. As he came toward her little house, he heard her footsteps and looked up to see her coming toward him. Her face aglow with beauty and happiness, she seemed to have found her own answers. He took her in his arms, and they felt the love and hope they both yearned for. Tomorrow would be another day, and they would face it together.

ABOUT THE AUTHOR

KARL GOODMAN was born in Tucson, Arizona and was raised in the West. At age seventeen and just at the end of WWII, Karl joined the Army and ended up in the Second Infantry Division. He served a mission for the LDS Church in the northern states and Great Lakes area, where he met his wife, Wilma, a "lady missionary." They have eight living children—five sons and three daughters. Karl was engaged in a building business with a contractor's license, until, at the age of thirty-eight, he graduated from the University of Utah and began teaching along with running his building business. He and his wife have served missions together in Mexico, Costa Rica, and Tonga.

He has traveled extensively in Mexico and Central America pursuing his interest in archaeology. He became interested in writing as a youth and has previously published a novel entitled *Walk the Edge of Panic*. He says, "I enjoy writing exciting, romantic adventure. I let my characters strive in man's often imperfect way to live the principles of the gospel as they live in this world."